AN IMPRINT OF PUSHKIN PRESS

The Other's Gold

"Addictive . . . This novel will resonate with anyone who guards an inner circle forged in dorm rooms and dining halls"

Vogue (US)

"It's an ode to the turmoil and joy of female friendship, and the perfect book to read with your friends"

Bustle

"*The Other's Gold* is as beautifully written and epic in scope as *A Little Life*, but featuring women characters"

Refinery29

"*The Other's Gold* reads like an origin story for *Big Little Lies*"

Elle

"A powerful story of the bonds we form . . . I felt like these women were my friends and was devastated that my time in their world came to an end"

Marie Claire

"I found it ha⎯⎯⎯⎯⎯⎯⎯⎯⎯⎯⎯s book as it was so immersive a⎯⎯⎯⎯⎯⎯⎯⎯⎯⎯⎯were captured so viscerally"

⎯ Wood, *Bookseller*

The Other's Gold

Elizabeth Ames

AN IMPRINT OF PUSHKIN PRESS

ONE
An imprint of Pushkin Press
71-75 Shelton Street
London WC2H 9JQ

First published in Great Britain by ONE in 2020
This edition first published in 2020

1 3 5 7 9 8 6 4 2

Trade Paperback ISBN 13 978-1-91159-032-3

Typeset by Hewer Text UK Ltd, Edinburgh
Printed and bound by CPI Group (UK) Ltd, Croydon CR0 4YY

www.pushkinpress.com

This is a work of fiction. Names, characters, places, and incidents
either are the product of the author's imagination or are used
fictitiously, and any resemblance to actual persons, living or dead,
businesses, companies, events, or locales is entirely coincidental.

For Jenny

A circle's round, it has no end
That's how long I want to be your friend
Make new friends, but keep the old
One is silver and the other's gold

—Girl Scout song

What do you do with the mad that you feel,
When you feel so mad you could bite?
When the whole wild world seems oh, so wrong
And nothing you do seems very right?
What do you do?

—Fred M. Rogers

PROLOGUE

Each of the four noticed the window seat first when she walked into their common room. Alice balanced her knee on the ledge, did a calf stretch. Ji Sun ran her fingers along the edges of a tasseled throw pillow, thought briefly of the pasties she'd seen in the back pages of the free weekly newspaper. Margaret sat straightaway, crossed her legs at the ankles as if posed for a portrait, and gazed out the window while her older sister unpacked her boxes. Lainey stacked the cushions off to one side and did a secret spin on the bare bench, perched high above the courtyard. Framed in the window, backed by leaves blinking in the breeze, she celebrated the small spell of freedom after her parents left but before her suitemates returned to the room.

How they became friends was no great mystery, but how they remained so, braiding their lives together beyond their shared college quarters, transcended the usual alchemy of optimism and obligation that kept friendships intact, kept people from fading into other categories: old friend, college friend, just someone I once knew. None of the four would ever be *just* anything to the others, and the window seat was practice, then, for benches upon which they'd later huddle: in the antechamber of the dean's office; in hospital waiting rooms; in the parking lot outside the psych ward, gathering the courage to face their friend.

First, they were all second daughters, a fact they'd found so moving and improbable when they discovered it that first day in their suite together that they were certain the housing office had used this piece of information to place them, some kind of complicated, mystical algorithm that also accounted for their rainbow of hair colors: Lainey's dyed cherry, Alice's blond, Ji Sun's black, and

Margaret's brown. That they could all be bright enough to have gained admission to Quincy-Hawthorn College and not think first of their last names—an R, an S, two Ts—did not make them laugh until later, and then only to offset the disappointment that they had been brought together in a manner so base and clerical.

There was also the window seat—the luck and unlikelihood of having one in a freshman common room—with its picture windows overlooking the courtyard, burgundy cushions threadbare but still sumptuous with a kind of worn wealth that fit, better than the rest of the room, with its modular beds and box dressers, their imaginings of what college would be like. They didn't know they'd gotten the window seat suite thanks entirely to Ji Sun's family's contributions, but the seat kept them in the same suite for the full four years, and kept them in their room more than they might've been if, like other freshmen, they'd had to go searching for a space like theirs. They came back from holiday breaks with little embroidered pillows and hanging plants, stained-glass discs and dream catchers, made the seat the center of their place, their friendship, their lives. When they remembered their time in college, they saw the seasons from the window seat. They watched leaves and snow and rain and cherry blossoms fall from behind the black cutaways of one another's silhouettes. The memories faded or were replaced by photographs of the four piled together on the center bench of the bay windows, oblivious to the light streaming in from behind, eclipsing their distinct forms and making them one shape with four heads. The person charged with taking the photograph would become distracted by the four girls and their faces, the easy way they tossed their limbs around each other, how their hair fell on one another's shoulders, how their cheeks touched and shone. The four bunched together like one giggling living organism, blurred by their vitality, frenetic with the desires and powers of youth. But in the photographs they were stone, backlit

and blurred further together by the darkness, expressions inscrutable, made monument.

Others sat beside them in some pictures: boyfriends and girlfriends, strangers at parties, future husbands, the professor, their
parents and siblings.

Their worst acts sat beside them, too, though only Alice had
committed hers before they arrived. Ji Sun would do hers the
following year, when they were sophomores, and Margaret would
wait until after graduation. Lainey was last, wouldn't do her worst
until they began having babies.

Were they waiting then, huddled together on that bench? Could
they sense their gravest mistakes beside them, or know only that
they would need to stay within reach of one another as they tested,
in turn, how far they could wander from their shared shore before
they risked being swept out to sea? *Not waving but drowning*, they
read in a poem in a sophomore seminar, and though only Ji Sun
memorized it, all could understand the risks, saw in one another
the potential for loose footing, misjudged depth, rocks in pockets.
They stayed bound together to witness, yes, and to reassure the
others they were more than their worst choices, to measure their
own cruelties and mistakes against the others', same as they would
do with their joys and triumphs. But what kept them together more
than any of this was the hope that they might map this fine distinc-
tion in one another, between waving and drowning, between
merely being out to sea some and being swept away, swallowed.

PART I

THE ACCIDENT

FRESHMAN YEAR,
2002–2003

A fter their room, the four spent the most time together in the dining hall, so called as though anyone could mistake its vaulted ceilings, tree-length tables, and brassy chandeliers for anything so pedestrian as a *cafeteria*. Margaret managed, though. Despite being the one most dazzled by the space, she couldn't call it anything other than the cafeteria. When they entered the hall for their first dinner together, she stopped, the flow of new freshmen tripped up first over the obstruction caused by the four, and then by the scattered double takes at Margaret, whose face and body her own suitemates were also still stealing glances at, wondering why they hadn't been warned. Margaret had cheekbones that sliced each one of them open in turn: Ji Sun by their architecture; Alice by how smooth and bright they were, scar-free; and Lainey by the desire to touch them, compare their structure to her own, which she'd always considered the best thing about her face.

"Wow, we get to eat in *here*." Margaret looked around, oblivious to, or unmoved by, the people who turned to look at her—her long, gauzy white skirt and her heart-shaped face made her look like some kind of moon child princess bride, like she trailed glitter, didn't belong on this planet, let alone in a dining hall, even one with chandeliers.

"Didn't you see it when you visited?" Alice asked, ushering Margaret by the arm toward the tray stand.

"Oh, I didn't visit," Margaret said, choosing a fork as though it might play a song. "I *just* got in off the waitlist."

"Oh," Lainey said, and nodded, tried to think of how best to react. She couldn't imagine admitting this. She'd been wait-listed at Trinity College and even after being offered acceptance, the sting had manifested as lingering resentment toward all things even nominally Irish.

"Wow," Margaret said again when they'd finished piling their trays and stood, looking for a place to sit. "Just . . . wow!" She held her tray with one arm and used the other to gesture around the room, as though her suitemates couldn't see it. Her attitude was infectious. Ji Sun, the least impressed by institutional spaces, especially American ones that prided themselves on their "heritage," did feel now like the room was polished gold, sun dust from the fading day washing the students in honeyed light, glinty little sparks bouncing off the lowest glass facets in the light fixtures.

"Yeah, hey, wow," Ji Sun said, teasing but warm. They settled at a round six-top that they could tell in their bones would be their table, even as they shared it on this first night with two other freshmen, both of whom seemed more in awe of this foursome, somehow already solidified, than of their surroundings.

They traded the usual questions with the two other girls, *Where are you from? Which is your residence hall?* but none of the four bothered to listen to or remember the other girls' answers, especially after, when Lainey answered upstate New York, they asked again with new emphasis, No, but, where are you *from* from, like where are you *originally* from? Lainey rolled her eyes, a signal to her roommates to let Lainey decide when or whether to answer this question, which Alice and Ji Sun might have guessed, but Margaret wouldn't have known. The four had some basic background about one another, and now wanted urgently to know more vital information. Did they have boyfriends? Girlfriends? Had they ever? Had they had sex? Who was smartest? Who would be best loved by the others among them? Who would lead the way?

Four was good in this regard, they could see it already, better than three because there was less stasis. Three meant one could always think of herself as the nucleus, the reason, but four were enough to make a bridge, to link arms all sorts of ways, to have no center.

After dinner, they stopped outside the closed door to their room, the new whiteboard hung there, pristine when they'd left, now covered in frenzied letters that filled the space: *I ALREADY LOVE YOU. MARRY ME.* All of them looked at Margaret, who smiled and shook her head in a gentle way that suggested she both accepted and rejected that she was the proposal's intended recipient.

She inched closer to read the small footnote scrawled at the bottom of the board aloud, *"hook up w me at least? Oh, please."* She groaned and smiled and pushed open the door to their room, leaving the other three to consider that maybe the message hadn't been meant for just Margaret, and anyway, who cared about marriage when they'd just arrived at college?

Inside, a scarf Margaret had thrown over one of the lamps gave the room a maroon glow, and though they were tempted to varying degrees to retreat to their bedrooms and make phone calls or arrange the photos they brought (some chosen because they wanted to see the faces therein every day; some brought along out of obligation; and the largest set selected because they liked how they looked in the pictures, either their face, or the way they were surrounded by smiling friends: loved). But none of this felt as urgent as they'd expected it would, and instead they found places on the window seat, Ji Sun cross-legged and upright, Alice stretched out on her stomach, Lainey with her chin resting on her tucked knees, and Margaret seated as though on a porch swing, tapping the brass vent along the baseboards with her heels.

The note made it easier to talk about sex and romance right away, earlier than they thought they would. But together on their bench, they shared the sense that their fears and desires couldn't tumble out of them fast enough, and they soon discovered that Alice was the only one who'd had real sex, good sex, the definition

of which—they came to a provisional agreement—included pene-
tration (a detail that embarrassed Lainey once she started her first
gender studies course later that term) and an orgasm. Margaret
admitted that though she'd had sex with two people, she'd never
had an orgasm except in sleep.

Alice looked blankly at Margaret. "But what's the point?"

"I don't know." Margaret blushed. "It's still fun!"

"I guess," said Alice, not pretending to look convinced.

"You don't have to have sex to have an orgasm, Alice," said
Lainey, who would give Margaret her first vibrator for Christmas
the following year. Her defense of Margaret reified the sense that
they were all seeking Margaret's approval, something Margaret
could see and was accustomed to, and which she went out of her
way to give to people, so they could relax and fall into a friendship
that would be, like any, dictated by jostling for position within the
group, but not with her as its prize. Margaret had already touched
each of them in turn, squeezed a surprised Ji Sun when they left
the dining hall; clasped Alice's hands when Alice offered to take
Margaret sailing; and lightly rubbed Lainey's back after she'd
mentioned falling out with her high school best friend.

"Obviously I know that," Alice said, and made a jerk-off motion
with her hand, part dismissal, part instruction.

They all laughed at this, and inched closer together on the
bench, settled in. Ji Sun leaned back against the window, Lainey
loosed her knees, and Margaret swung her legs over Alice's back.
They were dizzy with how bound together they felt already, how
much of themselves they'd already given over to the others.

Alice and Ji Sun had both gone to boarding school, Alice near
here, in New Hampshire, for high school, and Ji Sun in Switzerland
starting when she was twelve. The way they told it, boarding school
all but required you to have sex to graduate, though more of Ji
Sun's own exploits had transpired back in Seoul, where she'd

grown up and her parents still lived, or in the Philippines, tossed off tantalizingly as where she "typically summered." A few nights later, after a party where they'd all gotten drunk off beer foam and foul tequila (save Alice, who'd smoked a joint she'd somehow procured before the rest of them even knew how to use the library, and who helped guide the other three as they stumbled back to their room, the inaugural act of an unspoken rule that one of them would always stay sober enough to help protect the others), Ji Sun would, in the hours as the sun came up and their buzz wore off, tell the group about the time her then boyfriend had gone down on her in the backseat of a limousine. After they recovered from the surprise of learning that she just went around in limos some-times, not only for prom, and in fact found them tacky, the details she shared—the heat outside; the mirrored partition where she could watch him work; and the way they'd almost been caught, someone knocking on the window while her dress was only a suggestion, straps down at her ribs and skirt up over her hips—stuck in their minds and lived there like a scene from a movie they'd memorized, or a memory that they couldn't be sure wasn't their own, even if they hadn't yet been eaten out, or set foot inside a limousine. They embroidered their friend's story further, so in some memories she wore a metallic dress, the color and move-ment of mercury, silk pool slunk around her midsection. One of them turned the partition purple, a kind of gas-in-a-puddle rain-bow color that cast everything in the car in a plummy, bronze light. On the way to her own rehearsal dinner, in a stretch limo that embarrassed her (on some level thanks to Ji Sun's dismissal), Margaret let her fiancé go down on her, an act less like the realiza-tion of a fantasy and more like the satisfaction of some foretold prophesy, further confirmation that the four were as enmeshed as they believed themselves to be, for better or for worse, married already, in a way, to one another.

Sex addressed, they could move on to the sort of hungry questioning where they wished equally to reach the end, to learn everything about the others, to *know* them, and also to never stop talking.

When their throats got sore, Lainey put on music, and they began to move and dance. Alice plucked the scarf from the lamp where Margaret had draped it, mouthed *fire hazard,* and tied the scarf around her neck fifties-style, did a little sock hop to the beat. Lainey flipped through the pages of her CD binder, liberated from the usual need to impress with her music. There was time enough for her roommates to hear Bikini Kill wail and Black Star bounce from her bedroom, and she didn't need to prove anything on this, their first night together, only needed to give them that feeling she got in her chest when her favorite songs came on, that they *must* leap to their feet and throw their arms up into the air, that they *must* erase any self-consciousness that came from moving their hips in front of others, close their eyes or keep them open, up to them whether they wanted to sing along, but they had to dance together, had to feel some kind of ecstatic freedom from everything that had come before and would come later, bound only to each other for at least the length of the song. None of them had any idea how long they'd been dancing, but they were coated in sweat, hair matted, mascara running, when their RA knocked on their door and told them quiet hours had begun half an hour ago, and could they please start the year off on the right foot. "Think about how your decisions impact others," she'd said, tapping her pointer finger on her own chest, on the Quincy-Hawthorn crest on her T-shirt. But that night, outside the confines of their common room, there were no others. They considered only their roommates, and each one fell asleep to find the other three already waiting in her dreams.

CHAPTER 2

Though the four shared as many meals together as possible, there were already times, three weeks into the semester, when their schedules necessitated other permutations. Alice and Ji Sun took early dinner together every Wednesday night before Alice went to weight lifting, while Lainey was in rehearsal and Margaret met with her writing tutor.

Ji Sun liked these Wednesday nights. They attracted less attention just the two of them, and they sometimes sat at the lone table for two that remained in the dining hall because one of the college's two founders had proposed to his first wife there. She was seventeen to the founder's fifty, and he went on to leave her and their four children for a nineteen-year-old, whom he left, three kids later, for another seventeen-year-old, this time to his sixty-seven, who bore him two more children before he died, losing the chance to do it all again. "Different times," the student guide on their freshman tour had said, and shrugged, before putting his hand over his mouth to whisper-shout the rumor that every class of Quincy-Hawthorn College since 1874 had as a student one of Hawthorn's descendants. Alice and Ji Sun had exchanged raised eyebrows, Alice then pantomiming a glance around with a magnifying glass before shooting Ji Sun a wink. Of anyone she'd met so far at school, including professors, Ji Sun was most impressed with her roommate Alice: her square jaw, her candor, and the ease she had in her body. But Alice wouldn't have guessed as much, Ji Sun knew. If you were reserved and not unattractive, people assumed you were a snob, that you disapproved. Ji Sun allowed that, in her case, they were often right. Alice knew, of course, that Ji Sun cared for her, loved her even, as they all loved each other already, and had said as much, even though Alice and Ji Sun shared in common families that almost never expressed this sentiment aloud. But Alice may not have known that Ji Sun admired her. Alice, with her low, raspy voice and patrician accent, lank blond hair that she wore scraped back into a ponytail where others would surely want to show off its virgin corn-silk color, defied categorization in a way that appealed to Ji Sun. There was a kind of creamy toughness to Alice that Ji Sun found both reassuring and a bit intimidating.

Alice already knew she wanted to be a doctor, but she approached her studies with a kind of pragmatism that the other premed students—a number of whom Ji Sun knew from the campus Korean Cultural Association—forwent in favor of agonized rants about organic chemistry and hopped-up, almost masturbatory accounts of the rigors of their current schedules, and the gauntlet of semesters to come.

Then there was Alice's command of her body, even with a limp that made her right foot land a little funny. How she rose with the sun for crew practice, how she ran for enjoyment, how she did not agonize over what she put on her plate each night in the dining hall. Alice's tray looked to Ji Sun like a television advertisement for American dinnertime: meat, mashed potatoes, peas, tall glass of milk. No apple pie, but Alice's blond hair and sailor-knot bracelet gave the tray a glow so you might still see a slice of it there.

Alice bore the signifiers, too, of a certain shaggy New England wealth, which Ji Sun could recognize but did not care to adopt. Ji Sun carried purses alongside her backpack that could pay for three months' room and board, but the few students who recognized them probably assumed they were fake. She alternated between all-white and all-black outfits, and while financial status was signaled for most students by whether they used the laundry service or scrounged for quarters and braved the dank basement, Ji

Sun sent her clothes to an actual dry cleaner, a service her mother's assistant arranged before Ji Sun arrived on campus.

"Alice." Ji Sun waited for her roommate to sit. "How did you get your limp?"

"I told you." They had discussed it briefly that first night together, when Margaret had tentatively reached for, but had not touched, the pearled scar that ran along the left side of Alice's face. "I was in a car accident. When I was twelve years old." Alice went back to her meal. Her answer was practiced, succinct. The way she met Ji Sun's gaze when she said "twelve years old" was meant to shut down further inquiry, Ji Sun could see.

"Oh. I'm sorry." American women said they were sorry for everything. *I'm sorry, can you pass me the salt? I'm sorry, do you mind? I'm sorry, just squeezing by here.* Ji Sun had heard Lainey apologize to a door in their suite.

"Who was driving?" Ji Sun asked, and knew by the way Alice's jaw tightened that she had landed on the exact question she wasn't meant to ask, and that Alice never answered. This she admired about Alice, too. She wasn't shy about her life, but she wasn't desperate to give up its secrets the way their classmates were. They couldn't wait to play Never Have I Ever at parties, a game that afforded drunk girls the chance to share that they cut themselves or gave their swim coaches hand jobs in high school, hoping the damage would help pass them off as interesting.

"A relative," Alice said, and looked down at her plate. "Inclement weather."

"I see," Ji Sun said. "I'm sorry. Were you close?"

"What?" Alice said, face flushed above her cheekbones. "Close to what?"

"You and the relative, were you close?"

"He was fine." Alice answered a question Ji Sun hadn't asked, but the way she'd finally veered from her script held promise.

"And you, you're varsity crew now, as a freshman."

"Yes," Alice said, looking up, back on steadier ground. "A child's body is remarkably resilient." She touched the back of her head and looked away. Ji Sun worried Alice might cry and then Ji Sun would have to say she was sorry yet again, and the conversation would be over.

"That's true," Ji Sun said. "My mother used to say our skulls were rubber and our brains congee. Porridge," she added, disappointed that Alice hadn't known.

Alice laughed, and then, almost as if by accident, said, "It was my dad. Driving."

Oh, Ji Sun thought, a drunk, then. She'd read John Cheever, and expected every wealthy New Englander she met to have a drunk, distant father and a pill-popping, resentful mother.

"Oh," Ji Sun said. She should say I'm sorry now, she knew, and she was sorry that Alice's father had imperiled her in this way, when she was a child. She wouldn't push Alice any further, but she didn't look away.

"It was . . . I don't like to talk about it, to be honest," Alice said, and rested her fork beside her peas and potatoes.

"Yes, sorry, of course," Ji Sun said. "I've just wondered. If you ever do . . . want to talk about it. I'm here." I'm curious, she almost added, still negotiating the terrain of their friendship, new but deeper already than any she'd known before. In boarding school she hadn't been part of a tight-knit group. Her wealth had made it easy to dip into different cliques, accumulate certain expected markers of an international boarding-school experience: trips to European capitals, elaborate meals shared for various cultural New Years, dances in the ballrooms of Swiss hotels. Looking at the pictures she'd brought to hang on her wall, she felt sometimes that they belonged to another student, had landed in her bedroom by mistake. She could find herself, her closed-mouth smile set apart from her classmates' toothy grins, their peace signs and high kicks, their goofy ease. Here at college, she had a real chance for that kind of coziness, felt near to the warmth of that comfort already, knew she shouldn't risk it the way she was now. You could go years into a friendship before learning how someone got her scars. Why push it? The four had hurried into intimacy, but they were not yet family. They didn't know the whole of each other's histories, and they had not yet built up their own together.

Should she put her hand out, make some kind of gesture of caring? Ji Sun thought again of Margaret, how she seemed to find a way to hug them—each of them—every day, how she flung herself alongside the others in their narrow extra-long twin beds, nestled like a puppy. Her touch was easy and welcome; Ji Sun hadn't known how much she craved it, this fraternal physicality, the closest prior approximation of which she'd experienced with her older sister before she'd left for boarding school when Ji Sun was nine.

"Thanks," Alice said, and it occurred to Ji Sun that Alice might be glad Ji Sun didn't try to touch her now. The way Alice sat, so straight backed, made it feel as though she'd moved across the room even though they still sat together at the small table, tucked against the wall.

They ate together in silence for a stretch, the din of the room recessed. It felt to Ji Sun, with each bite, that their table, already on the room's perimeter, was moving further and further away, enclosed by some kind of force field of loaded silence.

"My brother." Alice put down her fork again. "He nearly died in the accident."

Alice looked at her tray while Ji Sun stared at her scalp, a zigzag of skin pinked by sun. Alice had this impossible blend of clean and dirty that intrigued Ji Sun, like she'd been at a boys' sleepaway camp all summer but showered in an upscale hotel.

"And he's still . . . compromised. Mentally. Because of it." Alice met Ji Sun's gaze. "So I don't, well, I don't . . ." Her eyes filled but didn't overflow. Ji Sun watched as her friend's chin trembled, and lifted her hand to reach across the table to finally touch Alice's.

"No, it's okay," Alice said, lifting her two hands in surrender. "I'm fine." She touched her eyes with the backs of her hands and when she lifted them away, her eyes were dry and her chin stilled.

"Should we get ice cream?" Ji Sun asked after a pause, and pointed in the direction of the soft serve machine, which dispensed a substance suggestive of ice cream. "Sprinkles?" Sprinkles seemed like the right thing to offer Alice, who looked so like a child now, with her scrubbed-clean face and long ponytail, flyaways wild at her temples.

"I think it's mandatory," Alice said, and stood. Ji Sun followed behind as they deposited their trays and swirled their cones full, then dunked their ice cream in the sprinkle vat in clear defiance of the note requesting students use the "custom sprinkle implement." Ji Sun still trailed a step behind as they left the cafeteria, and watched Alice navigate the crowd, her one foot turned the slightest bit inward, tapping an extra heartbeat on the floor. Then they were outside, side by side, hands sticky and swinging. When their knuckles bumped for the fourth time, Ji Sun took Alice's hand in her own, a move her hand remembered with no hesitation, a hold-over from her primary school days, dormant in Switzerland, where hand-holding had been reserved for couples intent on broadcasting their status. Alice didn't turn to look at her, but Ji Sun could feel her face unclench, and when she glanced over, Alice had her eyes closed and mouth set in a small, relaxed smile. A bit of chocolate ice cream had dried above her lip, a half mustache. Alice's hand, covered in calluses from crew, made Ji Sun aware of how soft her own hand was, and she swung it a bit, carried Alice's along. Alice gave her hand a small squeeze and Ji Sun felt it as a thank-you, a lightness that reached even her feet, and she nearly skipped a little, or she would have, but she was in no rush.

CHAPTER 3

O n her way to meet Margaret and the rest of the small study group from their American history survey course, Ji Sun slowed to adjust the bobby pins Lainey had put in her hair after giving her a milkmaid crown that morning. Ji Sun had admired Lainey's hair worn this way, and was surprised by how eager Lainey was to replicate it, and then again by how she liked it on herself, the relief of the weight off her shoulders in the heat, and the way it connected her to Lainey, the only one of them who might pass for a sister to each of the others. As Ji Sun approached, she could hear Margaret, facing away from Ji Sun, explain to the other students in the group, "No, *GEE* sun, just think, like, Oh, gee, the sun is out!"

"Oh, gee, the sun is out," felt like the furthest phrase Ji Sun would ever associate with herself, but something about hearing it in Margaret's nasal lilt, the way she spoke to the other students like a primary-school teacher, singsongy and patient, filled Ji Sun with the warmth that Margaret so often brought, made her feel for a moment like the sun, which was out in force, was powered in part by herself, or at least that she might curl up in and enjoy it, a black cat with a glossy coat.

It was easier for Ji Sun to appreciate Margaret than it was for Alice, who grew impatient with Margaret's flightiness, or Lainey, who distrusted Margaret's earnestness. Ji Sun found both of these traits unobjectionable if not endearing, having encountered them less often than her roommates had. She also struggled less against Margaret's beauty. Her father had a penchant for hiring women who stopped people in their tracks, and Ji Sun's own older sister, Ji Eun, was beautiful in a way that made people say stupid things around her.

Ji Sun also appreciated her own aesthetic presence in a way that it seemed few women her age did. She loved the way her body wore clothes, and she didn't have problems with the way it looked naked, either. She wished, on occasion, that her butt were less flat, but not enough to do squats or anything more than imagine what she might look like in certain skirts with a rounder ass.

If anything, she worried that sometimes she was tokenizing Margaret, that she enjoyed her company as an ornament, look how nicely this Renaissance painting of a girl pairs with this living creature in sculptural clothing, one petal soft and diaphanous, the other crisp and angular, jagged to the touch. Ji Sun didn't view the attention as people locking in on Margaret, comparing everyone within radius unfavorably. Rather, she thought Margaret had a beauty so encompassing that it cast an aura out around her, and Ji Sun herself was made more beautiful because of this. She saw this especially when, like now, she heard Margaret describe her as sunshine. Did Margaret see everyone as sunshine because her beauty lit them up somehow?

Ji Sun joined her roommate and their study group.

"It's me, sunny Ji Sun. Here comes the sun." She smiled, but the group didn't know her well enough for the joke to land. She gestured at her all-black outfit and sat.

"I'll just call you Jesse," Conner said.

"Fuck that!" Margaret said, her mouth hot pink with the word, its abrupt shift in sound and shape from the sweet coaching she'd just given them.

Ji Sun didn't need Margaret to stand up for her in this way, but she did enjoy it.

"Yes, indeed," Ji Sun said quietly, because she wanted to confirm their expectations about her in order to better mess with them later. She wouldn't blush, though, or hang her head.

"What, Conner, should I just call you, I don't know, Conehead?" Margaret crossed her arms.

They all laughed at the feeble insult, but Conner was a dog with a bone.

"It's not the same. My name's easy, it's, like, normal American."

"Whatever," Ji Sun said, wanting to save Margaret from the battle she was gearing up to do. Margaret had stood and kicked off her woven leather huaraches as if in preparation for some kind of hand-to-hand combat. "Perhaps we won't have much need to address one another in any case," Ji Sun said, looking first at Conner and then at the rest of the group, on his side in their silence.

Margaret was still flushed pink, too angry to be articulate. "*American?*" She scowled. "Normal? What does that even mean?"

"Man, you're hot when you're mad," Conner said, and reached for Margaret, as though instead of a fight she might consent to his embrace, roll around with him right here in the grass outside the library.

Instead, she jumped back as if even the suggestion of his fingertips burned. "God, Conner, you're such a boor!"

Boor was a word they'd all put into rotation care of Lainey, who also called people dullards and cream-faced loons, and other Shakespearean insults that broadcast her plans to be a drama major, and that they all loved since none of what they'd memorized in school could be used outside of standardized tests in this way. They'd all adopted Lainey's taxonomy of Conner's contemporaries—three-inch fools, incharitable dogs, base football players—but Margaret, who acted oftentimes as Lainey's student, had done so most heartily.

"Don't touch me!" Margaret brushed the grass from the skirt of her sundress and wobbled a bit. "Shit! Fuck!"

"All right, Jesus, calm yourself, woman." Conner smiled at the two others in their group.

Margaret grabbed at her ankle and flopped back into a seated position, pulled her foot into her lap. Ji Sun saw the blood bright on Margaret's white dress before she could tell where it came from.

"Oh no, Margaret, what happened?" Ji Sun rushed to her side.

"I must have cut myself on something," she said, tears bright on her cheeks before Ji Sun had seen her eyes fill. "Be careful, Ji Sun, I don't know where it is."

Ji Sun pulled loose the scarf she'd tied to her satchel. It was vintage Hermès, an old one Ji Sun had decided she liked after her mother deemed it garish, the goddess Ceres with blue-stone skin, wings, and a tree-trunk body below her abdomen. She wrapped it around Margaret's foot, made the tightest knot she knew.

"We've got to get you to the infirmary," Ji Sun said.

"Fuck is an infirmary," Conner said. "I'm gonna carry you to the student health center. If you'll allow it." He stood before Margaret, bowed.

"It's not far," Margaret said, her hand on Ji Sun's shoulder.

"But you can't walk," he said, this time appealing to Ji Sun, who looked at the blood-soaked birds on her scarf and agreed.

So boorish Conner got to be a knight after all, lifting Margaret in his arms and carrying her, as though over a threshold, all the way to the student health center. Ji Sun, running to keep up with Conner's huge gait, trailed close behind until Margaret called her name, reached out and grabbed her hand, and then for the rest of the way Conner had to carry Margaret with Ji Sun attached at the limb, their link forcing what he must have imagined as a heroic dash into something more cumbersome, and, to onlookers, more confusing.

"Stay with me, please, Sunny," Margaret said, and Ji Sun got her absurd nickname then, given to her by the girl who'd go on to get eleven stitches as an indirect result of her defense of Ji Sun's right to have a non-Anglo name, whom it was impossible to deny, Ji Sun knew already, heart racing as she held Margaret's hand across Conner's broad chest, all their sweat intermingling, breadcrumb trail of blood dotting their path—anyone would let Margaret call them anything she liked.

CHAPTER 4

B y the start of fall reading period, Conner had become Margaret's boyfriend. Their courtship flourished over the objections of her roommates and the unsung but palpable dissent of others whose hearts were broken by the news that Margaret was in love, and with someone, as Lainey put it, so disappointingly predictable.

"He's rich, he's tall, he's *handsome*." Lainey stuck out her tongue to indicate that this was not her preferred flavor of handsome. "He has hair like a Ken-doll wig. He's wears *rugbies*. With, like, *boat shoes*."

"What's wrong with boat shoes?" Margaret asked, and traced her finger along her bare foot, forcing Lainey to consider its shape, land only on *elegant*. A foot! She'd learned new things about beauty from Margaret, that it wasn't just about a symmetrical face, good hair, and a nice body. There was a harder-to-quantify quality, a pore-lessness and impermeability, something to account for how Margaret never seemed to have bruises or scratches on her legs and her feet were always clean, heels uncracked, toes hairless and unbarnacled. Lainey had seen Margaret apply body lotion in a haphazard way, smear tinted Clean & Clear moisturizer on her face in the morning without even looking in the mirror. It frustrated Lainey that Margaret's beauty didn't seem to require a scrupulous upkeep commensurate with such results, but it taught her that Margaret was formed differently, cast from different materials.

"I like his feet. He never wears socks, have you noticed?" Margaret touched the spot she'd sliced on the underside of her own foot and didn't wince, instead retreated into some private reverie about Conner's feet, which Lainey was sure were sweaty and fungal.

Conner was a basketball star but read more like a football player (*base football player!*) with his broad barrel of a chest, shoulders that appeared prepadded, and jocular, heartland, head-injured demeanor. He was a junior but his body made the nonathletes in his year look like pollywogs. Like Margaret, he was midwestern, from Minnesota. Lainey loathed him on sight. Alice wasn't a fan either, failing to find much beyond a familiar, rich-boy school of studied charisma to nudge her past the first impression she'd formed of him when she'd learned how he'd treated Ji Sun in study group.

When Conner had apologized to Ji Sun for his "boordom," Ji Sun had only nodded, so slight that it was clear that while she acknowledged what he offered, she made no commitment to accept. He seemed to take this as a challenge, and launched a campaign of interest in both Ji Sun and Korean culture, asked to try the boricha she kept on their little kitchenette counter, and performed his enjoyment as though auditioning for its ad campaign. Her roommates had all tried the tea out of politeness, but only Conner liked it enough to pour himself a tall glass whenever he came over, and she was surprised to find that his enthusiasm for the beverage offset her irritation at how much he consumed. He reacted with genuine shock when she told him she'd never been, and didn't plan to go, to North Korea.

"Did you not go to high school?" Ji Sun asked him, taking pleasure again in the surprise on his wide, generic face at being spoken to this way. "Was North Korea not the villain in like a million of your action movies?" She added the "like" consciously, as though without it she might as well speak to him in Korean.

"Well, yeah, but like, I guess I thought it was different for uh, other Koreans, *South* Koreans." The way he said this, so proud to have remembered this basic biographical fact about Ji Sun, again filled her with a kind of pity and contempt that somehow endeared him to her. Like the rest of her roommates, she told Margaret to break up with him. But privately she was beginning to understand his appeal, his dogged, dopey attempts to win her over, his frothy, lopsided grin. Even his ignorance troubled her less than some of his classmates', paired as it was with real curiosity. He didn't try to pretend he knew more than he did, and this was refreshing on a campus full of students from the tops of their classes who, in reading seminars, had read every book "at the start of high school," and, how convenient, had "probably forgotten most of it by now." Ji Sun didn't smile at Conner, or offer him any evidence of this begrudging affection, but she did invite him, along with Margaret and the others, to attend a Chuseok event hosted by the Quincy-Hawthorn Korean Cultural Association, made up mostly of Korean Americans, along with nearly every member of the Korean Christian Campus Fellowship, which Ji Sun had joined in part to appease her parents but also, though she'd never admit it, to remind her of them.

He reacted as though she'd asked him to escort her to the Nobel banquet.

"Oh, wow, of course." He put his hand over his heart, his chest, its shape, like a mold for armor, clear under his thin polo shirt. "And I hope, when the season starts, that you'll come to a basketball game. To learn about *my* culture."

He was such an idiot. He grinned, and Ji Sun pictured herself in the stands, her all-black outfit a buoy in the sea of navy and forest green, school colors she did give Quincy-Hawthorn some credit for choosing, a kind of sports-appropriate arrogance implicit in the monochrome, how you had to work to distinguish their mascot, an ocelot.

"You have yourself a deal," she said. She put out her hand, and he shook it.

Conner brought her two red pears. She recognized them from the dining hall, but he'd taken the trouble to wrap them in a piece of crinkled gold tissue paper, and when he handed them to her he whispered, "Happy *Chuseok*, Ji Sun."

She smelled booze on his breath and saw the screw top of a flask poking out from the pocket of his cargo shorts. He'd brought along two friends who, while they at least wore full-length cargo pants, were red-eyed and loud. Unlike Conner who'd practiced pronouncing Chuseok and stood up straight in his beach-bum outfit, they skulked around like wolves, shoved food in their pockets even as they said *Ew* about dishes they didn't recognize, laughed too loudly, and looked as though they'd been loosed from their enclosure and weren't sure whether to hunt or mate.

Ji Sun steeled herself to run interference, but the Korean Christian Campus Fellowship, or KCCF, was populated by the most aggressively friendly people she had ever met. There were times when the boundlessness of their generosity and apparent joy made Ji Sun wonder if there wasn't some way she could believe in Jesus, if only for long enough to know whether this goodness was genuine, and what it felt like to feel that way. A few members approached Conner's friends, and Ji Sun thought the two werewolf pups would probably wind up agreeing to come to church by the end of the party. There were other non-Korean students in attendance, too, brought along by their friends and roommates in a kind of liberal arts tourism, to learn about the world via free food, paper plates, and congealing entrees scooped from aluminum tins. It all added up to a welcome departure from the dining hall, where everything had started to taste vaguely similar, cooked or raw, animal or vegetable.

Cat, Ji Sun's closest friend from KCCF, spotted Ji Sun and came over. She hugged Ji Sun and said hello to her roommates. Margaret pulled Cat into an embrace, and, released, Cat laughed and blushed. She looked at the group with what seemed to Ji Sun like an equal measure of longing and befuddlement. Ji Sun had gathered that

Cat both wondered if there was space for her in this foursome, and trusted that Ji Sun would eventually abandon its stricture for a closer friendship with her and Ruby, who came over to join them now.

Ruby wore a pale peach and gold hanbok, but it didn't soften her. She smiled at Ji Sun and gave her roommates a cool nod.

"Lots of new people here tonight," Ruby said, and pointed at Conner's friends. "Fun."

"Ruby, don't be mean. That's part of the point of this!" Cat said.

"The point of Chuseok is to feed sloppy white boys?"

"Kind of!" Cat laughed. "No, but *fellowship*," she said, and nodded at Conner, who approached with his loaded plate.

"Are we going to talk about our ancestors?" Conner leaned close to Ji Sun.

"No, ugh." Ji Sun reacted more to his hot breath than his question, but both felt stifling. "Just eat, listen to music. It's a party." She gestured around weakly, as it didn't look like much of one. The food table was laden, and a good effort had been made to decorate, but the basement room was too large and well lit, the vibe that of a primary school birthday party where the kid's parents had made him invite the entire class.

The full moon had been visible all day, gauzy in the afternoon and sharpening as the sun went down in a cloudless sky. Each of the four felt like she could burst out of her skin. They took the full moon as both warning and permission: anything could happen that night. They could crawl out of their bodies. They could metamorphose. No one was wearing the right thing; they should be naked and howling in the woods somewhere, not listening to quiet K-pop and switching on battery-powered tea lights to place on a lectern-cum-altar.

Ji Sun had brought along a huge tray of songpyeon that her mother had shipped from their favorite bakery in Seoul. It arrived in the mailroom inside a large wooden crate packed with dry ice and a smaller Styrofoam cooler, and a student worker had been dispatched to alert Ji Sun that she should collect the parcel *immediately* as it was marked PERISHABLE and URGENT and had come "from a different country." There was no note from her mother, but there had been one from the baker, who had known Ji Sun since she was a child.

She felt a pang for this baker that surpassed any longing for family, or home. She'd spent a third of her life celebrating holidays away from home, and she was used to gatherings where students would stand to present on their cultural traditions to a group of people focused on their food, impatient for a dessert they'd dismiss as not the right kind of sweet. But she'd never felt so far away, even surrounded as she was now by people speaking Korean. She didn't wish to share any memories of the baker, or her family, with these people; she barely wanted them to eat the cakes she'd brought, her least favorite flavors. She wanted to leave, with just her roommates, go back to their window seat, swig straight from the jug of Carlo Rossi that Conner had given Margaret, and gorge on the good flavors of cakes that she'd tucked away in their mini fridge.

"Sunny," Lainey called her Margaret's pet name from time to time, in a theatrical way that mimicked Margaret's accent and sweetness, "no offense, but if I don't get out of here I think I'm going to explode." Lainey's own older sister was adopted from Korea, contributing to the sense Ji Sun had sometimes that Lainey could be her half sister, though Lainey herself was not Korean, and had told them that her birth mother was white, and her birth father was Mexican and Vietnamese.

"Me too!" Margaret squealed. "I feel so, I don't know—*scratchy.*" She did a full body wiggle and Ji Sun saw some students turn to watch.

"Yeah, it's the full moon, man," Alice said, mouth full of food. "It's no joke."

"But we just got here!" Conner said. His cronies had by now been absorbed by the KCCF crew, and they laughed together like old friends, heads tossed back.

"We should be outside, don't you think?" Margaret asked, wiping powdered sugar from the corners of her mouth. "This feels like one of those nights full of *potential*." Margaret said *potential* like she was proud to know its meaning, and Lainey and Ji Sun exchanged a glance.

They had a private ongoing investigation, about which Ji Sun wished she felt more ashamed, into how Margaret had gotten into Quincy-Hawthorn College. Margaret struggled in all of her classes, met with her writing tutor twice a week, and still got Bs—considered Quincy-Hawthorn Ds—on her papers.

When they'd last whispered about it, Lainey had asked, "Do you think they knew?"

"Knew what?" Ji Sun asked.

"That she looks like that!" Lainey couldn't bring herself to say, *that she is so beautiful*, was tired of affirming it all the time.

Ji Sun had said no, but she couldn't remember whether Quincy-Hawthorn had given the option to attach a small photograph of yourself if desired. Her father had graduated from Q-H, and the family had made donations large enough that Ji Sun knew she could have attached a photograph of Kim Jong-il and still been admitted.

"Yes, let's do get out of here," Ji Sun said now, and took Lainey by the arm. "Conner, you can stay," she said, and linked her other arm through Margaret's.

"Hey, wait up," Alice said, loading her napkin with cakes. "Am I supposed to stay here and mind these hooligans?" She pointed at Conner's friends, who'd started a dance party with three giggling freshmen.

Ji Sun took note of the looks they gave the girls, the way they licked their teeth. Did the boys know the girls' names? This didn't matter. Could they tell them apart? This did. But it wasn't her problem, and she was tired of feeling like Conner's friends, or Conner, were connected to her, even tenuously. She knew they'd say something stupid and racist, but she didn't need to stick around to hear what.

Cat was dancing with Ruby and some others, and when she caught Ji Sun leaving, she stopped. Ji Sun waved and mimed that she would call her, left without looking back to see whether Cat was dancing again. She might have invited Cat to come, but felt sure that Cat wouldn't leave, and more, Ji Sun didn't want to broker any getting-to-know-you conversations, wanted only to dance wild with her roommates, none of them observed by anyone, all of them free.

Outside, Margaret waggled the silver flask that she'd snagged from Conner. She held it aloft, a beacon, and they chased her to a quiet corner of the brick fence, the least lit by salt lamps, sunk together into the damp grass.

Margaret opened the flask and Lainey leaned in, took a sniff, "Ugh, smells like cleaning solution."

Margaret held the silver lip to her nose. "Smells like fire. No, like candy!" She took a swig and bowed her head, raised it with a sucked-breath *Yow*, eyes gleaming. "Black licorice!"

"Let me try," Alice said, and took a long gulp. "It's cinnamon." She shook her head, took another draw.

"Whoa, slow down there, cowboy," Lainey said. "Save some for the rest of us."

They passed the flask among them until it was finished, each feeling fire on her tongue, fuzz in her head. They skipped and staggered past empty lecture halls on their way to the arboretum, where they held hands, spun one another round, belted out songs from *The Little Mermaid* and *Beauty and the Beast*.

Quincy-Hawthorn's campus was ringed by woods, with the arboretum as its crown. It butted up against a state park, on the other side of which was the nearest town. The arb was open to the public, but even the trees seemed to sense the divide, with the arb's entrance and far perimeter marked by rows of huge sycamore trees, standing sentry, mighty enough that they seemed both to guard against and to be the menace.

The leaves had just begun to turn, and the buildings on campus were the color of burnished brick in the daytime, reds bright against the manicured green spaces that anchored the grounds: the courtyard and its horseshoe of housing; the library lawn with its willow trees; and the big hill and birch-lined quad below, where most of their classes met. Now, in the moonlight, the leaves looked bruised purple and metallic, as though they might chime if there were any breeze.

They walked it off beneath the trees, talked about their classes and their crushes and their dreams, same as they did most nights, but in the woods, with the moon fat and full of longing, it felt like they might find what they sought together. Maybe tucked among a small clot of trees there would be a cottage with a secret door, a portal, and they could pass through this last stretch of their child-hood together, emerge unscathed. None would call herself a child; but none would say she was grown-up, either. Arriving at college brought with it much self-conscious talk about how they were really and truly adults now, even as they slung their backpacks over both shoulders, tucked their stuffed animals beneath pillows, called their parents to ask for checks.

Later, when even the moon seemed tired, they headed home along the bike path, deserted at this hour, and felt a presence behind them, big as a bear.

The four drew closer together without saying anything. The knowl-edge that they were in danger was immediate, transmitted without a word, and they bunched two by two, Alice and Lainey behind, Ji Sun and Margaret in front. They left very little space between their pairs, made of themselves a small house, a locked room.

Lainey dug in her coat pockets for her keys, stuck them up between her fingers like talons, though she had fewer now, just their room key, her old house key, and a runty key to her bike lock, barely big enough for her makeshift claw.

Alice took a quick look over her shoulder, and in a flash saw two men, hulking, dressed in dark clothes and wearing hats, shearling inside one of their sweatshirt hoods sticking in her mind so that that they remained bearlike even now that she knew they were men.

Lainey tried to remember what she had learned about bears. She hadn't looked yet, but she could feel them there, hear their ragged breath, sense from Alice's skin that they were animals. There was the type of bear that you were meant to stun by punching it in the nose, and then there was the type you just needed to run from, fast as you could. Was there a type you played dead for? She felt in a panic that they might try this now, all four of them, fall to the ground and see if they could fool these monsters into believing their prey were asleep, already dead. She wondered if she should whisper her plan, but it was too quiet, dead silent in an understanding shared by all six that if they didn't speak, maybe everyone could pretend there was nothing here to fear.

When had they learned to behave like this? In other peril it was clear that you should run, scream for help, throw your weight against whatever assailed you, holler fire. But this way of attempting escape, not daring to look at or speak to one another, this silent lockstep march—Had they learned it in school? Had they seen it in a film? Was it passed along by their mothers?

The sounds of the bears' footfalls grew closer, and there was a jingling noise, as though maybe the men had made weapons of keys, too. Maybe they had strung small blades and bones and teeth around their necks. Lainey began to imagine how she would remove herself from her body, and some base part of herself surfaced, wondered whether they would want Margaret first, and would the rest of them run, then, or stay and fight? She told herself she would stand in front of her friends, fought her shame with the resolve to be brave. She drew in deep breaths and willed herself to turn around, but before she could she felt the air cool beside her as Alice unlocked herself, spun on her heels, and shouted.

"Hey! Fuck off!" Alice threw her arms out and started windmilling, dropped her left arm and reached for the flask in her pocket, drew it out slowly, as if it were a grenade.

"Lainey, the call box!" Her one arm still wild, flash of silver near her hip—did Alice have some hidden weapon?—the men seeming to grow larger, closer.

"The what?" Lainey felt a hand on her arm, was it Margaret's, was it a claw?

"The emergency call box! Get to the box!" Alice screamed, but Ji Sun was already running ahead, toward the narrow blue beacon that would connect to campus police. Lainey recalled now how these had been pointed out on their campus tour, but she hadn't known there was one here, hadn't even thought to look.

An intercom crackled and a white light flashed on. They heard the sounds of a car and the men fled. The men were gone, into the woods, by the time the car—not campus police—came into sight, but the way they'd run confirmed for everyone that they had meant to do harm.

The four of them stood there, Ji Sun on the small slope of grass by the call box; Alice, closest to the woods, their sentinel; Lainey and Margaret in between, breathless. Margaret had her arms wrapped around her body; Lainey's arms were out at her sides, waiting. The four came together and began to run before they exchanged a word. When they'd put enough distance between themselves and the woods, Margaret asked whether they should stay and wait for the police, tell what happened.

"I'm not sticking around!" Alice said. "They could come back. And I don't want to spend all night talking to the campus police."

"We reek of booze besides," Ji Sun added, though she knew that calling upon campus safety services exempted students from penalties related to underage drinking. She knew, too, that she was exempt from these penalties because of her family name.

All had sobered the moment they sensed the men, the alcohol evaporating from their bloodstream in the same collective osmosis that told them not to speak. But now, exhilarated, exhausted, they circled close to intoxication again, drunk on relief from the unspoken imaginings of what they'd escaped.

Home, they huddled together on their window seat. Margaret brought her big quilt out from her room, and they scooched close enough together that they could share it. No one wanted to be alone. Their eyes were wide, unblinking. As the night hung between the deepest dark and the first hint of light, Lainey was reminded of the first time she'd tried Ecstasy, how she could feel it drain from her bloodstream as the sun came up, suck the joy from her brain, replace it with depression and daylight.

Lainey wanted to thank Alice, but again, Alice preempted her. She opened her mouth, said, "I," and let out a sob.

Margaret reached across Lainey to hug Alice, said, "Oh, Alice, it's okay! We're safe."

"It's not that," Alice said. She touched her face, thumbed along the scar at her jawline. She placed her hand across her cheek, a shield. "I'm the one that caused this. I caused the accident. It was my fault."

"What are you talking about?"

"My limp, my face, my"—another wail escaped—"brother." She put her head in her hands and cried.

The others were quiet, relieved not to talk about the men. They knew what might have been. But they had escaped! They were heroic. And now their brave rescuer, bearer of the blue light, sat defeated by some other danger, one she was dredging up.

"It wasn't a car accident," Alice said. "It was a tractor. We were visiting my grandparents' old farm in Western Mass. And—" She stopped, took a deep shudder of an inhale that silenced her tears. Her eyes were red, but dry. She didn't look at any of them.

The others stayed silent. When someone points to her scar and begins to speak, you listen. You don't say a word until she wants one from you.

CHAPTER 5

I was twelve. That part's true. My brother and I, we were riding together, and it was my fault. I . . . caused it," Alice said.

Her sisters didn't know. Her brother didn't even know! Since the accident—everyone in her family called it this—the bit of fuzz around his brain had remained there, fat on a pork chop. Only her parents knew that Alice had pushed him, and they were the ones who named what happened an accident and made it so. Her grandparents were both dead now, took whatever they suspected with them.

"I say it was a car accident since there's less to explain. People don't ask as many questions."

Alice looked at Ji Sun with what Ji Sun took as both accusation and understanding. Alice had a secret, and she was giving it to them to hold. They inched closer to Alice; they wanted her to know they would accept.

"I don't know, I started saying that, that it was a car crash, in boarding school and it stuck." Alice stopped again. She could not tell them what she had done. She wanted to; she felt it burn in her throat, thicken around her heart, threaten to stop it beating. If she could tell them, what hardened there would open, her heart would beat. But she couldn't. She could say she was to blame, that what happened was her fault. But she couldn't say she pushed him.

She crossed her arms over her chest, a reflexive holdover from that time, though her breasts were not quite as flat as they had been then, and no one had poked them in the years since. The space around her sternum had been stroked and grabbed and licked, but not needled in the way it had been by her brother, with pens and sticks, his toothbrush, whatever he could find, but most often his long pointer finger, its touch rough enough that it felt to her he bored a hole in her chest, and she did find bruises on some days when he didn't wait for what she imagined then as the clay of her skin to reseal before jabbing at her again, fast and hard, finger in that same divot he'd made.

Her brother had been a brat, later a pill, and at the time of the accident, a jerk. These were the ways her parents referred to him when they told her, as they always did, to ignore him. Her older sister, Eleanor, called him worse, but advised Alice to ignore him, too, all of them unaware or uncaring about whatever shift in adolescence had made him malevolent. He took Alice's body as a personal affront, registered his disgust with it every day. Called her worthless. Poked. Said no one would ever want her. Poked. Her ugly boy body, her disgusting nothing chest. Poke poke poke.

Alice had spent her childhood outdoors and muddy, one of the fastest in her class, a natural in every sport she tried, with almost no pressure to behave more like a girl from her parents or from anyone at the small Quaker private school she'd attended since pre-K. So her brother's insistence that she wasn't what she should be confused her, served as her introduction to the idea that she was meant to be sexually desirable at all, and that already she fell short. She was shocked by how cold his gray eyes were when he appraised her, told her she made him want to puke, just the sight of her, her ugly little tits. She had come to pride herself on her potty mouth in boarding school, to capitalize on the way raunchy words registered as extra scandalous from a small, neat girl. But she never said tits, ever. Her brother had made it the worst word, a weapon. When she heard it said with the right fleck of disdain, she still felt a rush of heat in her underwear—not desire, but a wetness that served as warning, that she might pee herself as she had done that day on the farm.

She could still feel the sticky heat of the tractor's vinyl bench beneath her thighs, remembered seeing her pale khaki shorts in a pile on the porch later, wondered how she could have peed that much, how the stain could be so dark, before she could understand that they were brown with blood.

Earlier that day, she'd had to strip down into her undershirt, cream with lemon-yellow Swiss dots, after her T-shirt got covered in egg, one she'd been tossing with her brother, lightly, just fun. They'd toss and take a step back, toss again, see how much space they could put between them. He hadn't rocketed the egg at her, she didn't think, just thrown it with enough force to reach her. She'd been the one to crack it in her hands when she tried to catch it, and they had both laughed. She lost, but she didn't burn with shame. He wasn't a monster every moment, and when she thinks of her life at home before she left, she is almost always with him. They are the middle children, Irish twins. On the farm that day Eleanor was inside the house, on the phone with her boyfriend, and her younger sister, Brianna, still a toddler, was on the porch with her parents and grandparents.

She worried the undershirt's little yellow bow. Why hadn't she yanked it off? Now, she finds those same bows on women's bras infantilizing, something Lainey taught her to believe. But as a child, she found them something akin to sexy, and so, nervous making. Even tiny as a fingernail, her yellow bow blazed, and her brother didn't need the signpost. He reacted just as she knew he would to the undershirt, told her to stop showing off her awful nothing tits, to cover up.

On the tractor, even above the roar of the motor, he continued, and she could make out *fucking tits*, extrapolate *stupid*. His mouth was cavernous. She inched as far as she could from him on the tractor's small bench seat, designed for one adult. He was shouting, laughing, licking his teeth, exhilarated by the distance from their parents, his perch in the driver's seat, the noise that gave cover to shout his worst. The sun was too hot on her skin and she could feel it tighten on her shoulders, begin to burn. Her parents never made her wear sunscreen.

He took his hand off the wheel to poke her, and they swerved. They were near a small slope of land beside the barbed-wire fence that enclosed the horse pasture. Later, Alice would tell herself that he might have fallen off anyway, caused an even worse accident, killed them both. She had wanted him to die. She wasn't thinking about hurting him. She was thinking about killing him.

He took aim at her bow, but the tractor jostled, and he connected with her small breast instead. He poked anyway. The bite of his fingernail on her body. He widened his eyes and poked again, in the same spot, harder. He wasn't even looking at the wheel, and when they swerved again he still kept one hand aloft, accusing her nipple, ready to poke again and try to push into her bones, through her body and out her back. As he tried to right their path one-handed, Alice reared back with all her strength. She read later about mothers lifting cars off their babies with one hand and had no trouble believing in that boundless strength. When she pushed, she didn't picture her brother crumpled beneath the tractor. No, she felt her rage was enough to rocket him up into the sky, where he would explode in the sun's fire, burst into a billion bits, drift back down to the dirt as dust. She pushed him with all her might.

"Where were your parents?" Margaret asked. "They weren't watching?"

"They were on the porch, back at the house. They didn't hover, they weren't like that."

They had come running after her mother noticed the second swerve, just before Alice pushed. But Alice didn't remember when they appeared, didn't remember their screams or her father pulling her from off her brother's motionless body. Didn't even remember the pain of the two injuries she sustained on her leap: the broken bones that caused her limp, and the nub of a barb that caught on her cheek, sliced a jagged line from her dimple to her temple. Didn't remember much of anything about the time before her brother returned to consciousness beyond her plan to kill herself, a concept heretofore so foreign that at first she thought she'd invented it. When her brother woke two days later in the hospital, her desire to die morphed into a wish to vanish from her family, a plan facilitated by her parents, who signed her up for so much in the way of after-school and summer activities that she barely crossed paths with them in the year and a half before they sent her away to boarding school. And she'd spend the summers mostly away from home, too, doing wilderness courses and sailing camps, spending as much time on the water as she could, where she could be distant from her family's pain, unreachable. In every sport, subject, and club, Alice told herself she would be good, do good. That her brother lived made her feel as though her own life had been saved, and it had to be for a reason.

Lainey, Margaret, and Ji Sun were quiet, waiting. They looked to Alice now like children in their oversized sweatshirts, staring up at her, hands folded, eyes wide.

How inadequate it would be to tell them, what, that he was teasing her—her parents' name for it—and she'd had enough? He poked her in the chest sometimes? These weren't reasons to kill someone.

"I, anyway, I distracted him." Hadn't she? She distracted him to such a degree that he wanted to rule her, ruin her. Lainey had described the cruel girls at her middle school as terrorizing her, and Alice knew that Lainey would call what Alice's brother did a kind of terrorizing, too. But she was too tired to tell them the truth now, even if she'd had the guts. She felt acid roil in her stomach, some knowledge that she was missing her best chance to unburden herself, here with friends who, at least tonight, were grateful to her, believed her to be good.

"Oh, Alice, but you were so young! You can't hold yourself responsible for that!" Margaret squeezed Alice's arm while Lainey and Ji Sun murmured their agreement.

She couldn't explain to them how quickly she'd dove off after her brother, how immediate and all-consuming her regret. And if she ever managed to tell them the truth, to let them coo and call it self-defense, an impulsive mistake that anyone might have made, let alone a child!—there would still be the moment, sliced smaller even than that split second when she decided to push, when she saw her brother's body motionless beneath her and felt something other than regret: power.

"Alice, let's go to bed, huh?" Lainey stood up from the bench. "This was such an intense night, and we're all going to crash at some point."

The best work Alice had done in the years since the accident was in forgetting, embroidering over the truth quicker than the stitches were removed from her scar. She'd kept them, small black barbs themselves, in the yellowed plastic saltshaker from her Hello Kitty picnic set. She'd taken the saltshaker to boarding school and it was with her now, in a wooden cigar box at the back of her underwear drawer, along with her passport and the jewelry she never wore.

She wanted to yield to Lainey's touch, but she felt stuck to her seat, to the picture of her brother's body that surfaced now, pinned to the ground beneath the tractor's front wheel. He was motionless, but in her mind's eye now he is waving, thrown overboard by his sister into this sea of grass, signaling to anyone above who might come save him. But it's only Alice who can see him, and when she lands at his side she covers his face in the blood from her own injuries, so that when her parents finally do arrive they first believe both of their middle children to be dead, even as Alice's screams surround them.

"Go ahead, go to bed. You're right, we should," Alice said. "I think I'll sleep here tonight." She allowed them to arrange the pillows beneath her head, tuck her in.

Once they'd gone to their rooms, she turned to face the cold glass that looked out onto the courtyard, looked for the blank relief of sleep.

CHAPTER 6

Lainey abandoned the Dump Conner campaign when she started hooking up with, and then legitimately dating, Lesley, one of Conner's teammates. Like Conner, he was a tall junior who looked like a man, but unlike Conner, who was white enough to pass for a stock-image photograph from a fifties country club, Lesley was black. And golden in the cheeks, burnt sienna where his hair and neck met, the rusty glow at the ends of his curls an auburn corona.

"Yup, the rare black redhead," he said, when he caught her staring. She knew better than to ask to touch.

"Seems you know something about unusual hair color yourself." He nodded at her, and the way he said *unusual*, stretched the vowels—she had to see his tongue again.

"Oh, right," she said, touching her own hair, violet for October. "Mine's natural, too," and then, voice lowered, she heard herself add, "And the carpet does indeed match the drapes." The cliché had been stuck in her head since he'd called himself a redhead, and burst out in reaction to how hard she'd been trying to suppress it.

He gave a big, full-throated laugh and she was filled with joy for having said something so stupid, as his laughter gave her a long look at his perfect pink tongue again.

"No cavities," she said, learning already that being near him made her incapable of keeping her mouth closed. She worried now that she'd say something offensive, that the effort to avoid doing so would rocket back around like a racist boomerang, knock her square in the face.

"What's that?" he asked, a smaller smile this time, and one raised eyebrow, the hair of which was black, but maybe a little reddish, though she couldn't be sure without a closer look.

"Nothing, no, I was just thinking of I guess not getting dessert." She waved toward the soft serve machine.

"You live with Margaret and them, right?" he asked, and put his tray down beside hers. "I play basketball with Conner. That's my boy."

"Oh," she said, irked at being "Margaret and them" before allowing that this was fair if he was Conner's teammate.

"All right if I eat with you? I've got to jet soon, though." He was already sitting, and she stood there, staring at the top of his head.

"Sure, yes, why don't you," she said, unsure how to speak or sit. "Alice is joining me in a bit, but—do you know Alice? She rows crew, she lives with us, too. And Ji Sun."

"Yeah, I've met Ji Sun," he said. "What's up with her outfits?"

"How do you mean?" Lainey finally sat down, hands still on her tray.

"She's kinda . . . monklike or something. Not sure. Like she's wearing the world's nicest bathrobe?" He was so adorable. She wanted to crawl into his lap.

"I think it's just higher fashion than we're used to seeing around here, to be honest." Lainey was only realizing this herself, unfamiliar as she was with some of the brands in Ji Sun's full, neat closet, outfitted with organizers that no one seemed to remember her installing.

"I like what you've got on," he said, and gave her a different smile, slyer.

"Oh, so you *are* one of those."

"Excuse me. One of what?" he teased, but it felt loaded.

"An *athlete*," she said. "A flirt." She was wearing her shortest cutoff jean shorts with dark purple tights underneath, a ratty V-neck Sleater-Kinney T-shirt, and an oversized cardigan. It was her favorite Friday outfit, and it pleased her that he noticed.

Now he clicked his tongue in his cheek as a confirmation. She was exhilarated to be flirting like this, over a meal, with the lights on, rather than drunk at a dark party, hoping the person she kissed still appealed to her when she could better make out their face. By the end of the meal, they'd exchanged numbers and he'd touched her knee, lightly, just the softest skitch across the nylon there. Alice had had to stay late at the lab and Ji Sun decided at the last minute to eat at a restaurant. Lainey was glad for the luck of both of them skipping this dinner, but part of her wished they'd been there just to watch, to confirm for her that there was something visible in the air around her and Lesley, some kind of orb that lights up when there is potential for love between two people, not yet confirmed, but activated, radiant, irresistible.

One month later, at the start of November, Lesley and Conner planned to come over with two of their teammates. Alice was away for a crew meet, but the boys had already planned to come as a foursome.

"More for you to choose from!" Lainey said, as Ji Sun sat on her bed, rating Lainey's outfit options. "Or you could hook up with both?" Lainey was already drinking, sipping wine from a beaker that Alice had brought home to use as a vase. Lainey waggled her eyebrows and flopped back on the bed, giggling.

When the boys arrived, Lainey went to bring them up from the small lobby. They brought the smell of the cool fall night in with them, damp and smoky.

They settled around the window seat, with Margaret going to sit in Conner's lap, like usual. She did so even in the dining hall, and it drove Lainey nuts. Lainey set out a cafeteria tray of snacks and offered the boys some of the boxed wine that Conner kept them supplied with. "I can do you one better," Conner said, and took out a flask, larger than the one that Alice had kept after brandishing it that night in the woods.

The two teammates were cute enough, though neither pulled any cord in Ji Sun's core. She appreciated the way their shoulders looked in their sweaters, but she tended to be attracted to moodier boys, with longer hair and more sullen expressions. Her sister said it was because she'd watched too many Boy George videos as a kid, ruining her for anyone but androgynous white boys. The cuter one, Ruben, wasn't white, but Blasian, a word Ji Sun had learned earlier that night from Lainey. He had kind eyes and a mean smile. As the wine warmed her cheeks and belly, Ji Sun could imagine a good night rolling around with him.

They drank and made fun of each other's favorite bands from high school, and the taller teammate, Jeremy, whom the boys called Jerm, took a baggie of weed out of his pocket.

"Wait, should we hold off?" Ruben asked. "Isn't there a piss test Monday?"

"Nah, only scholarship kids have to take it," Jeremy said. He'd dropped to the floor to roll the joint, kneeled over the window seat as if hunched down in prayer. Before he'd finished, Margaret had gone to her room for a rolled-up towel that she placed beneath the door to the hall, draped a cream pashmina around her shoulders, opened two windows, and reached for the just-lit joint. Lainey stared at her, stunned by how she could move so quickly and still seem unhurried, elegant. So often it seemed as though others were waiting on Margaret—returning her library books, giving her lecture notes, heating up her ramen with their own—that when she whirled into efficiency like this, Lainey took notice. It seemed only to happen when boys were around.

"That's so fucked up!" Lainey said, taking the joint from Margaret. "Only students on scholarship have to take drug tests?"

"It's a condition of some scholarships, yeah," Jeremy said, rolling his eyes at Lainey and taking back the joint.

"Do they not just administer them to the entire team?" Ji Sun asked.

Jeremy turned to pass the joint to Lesley.

"Do you not . . . should you?" Lainey asked Lesley.

"I'm not on scholarship. My parents are pretty rich." Lesley took the joint and passed it to Ji Sun. "Ladies first." He nodded.

"Oh, I didn't—I wasn't trying to—" Lainey felt her cheeks burn.

"Not like a lot of these kids' parents, mind, but they do all right."

He hadn't tried to reassure her, and she felt a frantic rush to prove herself not-racist.

"I just meant, like, a sports scholarship."

"Q-H doesn't give those. Girl, retreat. You don't know my SAT scores." He winked, but he'd hurt her. She'd hurt him, rather, and it smarted to feel so foolish. She had taken such pains to differentiate herself from the entitled students that surrounded her, and here she was, one of them.

"I'm sorry," she said, feeling a blush so deep she thought it must be purple.

"All right, then," he said, and pulled her close. "Aren't you gonna ask?"

"Ask what?" Lainey wondered at what she didn't know. Was there a code to undo this? A question to prove she wasn't like those who assumed any black student who got in did so thanks to affirmative action?

"My SAT scores! Bet I schooled your fine ass in math."

She loved to hear him call her ass fine, felt a wash of relief. At home, she was one of few nonwhite students in her class, and she'd realized already that she'd arrived at college thinking this made her exempt from accusations of racism. But here she was, assuming her own *boyfriend* was on scholarship because he was black. She was on partial scholarship herself! And Lesley had all the usual markers of wealth, which Lainey was expert at identifying: the new iBook; Ray-Ban sunglasses; a different pair of fresh sneakers for every day of the week; and, most of all, an ease with all these things, an assurance that there was more where they came from.

She had made herself a student of Lesley, her cultural envoy into Southern California—*SoCal*, he called it—blackness, and basketball. She dropped *hellas*, used his cocoa butter on her elbows, borrowed and belted his Kobe Bryant jersey to wear over gold tights. She wondered what it would be like to move beyond the bubble of campus with him, what kinds of looks they might get. She wanted the chance now to grip his hand tighter, puff up her chest, stare down—even from half a foot lower than Lesley— anyone who looked at them askance.

Lesley smiled at Lainey now, but Ji Sun had seen his lip curl. In their Intro to Human Psychology course they had just learned that it was disgust—not jealousy, not fury—that was the most common predictor of divorce. Ji Sun wondered if Lainey had seen it, if she should warn her. Ji Sun thought she should adopt Alice's approach to boys. Alice was the only one of the four who had no interest in a boyfriend, who was against the very idea. She was too busy, she said, and what good would it do her? She could hook up with people whenever, and why would she want to spend time with them beyond that? Ji Sun understood this as she, too, was so enveloped in their friendship that the idea of devoting emotional energy to another person seemed exhausting. She would hook up with Ruben, she decided, and when Alice got back on Sunday afternoon she'd tell her all about it, together forge the no-boyfriend contingent.

Everyone was drunk now, and stoned, and Conner and Margaret had already tangled themselves up in a mess of limbs on the window seat. Lainey held Lesley's hand, led him to her room, hers alone for the weekend with Alice away. Ji Sun saw now that Ruben was asleep on the futon, a trail of drool pooled on the cushion beneath his mouth. She looked at Jeremy, who watched Margaret and Conner with a kind of open hunger that did arouse her a little bit. He was very tall, with stubble and acne on his cheeks. The best thing about him was his big nose, which reminded Ji Sun in some way she couldn't explain of a cruise ship, impressive and absurd.

"They'll have to get a room or we will," she said, and covered her mouth as a hiccup escaped. If she wanted to, they would. They were the last two; it was as simple as spin the bottle.

Ji Sun loved kissing and Jeremy was competent. He tasted smoky and astringent, and not like beer at all, a welcome change from her most recent drunken hookups. He put his hands in her hair and began to kiss along her jaw and neck; she stood and offered her hand, and he followed her.

In her room, he changed. He opened her shirt before she could, grabbed at her nipples, lowered his face so he could bite and suck, a hickey forming already on her breast. He seemed not to want to have sex with her, and she was relieved. She could kiss for hours but most of the boys she'd kissed in college had been in a rush to do the next thing, to do more. Most of them seemed to think that it wasn't even worth kissing unless they might get a blow job out of it.

She moved Jeremy back up to her face and sucked on his bottom lip, hard enough that she knew it would be plum colored in the morning.

"The fuck . . . ," he muttered, and pulled away. He gave her a smile that seemed sweet until he said, "I thought Asian girls were supposed to be all submissive and shit." He laughed like he knew she would, too, but she pushed him off of her.

"Okay, we're done," she said. He came back for her neck, like he hadn't even heard her, and sucked in the way she had on his lip, to bruise.

"Stop it," she said. "I'm bored with you now." Submissive. She wouldn't waste her time trying to teach him anything, but she would make sure *submissive* wouldn't be among the words he'd remember her by.

"Fuck you, bitch." He stood and seemed both drunker and stone sober in a split second. He looked the height of the room. "I was bored with you before we began."

How could he turn so quickly? He had been affable, eager, game to maybe kiss until morning, when neither would make any promises to call the other, but both would have felt it a night well spent.

She thought of her friends, tangled up or passed out with their boyfriends. Should she call out for them? He didn't mean enough to her to make her cry, but the way he'd spoken, the snarl in his lip—she felt if he didn't leave soon she might cry anyway.

"Get out of my room," she said, and he stayed looming over her. She buttoned her shirt while he watched, unmoving. He seemed to grow taller.

She went to the door and he stayed standing over her bed. His cheeks puffed up, and as she opened the door she realized he was gathering spit, *hocking a loogie,* Alice called it, when she had to spit after a run. He dredged up phlegm from his throat and spat, loud and wet, on her pillow. Looked at her while he did.

"Get out," she said, wanting to shout now, but still afraid that if she raised her voice she would cry, not so much because of what he did, but because she'd been fooled by him. He stayed there, lips wet, staring her down.

"Get out!" By now Ji Sun was loud enough that she heard movement from the other rooms, and Margaret called out, "Sunny? Ji Sun, are you okay?"

Margaret came to Ji Sun's open door, wearing only her bra and a pair of boxer shorts.

"Jesus H.," Jeremy said. "Your body." He was still on the other side of Ji Sun's bed, mouth wider now.

Lainey and Lesley joined the commotion, and Lainey took charge.

"All of you need to leave." Lainey turned to Lesley. "I'll call you tomorrow. Get him out of here." She pointed at Jeremy, who had finally exited Ji Sun's room, but appeared to have done so only to get a better look at Margaret's breasts.

"What's up?" Conner came out of Margaret and Alice's room, rubbing his eyes.

"Get dressed," Lainey said. "Get Ruben and get out." She tossed Conner the pile of fleece basketball zip-ups they'd left on the window seat and put her arm around Ji Sun. Margaret kicked their pile of huge shoes out into the hall and wrapped her arms around Conner, gave him a long kiss before closing the door.

Once they were gone, Ji Sun did cry. But she couldn't bring herself to tell her friends about Jeremy's spit, only said that he'd turned racist, mean.

"He became too . . . aggressive," she said, though one semester into college, she already knew how "aggressive" had come to contain a huge swath of behaviors, from pressing too close against an ass on the way to a keg, to rape.

Lainey asked if they should call their RA, or health services.

"No, no, he didn't do anything . . . like that," she said. "He didn't assault me. He was just an asshole."

What might he have done if she hadn't shouted, if Margaret, still in her shirtless coat of armor, hadn't come to the door? Reduced to summary, what he had done didn't seem like much: he insulted her, he spit—not even on her, but toward her, on her bed. He stared at her with his teeth bared, refused to move. He called her *bitch* in a way that felt worse than the times she'd been called bitch before. These were not things to report to anyone, not even her friends, and she was feeling foolish now, for causing everyone to derail the party and toss the boys out.

"We have to look out for each other," Lainey said. "Freshmen women are the highest-risk group for date rape." Lainey was going to minor in Gender and Women's Studies, and she'd already begun to volunteer at the campus women's center.

"He didn't *rape* her, Lainey!" Margaret shivered, reached for a blanket.

Everywhere they turned this was the menace, and the only way to protect against it was together.

"I know, I'm just saying." Lainey turned to Ji Sun again. "I'm sorry, Ji Sun."

"Me, too," Margaret said. "Some of Conner's friends are jerks, but I didn't know Jeremy was so bad."

Which ones were okay? How could you tell?

"It's fine," Ji Sun said. "I'm fine." With the boys gone, and Alice arriving back the next morning, she felt there was a chance this could be true, even if it wasn't yet.

CHAPTER 7

I t was a surprise to everyone that Conner's relationship with Margaret outlasted Lainey's with Lesley. But Lainey was not yet ready to date someone so kind, nor could she commit to the cheer-leading persona she'd enjoyed for the length of the season, and now found as itchy and ill-fitting as the vintage polyester cheer-leading costume she'd worn for Halloween. She'd gone as a zombie cheerleader, hoping to make some commentary on the nature of group sports and mob mentality, one whose finer points were fuzzy even before she became too drunk to sputter anything beyond, "Undead love sports, but shriveled brains." She'd Sharpied her arms with "12" tattoos, Lesley's jersey number, and drizzled fake blood on her temples and midriff. Lesley had dressed as a wizard and they'd both hooked up with a blond girl dressed like a fairy, mostly Lainey while Lesley watched, licked his lips, and said how beautiful they both looked, *You especially, Laine.* He was thoughtful even when drunk.

She knew, even when she broke up with him, a process protracted by how much she cared for him, that it was a mistake. But she wanted to make still bigger mistakes with her body and her heart, wanted to fall in love as many times as she could, have the clarity of purpose and thought that came for her only when she was infatuated, when her focus on a new crush gave her fuel to discover the world through them, to learn everything about them, to try to become them, to swallow them. Once she was comfortable, felt herself with them, or felt that who-knew-who-she-was feeling once more, she'd have to break it off and start again. She was self-aware about the process, had had enough fights in high school with friends who accused her of "changing herself" for a boy or a girl. But who doesn't change herself when she falls in love? Wasn't that the point of love? To change for the better, to grow? In college she would fall in love as much as she could, she knew; she would learn as much through make-out sessions at dark parties as she would in seminar halls or in a basement carrel at the library, where she'd heard people hooked up sometimes, and wasn't this a box as worthy of checking off her college list as sledding down the big hill on a dining hall tray, or doing a work study at the crisis center? She had her own ideas for her education. Stand back.

But some of her exploits would have to wait, as finals period was upon them, and all four felt they'd partied too much at the start of the year. None were too far behind, save Margaret, the contours of whose learning disorder still remained somewhat vague to the others, though they knew she wasn't dyslexic, "not technically," she'd said, when Lainey had been bold enough to ask. She got extra time on papers and tests due to ADHD, and she took her Gen Ed courses pass-fail. They were studying now for their psych final, the only class in which they were all enrolled together.

It got dark so early in December. Every Friday they'd scurry home after dinner together, skip any meetings or study groups, and ready their space for a weekend of work. By this time on Sunday afternoon, the common room was littered with crusted plates and snack wrappers, half-filled mugs and water bottles, blankets and sweatshirts, notebooks and textbooks, loose-leaf papers and worksheets, Ji Sun's cache of ultra-fine-point pens from Japan, Margaret's rainbow of highlighters, Lainey's scatter of random pens, and the troll doll totems they'd all adopted after Alice revealed the tiny one stuck on the end of her pencil was her good luck charm.

"Have y'all never heard of the library?" Melinda, their RA, asked. She'd come to remind them about an all-hall meeting later that night. "It pains me to say, but it looks like a hamster cage in here."

She poked her head past Alice, who had answered the door. "Smells a little bit like one, too, if I'm being honest."

"The library doesn't have our good study juju!" Margaret said, positioning her body in front of a contraband cedar candle, lit on the bookshelf. "This place is just *riddled* with good study vibes."

Lainey didn't feel this way precisely, but she had enjoyed the bolstering effects of Margaret's Ritalin, which Margaret had offered to her like a mint, as long as Lainey promised not to get addicted.

"I don't think that's how addiction works," Lainey said, but she felt too strung out after its effects wore off to want to abuse it, as much as she loved how quickly it allowed her to write a paper, to blaze through with enough time to spare that she could read for pleasure, a pursuit that vanishingly few of her fellow freshmen seemed to share.

Roe, a point guard on the women's basketball team about whom her roommates couldn't make enough *rebound* jokes, teased Lainey about how much she hung out in the college bookstore, camped out in the essays section. Lainey had even begun toying with the idea of a creative writing minor, scribbling down observations she thought she might weave into the sorts of strange, dense essays she wanted to read. Her admissions essay, a sideways look at the makeup of her group of siblings, she and her sister adopted, their younger twin siblings biological, from the imagined point of view of someone watching them ride the school bus together, had been called by interviewers from three different schools "one of the finest" they'd seen, in that same language, bolstering Lainey's belief that alumni from all these elite schools were part of some kind of cabal.

Even Alice and Ji Sun didn't read outside of class, not that they had much time for it. Ji Sun had her stack of art books, mostly architecture and photography, and Alice had the rainbow-corner pocket copies of a few J. D. Salinger books on a shelf in her room.

But both Ji Sun and Alice shared a robust familiarity with key classics, which it was easy for Lainey to attribute to their private school educations. They both seemed to have actually *learned* so much—about history, about science, about the world, even about how to learn: how to talk to teachers, how to organize their time—so many things that Lainey felt she was only beginning to learn now. Her high school experience, at her small-town public high school, had been a lengthy exercise in test taking. She both resented and envied their head starts—prided herself on being at Quincy-Hawthorn without having come from a feeder school, and wondered what she'd be like now, had she been able to attend one.

Margaret's high school outside St. Louis was more like Lainey's, but she hadn't fared as well as Lainey on the tests. Ji Sun had recently told Lainey that she thought perhaps Margaret had gotten into Quincy-Hawthorn in part because of her Native American ancestry, something Margaret had mentioned in their American history discussion section.

"Oh, God, everybody claims their great grandmother is Native American." Lainey rolled her eyes.

"No, but Margaret's really is. You can read about her. She was the first female physician on her reservation. She was Coast Salish."

"Huh," Lainey said. "You should tell Alice."

"I did. She's the one who looked her up."

Lainey bristled. Even with a reciprocity of intimacy unlike she'd ever known, there were these avenues, bits one told some but not the others, things some wondered if the others knew.

Lainey looked at Margaret now. She'd unclipped the milkmaid crown that Lainey had given her earlier that day, and two long braids hung down over her shoulders. She looked up, smiled at Lainey. Margaret didn't think twice, it seemed, about why her friend stared at her. She was used to being looked at, Lainey knew. Other women looked at Margaret when she came into a room and then quickly looked away. Men sometimes just kept looking. Of course people looked at Lainey sometimes, too. But there was something particular about the ways in which people tried to disguise or sustain their gaze where Margaret was concerned. Lainey wished she could ask Margaret about it, but she was still inwardly insistent that she not convey to Margaret how overwhelming she found her beauty, that she not be counted among those who reduced—or elevated—her to that.

Lainey tried to map Margaret's features onto the face of the weathered Sioux woman she remembered from her own American history textbooks. She thought of Disney's *Pocahontas*, but Margaret's face looked more like the earlier Disney heroines: its heart shape, those moony mammalian eyes, the sense that she was always gazing up at someone with a tantalizing blend of pleading and mischief.

Margaret gave this look now, as she passed little packets of her lecture notes to the group. Alice grimaced, and Lainey knew why. Margaret's lecture notes typically contained the briefest bullet points, elaborate doodles, and a few cryptic questions that they couldn't even be sure were about the course material: *America for real? Stages & fixations = beaches vs. coastlines? Oral fixation source of Trust & comfort*

"Are these for real?" Lainey asked.

"Everybody's going to pass this class anyway," Margaret said. She uncapped a bright orange highlighter and squinted at the packet of notes from Ji Sun.

"But we don't want to just *pass*, Margaret! Some of us care about our grades." Lainey looked at Alice, who shrugged but then nodded.

"Yeah, I've got to stay at 3.85 or above if I want to get into the best med schools." Alice had her own notes from every lecture, but contributed to the rotation out of principle.

"Well, I'm sorry that my notes aren't as *good* as yours, okay, Lainey?" She pulled the rubber bands from the bottom of her braids and started to unwind her hair. Waves sprung out, seemed to grow with Margaret's frustration.

"It's not my *fault* if I'm not as *smart* as you, okay?" Her hair was a wild mane around her face, now reddened. "Grades are not, like, the only thing in the world for me, okay?" She burst into tears.

Lainey first wanted to comfort her, but she was irritated by her tantrum. "They're not the only thing in the world for me, either, Margaret, but I was counting on these notes to help me study efficiently."

"Well, why don't you study efficiently without me here, then." Margaret stood up and kicked a bowl by accident, kicked it again on purpose. "I'm going to Conner's."

"Margaret, sit down, it's fine," Alice said. "It's not that big a deal." Lainey stayed silent.

"Lainey, we have plenty of notes." Ji Sun said. "And we have the review session tomorrow to fill in any gaps."

Margaret dropped her notes, watched them flutter to the floor.

"Stop acting like a child!" Lainey said. She had the urge to pick up a book and toss it at Margaret, but she crossed her arms over her chest instead.

"You're both acting like babies," Alice said. "Let's get some air. Should we go to dinner?" She looked out the window, but there was no telling if it was four or ten; it seemed like it had been dark for days.

"I told you, I'm going to Conner's," Margaret said, not picking up any of her mess. She pulled a knit Q-H basketball hat down over her hair, its pom-pom bobbling.

"I think we missed dinner," Ji Sun said. "But I could go for a burger."

"Let's do it," Alice said.

Margaret grabbed her bag and went out the door without another word.

"Lainey?" Ji Sun asked, and put on her coat.

"No, thanks," Lainey said, avoiding eye contact.

They left and Lainey stayed in the mess they'd all made, hungry.

It took her a while to remember that no one's mother was going to clean up after them, or bring her something to eat, so she decided to take one more of Margaret's Ritalins and do it herself—not from kindness, but because she knew it was the best way to win this fight.

When they woke up in the morning, the sun would stream into the clean room, and they would sit together on the bright window seat, say how stupid they had both been, hug and cuddle and watch a movie. Lainey would get to feel virtuous for having cleaned the room, though Margaret would never ask or even wonder who did it.

CHAPTER 8

The cold, wet stretch of the year between Thanksgiving, when none of the four went home, and winter break, when they all would, did sustain one parental perforation to their private universe. Alice's family came from their Boston suburb for the Serpentine Regatta, a weekend-long event they'd attended for generations prior to Alice matriculating at Quincy-Hawthorn, a tradition they broadcast in head-to-toe vintage Q-H paraphernalia, including a gold '46 Varsity crew pin that Alice's big brother wore pinned to the polo collar that peeked out from under his Q-H sweatshirt. He worried at the pin, twisted it, and told everyone he met to check it out.

"What a wild year to have been in college, right?" Lainey said, to which Alice's brother only smiled and laughed, the same response he gave most questions.

When Alice's parents arrived in the room, emissaries from a forgotten realm, they transformed the four into children. Each thought she might feel more mature by now than she did, that standing in front of even someone else's parents it would be so obvious that she was a *woman* now, not a girl. But instead, bunched together on the window seat, they felt like they were posing for a photo at a grade school birthday party, and their mismatched mugs, so funky and grown-up most nights, looked, in actual adults' hands, like a play tea set.

Lainey watched the awkward way Alice and her parents hugged, as if pantomiming the act from across a traffic cone, their bodies barely touching. Lainey thought back to her mother on drop-off day, how she smoothed Lainey's hair, squeezed her shoulders, looked for any excuse to touch her. She said good-bye one last time and one last time again just for the hugs, which Lainey would admit to having wished would last longer, too, though more from fear than from longing to be in her mother's arms. Maybe those two feelings were more alike than she had known before that day, when her parents left her.

Alice's father gave Ji Sun an especially vigorous handshake, no doubt due to his conversance with the alumni magazine, Ji Sun thought. Ji Sun's roommates knew that she was very rich, but they didn't yet apprehend that she was name-a-building rich. Anyway, none of the buildings on campus were named for her family, but that was because Ji Sun's mother found the practice gauche, not because they hadn't paid enough for the honor.

Alice's brother and younger sister both widened their eyes at Margaret. Her brother kept staring, and her sister, Brianna, only eight, said, "You are so pretty!" and then, when Margaret laughed and thanked her, put her hand over her mouth as though surprised anyone had heard.

The others had made posters for Alice when she was at practice, and they were piled on the window seat now. Ji Sun had made a line drawing of Alice's face, captured perfectly the shape of her wily grin, and paid to have shirts professionally screen printed rather than use the iron-ons Lainey had suggested they buy. The minimum order had been thirty-five, all one size, and Ji Sun brought the box out of her room now.

"We got extras made!" Margaret said, pulling out four for Alice's family. Lainey noted how easy it was for Margaret to share in the credit for this kindness, even though Ji Sun alone had designed the shirts, paid for them, and lugged them out of her room.

Alice's sister swam in hers, even over her jacket, but she beamed to match the older girls, who had pulled the shirts on over their sweaters, too. Alice's brother pulled one over his sweatshirt, but her parents politely declined.

"Oh, thank you, but I'll be wearing my polar fleece anyway,"
Alice's mother said, and *polar fleece* rang in Lainey's ear as she
watched Alice's mother fold the shirt neatly and set it down on the
arm of the futon, not even tuck it in her bag.

"These are like, next-level WASPs, right?" Lainey whispered to
Ji Sun as they walked toward the river together. Alice held her
sister's hand, but her parents and brother trailed behind, only her
brother's shirt suggesting any connection between them.

"I'm not sure that's it," Ji Sun said. "They're only that cold
towards Alice."

Lainey hadn't noticed this, but she saw now, outside of the dorm
room, how easy Alice's parents were with her brother, how they
each placed a hand on his back when they crossed the street. When
they reached the boathouse and Alice was absorbed by her teammates, her family left together to meet their friends, and Lainey
saw that Ji Sun had been right: as a foursome they looked downright cozy. They jostled together, the parents pointing out land-
marks, their children laughing.

Conner had picked up a bunch of AliceFace shirts to share with
his teammates, so it was easy to find them in the crowd. Jeremy
wasn't among them, but Lesley was there, greeted Lainey with one
of his good hugs, sniffed her neck.

"Mmm," he said. "Still miss that smell, Laine."

She missed his smell, too, which today was layered with the
skunk of weed and the warmth of just-cooked rice. He never
smelled like his teammates, their blend of fresh sneaker and nauti-
cal body spray, beer breath emanating from their every pore. Lainey
had broken up with Roe and was nursing a crush on a sophomore
from her dramaturgy class, but tonight she hoped she'd hook up
with Lesley. He had a new girlfriend, Vanessa, who was straight
edge, which drove Lainey bonkers: the black Xs on her hands at
every party, the bottle of some twee herbal soda, the smug look of

reproach at all the drunkards who didn't know any better. Lainey's childhood best friend had had a long stretch of being straight edge that veered into all-consuming Christianity by the time they graduated high school, making it a little easier for Lainey to say good-bye, in that she felt she already had.

Lainey, Ji Sun, and Margaret had planned to only stay through Alice's event, and then go home and study before meeting Alice later for the Serpentine party. But Conner had brought his flask, as usual, and soon they were too buzzed to think of studying. They shared a bag of kettle corn the size of a toddler and watched the boys eat little bowls of ground beef with bright yellow cheese sauce, a Serpentine tradition. When Alice's boat finally sliced through the water, they stood and hollered, waved their signs, and whooped her name.

Even in their frenzy, they were struck by how little they had appreciated about this huge part of Alice's life. Crew was mostly facts and figures to them: when Alice would be away, whether they'd won, what their team standing was. They didn't encounter the physicality of the endeavor, and as they watched Alice now, even in a line of girls moving in absolute unison, they were certain it was Alice alone who fueled the boat.

They couldn't see from the riverbank that she was sobbing. She had her team visor pulled low, but they weren't looking at her face, could only take in the whole of her, lit by strength: the glow off her forearms as they cut the air against the dark angle of her torso, determined to leave everyone behind, to *go go go*. They could see only her power.

Her brother didn't usually travel, and Alice had been stunned that her parents brought him, and without mentioning it in the emails they'd sent about their plans. From their messages, it seemed as though Alice being on the crew team was more an imposition on their regular Regatta plans than a pleasure, and they'd been noncommittal about the parent barbecue and cocktails that followed the final race.

But here they were, waiting, as Alice and her teammates emerged from the boathouse, victorious, Alice's sister rushing to embrace her and her brother offering a high five. Her parents congratulated her, and swept up in the open camaraderie of the families surrounding them, Alice could pretend for a moment that they were functional.

They chatted with her teammate Clarissa and her parents, and as Clarissa left, she looked from Alice's brother to Alice and asked, "See you both at the party?"

"Oh, Serpentine weekend parties," Alice's father said, looking at Alice's mother, who had her eyes locked on her son. "Nothing like them, truly."

"Wow, can I go, Mom?" Her brother's face brightened in a way that made Alice want to weep. "Can I go?"

Alice's parents exchanged looks. "I'm not so sure," said her mother.

Alice knew that her parents interpreted the advice not to drink after a traumatic brain injury as referring to hard alcohol. Her brother had been drinking beers at dinner since he was sixteen, even though Alice wouldn't dare have a sip of wine in front of them now. She didn't think it was because he was a boy, but rather an allowance made since so many pleasures were already off-limits when you lived at home with your parents and couldn't drive.

"C'mon, I never get to go to college parties!"

The sound of a cheer had erupted over *parties*, so Alice and her parents both heard from her brother a lament at how he never got to go to college, not then, not now, not ever. He hadn't even graduated from high school. Alice's mother hired a tutor to help him get his GED, but Alice got the impression on her few visits home that by now her mother was paying the tutor to play video games with her brother, to come over every week and stay longer than his old friends ever did anymore. Her brother could retain some things, but not enough to hold down an office job, let alone manage an investment firm, or join a pediatric practice, or do any of the other things that Alice's extended family did, filled as it was by aunts and uncles and older cousins who loved to work and found more satisfaction in accruing money than in showcasing wealth.

Her brother was a gardener. He worked year-round at a family farm, in their greenhouse during winter, and outside all summer, refusing, as he had since the accident, to wear a hat. He never bothered with sunscreen, and he had turned red and weathered, with a hairline in sync with his skin, creeping back earlier than Alice imagined it might have had his life gone according to plan. This made the disconnection between the affable, childlike way he behaved and his appearance more pronounced. He was only twenty. But when he'd turned up at her dorm room, Alice had thought for a moment that he was a family friend before he laughed and his eyes crinkled, and she saw that he was her brother.

The summer before college Alice was a gardener herself, living and working on an organic farm in the San Juan Islands. She'd felt a tentative kinship with her brother as she imagined their fingers in the dirt at the same time, wondered how someone who didn't really know what happened could ever forgive her.

"I really wanna check it out! It's cool, right, Al? It's cool?" Her brother looked as though he'd been the one to win a race that day, his smile so wide it made Alice want him to tag along in spite of how ill it made her to imagine bringing him.

"It's cool with me," she said, counting on her parents to veto the plan.

"I suppose, if you're back by midnight. And bring your mobile phone."

"Can I go, too, Mom?" Brianna had gotten her face painted with the Q-H Ocelot, a little green paw print on her cheek, claw slices on her temple.

"No, sweetie. You're far too young for that kind of party, I'm afraid," her mother said, and tried to talk up the hotel pool.

"You might be, too, Alice," her father said, and gave her the kind of stern, protective look that she'd seen fathers make on family sitcoms. She tried to squelch it, but her heart rose.

What harm was it to bring her brother to the party? It was her fault he never went to college after all, and the least she could do was bring him to the kind of party that, if things had gone another way, he might be bringing her to, pretending to punch his frat brothers when they offered her shots.

He kept his AliceFace shirt on for the party, and this nearly did her in. She'd wept on the boat, the shame. Of what she'd done, but also at the relief she felt whenever she saw him now: that he didn't remember. The shame again that she liked him better now than she had back then.

"This is so cool of you, Al," he said on a loop as they walked to the party together. "I'm pumped. Are you pumped? This is so cool of you, Al." No one else called her Al.

At the party, she was grateful to see that her roommates still had their AliceFace shirts on, too. It might have embarrassed her, but now it made her brother seem less pitiful, and seeing them in their oversized fluorescent shirts, nothing like the party clothes worn by the girls that surrounded them, she was overcome with love. She threw her arms around them, each one in turn, and then they all clustered together, a group hug that displaced several partygoers in the crowded kitchen, and lasted until they needed their hands to take paper cups off a tray of Jell-O shots. Alice was relieved that her brother passed on them and accepted instead a red cup of beer from Conner, who had come sniffing around for Margaret.

Alice could feel herself relax as the booze took hold, and her friends took the lead on entertaining her brother. He had the same shirt on as half the basketball team, after all, and some students might mistake him for one of them. Alice wondered if he could feel this, too, that he'd changed lanes into another life, one that might have been.

Her brother was in the bathroom when a lacrosse player bumped into Alice, burped, and called her a dyke.

"I *wish* I were a lesbian. Men are pieces of shit. But they've got those cocks!" She could scandalize even college boys saying *cock* with her Boston Brahmin vowels, leaned against the counter in her cream sweater, hair a glacial blue in the bit of black light that streamed in from another room.

A few of the boys clapped and put their hands over their mouths. *Ho ho! We've got a live one!*

Her brother reappeared from the bathroom and they went to the basement to find the keg.

"Later, boys," Alice called over her shoulder, confident that at least one would be fantasizing about her now, would find her later. Probably the one who'd called her a dyke. It would feel good to reject him, maybe let him grind up behind her first.

She shouldn't get too drunk, she thought, embarrassed to be thinking about sex with her brother back by her side. She hadn't eaten much and she had never felt so many emotions at once before, nervous and sad and elated and relieved and ashamed and grateful. The combination made her more out of it already than she'd planned to get, made her feel like centipedes had been injected into her veins. She loved her friends. She was so glad to live with them, far away from her family. She couldn't believe the horror of what she had done. With her brother so close to her on the stairs she felt off balance, like she could trip, tumble straight through the basement floor, down to whatever hell deserved her.

On their way to the keg, her brother stopped, she thought to tie his shoe. He stayed hunched for so long that Alice wondered if she should offer to help him. Did he need help tying his shoes? How horrible she was. But when she bent low, she heard him mutter something about a pin he'd lost. She tried to tell him they would find it, though she wasn't sure what pin he meant, and before she could ask, someone shoved her brother, said "*Move* it," and he fell from his squat onto his bottom.

"Fuckin' worthless," the boy who'd pushed her brother said, and Alice felt the words like a phantom limb, just above her breasts, an ache in her sternum, some kind of growth that had never belonged in her body, but had lodged itself there nevertheless. *Worthless.*

Alice stood, reared back, and shoved the boy as hard as she could, knocking him into a wall.

He had tossed it off, *worthless,* just because her brother slowed his path to the keg, but Alice was transported back, to the barn where they'd tossed the eggs, to the vinyl bench where her thighs had stuck, to the too-hot air her brother had pushed his finger through to reach her breasts. *Worthless.*

"What the *fuck*?" The boy lifted his fist in the moment before he saw that she was a girl, loosened his fingers, but didn't manage not to strike Alice. The flat edge of his hand landed against the long stripe of her scar.

She put her hand there, in the exact spot she'd sliced open. The scar had mostly felt like nothing in the intervening years, and she didn't even remember the itch she only learned she'd complained about when she snooped in one of her mother's old daybooks last Christmas and read: *Alice won't stop scratching her scar and we're at a loss about it. Have no idea how to address. Cone à la Nancy???* Nancy Reagan was their terrier.

But now it burned and itched; she felt sliced anew.

The boy stepped back, seeing his mistake maybe, but more likely seeing on her face something with which he did not wish to contend. By now, Lainey had come down from upstairs and joined Margaret and Ji Sun, who already formed a circle around Alice, a human shield to guide her up out of the basement.

Lainey took Alice's brother's arm, trailed by Lesley and Vanessa up to the kitchen. Vanessa was the only sober one among them, and she volunteered to go in a cab with Alice's brother back to the hotel. Lainey agreed after making sure Alice's brother had his cell phone, and that he hadn't been hurt. He had the strange look of someone slapped awake from a pleasant dream: a smile still on his lips, but eyes worried.

Alice was sheet white and shaking, not making eye contact with anyone but the middle distance. Ji Sun and Margaret each had an arm around her, but they could feel, too, that she was not in her body, and she didn't respond when they asked her whether she was okay, if he'd hit her head, and finally Margaret, growing nervous, "Alice, are you in there? Earth to Alice!"

"Where is my brother?" she asked when they were nearly back to the dorm.

"He's on the way back to the hotel. He's safe."

"It was so stupid to bring him to the party," Alice said. It was a relief to her roommates that she spoke, but she castigated herself the rest of the way home, continued on into their room, over their objections.

"Alice, sit down, have some water, it's okay!" Ji Sun said.

Alice rocked back and forth on the window seat. She kept one hand pressed against her scar, and hammered the other into her knee like a mallet, too rough and irregular to be a tic.

"Alice, stop it! It's fine! He's fine." Lainey grabbed Alice's fist and tried to hold it, but Alice yanked it loose.

"He's *not* fine! He will never be fine. And it's my fault!"

"It's not your fault!" they all tried to say. They understood Alice's guilt as a version of survivor's remorse, that she had been in the tractor, too, and was unscathed compared to her brother, felt responsible in some convoluted way for distracting him. But now that they had seen the way Alice's parents treated her, and the way Alice wouldn't look at them now, something was shifting.

She rocked and keened, and they saw their reassurances were lost on her. They needed to wait in silence until she was ready to speak.

They waited until the light was pulled evenly in both directions, when you couldn't tell if it was darkest night or earliest morning, the only time of day to share certain things. And Alice did.

What is the right way to react when someone tells you that she wanted her brother dead and she almost made it happen?

They said nothing, for a length of time that had no measure, but seemed interminable, and then they rushed to fill the silence with reassurances for themselves as much as for Alice.

"It wasn't your fault," they said. "You made a mistake!"

"No," Alice said. "When I say it's my fault, I mean it. It wasn't an accident. I—I pushed him off the tractor." Only a second passed before Alice said *pushed*, but it felt to the others like far too much time, time enough to have to rearrange what they believed possible about their friend.

"But still, it was an accident, you were a child!" they said.

"No. I used all my strength and I shoved him out of the seat. I wanted him to die," Alice said. She wasn't crying, and she didn't look at them. She seemed to be answering the questions of an invisible interrogator.

"But, but, *you* could have died, too! You put yourself at risk. You didn't know what would happen!" one of them said.

"Haven't we all been that angry?" one of them asked. The others nodded, but they weren't sure. "You were just, you got that mad when you were in a moving . . . vehicle. Anyone might have . . . made the same mistake." They were struggling to find the right things to say.

All could understand the shoving and the wanting dead. But that they'd happened in the same moment: this separated Alice from them.

"But still, you were only a child!" one of them offered.

"I was older than my little sister is now! I was old enough to want him *dead*."

The way she said *dead* again, definitive, as though he had died. Had they met his ghost? They all thought back to the exchanges they'd had with her brother. Margaret's family might have called him "touched," and Margaret wondered now what it meant, *touched*. Touched by whom? By God? Was it a gift to go through the world a dope?

They thought of his lined face, his big smile, how eager he had been to see Alice, to meet her friends. He'd said to each of them how cool they were, more than once, and even though this embarrassed them, they weren't immune to compliments, even from someone who gave them so freely.

"It was still an accident really, though, right?" Margaret asked. "I mean, you didn't kill him."

"But I wanted to. I tried to. Please," Alice cried now, instead of answering, as though under oath. "Don't make me say it anymore."

"You don't have to! You don't have to say it at all," they said, and then they said they would never tell anyone what she had done.

The look on Alice's face told them that this hadn't occurred to her, that they might tell what she had done.

"Oh, God, please don't tell anyone. I don't even, don't even mention it to me. Let's never talk about it again," she said. "Promise me."

They promised, but it didn't seem enough. Lainey removed the pin from her kilt and suggested they become blood brothers, not changing the word, but adding moon sisters. They could be both. The kilt pin was too dull, so Ji Sun stood and took a NOT MY PRESI-DENT pin and a lighter from off the bookshelf. She bent back the pin and burned its tip, poked it into her pointer finger until a spot of blood appeared. She passed the pin along to Alice, who poked hard without a look, and Lainey, who poked and sucked the blood, caught herself, and let it bloom again.

"Can you do me, Alice?" Margaret asked. "I can't do it myself."

Alice looked newly bereft. "Why me?" she said, her face crumpling.

"You're the doctor," Margaret said. Her eyes widened and Lainey wondered again why Margaret seemed so much younger than the rest of them, even now with Alice looking like a kitten in the days before its eyes opened, a fresh pink grub of pain.

"I'll do it," Lainey said, and counted, "One, two, *poke!*" to Margaret's *Yow*, and they pressed their fingers all together, like a toast where each made sure to touch everyone, to look in her eyes.

They were locked together now in this new way, by blood, by Alice's secret, her worst act. They'd sworn in blood under the moon to keep Alice's secret, and in this way they vowed to keep future secrets, too.

Alice didn't tell them what had enraged her enough to push. She knew they might have ideas from their own childhoods. It seemed to Alice the only way she could atone at all, to try not to make her friends see this puppy of a man as a wolf of a boy.

None of them were afraid of her, not even for a second, and this Alice must have sensed when they held her in their arms. They hadn't known twelve-year-old Alice, but they loved her, and if they had been on that bench with her, they might have pushed her brother, too.

But in this fearless embrace there was a bit of gratitude, too, a feeling that Alice had gone out ahead and done the worst thing, a child's belief that none of them would ever hurt anyone so much.

PART II

THE ACCUSATION

SOPHOMORE YEAR,
2003–2004

CHAPTER 9

The four felt lucky to be headed together into Professor Walker's classroom at the start of their sophomore year, reunited after a summer spent pining for one another, pinging emails and cascading chains of phone calls from their points around the world: Ji Sun luxuriating in the Philippines and interning at an art gallery in Seoul; Alice sailing and camping all over New England as part of a wilderness medicine course; Lainey in Vermont, itching in an over-warm usher outfit at an outdoor theater-in-the-round; and Margaret, home in Missouri and working at a new ice cream shop that required her to sing its theme song every single time a customer dropped money in the tip jar. Walker's was the largest course in all of the humanities, crowded with students and even some faculty members who sat in on his lectures, but the four had lucked out in the lottery and secured spots in discussion sections, too. The class met in Loeb Hall, a small but stately building perched atop the big hill that mainly housed offices for the college's higher-ups, but also contained a large lecture hall that looked carved from the gilded guts of a roll-top desk. Before the semester began, only Lainey, also the only one who'd read Walker's work, had said she'd sit in if she couldn't earn credit, but Margaret had promised to give her spot to Lainey if she got one and Lainey didn't.

"That's not how the waitlist works," Ji Sun had said, and even knowing this, Lainey was steamed that Ji Sun hadn't made the same offer.

Ji Sun was skeptical that Walker would be all he was cracked up to be, but when she entered the lecture hall, she gasped. He stood in silhouette in the front of the room, an enormous Jenny Holzer slide illuminated behind him: ABUSE OF POWER COMES AS NO SURPRISE.

Ji Sun had hung her treasured wooden PROTECT ME FROM WHAT I
WANT postcard, a gift from her sister, on the gallery wall she and her
roommates put together earlier in the week. One panel adjacent to
the window seat was randomly painted lilac, and last year they'd
hung snapshots from parties and postcards from high school
friends there. But they wanted to show they'd grown. Their walls
weren't just bulletin boards, and their dorm room was their home.
Jenny Holzer was Lainey's favorite artist now, too, along with
Barbara Kruger, whose postcards Lainey had contributed to the
wall.

"Hey, it's Holzer," Lainey said now, and elbowed Ji Sun lightly,
but Ji Sun was too transfixed to be irked that Lainey would think Ji
Sun wouldn't know.

It wasn't that Walker was beautiful, though he was: tall and
shaggy haired with perfectly tailored pants and a crisp Oxford shirt
in the only shade of blue that Ji Sun found an acceptable alternative
to white. He stood before the line of students waiting to talk to him,
flanked by teaching assistants who alternated between staring at
Walker with open adoration and shooting glares at the students
who no doubt wished to make the case that they alone deserved to
come off the waitlist. But more than Walker's beauty, it was a wash
of feeling: Oh, *this* is what college is supposed to be like! The late
summer light streamed in, painted gleams on the dark wood mold-
ing in this, one of the oldest and most stately rooms on campus,
retrofitted with modern implements that could slide out of view
like Murphy beds and send the students back to earlier eras, when
they might have come to college not just as a launching pad to their
professionalization, but to be awakened, politicized, even radicalized. This is what Walker promised with his course, Protest Songs:
American Unrest from Vietnam to Operation Enduring Freedom.
They admired even the course title, that he was so willing to engage
with the war that was barreling down on them, the one they all felt

there had to be *some* way to stop, with this bumbling pet monkey of a monarch mixing up countries in the Middle East, forsaking any global goodwill left over in the wake of September 11, when the four had just been finishing high school, Lainey and Margaret terrified to leave their hometowns just as the world seemed ready to collapse around them.

In Lucerne in 2001, Ji Sun had stood alongside her American classmates for an international moment of silence, and she'd spoken to her mother and sister that morning, knew they were doing the same in Seoul and in Brussels. What a show of love, from everywhere! What would it feel like to be on the receiving end of that, Ji Sun wondered, eyeing the Americans, most of whom stood, huddled together, faces streaked red, clutching one another as though even here they were under siege. Surely, Ji Sun thought, after their grief wore off some, the Americans would be jarred into a recognition that they were part of an entire planet of people, some of whom, her own parents included, had been facing fears of buildings falling out of the sky for many years. But it seemed September 11 had had the opposite effect, and the Americans she knew became more obsessed with their Americanness than ever before, with what America meant, what America would do, and what that would mean (for America). The rest of the world was mere audience, at best, waiting to be gifted with American pop culture exports, or expected to offer sympathy, support, or troops for whatever war, or "operation" (who cares on what country!) Dick Cheney was drumming up next.

Bush had made Ji Sun Axis of Evil–adjacent during the previous semester, and Ji Sun had stopped being stunned that even Quincy-Hawthorn students would still sometimes look at her hangul askance, unsure of her allegiances.

So her heart lifted when Professor Walker asked them, "What is America?" and after listening to their volleys, laughed, said, "You're all wrong. America is a corporation! And its current CEO is not fit for the job. And this place," he gestured around the beautiful room, his palm open as though he carried something fragile there, "this place is a corporation, too. Are you the customers? Am I the product? Who is getting rich?"

Walker would know. He'd made millions creating an election-results-prediction algorithm and website, selling a majority share of both to Google. That he'd had extraordinary luck in a dot-com boom that few understood made his success still more dazzling. Most people who made that kind of money quit teaching, moved west. That Walker stayed gave him credibility as an intellectual, devoted to shaping young minds when they were still malleable, plus the wholesome patina of a family man, having said in interviews that he stayed in part for his young family. He talked about the worth of a liberal arts education, what a gift it was to work at an institution that not only helped advance human thought, but welcomed, even encouraged, interrogation and dissent from within.

The university couldn't dip his form in bronze fast enough. His dark fop of hair appeared all over Quincy-Hawthorn's website, a snapshot of him lecturing in the banner on his department's page; his headshot popping up often on the News page; even a candid of him and his wife, a Japanese-American ceramicist, and their beautiful hapa babies on the Campus Life page.

"Q-H has such a boner for this dude," Conner had said when they'd told him they all got spots in his class.

"Everybody has a boner for this dude," Lainey said. "Me included. *You* included."

"Not really my type," Ji Sun had said then.

"Listen to him talk," Lainey said. "He's everybody's type."

They had all heard the rumors, of course. But they seemed fuzzy and unfounded, and were mostly met with jokes.

"I'd like a little of that *sexual* harassment pointed in my direction," someone would say, and even Lainey, who was starting her second year of work-study at the campus women's center, would laugh.

On the walk home they floated in the postlecture glow, talked about neoliberalism and Walker's hair until Margaret stopped on the sidewalk.

"Do you think it's true? What people say about him?" Margaret asked.

"What, that he's *magnificent*?" Lainey asked, smiling.

"Not that," Margaret said. "I mean, that he sleeps with his teaching assistants."

"Of course not!" Alice answered. "He wouldn't have a job!"

"Oh, right. No! I don't know." Margaret sat on the low brick fence beside the bike rack and the others stood around her. "I just thought about it today, with the way some of the TAs were looking at him."

"It's not illegal to have a crush," Lainey said, hand on her hip. "And besides, even if he did sleep with a graduate student, which I am *positive* he did not, I'm sure it was consensual, and only problematic because it's outside the bounds of convention."

"But he's married!" Margaret said.

Lainey rolled her eyes. "That's what I mean. Who knows what arrangement he has with his wife!"

"Have you seen her?" Ji Sun asked. "She's quite striking."

"What does that have to do with it?" Lainey asked. "Ugh. These rumors persist as a way to undermine the work he's doing at Q-H, which, like, obviously has its detractors." Lainey hitched up the straps on her backpack and looked around at the stream of students passing to their next class. Freshmen made furtive glances at their folded maps, and Lainey thought how much smaller the campus had become to them after just one year, the entirety not visible from the base of the big hill, where they sat now, but feeling nearly so.

Margaret nodded. It was unusual for her to disagree with Lainey, whose confidence and smarts always won Margaret to her side. "I don't know, though, isn't it against the rules anyway? Even if it is consensual? What do you think, Alice?"

Lainey scowled.

"I dunno." Alice looked at her watch. "I guess it's frowned upon. I've got to run, though. See you for dinner?"

"I might have a meeting," Lainey said, looking at Margaret.

"Yeah, okay," Alice said. "Well, I'll be at the D-hall by six. Let me know where we land on this guy, 'cause I should probably have the info before I fuck him." She winked. She didn't even think Walker was as dreamy as the others did, but they were grateful to her for making a joke that let them laugh and leave for their next classes feeling that they all desired the same thing, and that they would be okay whether or not they got it.

CHAPTER 10

F lames had begun to lick the leaves outside their picture window, and Lainey felt their heat in her limbs. As it cooled into fall, she grew electrified, molted the sluggishness of late summer, felt on fire to become. Become what? Become what? Become *what*? And when would she know? She wasn't even sure she wanted to act anymore, and theater had been one of the few things she'd come to college certain about. Her Improv Activism troupe had stalled and then imploded. Their most recent efforts—impromptu antiwar sketches staged in library reading rooms—had been met with strident shushes and the wrong kind of laughter, and Lainey had told the troupe they needed to use everything at their disposal to break students from the trance of myopic apathy disguised as ambition. But the men in the group only wanted to recite long passages from Marxist philosophers, and the women only wanted to perform their slam poetry. Everyone wanted drums. At the last meeting, the group's founder, Shane, had begun to wonder aloud whether the invasion of Iraq was, while a terrible thing, perhaps an unavoidable and even necessary one, and the night devolved into wails, accusations, and breakups, including Lainey's with Shane, whom she'd been seeing all summer since they met as ushers at the theater-in-the-round. She was pretty sure the troupe was disbanded, at least for now.

At home, the change from summer to fall was marked by shopping for school supplies with her siblings, and she'd received a small package from her big sister, Rachel, the second week of school, filled with sheets of stickers Lainey remembered from the desk in their shared childhood room: scratch-'n-sniff food cartoons from their cafeteria, neon puffers of 1980s cartoon characters, tiny animals and flowers smaller than her pinky nail. *Found these at home last visit & thought of you. Maybe you want to mix up some of your damn-the-man paraphernalia, keep the man on his toes. Love you the most, xR.* Both of them had been sticker hoarders, preferring to file their stickers away rather than stick them into the albums that were popular with their peers. Scarcity reserves, her sister called it, when Lainey had called to thank her for the stickers, and all adoptive kids had it, according to Rachel, who said it was passed down in their genes. She studied genetics at the University of Pennsylvania, so she should know. But when Lainey wondered aloud what, specifically, their respective biological parents might have lacked, her sister had huffed.

"The means and agency to raise their own children, for one," Rachel said.

"I meant which *stickers,*" Lainey said. Her sister hadn't laughed.

Lainey had tucked her stickers away not because she wanted to keep them, but because she'd been waiting for the right place to put them. What sense did it make to move them from one sheet in a drawer to another on a shelf? They should be seen and enjoyed, and she shared them with abandon now, putting them on Post-it notes about her whereabouts that she stuck to the whiteboard, or on little mash notes she slapped on their mini fridge. The stickers delighted Alice and Margaret, who remembered similar ones, and Ji Sun loved them, too, though of course she had known more impressive stickers in Korea, knew the best of everything, it seemed, and Lainey would admit that Ji Sun's office supplies did make their stuff look like garbage.

The note from her sister was written on the back of one of their mother's old recipe cards for seven-layer sour cream taco dip. When it was discovered that both Lainey and her older sister were lactose intolerant, her mother found dairy substitutes before it was easy to do so in upstate New York, and learned to use her cheesecloth to make nut milks. Their dad had once driven fifty miles to buy a pint of ice cream made from coconut milk that advertised itself as even more delicious than the real thing.

What more did her sister want from them? Rachel looked to attribute most of her own problems, and all of Lainey's, to their both being adopted. Lainey had long accepted that being adopted had real bearing on her peripatetic sense of identity, and her parents had put her and her sister in counseling specific to adoptive issues starting when Lainey was in second grade. But Lainey was sure in a way she was about few things that she'd be even more of a mess if she'd grown up without two parents who supported her in every way, knew this better now than she had before college, now that she'd met Alice's parents, and Ji Sun's. She hadn't met Margaret's, but she'd heard enough to know she'd never wish to trade. They had a study break that coincided with Sukkot, and her parents had suggested she visit and bring along these roommates they'd heard so much about.

Margaret's friend Mac, a law student with an obvious crush on her, let Margaret borrow his car, a cream Saab, and the four filled it with enough junk food for a journey five times as long as the three and a quarter hours it took them, Lainey at the wheel, all of them hollering along with the mix tapes they'd scavenged, windows down and heat cranked up. Driving through Saratoga Springs, Lainey felt a lick of shame at wishing her parents lived there, or in one of the other chichi enclaves that she knew people at Quincy-Hawthorn pictured when she said she was from upstate New York, imagining, as they likely did, second homes and trains into the city, not the dinky nowhere town where she'd grown up.

Pulling into her driveway, that longing vanished, replaced by one for her parents, even as they stood there, a longing so pronounced that she had to catch her breath. There was some new layer of pity folded into her love for them, something about her being so clearly at the start of her life, arriving home with a carful of her college friends, and her parents, disheveled and grinning, at the door to the house where they would likely live out their days. They had a good life, Lainey knew; they loved their life. But so much about it was already determined, and from her vantage now, this seemed too painful to consider. She shook her hair, aubergine for fall, and got out of the car, took the stairs in only two steps, and nearly knocked them over, let them hold her in their arms.

After they'd had breads and spreads, Lainey's favorite childhood snack, and tea with her parents and were alone in her old room, Ji Sun described Lainey's house as a museum exhibit for wholesomeness.

"Yeah, it is incredible how cozy it is here," Alice had said.

Lainey felt defensive at first. Did they mean shabby? Her parents had a rambling Victorian, large but crowded with books and plants and threadbare antique rugs. She knew it was smaller than Alice's or Ji Sun's houses.

But as the weekend went on and her roommates accepted every offer of cocoa, wrapped themselves in her mother's afghans, laughed at her dad's corniest jokes, and delighted in the books and puzzles and VHS tapes in the den, Lainey could see that their enjoyment was genuine, and she relaxed, began to savor how at home they were here, in her home.

"I am so freaking comfortable," Alice said, laid out on the over-stuffed orange corduroy couch. "I've never napped so well in my life." She stretched her arms above her head and knocked over a framed photo of Lainey that sat on the end table.

"Oh, my God, look at little goth Lainey!" Alice held the portrait in her hands and sat up, passed it to Ji Sun.

Lainey knew the photo: her outfit from Hot Topic in the mall, her bleached bangs and black nails. For all of sophomore year of high school she'd powdered her face porcelain and raccooned her eyes black.

"It's hard to believe all that," Ji Sun tapped the picture, "emerged from all this." She gestured around the living room, fireplace roaring, music playing, Lainey's parents singing along, voices audible over the sounds of their cooking dinner together in the kitchen. In Ji Sun's other hand was a mug, hand thrown by Lainey's dad at the ceramic studio at the local high school. Ji Sun clutched it close, near her heart, even as Lainey noticed it was empty.

"It's *wonderful* here," Margaret said, snuggled up in the basket chair in the corner that Lainey and her siblings called the jungle, surrounded as it was by hanging plants, a ledge of aloe and medicinal herbs, and a giant pencil cactus that poked at the closest bookshelf and into the chair's wicker weave. "I don't even want to go back to school! Do you think your parents would adopt *me*?"

They all laughed then, and Lainey said "Probably," but she bristled, felt aware all at once of how this was her wealth. Margaret had her excess of beauty, and Alice and Ji Sun were both rich, Ji Sun extraordinarily so. Since starting Walker's class, Lainey had attended two meetings of the campus democratic socialists, but here she was, in her own home, counting the ways in which she didn't wish to share.

Rachel hadn't made it home as planned, claiming too much work. When she started graduate school, she became very angry with their parents, though she was always quick to say she was not angry at *them*, but at the system that made it possible for them to raise other people's children. Lainey had grown more protective of her parents in the face of Rachel's fury, let her sister have this crisis for the both of them. The thought of piling on when her parents were so receptive to Rachel's criticisms, so supportive of her rejection of them, made her miserable to even consider. They were her parents. Before she left for college, Lainey told her parents that even if her own adoption had not been closed, she would not seek out her biological parents. She didn't believe this, but she badly wanted them to. The information she did have about her biological parents had been distilled for some years down to one strike-through on a sparsely filled out photocopy of a form, which for a time during the second half of high school she trotted out as an anecdote for painful laughs, before putting it away, only to share with people like her roommates, whom she trusted and loved, and knew would let her be more than this black bisecting line. The strike-through came in the Ethnic Background section of the form, where—in handwriting that Lainey's mirrored exactly, whether through repeated viewing and intentional modeling or biology, she would have to ask Rachel—her biological mother, white, had written of her biological father, *Mexican and Chinese*, and ~~Chinese~~ had been crossed out, replaced by *Vietnamese*, in a different handwriting, with a set of inscrutable initials beneath. Her parents assured her that Vietnamese was accurate, and that the caseworker had "verified that bit." It wasn't lost on her that her bio father wasn't there at all, to fill out the form for himself, but she still felt angrier at her birth mother, that she hadn't known this, or had had to be told, or even, best-case scenario, had remembered later—what this told her about her biological parents' relationship was too painful for her to contemplate most days, in the house where she lived with two white parents who could trace their lineage down to neighboring shtetls in Poland, and who could have entire arguments with only snorts and sighs and farts.

Other people didn't know their parents like this, Lainey knew, didn't pay such close attention. But she'd learned from her parents that attention was a form of devotion, and this was the love they practiced in their home: of careful observation, of seeing and being seen.

Her younger siblings, the twins, Oliver and Edith, were her parents' biological children, born when Lainey was eight. They sealed the family for her in a way she struggled to explain even to the counselor she'd begun seeing shortly after her mother became pregnant. When Lainey first met the twins she felt they were of her in a way that was almost agonizing, as it was the first she could remember really reckoning with the idea that she was not of her parents in the same way that the twins were. But she saw that this was her sister and her brother, and they were her flesh and blood. She couldn't understand why Rachel, twelve at the time, didn't feel this way, and in retrospect seemed to first turn from their parents when the twins arrived home. When their mother had been on bed rest in the weeks before the twins' birth, Rachel and Lainey had both nuzzled up with her in bed every afternoon, carried in trays of snacks and read and watched their afterschool TV in her room, on a crummy old TV their father had brought up from the basement for just this purpose. The color on the set was off, and you had to stand up to turn the channels, but it was mostly an excuse to be with their mother anyway. Those months before the twins were born, Lainey felt sometimes that her mother was pregnant with her. She dreamed it some nights, and the dream bled into the day in a way that she wished she could share with someone. But curled up against her mother's body in bed, she could feel the feet and fists of the twins and it seemed selfish to claim that space as hers. She wondered if Rachel understood, with the tender way her sister rested her hand on their mother's stomach, the way Rachel kept one eye on the round rise of it even as she watched her favorite shows. Who was she guarding? Lainey had never asked.

At dinner, Margaret revealed that she'd never been to a Sukkot dinner, or even a Shabbat, didn't think she knew any Jewish people in the small town she'd grown up in, too far outside St. Louis to claim the city as she did at school. She explained to Lainey's parents that no one had heard of Boonville, and Kansas City confused people.

"Well, what a pleasure for us to introduce you to a taste of reform Judaism." Lainey's dad winked and gestured toward the challah, unblessed and with a hunk already torn off by Oliver.

"Yeah, but lighting Shabbat candles is like the only Jewish thing we even do," Edith said. Both Rachel and Lainey had had bat mitzvahs, but it seemed that Edith and Oliver may not. Their parents had never been observant, and Lainey understood her bat mitzvah as at least in part informed by her adoption, as a way to celebrate her membership in a community that she'd since learned some didn't consider legitimate. After a Birthright trip in college, Rachel had undergone a conversion to become a true Jew, as she'd put it, but Lainey didn't notice any changes in her sister after that, apart from the fact that she only dated Jewish boys. Growing up, Lainey felt Jewish, but mostly compared to non-Jews. Her parents' version of Judaism asked over and over how to be Jewish, and more, how to *be*, without ever providing an answer. Sitting at the table now, she felt how much this latter question had been forged in her bones, and how asking was the only answer. At Quincy-Hawthorn, most of the Jewish kids in her circles wore keffiyeh and *Free Palestine* patches on their backpacks, and ate at Hillel on Fridays, but mainly because the food was better. They were big into the antiwar movement, and Lainey brought up one of their recent efforts now, as dinner wound down, knowing it would be of interest to her parents.

"Are you all as involved as Elaine in these antiwar efforts?" Lainey's mom asked her roommates.

"Not as active as Lainey," Ji Sun said. "But we all show up."

Alice nodded and Margaret bowed her head.

"I'm not sure," Margaret said. "I know Lainey doesn't like to hear me say this, but I don't know if it's completely wrong."

"I'm against the war," Alice said. "Full stop." Alice looked at Lainey. "But I understand that."

"I understand that, too," Lainey's dad said, and rubbed his beard. They all waited, as they were used to men lecturing them after claiming understanding. But he only nodded until Lainey's mom picked up the nod baton and spoke.

"I do, too," she said. "I think we all do. But how does visiting that same terror on others solve our problems?"

"Mr. Bucholz said there's no way we can be safe without bombing them into oblivion," Oliver said, and shoveled a giant forkful of apple cake into his mouth. Lainey knew the cake so well, could anticipate the way the apples, even with so much cinnamon, would still taste the slightest bit of garlic and onion, the way everything chopped on her parents' ancient cutting boards did.

"He what?" Lainey's mom slapped her hand on the table, a loud knock softened by the batik tablecloth. "In what context could the *gym teacher* possibly have offered that bit of insight?"

Lainey's mother gulped down a slug of wine, and Lainey thought of how Rachel had also of late taken to accusing their parents of being snobs. Lainey had laughed. "Dad has *one* pair of jeans, Rach. I think you should come visit me at Quincy-Hawthorn to learn what a snob is."

"Intellectual snobbery, dear Laine," Rachel had said. "Something of which you yourself may wish to be wary. There are many kinds of knowledge that don't come from institutions."

"Okay, but aren't you in *graduate school*?" Lainey had wished they were having the fight in person, instead of over the phone, so her sister could see her face.

"That doesn't mean I can't appreciate the wisdom we've been deprived of by not having access to our family of origin."

They didn't have the same birth parents. But Rachel didn't seem to accept this. For all her obsession with finding her birth parents and righting the wrongs of having been wrenched from them, she couldn't even acknowledge that Lainey could never do this, didn't have the option. Rachel's studies had only made her more resolute in this strange blind spot, referring, as she often did, to their parents as if they were the same people, and not the ones at the table with Lainey now.

"Who is *them*, though, Ollie? We always talk about 'them' like this, like they're not people! You realize people in Baghdad are having dinner with their families, just like us, right now," Lainey said.

"Well, not *right* now, probably, since it's in the Arabia time zone," Edith said.

Lainey smiled at her little sister, but thought of the one aspect of her older sister's research that nagged at her, around intelligence. Just as she envied Alice and Ji Sun their exclusive educations, she fretted over whether the twins would grow up to be much smarter than even Rachel and Lainey, both of whom had graduated at the top of their class, and gotten academic scholarships to college.

"I can't believe you even talk about all this at the dinner table!" Margaret put her hand over her mouth as if she'd burped. "I'm so sorry," she said. "I didn't mean for that to come off that way. I just meant that my family . . . well, my mother always said if you look too long down the well you'll lose the light."

"Hmmm," Lainey's mother said. "I've never heard that saying. As I've known it, only light can root the darkness out."

"Yes. Dr. Martin Luther King Jr. 'Darkness cannot drive out darkness, only light can do that.'" Lainey's father reached out and took his wife's hand, and they exchanged a kind of look that made Lainey feel embarrassed but also made her think that someday finding a true life partner might be the only goal worth having.

The sun had gone down completely by then, and the light that remained in the room came from the warm overhead bulb and the flickering beeswax tapers, down nearly to their carved-wood holders now.

The twins got up from the table and started to collect everyone's dishes. Lainey's father offered coffee and her mother said they could each have a teacup's worth of wine if they preferred. Lainey felt a warmth in her belly as if she were already drunk, to have everyone she loved best around one table together, talking about love, and war, and the world, and how they might make it better, or how, at least, they could stop the government from making it worse. Her father had always said Lainey had a fire in her belly, when she'd rage or wail, even when he was the target of her screeds against injustice, and she thought now of how that fire was not cooled, but at this table it felt more like fuel than destruction. That warmth didn't make her want to sink into bourgeois complacency, but it did make her understand what everyone was so desperate to protect, what they'd fire blind missiles into the sky to save.

CHAPTER 11

When Professor Walker sang in class, Ji Sun was sunk. His voice, rich and smooth when he spoke, commanding in both its tenor and its near terrifying speed, became thin and tremulous when he sang, like a boy whose range had just begun to change. He sang like a child without much talent who had been given a solo in the hopes it would boost his confidence, and she felt something akin to actual love for him then, standing in front of the room singing so poorly, *closing his eyes*. The confidence it took, to be so vulnerable! Where did it come from?

Anyone on campus could answer this: from wealth, status, looks, charm, intelligence, privilege, lineage, luck. Anyone who spurned Silicon Valley in favor of the small stage at the front of a lecture hall, even the most ornate one around, was comfortable singing no matter how he sounded.

Ji Sun hadn't expected the depth of her enchantment. Walker rode a *bike* to campus, for chrissakes, didn't he sometimes feel like a parody of himself, removing his sheaf of papers from his leather panier, tucking the newspaper under the arm of his wool jacket, elbow patches, of course, just in case anyone missed the memo that here, boys and girls, was a man of the mind?

Now, eyes closed, hands at his sides, wave of dark hair cresting over his forehead, his voice rang out across the hushed room. He sang the verse to "Ohio," one hand over his heart, chin jutted forward as though he might direct them to the same well of ardent conviction from which he drew.

Finished, he opened his eyes and broke into a wide smile, dimples and accompanying creases nearly too much to endure.

"I felt so *certain* you would join in." He laughed. "Thanks for leaving me hanging. Unless—don't tell me you didn't join in because you don't know the words to this iconic American protest song? Homework. Write this down." He went to the board and started his wild scribbling, a playlist.

Ji Sun sighed. She felt, as she copied down the list in her neat script, that she was in a film about a star-crossed campus romance. The lecture hall, both dusty and gleaming, made her feel as though she sat inside an antique organ. It smelled of chalk dust and wood varnish. She wore her usual, a black tunic and black creepers, new ones with spent bullet casings embedded in the heels to look like studs. But in her mind she wore a perma-press cotton short-sleeve blouse with a Peter Pan collar, pilled cardigan in deep plum, pleated plaid skirt of the universally agreed-upon least flattering midcalf length, and leather Oxfords with no heels, in oxblood and cream— the uniform from her Seoul primary school days, transposed and updated only in size for this costume in her fantasy.

The students around her wore their usual, too—a smattering of sports sweatshirts, rugbies, and velour tracksuits with the word *Juicy* on the rear that had inexplicably become not only acceptable to wear outside of the house, but desired status markers. Even Margaret had one, in pale blue, purchased after a fair amount of agonizing since the set cost nearly two hundred dollars. But these students receded easily when she looked at Professor Walker, became background in the story of their romance. Even her roommates were bit players in this film.

He caught her eyes and returned her gaze, smiled. He could feel it, too.

CHAPTER 12

B y semester's end, Lainey had become cochair of the campus Code Pink antiwar women's movement, and she tried on a Saturday morning to get her roommates to join her for a peaceful resistance strategies workshop that she'd helped to organize.

"I'm just not sure how this is relevant to us?" Margaret said, which was met with a "*WHAT*" from Lainey before Margaret could even finish her sentence-question, that upward lift to every line that drove Lainey nuts.

"I don't mean protesting!" Margaret said. "You know I am against the war. I mean the nonviolent, what-do-you-call-it, the training in peace resistance."

It was hard for Lainey to know how to answer this, because the idea that the US would go to war in Iraq made her want to do violence. She knew Margaret meant that they probably wouldn't get into any skirmishes in their pint-size campus protests, but still, it felt disingenuous for Lainey to preach about civility when she wanted to burn the White House to the ground.

"Walker will be there!" Lainey said. She waggled her eyebrows. There would be pizza, too, as they'd had to add to all the flyers, heaven forbid anyone turn up to oppose an unfounded *war* without the promise of free food.

"He will?" Ji Sun asked. "I thought you said he had a scheduling conflict."

"He got out of it," Lainey said. "This is more important, and he knows it. You guys do, too."

"That's some mom-grade guilting, Laine, but I can't miss my Orgo review session. I'm sorry," Alice said. "Plus I have the worst cramps." Alice rolled her eyes toward her menstrual cup, which was drying atop its drawstring pouch on the strip of heat vent beneath the window seat.

Lainey looked at Alice's mooncup and felt washed with the horror of being a woman. It wasn't horror at this stupid little cup— its tie-dyed pouch, its toasted yellow silicon—it was the horror at her own disgust, its permanence, the way she knew, *knew*, as long as she lived, no matter how many women's studies degrees she earned, no matter how radicalized she became or appeared to be, there would be this at her core, this disgust at her own disgust, this discomfort at being made to feel from birth and on some cellular level, horror at her own body, what it was capable of, what it might be meant to do.

Her failings as a feminist felt so acute to her as she considered her roommates now: Alice, with her comfort in her own body, its strength and resilience, the pleasures it afforded; Ji Sun with her insistence on dressing like abstract art, shrouding herself in impenetrable layers and refusing to date anyone until she was twenty-five or secure in her career, whichever came first; and Margaret, with the easy way she showed them love, snuggled up, rested her head in their laps or on their shoulders, brushed their hair, held them like a mother might when they were sad, grabbed their hands and swung them in hers when they walked home together after dinner, this more like a child than its mother, but all of this easy physical affection for women felt to Lainey like more of a feminist act than the ones she herself embraced: affixing buttons to her backpack, shaving the hair on her head in an undercut, leaving her underarm hair unshaved, drinking from a mug that read FUCK THE PATRIARCHY on one side and WITH YOUR STRAP-ON on the reverse.

Lainey was tired of her own performance, too, tired of talking in rooms, talking in bigger rooms, even shouting into megaphones. Code Pink said wearing all pink was about visibility, but who was watching? She should go to New York or DC, join some real protests. But she was as bad as her roommates, wanting to make sure she had time to study, too, and not wanting to miss Walker's class.

She'd been the one to remind them to register the moment Walker's enrollment opened, to give them the best chance at getting spots. And she was the only one who had read any of his articles before they'd been assigned. She felt like a brat whose favorite indie band had made it big, though Walker had hardly been under-ground. Professor of the Year every year for the last seven, save one, when he'd been on sabbatical coming up with the algorithm that made even the young Republicans crush on him.

"He's actually having it at his house," Lainey said. "I thought I told you?"

"I'm planning to be there," Ji Sun said, and then, to Margaret, "and you're welcome to come along if you decide you're interested."

Ji Sun had it bad. Lainey was in love with Walker's *mind*, and though she appreciated that he was incredibly sexy, she felt so moved by his work that she sometimes forgot how good-looking he was. But she'd never seen her roommate blush so much.

"Hmm. I am curious what his house is like," Margaret said. "Maybe I will come."

"Great," Lainey said. "Another *Architectural Digest* fan against the war. *Viva la Revolución!*"

When they got to Walker's house, anyone could understand why Margaret had wanted to see it. Lainey, Ji Sun, and Margaret got a ride with Seamus, one of Walker's TAs, and his girlfriend, Amy. The three of them squeezed in the backseat of an Oldsmobile Seamus had modified to run on fry grease. The whole car smelled like a fast-food restaurant, but its seats were plush velour, the same deep green as the trees that surrounded them, pine and fir and birch. Walker lived on the woody, wealthier side of town, but they hadn't realized he lived *in* the woods. When they'd turned off the road, it first seemed as though they were driving into the arboretum, but there was his sleek mailbox, Walker-Yamomoto 3021 in sans-serif font. His driveway was endless. Seamus and Amy had turned off the radio to argue some finer point about Frantz Fanon, but they quieted as the light left the sky, and a soft hush filled the car as they snaked along, feeling cocooned and cozy as the gravel crackled beneath the tires.

They gasped when they saw it: a beacon of light wedged into a hill. Ji Sun thought it looked exactly like the kind of house a computer programmer-cum-academic instigator would have, showy but so elegant that you couldn't call it ostentatious. It was all windows, and what connective wood there was looked to have been chosen to blend into the environment. Who could fault a man for wanting a giant cube of radiant light? And to build it right into a hill, both a rodent and a god.

The house was illuminated now, warm as a hearth, and they could see students bustling around in the kitchen. They could see, too, a few rooms down and to the left, Walker's wife and children in what looked like the library in a museum, a huge wall of books behind them, overstuffed ottomans artfully arranged like postmodern toadstools in a minimalist wonderland. None of them could wait to get inside.

There was the promised pizza, but the kitchen island also had huge trays of crudité, and little ceramic pinch pots full of pink salt and dark flakes of crushed pepper. Bottles of sparkling water were lined up behind stacks of the photocopied agenda, homemade signs, and materials to make more. Someone had filled a woven sisal basket with pin-back buttons: G. W. Bush's face behind a red strike-through; NO BLOOD FOR OIL in white letters on a black background; NO WAR IN OUR NAME in black on bright green. Though it was one of the nicest houses she'd ever been in, Lainey felt right at home. The warmth combined with the energy around protesting made her comfortable. Margaret touched her arm, asked, "Can we take a tour?" Ji Sun didn't ask, but began to look around for secrets of Walker's life. The fridge was photograph-free, but there was a row of framed finger paintings on the wall toward the hall that she thought led to a bathroom, which she'd claim to be looking for if anyone asked.

Before they did, she ran straight into Walker. She'd been looking at her feet, her socks too thin for this weather. Her roommates had grumbled when they'd had to leave their shoes by the door: Lainey said her tights stunk and Margaret said her outfit looked weird without boots. Nothing put Americans out like being asked to take off their shoes. And yet in this moment she felt a rare kinship with the complaint, with her thin little mesh socks, sent from Belgium by her sister, tiny mermaids and sea stars embroidered onto the nearly translucent fabric so that they looked like they swam along her feet. She saw Walker's slippered foot before she felt her body collide with his, before she could take him in. He smelled like his house looked: modern and elemental, like woodsmoke and pencil lead.

"Oh!" Ji Sun said.

"Pardon me," Walker said, and put his hand on her arm, near her shoulder. "I'm so sorry," he said, to reassure her that he wasn't wondering what she was doing, prowling around his halls in the dark.

"No, no, it was me. I wasn't looking—I was looking for the bathroom."

"Straight back that way and to the left," he said, pointing toward the kitchen. "I'm Professor Max Walker. Welcome to my home." He stuck out his hand for her.

"I know," she said, and stared at his hand, his wedding band glinting in the shadowy space between them. "I'm, I'm—" she was too stunned to know what to say. Should she say her name? Tell him she was in his class, sat in the second row every week, had been to his office hours? Did he not remember that he was, if not in love with her, at least quite taken with her, knew she was something special?

"Of course, of course," he said. "I didn't recognize you. In the dark." He took a step back and reached out, lifted a dimmer switch along the wall. The lights went from low and flickering to interrogation bright. Ji Sun could feel the heat on her scalp. She began to sweat. Even her feet felt clammy. She had to get away from him.

"Okay, well, I'll see you in there," she said. "Not the bathroom!"

He laughed. Ugh, he was so gorgeous! How dare he show his dimples, bare his teeth.

"We'll convene in the family room. Just off the kitchen," he said. "And we'll get started in short order." He looked at his watch and then back at her face. "See you in there."

She thought he winked, but she couldn't be sure as she was shielding her face with her hand, to block the light, to keep from crying.

"And thank you for coming, Ji Sun."

Had she reminded him of her name? Or had she imagined it? Was this some kind of mind game? She went down the hall, away from him, in the wrong direction for the bathroom he'd mentioned. She would find another bathroom, and then an exit that wouldn't take her back through the kitchen. She would climb out a window if she had to! She would get out, gone.

She couldn't sit through this meeting now. Her cheeks burned and she spotted a bathroom. Houses like this always had a million bathrooms—maybe the architects knew that people who visited places like this would need ample opportunities to close the door and cry.

But she looked at her face in the wall-wide mirror and saw that she wasn't crying. She was drawn and dry: hollow. Ji Sun turned on the fan and stepped into the shower, nearly as large as the rest of the room, just a sheet of glass and a change of tile to indicate it was a shower. There was a slotted bench and two showerheads. The bathroom wasn't even en suite! Was this an invitation to guests? Maybe she'd been wrong about the reasons for so many bathrooms, maybe new money meant wild parties where people paired off and showered together. But two showerheads in such a large space seemed more in the service of efficiency than romance. The other person would be as far away as at the gym, when you had to shower before entering the pool. Ji Sun stood under one showerhead now and imagined Walker under the other, looking at her, his eyes narrowing, struggling to make her out.

She used her mobile phone to call the single car service in town, quicker than a taxi since fewer people used it. Louis said he'd be there in fifteen minutes, but Ji Sun thought it would take him that long just to get down the driveway, so she told him to meet her on the main road. Lainey had a cell phone, too, and though she rarely checked it, Ji Sun tapped out an SMS: Feeling unwell. Ducked out. See you at home. Sorry.

She was sorry. She should have sucked it up, filled a compostable paper plate with crackers and cheese and joined the meeting. It was just a misunderstanding! She could sit among the students and his eyes would lock on hers again, she knew. She could hear laughter as she made her escape, and Walker's sonorous voice, but she couldn't change course now.

The woods looked different now that the sky was dark. Though she'd just come down the driveway and knew it led to the road, she feared now that it would be easy to take a wrong turn, veer off into some dark copse of trees and never find her way home. Why was she walking away from the warm house, the bustle and hum of the gathering? Because he hadn't known who she was with her head down in the dark? She didn't want to feel so foolish while she was also scared. This was silly. She could still turn back. But her feet were moving not so much without her consent as without her knowledge, and with every step away from the house it seemed more impossible to change her mind. By the time she climbed into the backseat of Louis's town car, she was sweating, out of breath. The woods were no longer magical, but as they receded she saw they weren't foreboding either—just dense, just trees. She was too far away to even glimpse the box of light built into the hill, and as they drove back to campus, she started to feel that she'd imagined it. It wasn't until Louis asked her, "Miss Ji Sun, you all right?" that she realized she'd forgotten to retrieve her shoes. Her mermaid socks were shredded, the undersides more hole than fabric, and the sea beauties who remained were covered in mud, tails obscured, faces—she swore it—scowling, forced to adapt to land, forced to lose their wonder and live among all the dirt of the dry earth.

CHAPTER 13

W ith finals approaching, the four cocooned in their room again. Lainey had a pack of Ji Sun's fancy markers and a sheet of stickers from Rachel, was making new name-tag cards for their door. She'd drawn *APlus* for Alice, *Elaine the Brain*, as her roommates sometimes called her since overhearing her parents do so, and *Sometimes Sunny* for Ji Sun.

"What's your nickname, Margaret?" Lainey looked up from her work.

"Yeah," Alice said. "It's funny, you don't really have one! We always call you Margaret."

"Well, I guess Margaret *is* my nickname," she said, and went back to her book.

"Huh?" Alice scrunched her nose.

"Oh. Well, it's not my real name." She stood and turned away from them, took a bottle of apple juice from the mini fridge. "My birth certificate says Majestic."

"Your given name is *Majestic?* Are you for real?" Lainey sat up straight on the futon.

"How could you have never told us this! This should have been the first thing you told us!" Ji Sun waved her arms. She sat next to Alice on the window seat, and both of them had put down their textbooks, too, to stare at Margaret.

"I've gone by Maggie since I was a kid. But when I met people who didn't know me, know my family, they'd sometimes ask if I preferred Margaret. I decided that I did, and that when I got to college, I'd go by it. Maggie seems like a little girl's name."

"Why not go by *Majestic?*" Lainey held her arms out, a full wing-span of *What!??!*

"Majestic is a stripper's name."

They all laughed, even Lainey, who had been the one to tell the rest not to use *hooker* or *whore*, but instead to say "sex worker."

"No, I mean, really. I'm named after a stripper that my mother says saved her life." Margaret took a deep breath, like she was already bored of this story. "I was born nearly three months early, and my mom didn't realize she was in labor. She knew something was happening, but she thought it was Braxton Hicks, which she got with my sister. So she kept on grocery shopping. But Majestic saw her and knew she was in labor, and she drove her straight to the hospital, and they made it just in time. The doctors said a minute later and I'd'a been born in the car, probably not made it. I needed to be hooked up to a respirator immediately." She looked at them. "Fluid in the lungs." She placed both hands over her chest. They waited for her to take a bow.

"Wow. Just—wow," Lainey said.

"What was the stripper's real name? Did they think about naming you that?" Alice asked.

"Huh," Margaret said. "I don't even know! My mom loved Majestic. She thinks it's the most beautiful word in the world. She doesn't know that I don't . . . really go by it."

Lainey thought she should give Margaret more credit, having dropped her given name out of some sense of decency, since how could she walk up to someone looking like she did and say, Hello, I am *Majestic*? But even this rankled Lainey, to learn that Margaret knew they needed some safeguard from her beauty.

"Wow. Well. Majestic!" Alice shook her head. "That is really something else."

They all stared at her in confusion and awe. What other secrets was she keeping?

"I dunno," Margaret said. "Maybe I should have gone by Jesse?"

They laughed again then, this time for what felt like forty minutes, until their cheeks and stomachs hurt. One would stop, or try to, but the others' laughter would catch them up again, and they would tumble into it, the kind of laughing fit that started to feel more like punishment than pleasure. One would fall back into hysterics, slap the window seat, kick the baseboards, plead *Stop, stop, stop.* Finally, their RA knocked on their door, asked if they were all right.

Lainey managed to answer it. "We're fine," she said, through hiccups. "We're downright *majestic.*"

They could die behind this door together, gasping for air, and tonight they wouldn't mind. They *were* majestic, transcendent, in love. They were stupid and awful and they were fools. They hated one another, but only because they sometimes hated themselves. They loved the others more than they had loved anyone before, more than they would ever love anyone else on earth, they were certain.

CHAPTER 14

B ack after winter break, the four planned a surprise party for
Margaret, who had turned twenty-one the day after Christmas.
The others wouldn't turn twenty-one until junior year, but Margaret
had repeated fourth grade. They took Ji Sun's car service to the party
store and loaded their cart with self-consciously kiddie stuff: party
hats with pom-pom tops; a piñata and prizes to put inside; tiny
cupcake-shaped erasers and Matchbox cars; a whole suite of unicorn-
themed paper tableware; and a sparkly plastic tiara, its crowning
jewel a huge pink heart that read *Birthday Girl*. Lainey had wanted
them to dress like the empress from *The NeverEnding Story*, at least
wear necklaces draped on their foreheads like that. They'd had the
idea to have "Majestic" be the party's theme, but Margaret didn't want
anyone else to know her real name, and they were also struggling to
upgrade the party now that actual adults were coming.

They'd invited Seamus and the other TAs from last term, and
Walker had overheard, asked after his invite.

"Oh! Of course you're invited!" Lainey had said. She blushed
and shot Ji Sun a shocked look while Walker took out his datebook.
"We didn't think you'd . . . want to come? We're in Birch Hall and
it's this Friday. Margaret's turning twenty-one."

"Turned twenty-one already," Ji Sun added. "But anyway, it's a
surprise."

"Right," Lainey said. "So we're asking everyone to arrive *before*
seven or after eight."

"Smart," Walker said. "I'll just stop by at the start with Sachi?"
He penciled neatly into his planner while Ji Sun and Lainey nodded,
tried to keep their squeals swallowed.

*   *   *

Most parties in the dorms had an open bag of chips that was all crumbs by the time guests arrived. Their friends swarmed on the cheese and crackers they'd put out on unicorn paper plates atop a cafeteria tray, a bunch of grapes plunked down in the middle, satsumas with their leaves still on forming a border. Ji Sun felt more anxious about the food being gone before Walker arrived than before Margaret did, but she busied herself filling the piñata with the little plastic shot bottles Conner had dropped off earlier in the day.

Just before seven, they quieted and hid, Lainey near the door with her Polaroid camera, Alice planning to answer it, and Ji Sun behind the futon. The look on Margaret's face when they shouted surprise was magnificent—a gift to them all. They'd feared Conner would accidentally tell her, but they could see on her face that he had not. Her eyes were wider than ever, glassy and exhilarated, and she put her hands on her cheeks, framing the O of wonderment her mouth made. In this moment, her beauty had nothing to do with symmetrical features or clear skin. She was elated, alight.

"Oh!" she said. "Oh! Oh, wow!" She burst into tears. "You guys," she said. "You did this?" She touched the streamers they'd hung to frame the door. "I've never had a surprise party."

"Looks like *someone* had a bit too much wine at dinner," Conner said. He was red-faced and laughed too hard at himself, and more than one person answered him with, "Who, *you?*"

Margaret spent the first hour of the party running around and hugging everyone. Conner and Lainey bickered over the music, with Lainey wanting to keep it at synthy and poppy until the adults came and went, and Conner wanting the nineties rap that he thought made him a true OG. Seamus and Amy were already there, and while Lainey argued over the volume with Conner, she realized that Walker was there, too, in a scarf and jacket, a bottle of wine under his arm.

He moved easily among the students, shaking hands and offering his big, easy laugh. She watched as he shook off his coat and joined the TAs who were clustered around the window seat, drinking warm beers that they'd brought.

Ji Sun joined the group just as Walker was recommending a film whose title Ji Sun couldn't hear, with Amy answering that she "didn't do subtitles." Seamus, an international student from Northern Ireland, who Ji Sun knew spoke Irish, shrugged. "Me neither," he said, "Eurotrash."

He laughed, but Walker frowned. "Consider how we replicate the insularity of our government with our artistic consumption."

"But why engage with the rest of the world only through what we can consume, right?" Lainey had nudged into the conversation with an ease at which Ji Sun marveled. "You taught us that."

Alice and Margaret sometimes watched K-dramas with Ji Sun, and Alice had picked up some Korean phrases by now, but she still seemed somewhat mystified by the fact that millions of people would choose these shows over dubbed American programming. Ji Sun struggled to explain to her that America was the only place, as far as she could tell, with so little interest in artistic imports, other than ones it could chew to bits and remake, and that everyone else on the planet was all but forced to take their entertainment with a side of the American flag. She wanted to ask Walker to repeat the title, but she couldn't figure out how to gain a foothold in the group.

"Ji Sun, join us!" Walker said. "We could use your level head and cosmopolitan perspective on this."

This was what she had imagined college would offer! The chance to be treated as a contemporary, to sidle up to professors at a party and debate the aesthetic and ethical merits of art. She held a red Solo cup with vinegary white wine in it, but she could almost picture it as a coupe, champagne bubbles tickling her hand as she held it aloft, laughing with Walker, positively *cosmopolitan*.

Before she could take her spot in the circle, now inched open to include her, she felt a hard squeeze on her left tricep. She yelped and turned to see Ruby, her friend from KCCF.

"Ji Sun, can I talk to you?" Ruby asked.

"Oh, now?" Ji Sun asked, and glanced back at Walker.

"It's kind of important."

"You'll excuse me," she said to Walker and the grad students, who'd already begun to argue about car chases as neocapitalist propaganda. "I'll be right back."

Ruby grabbed Ji Sun by the wrist. "Can we go in your room?" she asked.

Once inside her room, Ji Sun freed her wrist from Ruby's grip, tried to shake out the pain.

"What's he doing here?" Ruby asked, trembling.

"What? Who?" Ji Sun said, rubbing her wrist.

"Him! Walker, Professor Walker! Who do you think?"

"We invited him?" Ji Sun said. *I'm in love with him?* She almost said the words, thought they might be swallowed in the sound of the bass thrumming just outside the door.

"You really don't know?"

"Know what?" Ji Sun said. She looked at Ruby now, her face drawn.

"I'm one of them," Ruby said, her scowl deeper than usual.

"One of who?" The bass had grown still louder, and Ji Sun had to shout.

Ruby took her wrist again, this time gently. "Come with me!" she said. "We have to go somewhere you can hear this."

It was too cold to go outside, so they went down to the first floor, to a private, wheelchair-accessible bathroom. Ruby locked the door and paced a little before she turned on the sink, drew the shower curtain open, and gestured at Ji Sun to step inside.

Ruby pointed at the plastic bench in the corner of the shower.

"You might want to sit down," she said, "if this is really news to you."

In the fluorescent light, Ji Sun could see how worn Ruby looked, her eyes bloodshot and her lips cracked and flaked. Ruby closed the curtain around them, and scooted right beside Ji Sun on the small bench. Darker now with the curtain drawn, Ruby spoke softly as she explained to Ji Sun that she was one of the students filing a formal complaint against Professor Walker for sexual harassment.

The rumors had intensified that semester, but so had their inoculation against them. The sting of the incident at Walker's house had evaporated when he'd written on Ji Sun's final paper to "entreat" her to take his seminar, that he "couldn't imagine the conversation without her singular voice." She hadn't even shown Lainey, who was also enrolled in the seminar. Alice and Margaret didn't have room in their schedules, but reasoned they'd still get enough Walker secondhand, from their roommates, and at the antiwar protests that had increased in frequency in the new year. But they all agreed that surely, someone so righteous and good, who stood up to the man—in the man's own house!—was not the type to take advantage of anyone, let alone someone like Ruby, who Ji Sun hadn't even imagined capable of pinching her arm this hard.

"He's a creep, Ji Sun," Ruby said. "And I don't think you want him in your *room*."

"What did he do? What happens when you . . . you file a formal complaint?"

"Probably nothing," Ruby said. She shook her head and looked like she might spit. "He's had complaints filed against him before. Did you know that? Like a *bunch*."

"For what?" Ji Sun said. "And why won't you answer me? What did he *do*?"

They heard a bang on the door.

"I don't feel like I should have to revisit my trauma right now for you to believe me."

"Your *trauma?*" It sounded to Ji Sun like a line she'd learned to rehearse. "What did he *do*, Ruby?"

"He . . . propositioned me," she said.

"And?"

"What do you mean, *and*? He asked me if I wanted to suck his dick!" Ruby put her hand over her mouth like she couldn't believe what she'd said.

Ji Sun felt a tightening in her stomach, and lower, something that butted up against arousal but was squeezed by shame. There was another bang on the door.

"Occupied!" Ji Sun shouted, and Ruby winced and hopped up.

"I should go anyway," Ruby said. "This is feeling really hostile."

"Hostile?" Ji Sun said, and tried to touch Ruby's back. She had a foggy, underwater feeling, as though the room had filled with steam. Ruby pulled back the curtain and went out the door, turned down the hall, away from her.

Ji Sun returned to a different party. The music was louder, and the furniture had been pushed to the common room's edges. Walker and the TAs were gone and everyone else was dancing, bodies grinding and bouncing in a throng. Someone had plugged in a rainbow party light but it was stuck on red, giving the room the look of a dance club on one of the crime procedurals Lainey was always watching. Ji Sun couldn't find her roommates in the crowd, and she needed to see them, ask what they knew.

She pushed through the dancers and found the three of them in Alice and Margaret's room, Margaret sobbing on the bed.

"What happened!" Ji Sun asked. "What's going on?"

Margaret wailed. "Tell her! I can't even say it. It's my birthday!"

"She caught Conner getting a blow job from some chick. In our bathroom." Lainey leaned close so that Ji Sun could hear. Alice rubbed Margaret's back.

"From that fat pig, too," Margaret said, and sunk from the bed's edge to the floor.

"Fuck that," Lainey said. "Talk about him that way, not her."

All cruel judgments of girls made by other girls were by-products of the patriarchy, and Lainey let you know it. Ji Sun noticed that when Lainey herself passed judgment on other girls, this rule did not seem to apply.

"I like Kiersten," Margaret said. "We're in Spanish together. But it's my *birthday*," she said again, as though she had been guaranteed that this was one day nothing bad could happen to her.

"I know, sweetie," Alice said, a bit tipsy and trying to assume the comforting maternal role that was usually Margaret's. "It's really fucked up. Conner's a dick."

"Yeah, he's a huge tool." Ji Sun was jarred from her crisis into this one, felt a small pocket of relief to think that Conner, for whom her begrudging affection had recently worn thin, wouldn't be around as much anymore, turning on their TV and pawing Margaret. "He's nowhere near good enough for you," she said to Margaret.

"Maybe so," Margaret cried. "But I love him!"

She was so pretty in her baby blue party dress, tulle skirt that might've looked like a costume on someone else, but even splayed out around her on the floor, paired with the jokey party crown they'd bought her, looked almost regal.

"This is the second time he did this, too," Margaret said. "The second time I *caught* him, I mean! Who knows how many other blow jobs he's getting in *bathrooms*."

"You didn't tell us that," Ji Sun said. "Did she tell you that?" She found a way to feel hurt even as Margaret was unraveling.

"I knew you'd just tell me to break up with him! Don't be mad at me, please!"

Lainey wondered aloud why so many girls wanted to get on their knees for this asshole, but in truth it was not mysterious to her. She'd imagined sucking Conner's dick herself, precisely *because* he disgusted her, and because he was Margaret's boyfriend. Would sucking his dick be about hurting her friend, or becoming closer to her? Having a secret from her, but also sharing something with her? Lainey would never do it, but she'd thought about it more than she would admit.

"Of course we're not mad at you." Alice leaned up against the mattress beside Margaret. "What do you think, should we shut this party down? Weekend quiet curfew starts in like twenty minutes anyway. We can get in our pajamas and eat cake." Alice was exhausted, and looked forward to shooing out the crowd, who hadn't even noticed that their hosts went missing. It felt to her like any party, absent the four of them, would evaporate anyway.

"I'm not hungry," Margaret said. "I keep thinking of the face he was making, ugh!"

Ji Sun thought again of Walker, of what Ruby had said, of the men and boys who it would seem were just wandering around campus looking for blow jobs wherever they could come by one: in the office of the building where they taught, in the bathroom at the birthday party for their girlfriend, while she twirled in her perfect skirt just outside the door.

CHAPTER 15

Lainey dyed her hair Manic Panic Hot Hot Pink for the February antiwar protest. Students at the state school had been teargassed the week before, and Lainey was secretly hoping for this, would chain herself to anything, wanted to get arrested. The rage she felt at the government was neck and neck with her rage at her own impotence, about which she felt her liberal arts education had, for all its promises, so far mainly only enlarged the scope. Some days, Margaret's friend Mac swiped them into the law library and Lainey sat in a private cavern of books, rules, and rulings that men had made, her best hope, and even it seemed outlandish, to add a volume that would be kept in some other, dustier library with all the plays and essays until they disintegrated or were obliterated in the nuclear war her government might initiate out of sheer stupidity.

Outrage gave her an energy she couldn't get at the library, and she was alive in her indignation. She felt a thrum of anticipation, for the crowd, for the chance to be part of something that moved and was moving, something that was beyond shifting the course of history, that also had the chance to change something right now, at this moment, for living people. At protests sometimes she felt she traveled into the future, could see herself in a photograph clipped from the newspaper, chose her outfit with an eye for the nostalgia that she already felt for her own young body: cutoff black jean shorts, tendrils licking down over unshaved legs under bright pink tights, vintage motorcycle jacket, and a cropped hot pink tank top. Showing her stomach made straight girls jealous more than it made anyone desirous, but she wanted any longing aimed at her, as much as she could get.

Margaret emerged from her room looking like a flower child gone glam. She wore one of her gauzy, long white dresses, layers of which wafted out around her like angels' paperwork. She had on a pale pink angora sweater that Lainey recognized as one from Alice's closet that she rarely wore, so soft it seemed to breathe. Margaret had stuck pink carnations at random intervals in a long braid that hung down over one shoulder, plenty of waves still loose. A few carnations were in her hair, too, seeming just to float there, no need for bobby pins when your hair was spun from candy floss. Lainey reached out to touch one and Margaret grinned, thick pink gloss on her lips.

"You want?" she asked, and held out the tube of lip gloss in one hand, a carnation stem in the other.

Lainey did want. She wanted to say that this wasn't a costume party, but she looked down at her own steel-toed Doc Martens, ordered special in her size from the Army-Navy surplus store just for this, and kept quiet. She felt the urge to make her own ensemble rougher, less calculated.

"No," Lainey said, and scrunched her nose at the lip gloss. "Why not." She took the flower from Margaret, stuck it in her breast pocket, and zipped, let the teeth tear the thin stem, seal the flower there. Pale fluted pink on scabbed black leather made her look tougher, she reasoned, and thought that standing alongside Margaret would do the same. Lainey had had a serious girlfriend last semester, but even after all their PDA, and all the time spent at the LGBT co-op, cooking lentil dishes, the lesbians she knew still looked at her like a tourist. She wanted fluidity, but only if every shape she shifted into was one she could fully inhabit; any resistance from others and she doubled down, insisted she had always and forever been the way she was today, even as she was already imagining who she'd feel like loving, and being, next. She decided she'd shave her head after the protest, something to help people read her the way she wanted them to: angrier, uglier, and larger than she looked. Enormous.

They gathered on the library lawn, with plans to march into town and join a larger rally there. When they arrived outside the library, Lainey was disappointed to see there were no riot police, only campus security, a few of them with their hands rested on the billy clubs that Lainey hadn't even noticed they'd worn until now, when a part of her wished they'd brandish them.

She felt like part of a preschool stroll, pink pinnies and hands on signs, stay close together kids, don't stray. She hoped that when they got downtown the crowd would swell, and with it, her energy.

"Why isn't *everyone* here for this?" Lainey stuck her hand out at the students who scurried past the protest, entered the library. "What, their homework is more important than this unfounded *war*?"

"Hey!" she shouted at a cluster of girls walking together into the library. One carried four coffees nestled in a to-go tray, blew at the lids. Lainey could smell nutmeg, and the girls' tropical body sprays, so inappropriate in February in New England, when it had begun to feel as though variations on winter were the only seasons. She lifted her chin at the girl carrying the coffee. "You bring those for the protestors? Least you can do, don't you think, if you can't even make time to join us today?"

"Uh . . . okay," said the girl, stunned as Lainey lifted the tray from her hands. The other girls stopped and stared, mouths open. They were a matched set: long hair blown stick straight, tight black pants, puffer coats.

"Nuh-uh," said one, and snatched her drink back from the tray. "That cost me four bucks!"

"Buy a new one," Lainey said, handing a hot coffee to Alice, who shrugged.

"Best not to get into it with her," Alice said to the holdout.

"I don't need some random coffee," Ji Sun said. "I don't even drink coffee."

"It's barely coffee," Lainey said, sniffing the drink she passed to Ji Sun, a peppermint mocha. "And it's the principle of the thing. If these students can't even be bothered to register their opposition to the murder of innocent people for oil, the least they can do is support those people who can. Don't you think there're people in *Iraq* who might like to study today?"

"Whatever," the last girl said, and handed Lainey her steaming cup. "Good luck with that." She gestured at their signs. "I'm sure the government's going to really wake up once they see your fucking fishnets."

"What did you say?" Lainey yelled, head cocked. She had waffled on adding the fishnets over her tights, too much with her moto jacket. But it was so chilly that even a layer of holes couldn't hurt, and she liked the way they felt, didn't care if they were cartoon-sexy; they made her want to touch her own legs. Lainey felt her hand tighten around the coffee cup, a flash of desire to throw the coffee in the girl's face. She felt herself lift her wrist, take aim. Alice saw something in Lainey's expression and reached up for her arm, held it back. Instead of throwing anything, Lainey's grip tightened and the coffee geysered up, popped off the lid, and sprayed down on Lainey's hand, and Alice's.

"Fuck, damnit!" Lainey said, licking the coffee off her hand and wrist. Alice sucked breath between her teeth, pulled off the stretchy gloves she'd been wearing and tossed them on the ground.

The straight-hairs scurried into the library, their perky little butts a rebuke.

"What the hell, Lainey?" Alice bent down to scoop a handful of icy snow from a dirty drift. "That could have been really bad. That coffee was burning hot!"

"I'm sorry, Alice. Are you okay?"

"Yeah, lucky for you my hands are made of fucking rhinoceros skin. And I was wearing gloves. Are yours okay?" She scraped off some snow for Lainey, scowled as she handed it to her.

The backs of the fingers on Lainey's right hand felt so cold they were hot, and Lainey knew she'd think of the straight-hairs all day as her skin prickled and stung. The snow crumbled into bits as she tried to press it against the burn.

"Oh, no," Ji Sun said, and turned to look at Margaret, who had tears on her face and coffee all over her pale pink sweater.

"Oh, I'm fine! It just surprised me," she said. "I'm sorry about your sweater!"

"It's not your fault, Jesus." Alice sent another glare toward Lainey. "I was going to let you keep it anyway."

"Oh, that's so sweet, Al! I should run in and wash this off. I'll meet up with you." Margaret dashed off to the sounds of a drum circle before anyone could offer to join her.

"Were you going to throw *burning* hot coffee in her *face*, Lainey?" Alice shouted over the sounds of the drums.

"That is extremely messed up," Ji Sun said, close enough so both could hear her, before the drumbeats swelled loud enough for Lainey not to have to answer them.

When Margaret came back from the library, she had Reezus and Jamie from the women's center with her. They both wore all black with strips of hot pink duct tape X'd on their chests, sharpied to read *NOT MY PRESIDENT* and *FUCK THIS WAR.*

Reezus had given Margaret her leather jacket and Lainey had to swallow a gasp. Margaret looked so exactly like what Lainey herself wished to project: soft and rough, her chiffon skirt rippling out in the breeze beneath the oversized jacket, flecks of mascara stuck to her perfect pink cheeks. Reezus looked even more butch with Margaret on her arm, and Lainey felt again like a child in a costume, chicken skin on her bare midriff, idiotic in this weather. Lainey knew Reezus wore a dildo tucked into her men's briefs some days, and she wanted to grab at it, fuck someone with it, fuck herself in front of everyone, get some attention even close to commensurate with her rage. The student speaker had finished guessing at how many people around the world they were joining that day in protest, and the crowd had begun to chant "No blood for oil! No blood for oil!"

The next day in the student paper, there they were on the front page, Margaret and Reezus and Jamie with their mouths open and fists raised. They looked like they could be from any era, two androgynous warriors and their heroine, flowers in her hair like a crown.

Lainey could see herself, fuzzed in the background, and while she could only remember shouting until her throat went ragged, her mouth is closed in the photograph. In black and white behind the others, she looks almost like one of the straight-hairs, standing in judgment, nursing an empty coffee cup.

CHAPTER 16

Ji Sun hadn't set out to keep Ruby's secret, and she'd done so less out of kindness and more from the wish that if she ignored what Ruby told her, it might go away. But the rumblings on campus about Walker had only grown louder. Lainey's friend Adam had even written an editorial in the student paper; it didn't name Walker, but anyone who could read would know. Ji Sun needed proof, but the proof she really wanted—that Walker hadn't done it—was not possible to get. Ruby was still irritated with her, but Ji Sun had managed to extract from her that Cat was one of the other students who planned to join the formal complaint. Ji Sun was hurt that Cat hadn't told her herself, but she allowed that she hadn't spent much time with her, and none just the two of them, since the start of the year.

That there was another Korean-American student accusing Walker gave Ji Sun's investigation a new urgency. Hearing her friend's name, Ji Sun felt the first sting of something like certainty that he was guilty, and knew, at the very least, that she was done sticking up for him. If Walker had done this thing, it hurt her, too, and as much as she wished it weren't true, she would have to join with these women and stand up to him and so many men who had dismissed her, ignored her, erased her. She could see on their faces the first day of class which category she fell into: fetishized or disappeared. They would wipe drool from their chins or they would still, at midterm, mix her up with other East Asian students. She thought back on the looks she felt that Walker had given her alone. They hadn't felt lecherous, they hadn't even felt strictly sexual—they were *loving*. It made her sick to think of it now, how a tossed-off wink or grin could make her feel not just admired, but *enveloped*.

On a Tuesday before dinner, Ji Sun met Cat in the maps room of the main library. She followed Cat to a cluster of empty carrels where Cat opened her laptop and plugged in the Ethernet cable, pulled up her email. Ji Sun tried to make out the letters of her password, wanted to be able to log in later and read every word that ever passed between Cat and Walker, read even the emails that Cat sent to everyone else, to see what it was about her friend that drew Walker to her.

But Ji Sun was too nervous to catch which letters Cat hunted and pecked, felt her breath turn rancid on her own tongue, bile up from her belly at the conviction she had, sitting next to Cat and feeling aware now of how craven it was to wait for evidence of something she already knew, and to ask the victim to provide it.

Cat drew in a breath and turned the screen so that Ji Sun could see. Here it was, his email:

My cock misses your touch, Kit Kat. All the girls love it, but only you make it hard as a brick xxM

How sunk she was. Not that it was crass, but that it was so inelegant. So short and so ordinary. Ji Sun had thought him some kind of poet, a prophet! The language he used in class some days, the songs he'd sung them all. And this is how he flirts? Ji Sun corrected herself: harassed. Cat and the others were accusing him of sexual harassment, and here Ji Sun was, a beat of arousal at the word *cock*, and then fury that she couldn't read this message without feeling the wrong sort of rage at *all the girls*. Not: *How could he!* But: *Who were they?*

"I'm so sorry, Cat," she said.

"Oh, Ji Sun, it's okay!"

Ji Sun hadn't realized she was crying until Cat offered her a balled-up tissue.

"It's clean," Cat said. "It's just been in my bag for a while." She watched Ji Sun uncrumple the Kleenex and wipe her eyes. "I don't know," Cat said. "He's the professor. And he's, like, *the* professor, you know? I do like him! I mean I did. I did have a crush on him. Before he . . . before this." She closed the lid of her laptop. Her eyes looked like those of the animals in PETA brochures Lainey had brought home during a short stint as a vegan: resigned, done even dreaming of rescue.

"Me too," Ji Sun said.

"Oh my God, really?" Cat asked, and the wide hope in her eyes, the sudden change from what had just been so bleak, was all the reason Ji Sun would ever need to do what she did next, which was not to stop Cat in her misunderstanding.

"No wonder. I didn't get why you were so intense about this. I should have guessed," Cat said.

Of course Cat would think Ji Sun meant that she was also harassed by Walker! Why else would Ji Sun be *weeping*? She couldn't correct Cat now, tell her that she only meant to say that she, too, had a crush.

"It's okay. It's not your fault," Cat said. "I'm telling you, you can't blame yourself."

But Ji Sun did. For not seeing what so many insisted was there, for finding instead not only what she wanted to, but exactly what Walker was selling.

So Ji Sun crossed a line, and she joined Cat on the other side.

CHAPTER 17

E verything was on fire. The war was on and so was the case against Walker. Lainey could still feel the tingle of the coffee burn on the back of her hand a month later, when the president declared war by announcing war had already begun. A week earlier, the US had tested something they called the "mother of all bombs" at an Air Force base in Florida.

Lainey was embarrassed by how she'd reacted when Ji Sun told her what she knew about Walker. But it was too much! She'd wondered if it were possible that Ji Sun's friends were lying, and then, when Ji Sun assured her that they weren't, Lainey had asked if maybe they weren't overreacting now, to whatever had transpired between them.

"Excuse me, *transpired between them?*" Ji Sun made a face that Lainey had never before seen, at least not pointed in her direction. "Is this coming from the same person who practically tackled the counterprotestors at Take Back the Night? The same young *feminist* who taught me the word *vagina* comes from *sheath for a sword?*"

Lainey's face burned red; she couldn't speak.

"What will it take for you to see him for what he is?" Ji Sun said. She didn't need to raise her voice for Lainey to feel like it was the only sound in the world.

Lainey and Ji Sun hadn't spoken for three days after that, a standoff that Alice worried was going to send Margaret over the edge.

"You guys, you *have* to get over this. It's not worth it! He's not worth it!" Margaret said. "Isn't that what you're always telling me? You're fighting over a *guy*, you know. You're such hypocrites!"

Margaret had never called them names, and when she said this now, in their room on an evening when Lainey was about to head out the door and Ji Sun had just come in, both Lainey and Ji Sun were stunned by its truth.

"You're right," Lainey said. She put down her bag. "I'm so sorry, Ji Sun," she said, and explained that this was the hardest apology she'd ever had to make because she was still so ashamed at how she'd acted when Ji Sun told her what she'd learned, and she still wanted to think that Walker was better than that.

"It's hard for me," Lainey said, "to accept that someone I admire so much, someone I like basically *worship* is just this . . ." There was no right word. "Asshole! Just this *giant* asshole."

They laughed then, and hugged, and Margaret cried with relief and Alice went to her room to find the binder of notes she'd kept from Walker's class. "Let's burn it," she said, and climbed up on the window seat to try to disable the smoke detector.

Lainey got her copy of Walker's book, *American Algorithm: How Silicon Valley Scions Are Reshaping the New Global Capitalisms*, signed special for her with a funny little drawing inside. She'd planned to X-Acto out the title page and frame the drawing and inscription, it meant so much. Now she spat on the cartoon and dragged her finger across the ink, which didn't smear. The page darkened beneath her finger, but the tiny cartoon Walker had drawn, his arm holding a protest placard that squared around his own name, stayed smiling. She spat again and rubbed at the page with her finger until the paper rolled away into grubby bits under her nail. "I'm burning this, too," she said, and threw the book to the floor. "Burn this asshole to the ground."

Even the best man, their favorite one, was garbage. Protests were little more than farmers markets without the produce, and America was turning Iraq to ash. Everything decent could be undone, and they couldn't stop anything, save anyone. So when Ji

Sun mentioned, crouched in the parking lot where they'd taken their pyre so as not to get in trouble, in the glow of their small fire, that she may have inadvertently suggested to Cat that she, too, had been harassed by Walker, Lainey felt the click and spark of possibility, the power of a plan.

By now she knew how rich Ji Sun was, though the source of her family's money was still something of a mystery. The most enduring rumor was that her father had invented a kind of sealant used in nonstick pans around the world, but Ji Sun's friends knew that it was her mother's family that was truly, dangerously rich, the money from her father's innovations and real estate investments a convenient decoy, flashy and newsworthy.

Lainey only knew *how* rich because she'd stumbled on a trust statement last semester, written the number in her planner, and later, at the airport on winter break, asked for the exchange, asked a second time because she couldn't believe it, and then asked at another counter in the same airport because she'd been so sure it couldn't be true.

"It's just . . . not the kind of number you associate with money," Lainey had told Alice in January, when they returned from break.

"We can't, like, treat her differently," Alice said.

"Why would we? We already knew she was superrich."

"Yeah, but . . ." Alice shook her head. "Oof!"

"It was tucked in a book! Open on the window seat. It wasn't like it was hiding away. You would have done the same thing," Lainey said. "Wouldn't you have?"

Alice was silent for a moment. "Should we tell Margaret?" she asked.

"No," Lainey said. "I feel bad enough for nosing, and now for telling you. But I had to tell someone!" Lainey had been gratified to see how stunned Alice was to learn the number. Alice was wealthy, too, but that her pale eyebrows still hadn't returned to their usual spot told Lainey that she'd been right that Ji Sun's affluence was in another league. "I mean, I wanted to tell you. But I feel like if we tell Margaret it's more like this big secret we're all keeping from Ji Sun, and it gets weird."

"Yeah," Alice said. "I get that. Plus, Margaret does have a tendency to blurt out secrets she's meant to keep." Alice touched her knee, looked at the floor.

"She promised, Alice," Lainey said.

To have friends that could read her mind, even if it was just decoding her expressions after enough time spent together, felt to Alice like actual magic—that Lainey could look at her and know what she feared, know just what to say.

"I know, I know. It's just weird, you know? After so long keeping something a secret, to have people know. I . . . I trust all of you, but sometimes I remember that you know and I wonder what you must think of me." Alice kept her head low, but looked up, cautiously met Lainey's gaze.

"I think you're amazing, Alice. I think you're smart and kind and good. You can be all those things even if you did . . . a bad thing. You *are* all those things." Lainey could reassure with such magnanimity because she had not yet made a mistake for which it was impossible to truly forgive herself.

Lainey wanted to explain to her that she credited Alice with helping Lainey understand that people were not bad or good, and that they could do a terrible thing and still be a good person. This is what you were meant to learn at a liberal arts college, Lainey was pretty sure, but she had learned it better from Alice, from what Alice had done. But she couldn't figure out a way to explain this to Alice without acknowledging that there was a time when, upon learning what Alice did, she would have moved her friend into the "bad person" column, and that if someone else did what Alice had done, someone Lainey didn't know so well, maybe she would not be able to move them out of that column. But now they were teaching one another that these columns were not so neat, that few people lived their lives on just one side of that line. In the girls' bathroom in Loeb Hall, where Walker taught, someone had scrawled *Walker is a PREDATOR* inside the stall that Lainey used most often. In Walker's seminar, they had learned how they were both victims and perpetrators of capitalism, and when Lainey saw the word *PREDATOR* like this, tall as a fresh pencil, she'd had to fight the urge to get out her own Sharpie and try to start a conversation. But even if she agreed that everyone was both predator and prey in some way, what could possibly prey on Walker? Wasn't he at the top? He had everything he wanted and still it wasn't enough. He wanted something—someone—that *didn't* want him. He'd told them that they weren't any better than America's CEOs just because they didn't see the faces, or recognize the humanity, of the people they harmed indirectly via their late-capitalist splendor: closets stuffed with cheap clothes made by children, chocolate bars in their backpacks made from beans picked by slaves. But Walker did see the faces of the people he hurt. And he liked it, did it again. This was an uglier kind of power; Lainey didn't care what Walker said. She wasn't taking his word for it, for anything, anymore.

"You should join the complaint," Lainey said now, as they huddled close together, black tendrils of burned paper floating up from the pavement. Lainey rubbed her hands together and blew on her knuckles. "If Cat already thinks, you know, that it happened to you, you should join for real. Add your name." Her eyes met Ji Sun's and she could feel the shift of a needle into a groove, sense the satisfaction of having put something in action.

Ji Sun was still a little miffed with Lainey, and now by how quickly she'd gone from Walker holdout to pushing Ji Sun to take him down. But more than irritation, she felt profound relief that their silence had ended, that the four of them were together again.

She had thought of what Lainey was proposing, of course, and when Cat asked if she would add her name to the formal complaint, she'd said she needed to think about it.

She'd thought of little else. If Walker saw her across a table, if it came to that—and wouldn't it? Didn't this kind of thing always play out across conference tables, institutions such as this doing everything in their power not to be named in a lawsuit, not to have their dark secrets see the light of any rooms outside their own? But if Walker saw her across this table, sitting beside three young women that he did kiss, or fondle, or fuck, he would look at her and gasp. He would know, *know* that she was lying, but not have anything to say about it because in so saying he would be admitting guilt, that he had chosen *these* three students to prey upon and exploit, but not *this* one. Just imagining this made her hate Walker even more, for how it made her feel at this imaginary conference table to burn with shame not at having falsely accused him, but at how he hadn't chosen her to try to harm, how this, too, did hurt her in some perverse way.

Her parents, another such institution, would also do whatever it took to avoid making the news. They outsourced their scandals to her father's siblings, and now their children, too, enabling Ji Sun's cousins with a combination of vast resources, little work, and no incentive to clean up their acts. This kept Ji Sun's mother's family clear of much scrutiny. But if Ji Sun were named in a sexual harassment suit against a famous tech founder at her American college, it would bring some trifecta of public shame: that she was a sexual person, that she dared to speak up against a man in an authority position, and that she was damaged goods. Besides which, Walker hadn't sent her any untoward emails; he hadn't pressured her to touch his penis; he hadn't shut the door to his office behind her and then picked up her hand, put it on his own knee, waited.

"But she can't, you can't join, Ji Sun, right, because he didn't . . . take advantage of you. Did he?" Margaret's voice was pitched like a child asking if her parents were getting divorced. Beneath her puffer vest, she wore the pale angora sweater that Alice had given her, and she looked as skittish as the bunny the sweater had once been, nose twitching, cheeks pink.

"No." Ji Sun was clear on this. "He never did anything like that to me. I never even really felt uncomfortable around him. Did any of you?"

They all shook their heads.

"I get that he's this dreamboat," Alice said. "And this big-deal professor. But to me he honestly felt more like, I don't know, a camp counselor or something. I . . . trusted him. Which I guess is weird in its own way, right? Like, I don't really think about whether I *trust* teachers or not. I usually just take their word."

They shared who and how he'd been to each of them: a crush, a prophet, a counselor, a king. They went inside and thought of who and how he'd been to the girls who were accusing him: a creep, a lech, a pervert, a dick. None of these words were quite right, but the ones that might've been, they were not yet ready to say.

CHAPTER 18

Lainey had sworn off men in the wake of learning the truth about Walker. But she found herself falling into something unexpectedly serious with Adam, whom she knew from the articles he wrote about the antiwar protests, and whom she'd previously deemed a bit of a dullard. Now he was the only person, other than her roommates, with whom she wanted to spend time.

People always talked about being dizzy in love, but it wasn't like that for Lainey; it was the only time she could see clearly. Adam, ordinary Adam—apple pie no à la mode Adam!—was the only person with whom this clarity felt sustainable, less like the first hit of some new drug, its effect weakened with each use, and more like some kind of health food she didn't know she'd been needing all her life: nutrient deficiency, vitamin Adam. She felt a freedom to not adopt his habits or uniform (oatmeal for breakfast every day, the same boring clothes as his roommates and half the other boys on campus) and to instead relax into herself, freeing up space to read and write and consider questions about who she was, the answers to which seemed fascinating in their complexity rather than punishing. She studied better and slept better. She'd stopped taking Adderall from the cache Margaret had given her, but she felt energized with the edges worn off, rooted but not stuck. The skin on her face felt new: cheeks softer but tight, too, from laughing so much. Was she stupid now? She walked around grinning like a loon. For as long as she could remember, she'd had a voice that rang in her head like a bell some days: *I'm sad. I'm sad. I'm sad.* After a month with Adam, she realized it hadn't played in days. She'd kissed him when this occurred to her, a kiss so forceful she nearly knocked him over.

"Wow," he said, taking his hands from the pockets of his puffer vest. "What did I do to deserve that?"

The way he said it, like the kiss was both reward and punishment, made Lainey feel weak in the knees. "You make me weak in the knees," she told him.

"I don't know," he said, still a slight wobble in his own long legs. "You seem to be standing pretty steady to me."

She wanted to leap up into his arms, have him carry her not over a threshold, but onto the shores of his planet, a place where it was possible to cultivate a patient, steady appraisal of the world around him, to be truly curious about things without giving over to obsession, to listen to other people without thinking of what you would say next. What place made this person? Could it possibly be the same one that had trained her to believe that the most interesting people were the loudest ones, the shape-shifters, the lecherous lecturers like Walker, all flash and dazzle, rotten at their core? What a relief it was to be around Adam, steady and decent and true.

Margaret had also started dating someone. Mac was a second-year law student and in nearly every way an enhanced, or at least enlarged, version of Conner: richer, beefier, louder, a bit more boorish. He had a face that looked like it had been perfectly sculpted at one point, but then the artist couldn't resist going back in there, and had overworked it so that now his eyes were squinty and stretched a little too far apart, and there appeared to be a bit too much material at his temples and on his cheeks. He'd sent flowers to their room every Friday since Margaret's birthday, but Margaret hadn't been ready to date anyone until Lainey took up with Adam. Margaret's roommates felt about Mac the same way they had about Conner: suspicious, begrudging, wearily tolerant. "Asshole upgrade," they'd called him privately until Margaret announced he was her boyfriend, and they vowed to give him a chance.

Now they were all together in the girls' common room: Mac and Margaret snuggled on the futon, his meaty hand on her jeans; Adam and Lainey and Ji Sun on the window seat, books in laps; and Alice at the desk, peeling methodically through a bag of oranges she'd ferreted away from the dining hall. She'd previously hoarded bananas to practice her sutures, and was now focused on removing each orange peel in one piece.

"Is that like a surgical thing, too?" Margaret asked.

"No," Alice said, without looking up. "This is not for anything particularly premed other than stress relief."

The smell of orange oil crowded out the faint smoke from a spent beeswax candle and the vegetal, decaying smell of the dying lilies, Mac's latest offering, that sat atop the mini fridge. Lainey thought she could smell everyone in the room, too, the best smells beside her: Ji Sun of resin and suede, and Adam of sun-warmed sweater and a whiff of boyish funk muddled up with his piney deodorant. She rested her head on his shoulder.

"What do y'all think is going to happen with that?" Mac picked up a copy of the student newspaper, pointed at a headline about the allegations against Walker, below the fold on the front page.

Neither boy knew that Ji Sun was planning to be at the hearing, though Adam had interviewed Ruby—anonymously—about the complaint.

"Probably nothing," Adam answered, though the question was not for him.

"He's got quite a lot of admirers," Mac said, squinting at the newspaper.

"They're not his *admirers*." Lainey felt her shoulders tense, sat up straight. "They're his accusers." The pitch of the room had changed, and she felt trapped now instead of cozy. She could hear Alice's humidifier, which ran on high all winter, whir and burble, and she became aware of the condensation on the fogged windows, cold and wet on her back.

"Right, right," Mac said. "Lemme see here." He began to read: "Maximilian Walker—oof, Maximilian? Is this guy for real?" He snorted. "Pretty fucking handsome, though, am I right?"

No one answered.

"Alice, you get the appeal of this guy?" Mac asked.

After Margaret, Mac was most comfortable with Alice. Lainey tried to hope this was because they were both athletes, but she was starting to feel it was more likely for reasons of racism.

"Eh, not my type." Alice scrunched her nose. She liked thick-necked athletes and wan poets but didn't have much interest in the preppy sort of handsome for which Lainey insisted she was the perfect, catalogue-ready analogue. Sailboat beauty, Lainey called it, like you're always laughing on the dock at your lake house. Alice wanted to say something against Walker, but out of the corner of her eye she could see Ji Sun, frozen on the window seat, and Alice feared she would blurt out the wrong thing.

Mac went on reading, oblivious or unconcerned with his hosts' discomfort. "Blah-blah, accused of 'inappropriate amorous relations,'" Mac made air quotes, "with at least two graduate students in the course of his tenure at Quincy-Hawthorn College." He stopped, moved closer to Margaret. "Huh, wouldn't mind having some *inappropriate amorous relations* with a certain coed I know." He moved his hand from her knee up her thigh and squeezed. Margaret blushed and squirmed.

"Ugh, can you not," Lainey said.

"Not what?"

"Not make a joke out of all this. It isn't funny." Lainey stood up from her seat.

Adam sat up straighter, reached his hand out for her. "Laine," he said, and maybe "it's not worth it," but this last part was muttered, and Lainey's rage had begun to crowd out other sounds.

"I didn't realize you were so in the tank for this guy," Mac said, still leaned back in his seat. "Looks like you've got it pretty bad." He looked her up and down.

Lainey felt his eyes on her like they were slugs, sliming lines along her body. She was incandescent with anger, at herself for how in the tank she had been indeed, at Mac for thinking he had any right to say so.

"Those *women*," Lainey said, "have a lot of courage to stand up for themselves. To stand up to this whole place!" Lainey could feel Ji Sun, stock-still on the window seat.

"Seems like they probably just want attention," Mac said, and slapped the paper down on the futon. "I've got to run, girls," he said, looking at Adam. "Didn't mean to cause such a stir." He stood to go, an ogre filling the entire room.

"Aw, babe," Margaret said. "It's not about you. We all had class with Walker and we really respected him. Now we find out he's just like all the rest."

"Well, not *all* the rest, I hope," Mac said, and lowered his large cleft chin, pouted out his bottom lip, chivalrous again, to kiss Margaret on the forehead. "Call you later, sweetness."

When he was gone, Lainey had nowhere to unleash her rage but upon everyone else in the room.

"Where the fuck were all of you right then?" She trembled, felt anger course up from her throat.

"I'm sorry, Lainey," Adam said. "I just didn't think it was really my place to—"

"Not *you*," Lainey said. "This isn't about you either."

His face crumpled, but he nodded and looked down.

"Not like that," Lainey said. "But look, we need to talk." She raised a pointed finger at each one of her roommates and turned back to Adam. "Can I meet up with you later?" She wanted to leave with him, watched as he packed up his backpack and closed the door gently behind him.

"What was that? Not my type?" Lainey looked at Alice. She couldn't really ask more of Ji Sun, understood why she would clam up. "And you, you think these girls want *attention?*" She looked at Margaret, now charged with answering for what Mac had said, what everyone said: that the girls were confused, heartbroken, mad about their grades, bitter about rejection, jealous of Walker's wife. They wanted better grades, money, attention. Attention, attention, always attention. Even unnamed, they were desperate for the spotlight. There was simply no universe where Walker was in any way responsible for hurting young women. The girls were to blame, no matter what he had done.

"No, I don't know!" Margaret said. "I don't think that, but I don't know—I don't know what happened between him and the other girls! How am I supposed to know how they felt about each other? And I don't think, well, I don't think Ji Sun should say he did something to her if he didn't!" Margaret's eyebrows shot up her forehead, and she put her hands over her mouth.

Ji Sun, rooted to the window seat, only nodded. Her face cracked into a frown and she brought the backs of her hands up to her eyes.

"I'm sorry, Sunny!" Margaret leaped up from the futon to go sit beside Ji Sun, who waved her away.

"No, no. I get it. It's complicated. It's not clear-cut. But what is clear is that Walker shouldn't be a professor here, and I can help make that happen." Ji Sun's eyes were glassy, but she had stopped herself from crying. She wiped her nose on her sleeve, a move so childlike and incongruous with her elegance that Alice and Lainey shared Margaret's impulse to run to her.

"So what, you're like the Robin Hood for Title Nine?" Alice asked. "I mean, I get it, but just, like, what if it came out? That it

wasn't true, what you were claiming. Wouldn't that make them not
believe the other girls, too?"

"Why would it come out!" Ji Sun's wail came out more a whine,
like Margaret's. She looked at Alice. "I thought you agreed it was a
good thing, what I'm doing. Protecting future students. Believing
victims!"

"I do, I do!" Alice said. "I'm sorry, it's just, it still feels risky. I'm
thinking of *you*, Ji Sun. I'm on your side!"

"Yeah, but if it didn't happen to her, it's wrong, isn't it, to say it
did? He might lose his job," Margaret said, nestling herself back in
the corner of the futon.

"He *should* lose his job!" Lainey threw out her arms, tried to
shake some adrenaline loose through her fingertips.

"His kids . . . think of how they will feel. And they'll have to
leave their school." Margaret pulled her knees up against her chest.

"What, why?" Ji Sun asked Margaret.

"Well, he won't live here anymore! His wife doesn't work . . ."
Margaret trailed off.

"He has boatloads of money. Don't worry about his money. Who
cares about his money? Who cares about him at all?" Lainey said.

"Not his money, I mean, but why would they stay here if he
wasn't teaching here? And he'll be so ashamed."

"He should be ashamed! Why shouldn't *he* be made to feel
shame!" Lainey was trembling again, felt her cheeks burn. She
wished in a way that she could do what Ji Sun planned to do. That
it wouldn't make a difference if she joined the complaint made her
even more furious, though, and even though it wasn't Ji Sun's fault
that Lainey didn't have her money, she still felt a small burr of
resentment stick itself inside her ribs. She recognized that it came
in part from associating Walker's fall with Ji Sun, and from still
wishing on some level, even now, that they were all wrong, that
Walker wasn't really as bad as all that. So much of who she'd

become was staked on who he was, what he'd taught them. She couldn't hold in her head that he could have given her so much but taken so much from others, and it made her feel like she had to throw away everything he ever touched, even the parts of herself he'd helped forge. Where would that leave her?

"Okay, okay, we all need to take a breath," Alice said. She picked up the newspaper, opened it to the opinion page, where a small photo of Adam appeared beside his latest column. "You guys really don't think that Adam looks like him? He's like the nonevil mini Walker!"

It had been a running joke since before Ji Sun found out about Walker, that Lainey had befriended Adam in part because he looked like Walker. But Lainey and Ji Sun maintained that he looked nothing like Walker, other than their wavy hair and shared affinity for corduroy.

"Oh, what, all white people look alike to you?" Ji Sun said, smiling at Alice, glad for the break. She did feel that the two shared a certain lithe physicality that had less to do with looking alike than both looking good in pants.

Alice burst out laughing while Margaret looked hurt.

"Of course not," Margaret said. "I mean, they could be in the same lineup! A composition sketch artist would—"

"Composite," Lainey said, interrupting.

"What?"

"It's composite. A composite sketch artist. Made from multiple accounts. Not composition."

"Okay, sorry, gosh, but that's not the point!" Margaret said, and burst into tears. "All I'm saying is that, well, they're handsome. And the girls might have *wanted* to be with Walker, and they regret it now."

"For fuck's sake, Margaret! You sound exactly like a defense attorney!" Lainey shouted, and she caught herself, shook her head.

"I hope in your last two years here you manage to actually learn something." This, said quietly but so close on the heels of correcting her about composition sketches, proved too much, and Margaret's sniffling turned to blubbering.

"I hope *you* learn something about how not everything is so black and white!" Margaret paused to blow her nose, moan. "You say so yourself, that it's *nuanced* what Ji Sun is doing, well, can't it be *nuanced* what the other girls are doing, too, and even what Walker did?"

"No! He's in a position of power, Margaret, and maybe you don't understand that because, more than any of us, you're in that position, too."

"What do you mean?" she wailed.

"Look at you! People do anything you want!" Lainey could feel herself losing the high ground, but she couldn't stop now. "They'll let you believe anything! Has anyone ever told you you were wrong about something in your entire life? Am I the very first?"

Margaret cried without trying to respond.

"Okay, that's enough," Ji Sun said, and went to the futon to comfort Margaret. Lainey glared at her and Alice leaned back against the desk, hands across her chest.

"What? She's wrong, but she's not the enemy. Don't be so hard on her," Ji Sun said. Margaret folded herself into Ji Sun's arms, and Ji Sun found herself struck by how easy it was to misinterpret desires: for comfort, for knowledge, for acceptance. All these ways people wanted to connect with each other that weren't about sex, but that it was easy to mistake as such, especially here, with all their bodies so electrified by the urgency of awakening to their powers. She didn't feel sympathy for Walker, only disdain. But she understood him. Holding a girl in her arms—trembling, needy—she understood him well.

CHAPTER 19

Ji Sun's father immediately learned the name of everyone he met, no matter their station, so that he could better make requests of them. He'd given Ji Sun the advice to do the same in college, to learn the name of every student she met, but also every administrator, janitor, and mailroom worker, commit all these to memory should she need to call upon them. But he hadn't been able to explain to her *how* she would remember their names, seemed befuddled that it wouldn't come as naturally to her as it did to him. The lesson he offered was about the usefulness of the practice, not its mechanics. *What, your young brain has already so many holes in it?* he'd asked her.

Her young brain was nothing but holes, she felt now, as she failed to remember the name of the girl who sat to her right on one side of a long table, Walker and his white-haired, matched-suit cronies on the other. The righteous rage she'd felt when preparing for this meeting was gone now, absent her roommates—Lainey's fury, Alice's steadiness, and even Margaret's neediness—and sitting instead alongside Ruby, Cat, and the third girl whose name, should someone place a gun to her temple, she feared she still would not be able to produce, fallen as it had into the same cavernous space that had swallowed her courage, her resolve, any certainty that this was the right thing to do. Was the girl's name a noun, too? A ruby, a cat, and a revolver? Was it a Vietnamese name? Maybe she didn't have a name, maybe Ji Sun had imagined her, projected her, an extension of Ji Sun herself, the version who had suffered what Ji Sun was prepared to say she had.

Ji Sun knew the feeling of reaching for a word and finding it only in the wrong language—Korean at a gas station in rural Connecticut,

English at a dining table with her grandparents—but this was like that reach, only to grasp a handful of air, no language there at all. She searched and came up with only panic, fear at being found out. If she somehow failed to provide this girl's name—it didn't even occur to her that there'd be no reason for her to name the students who sat alongside her, that she wouldn't end up being asked or even allowed to speak—her fellow complainant, her comrade, surely they would know Ji Sun was an imposter.

At boarding school in year eleven, when everyone had been more preoccupied than usual with their grades, a pair of students had stolen a copy of a big biology test. It wasn't even the final, but everything contributed to their class standing, and everyone was obsessed with being in the top twelve, the spots that were all but assured to gain entrance into the Ivies. Ji Sun did well in her classes without having to work quite as hard as some of her peers, but what consumed everyone around you came to consume you, too. She wasn't immune.

When their teacher had closed the door to the lab and told them they would not leave until the culprits revealed themselves, the look of reproach he gave the room, before picking up his book and sitting down to read, had been so powerful that she had started to feel not only guilty, but as though it were possible she had stolen the test. Could she have done so and not remembered? In her sleep? She'd never sleepwalked before, but stress made people do strange things, and as the instructor turned the pages of his book, licking his pointer finger each time, sighing and smacking his lips, she felt as though her hand might lift itself into the air without her permission. She put her right hand down on top of her left, then feared she'd blurt out that she was to blame. She interlocked her fingers, leaned her chin and closed lips into her hands. Mouth covered, hands clasped, she felt her body start to stand, offer herself up as the guilty one, just as a boy in the front of the classroom said

"Fuck it!" and burst into tears before running out of the room. The teacher placed his bookmark calmly and followed the student into the hall. Ji Sun had nearly peed her pants in relief.

Now again she felt doubt and panic whirl inside her, incrimination she wondered whether she could invert somehow to make her accusation sound. That Walker had sent those emails to her. That when he put his hand on her shoulder in the shadowy, high-ceilinged hall of his home in the woods he had then moved his hand lower, down to the small of her back, let it linger there, looked not at her eyes but instead at her breasts, then down at his own groin.

Imagining this now sent no thrill of possibility up her center. In this room, Walker had lost his magnetism, though not his power over her. His skin was pale and dry, his hair seemed slick with grease. The clothes he wore were somehow both too shiny and too dusty, a sleek navy suit with a Silicon Valley sheen that seemed coated in the faintest fuzz of pollen or mold, like he'd walked through fog. His power now was that he knew the truth of her lie. But she knew the truth of his. So were they equals at this table? What kind of satisfying resolution could possibly be wrought when he sat alongside a whole slew of older men and one older woman, all in suits, all clearing their throats and crossing their legs and drinking coffee—comfortable—and beside Ji Sun there were only other young women: the law student; the two student Title IX advocates; and the three other accusers, all of whom were Asian, the fetishistic fuck.

But the other three had something else in common that Ji Sun didn't share, besides what Walker had done to them: they were all on financial aid. Ji Sun had known that Cat was, and Cat told her that Ruby and the other girl were, too, and Ji Sun might have guessed as much by the way the third girl, with her missing name, dressed: fake-leather shoes, a dress shirt and blazer that both looked polyester, the sale tag on the jacket having just been snapped off by one of the student advocates in the hall. There were long strands of her bleached-orange hair visible on the shoulders of her jacket, which Ji Sun could see was padded. She had the urge to collect these hairs, to return them to the girl, or to keep them in a locket that she would wear forever, as some act of apology for what Walker had done, for what Walker was, and for the part of Ji Sun that was the same as him. It was not lost on her that she and Walker were the richest in the room, and that she was richer. For a moment she felt strong again; they were both at the top of the food chain, but if he was a lion, she was a leopard, hidden in the shadowy trees until now, when she would tear his throat open with her teeth.

But then he stood, and cleared his throat, and began to speak. His voice had the same melodic quality that it had whenever he lectured, which she saw he was going to do now. He announced that he had delivered his letter of resignation to the dean earlier that morning, and would like to read a brief statement.

She thought she sensed contrition in his voice, but as he spoke, she realized he was sorry only for himself: *sorry to say that he would be taking an early retirement from the university in order to focus on the increasingly urgent demands upon the time and talents of a man with his particular atypical skill set. With his facility in tech and deep knowledge of American history, he had a responsibility to ensure that the future of democracy in the United States was not in as grave jeopardy as it appeared to be, especially on the eve of the upcoming election, and while at war.*

So he was leaving to save the world? Did he even know why they were gathered in this room? It seemed he thought they were all his students, here for a special lecture, fans who would be disappointed to learn he was leaving, but proud that it was for reasons so lofty and unimpeachable.

"I am sorry for the circumstances that muddy this departure, long in the making, and that the two brief, loving, and empowering relationships I had, many years ago, with fully consenting adult graduate students have become so misconstrued. I am sorry, too, for the misunderstandings and confusion that have led the students here to have reason to feel wronged by me, and to levy these unfounded accusations that I categorically and vehemently deny." He didn't turn to look at any of them, only continued his oration. "The trust between teacher and student, mentor and mentee, is sacrosanct. In my classroom, convention is challenged by design, but autonomy and safety are never threatened. I have endeavored to imbue my own admittedly challenging lectures with an encouragement to further question and challenge authority, and I can only speculate that the complaint by the assembled is a misguided response to that sincere entreaty."

This was his only gesture toward even acknowledging the four of them, *the assembled*, that their grievances were nothing more than misunderstandings, petty little nips at his heels, overblown now by being given audience in this room, though even here *the assembled* would not, it turned out, have any audience at all.

When Walker finished speaking, the mediator thanked him for his statement, and for his service to the university, and everyone on his side of the table stood and shook hands and patted him on the back and acted as though attending an impromptu retirement announcement, too subdued for a party, but much too cheerful for a wake.

So Ji Sun wouldn't have to say anything. None of them would get to say anything. She felt such powerful relief as she stood and filed out with the other girls, into the hallway together where they trembled, embraced, shuddered with the thrill of it: he was leaving, they had won. The time it took for relief to rearrange itself back into rage differed for each one of them. He hadn't lost his job; he had stood and given a speech; he was probably right now receiving an engraved golden pen. Whether they wept now, or cheered, or shouted, or cursed his name, what did it matter; the door to the classroom was closed, and no one on the other side could hear.

CHAPTER 20

S ince Walker didn't finish out the semester, Lainey and Ji Sun had a reading tutorial in the space where the seminar had been. They could read the remaining texts on the syllabus, or they could supplement their assignments with the approval of one of the TAs.

Lainey met with Seamus to talk about her plan for the final paper. She'd been working on an essay about Shulamith Firestone and the devaluation of women's antiwar efforts, the pitting of feminists and antiwar activists against one another. But she wanted to change her topic, write something that indicted Walker more directly, while still meeting the requirements to pass the class. She wanted to write something that would set the campus ablaze, reach Walker all the way in California, take him by the neck, make him hurt. She wondered if Seamus had any ideas how to do that. He had none.

"Figures," Lainey said, "that you'd come up short."

Seamus didn't say anything, just looked at her in his patient way, and then down at the table.

"I'm disappointed, too, you know," he said, his slow way of speaking so unlike Walker's, who'd crammed so much into his lectures some days he sounded like an auctioneer. Seamus had grown out his beard since Walker's departure, and with his woolly sweaters and thick Irish brogue, he seemed like a mossy teddy bear. Lainey was irritated by how comforting she found him, Walker's working-class protégé, his cuddly, rough-hewn foil.

"I don't know if *disappointed* really covers it," Lainey said.

She wasn't sure what she thought would happen after the mediation. That Walker would be held accountable. That he would apologize. That he would be fired, at least. That he'd flee in shame, fill his station wagon in the dead of the night, all the windows in that beautiful house on the hill gone dark. Instead, he'd gotten to ride off into the sunset of the West Coast, where he'd already been hired by some start-up in San Francisco and appeared in *Time* magazine's Innovators issue. In the photograph, she could see he'd cast off his professor look as easily as he'd shrugged off the rumors. He wore a quarter-zip crew in some futuristic material, new rimless glasses, a bit of scruff, and most jarringly, a close-cropped haircut, waves sheared away. He smiled his same smile, though, deep dimples, all those bright teeth. But now Lainey saw a kind of cheerful cruelty there, like he was celebrating having gotten away with it, with everything. Did the rumors not follow him there? Did no one know, or no one care? Silly crushes, broken coed hearts. Girls with axes to grind. Lainey knew what people thought. She scowled at Seamus.

"I know he, he had something with Amy once," Seamus said, and cleared his throat.

"What?" Lainey asked. "What do you mean?"

"Dunno," he said, and itched his beard. "I'd leave defining it to her, suppose."

"Well, okay," Lainey said, "but was it consensual, at least?"

Consensual was the one word that mattered, whatever happened between anyone, no matter what, was fine so long as no one shouted *no*, knocked anyone's teeth out.

"She'd say so, I hope," he said.

"What do you mean?" Lainey asked.

"He's very . . . charismatic, right? Very convincing." Seamus looked off into the middle distance. Lainey couldn't tell if he felt sadness, or anger, or regret.

"Not my story to say, though, Lainey. I'm sorry." He looked at her.

"Right, okay. I get that," Lainey said. "I can respect that." She looked at Seamus, waited for him to offer her something more, to explain why every conversation about Walker only left her angrier and more confused by how Walker managed to control the terms of the debate, even absent. How did he maintain his rule, still? She had not consented to this.

"I'm so sorry, though," Seamus said, and Lainey nodded, unsure what good it was.

The war dragged on, and people were saying that Bush would win again in spite of or even because of it. Lainey could feel her fury cool, begin to fossilize into depression. For a short while after meeting with Seamus, she tried to get in touch with Amy to talk to her about Walker, but Amy dodged her overtures. She tried to think of something she and her roommates could do to Walker, but all her ideas felt so juvenile, and none were practical with him thousands of miles away.

"What, do you want to *egg his car*?" Alice asked.

"I wouldn't mind, if it were here. I would take some satisfaction in knowing that at least he knew we were still angry. That we weren't . . . done."

"I think we should leave it alone," Ji Sun said. She felt anger, but also relief that she hadn't been found out. "I don't think it would make a difference," she added.

"Well, it wouldn't have to be eggs. I want to do something, something worse."

"No, I don't think it matters at all. He doesn't care if we show him we're furious, or that we know, or that we hate him. I don't think he's giving us a second thought," Ji Sun said. She looked at Lainey, but also somewhere else, inward.

Why should it still hurt, to think of the indifference of someone you hated now? But it did, and it burned. It burned and burned.

CHAPTER 21

J ust before summer break, Lainey broke up with Adam. She was headed to Paris to study abroad, and couldn't imagine anything more absurd than having a long-distance boyfriend while in *Paris*. It wouldn't be fair to either of them, she told Adam, practical, romantic Adam, who nodded and told her that he would wait for her.

"But I don't *want* you to wait for me," Lainey said, knowing already, someplace she couldn't name, that she would return to him. "I want you to sleep with a whole bunch of women. With men, too! Sow your wild oats."

"I've sown plenty," Adam said, and brushed the crumbs of a bagel from his pant leg. She wanted to jump his bones whenever he did something fussy like this. She couldn't understand it; he drove her up the wall.

"Well, I haven't," she said, though she was preemptively weary of her own insistence on this shopworn idea of a love affair in France, to be wine-soaked and puffing a Gauloise, sodden with tears, jilted and lusty along the banks of the Seine, a path she knew from books and movies to be the ideal place for a certain kind of soaring heartbreak that she both feared and sought.

She packed her best attempt at effortless French-girl clothes, though she could tell before she'd even left Charles de Gaulle that she'd gotten it wrong. As usual, not trying too hard involved great sums of money, as well as genetic gifts that allowed for neat little buns, bitten-bottom-lip pouts, perfect freckles that looked drawn on.

Lainey hadn't expected the depths of destabilization she felt in Paris, perhaps more potent after having enjoyed Adam's steadying effects. Now, in a new place, away from her roommates, she teetered into a kind of mania not to love Paris, and Parisians, as she'd planned, but to turn her small room into a garret, papered with passages from essays about French revolutionaries and post-cards of cafés and cathedrals, a collage of the experience she'd imagined she might have; its effect was oppressive rather than inspiring. She hadn't written so much as a postcard herself, beyond the bare minimum to pass her French course. She skulked around Shakespeare & Company, crept into the nooks inhabited by the booksellers who boarded there, succeeded more than once in nick-ing their personal items—a hairbrush, an address book, a small tube of lotion—only to feel washed with guilt and return what she'd stolen a few days later. The ability to both steal and restore made her feel invisible, as she couldn't see any other explanation for how she managed to escape notice: American, nonwhite, young and lovely, even as unkempt as she had become, her brown-black roots grown out and the bottom half of her hair a deep, inky blue that she'd imagined would look chic with her Breton shirts, but instead made her feel as if she'd crawled out of a *grille d égout*. Maybe she was a ghost now, haunted by her own evacuated optimism, by the war, by Walker. She'd let her love for Adam distract her, and now she was sinking down into the despair she should have felt all along.

Ji Sun and Adam both stayed on campus for the summer. Adam had a summer journalism intensive, and Ji Sun arranged to intern with the head curator at the college art museum. She'd pictured herself in the basement archive, away from people, humidity, and sunshine, alone with the art and her two gloved hands. Instead, she was put to work as "collaboration coordinator" for the digital archive, a project with which everyone at the museum was obsessed. It was as though the idea of looking at art in person were already obsolete, and all that mattered was getting everything they owned online, and fast, to win some kind of race against every other museum in the world, to "join the global conversation," as the museum's British-born director put it, sometimes with a pointed glance toward Ji Sun, as though together they could speak on behalf of all the world, its citizenry crying out for the pixelated versions of the museum's modest, incoherent collection. With Alice away, head counselor now at the wilderness medicine camp she attended every summer, and Margaret back in Missouri, babysitting and working at the ice cream shop again, Ji Sun spent most of her evenings missing Lainey with Adam.

Adam loved Lainey for the same reasons Ji Sun did, for the same reasons they all did. For how alive she was, how this made them want to be more alive, to go outside, to sneak inside, to go everywhere, to feel the sun on their skin, to dance in the dark until they fell down. A day spent with Lainey doing not much at all—trips to the dining hall, errands at the drugstore, studying on the lawn—could still take on an expansive quality that left you with that exhilarated, exhausted feeling that could, without Lainey, only be had after much bigger days. She made you long to spend more time with her the next day, every day. They all wanted to be with her, always, and when she had her moods and didn't want to be with anyone, they conferred together, guessed which one could draw her out. Might she want to go on an early morning jog with Alice? Might Ji Sun take her to a gallery in the city that would jar her storm clouds loose? Might Margaret do something foolish that only Lainey could help remedy? Or would it be another boy, or a woman as it sometimes was, who would clear away the clouds, lift her from the gray, light her up with infatuation once again?

Though forged around their mutual missing of Lainey, Ji Sun and Adam's friendship grew easily into its own comfortable rhythms, and they spent most nights together. She found she could talk to him about anything, and she trusted him. He'd shared the byline on the biggest story about Walker, even though he'd done most of the interviews and nearly all of the writing himself, because he knew how much it meant to his coauthor, one of Lainey's comrades at the campus women's center who was better at giving fiery extemporaneous speeches than writing. Ji Sun didn't know many people whose ambitions were tempered by generosity like this, and it interested her. He was smart in the well-read way that the brightest students at her boarding school had been, but more, he was curious. He asked her about herself and he listened to the answers; he wanted to know her.

They went to art-house movies screened at the campus theater, and took Ji Sun's car service to the two-dollar theater on the outskirts of town, poured 40s into Adam's Nalgene bottle and shared it as it grew warm and flat, the way they both liked it. They ate from huge tubs of popcorn with extra neon corn oil the concession stand called "butter food-product." They took to appending "-product" to other things of questionable quality: book-product, song-product, building-product, person-product. Ji Sun found dark circles of grease on all her black shirts, touched the stains and let them stay.

Each time they almost kissed, one or the other remembered Lainey, and stopped.

"The thing is, I'm still in love with her," Adam said, giving her eyes that she associated with baby seals rather than puppies, so round and doleful that she understood why whole factions would rally to save the seals, and also why someone might be driven to club one.

Another night, sweaty and sobering up by the lake, he leaned toward her with his eyes closed, and she put her two fingers on his lips, said, "I can't" in a voice lifted from a K-drama, breathless and triumphant, affording her the pleasure of seeing herself from above, being desired and denying that desire.

"She *told* me to mess around. She basically demanded I do!" Adam said.

Ji Sun could smell that other heat coming off him, not from the weather. One of precious few citizens on the planet to look good in shorts, he wore a pair that stopped well above the knee, unlike all the other boys that summer, who wore board shorts and cargo shorts, primed to surf or save the women and children of the village, both activities equally implausible in inland New Hampshire. She was exasperated by the lust she felt looking at his knee. His knee! She touched one finger to his thigh, just above the knee, as if to test its heat, and snapped it back with a gasp, stunned by how explosive it had felt, by the draw of the dark shadows further up his shorts.

But not with me! Ji Sun didn't have to say. She looked at her finger, and back at Adam, who looked at her finger, too. He licked his lips, not in a lascivious way, but in the way where the tongue tucks your two lips in, endeavors to swallow whatever it is you should not say.

When they finally did kiss, at summer's end, they still felt Lainey between them, and both experienced more pleasure from the relief of tension than from the kiss itself, though it was a good kiss, long and hungry—both with their hands grasping at the other's face and neck and hair, both so that they wouldn't move their hands lower, though if they had not been sitting, Ji Sun knew she would not have been able to stop herself from finding out what shape his ass took in her hands—but when it was over the freedom from that tension curdled, less from guilt or shame and more from the sorrow that comes when a longing is realized.

"We shouldn't, it's not worth it to do that again, right?" Ji Sun said, and Adam nodded so quickly, her spit still shining on his lips, that she was bereft in spite of herself.

It was not terribly difficult, though, to move him back into the category of unavailable crushes, where she should have kept him all along, and where he would stay forever, she knew, because he was Lainey's, his heart belonged to her. And she was Lainey's, also, in a way that included Adam, but transcended him, too.

CHAPTER 22

A year and a half after graduation, Ji Sun ran into Ruby in New
York at a party celebrating Asian American women writers.

"Wow," Ruby said, standing back to better appraise her. "I'm
surprised to see you here." They were at the main branch of the
New York Public Library.

"Why?" Ji Sun asked. "What about me suggests I don't celebrate Asian American women writers?" She laughed and made a
theatrical gesture around her *Celebrate Asian American Women
Writers* pin.

"No, I mean after what happened." Ruby crossed her arms over
her chest and tucked her chin, her eyes lowered.

Ji Sun searched Ruby's face, where she'd always found some
measure of reprove, but saw concern there. They hadn't been close
before the complaint against Walker, and they only grew more
distant in the fizzle of the aftermath.

"What do you mean?" Ji Sun asked, and thought, but didn't
say, "That was so long ago." College did feel forever ago in some
ways, but in others it seemed ongoing. She saw her former roommates often, and talked to them all the time. Margaret lived with
Mac, whom she was a month from marrying, on the Upper West
Side, while he went for his MBA at Columbia, and Alice was in
med school at Harvard, but came down two weekends a month,
cramming on the bus ride and studying while the other three fed
her takeout, claiming she still studied better with them in the
room. Since graduation, Ji Sun had been traveling, working as a
consultant for private art collectors, in part to put some distance
between herself and the insular, occasionally stifling postgradu-
ate Quincy-Hawthorn scene in New York City. More than this, she

wanted to keep America from becoming the only place—a risk that grew, she knew, the longer she lived there. Ji Sun's parents paid for an apartment in the West Village where she lived with Lainey when in New York. Adam was a research assistant at *The New York Times* and lived in a hovel in Bed-Stuy with four other underpaid would-be saviors of print journalism, but slept at Ji Sun and Lainey's most nights. The three of them stayed up late talking about their plans and dreams and ideas, and for the most part, it didn't even bother Ji Sun that after these talks, the two of them would retreat into Lainey's tiny bedroom and have what Lainey had once unforgettably described to her as sex that was "catastrophically satisfying."

"Oh, my God, you don't know, do you?" Ruby tucked her chin still lower, and Ji Sun thought she might unhinge her jaw to better illustrate her incredulity.

"What?" Ji Sun asked. "I've been out of the country. Just tell me!" Had Walker done something? Had something happened to him? Had he hurt someone, someone else? She would have heard, surely, if he'd been arrested. She felt a burble of fear at the thought of jail. Had Ruby found out somehow that Ji Sun had been lying? She didn't consider how it wouldn't matter now, only felt the panic of imminent exposure, and surprise at how easy it was to still feel guilt over what she had done rather than shame at not doing more.

"Alexa killed herself," Ruby said.

"We're meant to say 'died by suicide,' babe." A beautiful butch woman with bronze skin and a buzz cut appeared by Ruby's side with two drinks, put her arm around Ruby's waist.

"Here," Ruby said, and passed her cocktail to Ji Sun. "You need this more than I do, and we can share." Ruby took the tumbler of what looked like whiskey from her tall companion, who wore two thirds of a perfectly tailored navy suit, vest and pants, no jacket, her white shirt unbuttoned to show tendrils of tattoos creeping up from her chest.

"Ji Sun, this is Samadhi, Sam, Ji Sun. God, I can't believe you didn't hear."

"Should we sit down?" Samadhi asked, scanning the room for something other than the scattered cocktail-height tables. "Or go somewhere? Are you okay?" She put a large, soft hand on Ji Sun's shoulder and looked at her with concern unadulterated by judgment.

"What happened?" Ji Sun asked. "How?" She knew this was a craven question, but it was urgent, as always with death, to know, as though the details could inoculate you against this same fate.

"Pills," Ruby said. "Plus gas, from her car, so they know it wasn't an accidental overdose."

"Christ," Ji Sun said. "Both?" She pictured Alexa slumped over the steering wheel, wondered if there had been music playing, and whether Alexa had chosen it, or if it was just what happened to be on the radio. She remembered, in a rush, how she had forgotten Alexa's name during the mediation, and felt doubled over by the shame of this. She put her hands on her temples, steadied herself.

"Did she leave a note?" Ji Sun asked, though she had the sense that even if Alexa had, Ji Sun would never see it.

"No, no note," Ruby said, and leaned into Samadhi's embrace.

Ji Sun found it hard to absorb this news in the presence of this couple, how magnetic Samadhi was, how Ruby herself took on a kind of confounding allure beside her. Ruby nestled against Samadhi, who lowered her head so that Ruby could whisper in her ear.

Ji Sun felt still guiltier at this exclusion. She wanted to leave, find Lainey and Adam at their favorite bar, and tell them what had happened, have them reassure her that it was not her fault. She'd come to the party with a friend who worked in publishing, one she slept with on occasion. She looked around for him now, hoping less that he would come stand beside her, and more that he'd stay away long enough for her to extricate herself. She didn't want him to know this about her, though she wasn't even sure what *this* was.

"I can't believe it," Ji Sun said. "That is so awful." Ji Sun had known people who killed themselves. Just before she left for boarding school, two employees at her father's company had jumped to their death, together, from the Mapo Bridge. It had been major news, investigated as a possible murder-suicide, with rumors of a gang tattoo having been discovered on the chest of one of the men. Then, just as she arrived at boarding school, a Dutch student who had graduated the year before hung himself while on holiday in Greece. Ji Sun had the sense, that year, that suicide followed her, but she did not feel herself in any way to blame.

"I can't believe you didn't hear. This was *months* ago." Ruby shook her head. "Do you not talk to *anyone*? Are you not even on *Facebook*? Her obituary was in the alumni newsletter!"

Ji Sun had only ever skimmed the newsletter, its glossy content little more than one overlong solicitation. Her parents already donated enough, and everyone whose news she needed was still in her life.

"Were you, did you go to the funeral? Were you in touch with her, after . . . after college?"

Ruby gaped at her. "You are *unreal*, Ji Sun."

"What do you mean?

"She was my *girlfriend*," Ruby said. "My first!" She shook her head again and began to cry. She turned away from Ji Sun and let Samadhi, who looked at Ji Sun now with the worst, kindest sort of pity, take her in her arms again.

"Oh, God, I'm so sorry. I'm so sorry, Ruby! I didn't realize, I didn't know you were . . . so close." What she didn't know about

Ruby, she could see tonight, would fill a more interesting book than she might have guessed.

"Of course you didn't," Ruby said, her face flushed and wet.

"Babe," Samadhi said, "she's just hearing this. Give her a beat to process."

"Don't *babe* me right now," Ruby said, and loosed herself from Samadhi's arms to better admonish Ji Sun. "And don't defend her." Ruby's glare might incinerate Ji Sun. "She lives in a world of her own."

She did. And she had then, too, she knew. After the mediation, Ji Sun had left the room and not looked back. How quickly she'd tucked the whole thing away as some kind of narrow escape on her part, rather than a failure. Not even a failure to protect future girls, but a failure to defend one in the room, one whose name she hadn't even been able to remember, whose name must not have mattered much at all.

Now, nothing could convince Ji Sun that she was not to blame. No matter what she went on to learn about Alexa's troubled home life or history of depression, no matter what anyone tried to tell her about the fruitlessness of this particular brand of blame. Suicide made narcissists of everyone, and for the longest time it didn't even occur to Ji Sun how responsible Ruby must feel. She fixated instead on her own guilt, and regret that she hadn't done more, hauled Walker into a real courtroom, made him face a flank of lawyers paid for by her parents, not the sham of a mediation in that brightly lit classroom, all those schmucks in their suits, and Alexa with her bleached-dry hair, too much concealer, the shoulder pads Ji Sun remembered from her blazer growing in size in her memory until Alexa was, in some dreams, a shrunken husk of a face between two huge columns of coat, drowned little eyes struggling to find any point of contact. She knew Walker didn't dream of Alexa. She didn't know if he'd heard what had happened to her, but she was certain that he didn't blame himself, not even for a moment, and this, more than anything Walker had actually done, convinced her of his depravity.

She remembered a conversation she'd had with Ruby and Cat, long buried. They had been talking about Alexa, who was waffling on whether or not she would join the complaint. Ji Sun recalled how important it was to Ruby that Alexa join, and how Ruby had refused to share with Ji Sun any of the details about what had happened to Alexa. Ji Sun remembered asking again and again, how not knowing, especially when Ruby did, drove her mad. It boggled her now, to think of how brazen she was, demanding details that she herself had not provided, demanding details at all, as if her need to know his guilt was more important than anyone's privacy, as if the story belonged to her in any way.

"She had sex with him!" Cat had finally said, sick of Ji Sun asking. "Er, well, she had sex with him but didn't really want to?"

"*Rape*, Cat," Ruby said. "That's called *rape*."

Ji Sun had disagreed then, the word so wrong in her ear that she didn't even tell Lainey about the talk, had tucked it away until the news of Alexa's suicide forced an excavation. The vague language in the articles, everything an allegation: of sexual indiscretion, inappropriate amorous relations, harassment. All these ways to obfuscate what he'd done, and she'd shielded herself, too. Walker wasn't a *rapist*. He wasn't the man that they had believed him to be, but he wasn't *that* either. He couldn't be. He was a sleaze, a creep, a predator, even, but a rapist? She didn't want to say the word even now, and she wondered what of the conversation she might be misremembering, or what was colored by what had happened since.

When she googled Walker after the party, she saw that he was teaching again, this time at Stanford, and that he had a third baby on the way, or maybe she was born already. Ji Sun didn't wish to do the math, just stared at the photo of Walker and his family, his wife radiant in the bright California sunshine, belly swollen with the promise of a new life.

PART III

THE KISS

POSTGRADUATES,
2007–2012

M argaret's wedding, on the last night of 2007, made the national news, but not for any of the reasons her new in-laws would have hoped.

The proposal, which her roommates considered absurdly premature, had at least occurred after graduation, if only by three weeks, as though even Mac knew that it would have been unseemly to ask Margaret before she earned the degree he planned for her never to use.

On Margaret's wedding website, she'd written *The Other Great Loves of My Life* as the title for the section where she described Alice, Lainey, and Ji Sun, her maids of honor, all. Lainey read this and thought, *Oh, I have that kind of friendship that others dream of having.* She loved to see herself in this light, a starring role in the movie of Margaret's life, untying the gray silk ribbon around the dress box Margaret had couriered to them all, even though she, Lainey, and Ji Sun all lived in New York. The boxes were just the way you did things in this kind of spare-no-expense wedding that was, it seemed, Margaret's full-time job not to work as planner of, but as consultant on—since there were *two* wedding planners, and she was constantly meeting with one or both. The first was hired by Mac's mother, heir to a Kentucky bourbon fortune, and the second by his father's mother, a French socialite who still hadn't forgiven her son for marrying an American, let alone one who felt it appropriate to serve barbecue at a formal event.

Margaret marveled even at the fights, staged via their planner surrogates, and what they revealed about the terrain of weddings beyond what she had even known to imagine, from the venue (a private country club nestled in the woods outside Cincinnati, with a dance hall whose ceilings went straight to the moon), to the ice cubes (truly *cubed*, not oblonged or crushed, and king-sized cubes for the bourbon rocks), down to whether urinal cakes were déclassé (very much so, but what did the French know, didn't they *encourage* peeing in the streets?).

Margaret had been to a few weddings of high school friends, home in Missouri over summers, and none seemed all that different from the other, save the color scheme and the church. A bride could easily step from one ceremony into another, a few readings, and vows, and even some dresses unchanged. But this, Margaret's wedding, was a production: something to be mounted, *staged*. She felt some days like an understudy, even in the role of bride, like the real stars were Mac's mother and grandmother. But even this she didn't mind, as both women treated her with a kind of affection that, though she recognized as in part competitive, was a departure from the way they'd treated any of Mac's past girlfriends, and how they treated most people. She'd told Mac about a recent squabble they'd had about when Margaret should change from her first gown into the one she would wear to leave, though she and Mac weren't honeymooning until later in the month.

"Not to mention how heated they got about the dress itself! This is just *when* I could duck out and change without disrupting event flow."

"Don't let them railroad you, Margaret, Jesus. This is your wedding. And you're not their pretty pet!" Mac said. "You're mine." He kissed her and held her face in his hands.

"Ugh, barf," Lainey said later. "You're not anyone's *pretty pet*."

Margaret had told Lainey the story as an example of Mac sticking up for her, staking her claim to the space in this family overcrowded with domineering women. But, as with so many things told to Lainey, Margaret could see now how different this looked to a woman who would never take a man's last name.

"It's a term of endearment, Lainey," Margaret said. "He's not actually calling me a *pet*."

"Yeah, yeah, sorry," Lainey said, and looked at the door again. They were at the bar in a Mexican restaurant, waiting for Alice and Ji Sun to arrive.

But Margaret did feel like a stray dog sometimes, though she was too irritated to tell Lainey now: adopted by her roommates, and now by Mac and his family. All of them eager to provide shelter, none of them too concerned with why she might have cowered at their first tenderness. She felt her throat tighten and cheeks warm.

"Are you okay?" Lainey asked. "I'm sorry. You know I'm trying with Mac."

Having Lainey notice for once was enough, and Margaret recomposed herself.

"I'm fine, it's okay. Emotions run high around weddings, you know."

"Of course," Lainey said, and prepared for Margaret to recount in excruciating detail the difference between linen and flax table runners. She was surprised when Margaret said instead, "And I want you to *like* Mac." Margaret made the kind of eye contact that typically got her what she required. "Not *tolerate* him."

"I do! You know, in my way, I do. Of course I do," Lainey said, fidgeting with her many silver rings. "I care about Mac, and I care that he's good to you, that you feel supported by him. That he lets you be yourself."

"I feel more supported by him than by *anyone*! More *myself*!" She'd intended to sound assertive, but it came out like a shriek, and it hurt Lainey even though Margaret hadn't meant it to, and Lainey hadn't expected it would. But it struck right on the sensitivity Lainey was feeling about Margaret forging ahead into this next phase of life, what it would mean for the four of them, and for Lainey herself.

Of course Lainey would be in no rush to marry, Margaret thought, with parents like hers. Margaret looked for any reason to get invited back to their house, asked Lainey around every Jewish holiday whether she was going home, if her parents were hosting anything.

But so often Lainey stayed in the city, citing vague plans to workshop a play she'd been writing for more than a year. Margaret didn't know who she workshopped with, or what the process even entailed, and Lainey never offered up details, preferring to carve out some part of her life that was hers alone, as the others had seemed to do so much more easily, with Ji Sun traveling, Alice in med school, and Margaret ensconced already in Mac's world. Preferring also to keep from them that there'd been no progress on the play, an uninspired imitation of *This Is Our Youth* that had failed even to get staged at the Quincy-Hawthorn student theater. She spent the time she claimed to be workshopping holed up in her tiny bedroom watching crime procedurals, or high on Molly and dancing at Resolution, the gay club she frequented with friends from work often enough that she'd gotten a drink—well, whiskey, Sprite, and way too many maraschinos—named for her.

The country superstar who turned up, uninvited, to Margaret and Mac's wedding wasn't immediately recognizable even to the sizable percentage of guests who knew his catalogue down to the word. He wore a tuxedo like everyone else, but also a studded black Wildcats baseball cap, mirrored sunglasses, and a full beard as opposed to the artful stubble he typically sported. More obfuscating was how much smaller he was than anyone had imagined, and though they'd heard this about famous people, it was still hard to reconcile his stature as he danced up against Mac's sisters, not even close to towering over them.

Margaret's mother, nearly unrecognizable to Margaret with her hundred-dollar blowout and champagne Hervé Leger bandage dress, was the first to alert Margaret to the star's arrival.

"Do you all *know* him?" her mother asked, breath smoky with bourbon and menthol. Margaret could feel the tips of her mother's acrylic nails on the spot between her neck and shoulders where she rested her hand now, waiting.

Her mother's dress, a style that had been so popular a few years back, and that Margaret herself had worn to parties and weddings once Mac bought her one in red, was pale enough gold that Margaret's older sister and aunt both advised her mother not to wear it to the wedding, said it veered too close to white for the mother of the bride.

"It's not *silver*," Laureen had said, indignant. "Majestic bought it!"

Margaret shrugged. She had bought it, or Mac had, technically, though Margaret swiped the credit card when her mom had visited New York, and they'd taken a taxi to Bergdorf Goodman to choose a rehearsal dinner dress for Margaret.

Margaret had already chosen her wedding gown, with the help of her roommates and Mac's little sisters, twins who were juniors in high school.

"God, you can wear *anything*. It's like, a bit sickening?" Ashley, who was considered by her family and herself to be the "chubbier" twin, said.

"As can you!" Margaret said. "You're stunning." She kissed her soon-to-be sister on the cheek, the only place she could find much of this chub to which the family objected, and resisted the urge to say something self-deprecating, a habit Gavin, her best friend from home, had helped to break her of her first summer home from Quincy-Hawthorn, before she moved in with him.

"Don't do that," he'd said, after she brushed off a compliment on her new sandals, not technically allowed in the ice cream shop where they worked together, with some comment about her gigantic feet. "It's not a good look. It's tiresome. On you, I mean. In particular." Gavin had this way of speaking, all his sentences interrupted by himself. When Margaret had learned he was gay, she'd been delighted. *Sex and the City* had taught her that friend groups came in four, but she had been waiting for her gay best friend.

"What, football players can be gay, too, you know. *Lots* of them are," he said, and raised one eyebrow. "You may or may not be surprised."

He rode the bench at Missouri State, but trained like a fiend and ate buckets of the birthday-cake-flavored ice cream, with more toppings than Margaret could believe, so many heaps of brownie, Oreo, peanut butter cups, fudge, and caramel that the cream took on a solid texture, and had to be carved rather than scooped, into the cups. She liked the birthday cake best, too, but ate it with a few cubes of yellow cake and freckles of rainbow sprinkles, as God intended, she would say, and Gavin would roll his eyes, tell her she should add fudge while her metabolism could manage it. All the cute boys came in during Margaret's shifts, and even singing the stupid jingles became fun with Gavin, a confident if off-key baritone. Margaret was pleased by how well he hit it off with her roommates, as he was the only friend from home whom she'd invited to the wedding, the only real friend from home she had.

The buzz about the country star was quickly eclipsed by the fisticuffs that nearly broke out when Mac saw the way he was dancing with Claire, Ashley's twin.

"I don't care who you are!" Mac swelled, seemed double the star's size. Margaret found herself wanting to hold her new husband back from hurting the star, but also wanting to watch Mac punch him in the face. "That's my little sister! She's *sixteen!*"

"Seventeen!" Claire squealed, but only her twin seemed to hear.

The star actually tipped his hat, dressy as far as baseball caps went, with its black-on-black metallic embroidery, and Margaret gasped as he put his other hand over his mouth, catching what she feared would be vomit, but was instead a burp so tremendous that she felt swallowed by the smell from where she stood.

"Let's not, now hold up here, hold up, fella, congratulations, hey!" He looked from Mac to Margaret, and back to Mac, just realizing he'd wound up at a wedding.

Mac's younger brother, Sammy, had also joined the fray, along with their uncle, who was holding them both back, everyone else rapt.

"Let me tell you, let me tell you what, and another thing, I'm an *American!* Hey, what do y'all know, let me—*Congratulations.*" He uttered these phrases on a loop, staggered in his boots, and teetered so close to falling down that everyone stepped back, made a wide circle for his show. Mac and his brother stood down, ready to let him collapse into his own mess on the floor. But then the star leaned low, and rose up, a kind of bow in reverse, arms outstretched, smile set to mega-bright, and said, crisp as a two-dollar bill, "I do sincerely regret my dishevelment and disruption. If you'll allow it, I'd like to bless the newlyweds with a song?"

The twins and their friends cheered and whooped, as did all of the young people, and most of the Kentuckians, and the lingering sounds of confusion and resistance seemed to buoy him as he leaped onstage and launched into a song that even some of the French guests recognized, about warm beer, tight jeans, and an explosively broken heart. His voice was low and bourbon worn and the hackneyed nature of the song was elevated by the soaring chorus, the way his lust sounded like lament, his wails of woe like ecstasy. He even tried to sing the rap interlude that had helped make him a crossover success, and in this he was not so elegant, but his dedication and charisma, along with the enthusiasm of the backing band, got more people on the dance floor than could strictly fit.

"Is this a love song, like about a lover, or about his daughter?" Lainey shouted into Adam's ear, his hand in hers. They had snuck off before the scuffle to make out a little in an alcove behind the stage. Adam's willingness to break for kissing at any time was a quality of his that Lainey treasured. She felt a tepid moral opposition to marriage, especially if it meant you would kiss only one person for the rest of your life, but if she was going to enter into such a ludicrous contract, it would be with Adam, whose kisses still made her feel like she was tumbling headlong into some promising darkness.

"I think it's trying to be . . . *both*?" Adam said. "This is not a great song. But it is *such* a fucking earworm. Dance with me, daughter-lover!" he shouted over the music as he skipped with her closer to the center of the storm.

After the first song, the country star sang another, and another, and three more requests before he finished with a soppy ballad off his first album that was custom made for father-daughter dances at weddings, and that Mac requested, not knowing this, only that it was the star's biggest hit that he hadn't yet played.

As they danced, Mac whispered into Margaret's ear that he was sorry.

"For what?" Margaret asked. "Everything about this night is a miracle." She didn't care to know his answer: for requesting a song that called for the presence of the father Margaret didn't have, for nearly coming to blows with the country star, for letting the wedding veer off script at all, even in a way that made it more memorable to most of the guests than their own weddings.

When the country star left—seeming to vanish into a trapdoor under the stage—the band segued back into the bluegrass they'd been given the okay to play after midnight, and everyone danced until they were shepherded, still gleaming with sweat, to the stairs outside the estate. They were given the longest sparklers they had ever seen, along with instructions to hold them aloft for Margaret and Mac's grand exit.

Lainey, Alice, and Ji Sun found the fur capelets they'd been expected to wear when outdoors placed on their shoulders by the attendants who seemed to appear from behind the ceiling-height velvet curtains, a style Ji Sun had heard one of Mac's French relatives describe as "hillbilly Versailles" in the most pleasingly accented way. *Hillbilly* in her mouth sounded like a couture designer and *Versailles* sliced back lengthwise into French spoken too fast for Ji Sun to understand over the din.

"I thought we *were* the attendants," Alice whispered. "This wedding is unfuckingreal."

Ji Sun, who had seen her share of ostentatious celebrations, had been jubilant at the thrill of a real surprise stacked up against all the orchestrated ones, a wonderland of diversions—silhouette artists, custom bottles of bourbon with guests' names etched in the glass, vintage accessories, and a French 1920s crescent-moon bench swing in the photo booth—that, like a fun fair, made you sick to your stomach before you could sample them all. Her date, Evan, was a roommate of Adam's who had been asking her out for several months, describing her to Adam as his "dream girl." He'd only met her a few times, and Ji Sun was skeptical of his enthusiasm for her, as well as for the evening. He'd been repeating all night that he'd never seen anything like this, that this was for sure the best wedding *ever, of, like, ALL time.* After the country star showed up, his effusiveness stopped irking her, and she surrendered to his delight, felt it herself. She was giddy when the crowd parted for the country singer, when it looked like Mac might fight him, and most of all when he hopped on the stage and sang as if possessed. She knew the song, but she'd never *heard* the song, and no one had heard it sung like this, she was sure. She could have gone on dancing for the rest of her life if he'd kept singing songs like the first, and her adrenaline fueled her through his more saccharine follow-ups, moved her close to Evan during the ballads, where she felt in the heat between their bodies a kind of bright joy that wasn't love, but was the potential for it.

She would be thankful to Margaret for the rest of her life for this night, for this feeling, she knew. It could only be Margaret, given name Majestic, for whom this night could transpire. She'd felt sorry for her friend at the rehearsal dinner the previous night, by how outnumbered her guests were by Mac's family and friends, by the way in which Margaret's family would have been made invisible if not for how they stuck out, bewildered and belittled, wearing clothes too shiny, makeup too heavy, and perfume too sweet. But no number of people, no amount of money, not even an excess of beauty could guarantee a night like this. There was something else, something Ji Sun didn't pretend to understand but did recognize as a kind of magic.

"Magnum sparklers!" Adam said. "They even smell good. Like a fancy cigar."

Ji Sun didn't point out that a dozen men had lit long stogies, the puffs of their smoke mixing with the clouds of visible breath in the black sky of the cold Kentucky night. Instead, she grabbed Evan's swinging free hand and planted a fat kiss on his face, real sparks standing in for romantic ones. Falling in love was maybe a little like deciding to smile when you were in a foul mood; you tried it and then your face gave in and then your heart considered there might be something to it. Your mind stayed out of it for a while.

The enormous sparklers burned long after Margaret and Mac had clambered into their restored speedster, driven some kind of performative route off into the woods before circling back to the club where they, like their guests, were staying that night.

In their absence, the crowd had a stolen moment where no one appeared to usher them to the next bit of carefully orchestrated wonder. They all looked down the long row of flickering lights, the arches electric, wondered what might come down from the darkness next.

CHAPTER 24

Margaret was rich for having married Mac, and now she would be famous, too? It would have been too much if it hadn't felt to Lainey like a foregone conclusion somehow, a day they all knew would come.

The video was irresistible to tabloids, with its combination of how fall-down drunk the star was, how spectacular and stupid his monologue, and then, how chivalrous and how resplendent a performer, even when tanked. The grainy but glorious video, filmed on Margaret's friend Gavin's Flip camcorder, appeared everywhere, with its flashes to Margaret's face: beaming; wet with tears of joy and laughter; lit by the beads on her gown; the borrowed diamonds on her décolletage; her mighty, majestic smile. The dancing and whooping around her disappeared when she was onscreen and all anyone could see was her radiant, absolute joy. It wasn't even her beauty that was so magnetic, but how beautiful she found the rest of it, the way she looked at *them*.

The first article that focused on Margaret rather than the country star had lit up Lainey's Facebook feed: *Stunner Bride Gets Surprise of a Lifetime at Lavish Wedding*. The story was all screencaps of the video with links to things similar to Margaret's attire, since most of what she wore was custom, vintage, one-of-a-kind, "price upon request": so many ways of saying *Fuck you, plebe*. The same website did a follow-up article the next day on how to get Margaret's makeup look, this time with a clearer photo, gotten from a rogue guest, it would appear, who ignored instructions sent in an email cosigned by both wedding planners to please refrain from sharing any documentation with tabloids, as the family would like to showcase professional photographs, and in trustworthy media outlets. The

Southern planner had been disappointed when a feature in *Martha Stewart Weddings* had fallen through before the wedding, but Margaret mentioned they were "in talks" to do a story now.

Pity the reader adding NARS Orgasm to her shopping cart, thinking it would give her a face like Margaret's. Lainey clicked the link herself, toggled to swatches of still brighter shades. She could paint her whole face in neon pink and mica gold and she wouldn't light up as bright as Margaret in the video. She wanted to watch it again, but her cubicle was around the corner from the bathroom, and 10:00 A.M. was prime bathroom time. Poop time. She tried not to notice how long her colleagues stayed in the bathroom, but the tedium of her job, glorified data entry at a Broadway ticket broker's office, made it difficult not to look for any distraction. She pinched her own cheeks and took a slug of the coffee that had gone cold on her desk.

"Oh, my God, Lainey, your friend was on *The Late Show* last night! So fun!" Molly, her most cheerful coworker, appeared beside Lainey's desk with her ever-present, head-size Starbucks cup.

"What?" Lainey would have heard about this, surely, from Margaret herself, who had told them that she and Mac had been asked to appear on a few local Kentucky news programs, and even one national morning show. But she said the idea made her too nervous, and besides, Mac's grandmother thought it tacky, and his mother wanted to hold out for a better show—all this conveyed via the planners, now seemingly employed indefinitely to manage the postwedding flurry of attention.

That someone could say no to being on television astounded the rest, who realized they'd grown up thinking of it as a goal even if their respective ambitions had nothing to do with entertainment.

"Really?" Lainey asked Molly. How could Margaret keep this from them? "Oh, I fell asleep so early last night, I haven't had a chance—"

"Let's queue it up, girl!" Molly rolled over a desk chair and navigated to the clip.

The host played the infamous video, and the country star's drunken monologue was made still funnier by his good-natured laughter and endearing blush as he watched himself.

On one cut to Margaret's face, the host said, "Who is *she*? She should be on stage!"

"No shi—no crud, right?"

The host laughed, head back, mouth flung open, like crud for shit was the best joke he'd heard all year. The superstar hopped up from his seat, emulated the style of the leap he'd taken in the video, and took to the stage, grabbed the microphone and dipped it low, said, "This song goes out to all y'all newlyweds watching from home, but especially you Mac, and you, Margaret," he looked right at the camera, "belle of the ball, for your goodwill and neighborliness when a gnarly old drunk crashed your wedding."

The star appeared enormous again on screen, and Lainey marveled, as he crooned about blue jeans, at how perfectly his own fit, how the stones on his belt buckle seemed to twinkle with the beat. The wedding video projected behind him, silent now as he sang. When the rap verse began, the country star looked as if he would go for it, but then the rapper himself appeared from offstage and took over, and the studio audience audibly went bonkers. And there was Margaret's face again, laughing now, and beaming, and Lainey, as always, couldn't look away.

Lainey and Adam didn't appear, but you could see Ji Sun's date, Evan, at one point, dancing like a maniac, and a bit of Alice's strong arm, squeezing Margaret's shoulder. The only evidence of Mac was his ear.

Molly shimmied behind Lainey. "I love this song."

As the final chorus swelled, Lainey felt rise in her a familiar surge of something like fury. She had to make a change. She had to quit her job, focus on writing, do *something*. She couldn't sit here in this stale, gray room, her cubicle walls closing in on her while her best friends sparkled on television, became doctors, traveled the world.

"Wow," Lainey said. "That's awesome." She hadn't minimized the window with the blush compacts, so she gestured at a stack of meaningless papers on her desk. "Well, I should probably get back to work."

"Right, me too," Molly said, singing all the way back to her desk, "In those jeaaaaans, in my dreeeeams."

Lainey opened the group chat window she and her roommates maintained and typed out: Alice, wtf, your arm was on national television last night. Can I have your autograph???

Haven't watched yet—what are we talking about? Ji Sun was in Berlin, but was the easiest to catch online.

Oh, it's the video, it isn't me! Margaret wrote a few moments later, and the still-typing ellipses appeared. But yeah, pretty hysterical!!!!! She added the little plop-shaped blushing smiley face.

Alice wouldn't respond until hours later, when she wrote, Damn, he is wearing those jeans. Can I get his number, M?

After work, Lainey met Adam for a drink at the Bavarian bier haus between their two offices and broke up with him for the nth time. She and Adam shared an oversized soft pretzel, buttery and warm. She'd felt cruelty well up in her all afternoon, edging out ambition, and knew it would come out here, taste of mustard on her tongue, everyone in the bar loud and laughing, probably celebrating engagements or promotions or other capitalist milestones that Lainey both disdained and desired.

"I need to get in touch with myself, with my ambition. I feel like I've been putting too much into this, into us."

Adam gave a weary sigh, brushed salt from the corners of his lips. "But things have been going so well. Lainey, I thought we—I thought we'd get married."

"*Married?*" Lainey gulped, stopped herself from laughing—not at the absurdity of the idea, but at the fact that, had he asked her just before she broke up with him, she might have said yes. How could she feel so warm and behave so coldly? She didn't know what she was doing, or why. "We're twenty-four!"

"Not, like, tomorrow," he said, his eyes the same rusty amber color as his beer in the light.

"Oh, God, I don't even know if I want to *get* married, Adam. Ever."

Here he crumpled some. She'd said this before, but he didn't believe it, she knew.

"Is this, you find this stifling?" He gestured at their table, at his own body, broad shoulders and one of his soft blue sweaters.

She had the urge to touch him. She had just been feeling so full and so satisfied, something like content, coming in from the sludge of the city to this cozy spot, where they'd lucked into a table and gotten served right away. They loved and supported one another. They gave each other space to grow and become.

"No, I don't know."

"Is this about dating other people . . . or girls?" That Lainey sometimes dated women seemed both a point of pride and confusion for Adam, who'd been dumped enough times by her now that he feared himself, rather than women, to be the phase.

"Not just that, but I guess that's part of it," Lainey said. "Don't you think we're too young to be, like, monogamous? Don't you think it's nuts that Margaret and Mac are already married?"

"I mean, they're young, but . . . no, I don't think it's, like, insane that they got married. They're not teenagers." He touched his new iPhone, out on the table since he was too nervous to keep it in his messenger bag. "Lainey, I don't know how many more times I can go through this with you."

Him saying this felt perilous and thrilling. She could answer with love or rage; they came from the same place.

"Maybe this is the last time," she said, and waited for him to answer, *Because you'll come back to me, and you'll stay.* He'd said these exact words before; she'd memorized them. He would wait.

"Yeah," he said, "maybe it is."

The *yeah*, how readily he'd said it, how casual it sounded, tossed off like it was meaningless—she felt something go out from under her, and the free fall, there it was, that feeling she'd sought. Anything could happen, everything was still open to her, still possible. But when he stood to go, collected his precious phone, tucked money under a pint glass, and stooped to kiss her forehead like she was his wayward charge, she felt his shadow close around her. He left and the room grew more red but less warm, neon where there'd been candlelight, steam on the windows like smoke, everyone around her too loud and too hungry.

"Are you leaving?" a girl with foundation spackled on her face asked. She smelled like cotton candy and vinegar, and Lainey thought she might be sick. "We'd, like, *die* for this table."

"Be my guest," Lainey said, and stood to go. She paused as she pulled on her coat, considered what would happen if she asked instead for them to join her, paid for a round and listened to them complain about their ex-boyfriends, let some banker bros buy them ceramic boot steins, made her same old joke about managing to date a hedge fund manager while steadfastly refusing to learn what hedge funds even were, and gotten tanked enough to go home with one of them, sink down into the mediocre life that waited for her, jaws wide, at the bottom of whatever pit she was so intent to dive down into now.

CHAPTER 25

A lice got engaged next, to Kushi, on the night that Barack Obama won the 2008 election. Alice and Kushi watched the returns with some of her classmates and his fellow residents at the Back Bay apartment of one of the attendings from the hospital where they both worked. When CNN called it for Obama, Alice watched through her own tears as Kushi, whose observable emotions had so far run from riotous happiness to bemused frustration, wept. He was Canadian, the son of Pakistani immigrants, and couldn't vote. But he'd gone to undergrad in Chicago, and been on the Obama train early, with an enthusiasm that, along with the charisma of Michelle Obama, had won Alice fully to Obama by the primaries, in spite of her girlhood dream to vote for—to become, really—Hillary Clinton.

The others were cheering, toasting with tequila shots, while Kushi, still seated, shook beside her. She put her arms around him, brought him close, felt tears from his face make her own cheeks wet. When she remembered this night in the future, it would be this moment that rose above all the others—how they drew near in the overwhelm, how she gave shelter—even the elation that preceded it, the surprise that followed, and the immense rush that came from feeling like America the beautiful, the one in the songs and stories, was possible; hope was real; and humans were good.

They sent sprees of exclamation points by text, called their parents and other friends, collected their signs and sweatshirts— emblazoned with that sunrise O, and silkscreened with Obama's upturned, optimistic face—and then ran outside, joined the crowd in their impromptu parade to Copley Square.

Where had all this confetti come from? All these flags? Lainey had once observed that New York City was itself like a theater, always at the ready with any set and all the costumes, character actors for days, and Alice thought of this now as Boston, so dour in comparison, managed to send forth countless balloons from its own hidden trap doors, and the confetti that covered the sidewalk continued to rain down, the night sky a riot of red, white, blue, and gold.

"American Girl" began blasting from a boom box, and Alice shook her hips, did her finger-waggle shimmy invitation to Kushi to come dance with her.

"Alice, wait," Kushi said, and pulled on her hand. He bent low and she thought he was tying one of what she teased were his schoolboy sneakers, decrepit New Balances with ratty laces that were forever coming loose. But he looked up at her with a kind of beseeching wonder that made everything around her recede. She could remember having had this sensation only once before, where she could hear the record scratch in her own life, where the rest of the world blurred and she became one of only two.

"This is one of the greatest nights of my life—of American history! But also of my life. And I want you beside me for all the future greatest days, too. And the worst ones. All the days. All the joys. You saying yes is the only thing that could make this the best day of my life. Will you marry me?" He was screaming, she realized, to be heard above the crowd, and tears were pouring from her face in a way that made it difficult to see him, or the circle that had formed around him, their friends and also strangers who chanted and cheered, some with hands folded, hopeful—already stuffed with it, hope, but still, always, Americans, hungry for more.

"Yes," she whispered, and then shouted. "Yes! Yes, Kushi, fuck, of course!"

How had he come up with these lines, and when? How was someone so brilliant saying something so beautiful to her? What had she done to deserve a night like this, a life like this? He took her in his arms and they went into the crowd, where they danced and sang and were swallowed in the chaos of a joy that was all anticipation, all promise, all future forward, all confetti dust and hope and light light light light light

Three months later, the four were all together at a studio in Brooklyn to learn the mehndi dance they would perform at Alice's wedding. The ceremony was still six months away, but Ji Sun was in town, and the lesson replaced the meal they tried to share at least once a month.

Lainey was the best dancer of the bunch, and had learned the moves with ease. Ji Sun was graceful if labored, and Alice was competent if uninspired. But Margaret was like a giraffe foal, managing to land on her bum more than once, long limbs splayed out. She compensated for her lack of coordination with enthusiasm and her same old beauty, but Alice could tell the teacher was growing impatient. She'd had them break for twenty, and the four sat on the floor now with their waters, looking at one another in the mirror.

"Did you all take ballet growing up?" Margaret asked, eyes on Lainey's messy bun, hair dyed bright battery-acid yellow. Margaret was dressed like an extra in an eighties movie about ballerinas: grayish-purple leotard, pale pink tights, cream leg warmers. "I always wanted to, but we didn't have—well, we didn't really have the money, but we also didn't have a dance studio in town anyway, so . . ." She looked down. "I wish we'd done a choreographed dance at our wedding!" She smiled brightly.

This was their cue to say how Margaret had had the best wedding, why would she change a thing, her wedding was a dream, etc., but Alice had grown tired of this. She was sick even of planning her own wedding, which, were she in charge, would be at City Hall on a weekday afternoon when neither she nor Kushi were on call the next day, so they could gorge on happy-hour oysters and champagne after.

"It's just another thing to coordinate," Alice said. "I'd rather not have to deal with it."

Anything you said about your own wedding, Alice had learned, was taken by anyone who'd ever had a wedding or thought she might, as judgment or insult. She'd thought Margaret, whose wedding was famous, for chrissakes, would be immune to this, but here she was, scowling in her ballerina bun.

"I basically gave Kushi's mother carte blanche," Alice said.

"Your mom, she doesn't mind?" Lainey asked.

"What do you think?" Alice rolled her eyes. "I think she got her fix with Eleanor's wedding anyway."

Kushi had said his mother would keel over if they got married in a courthouse, disown him if they eloped. He was an only child, after his sister died of leukemia when she was eleven and Kushi was eight. Kushi couldn't remember a time before he'd wanted to be a doctor, and he still felt some guilt that he'd decided on radiation oncology as his specialty rather than pediatric oncology, as originally planned. But the ped-onk rotation had nearly destroyed him, he told Alice. He'd come home every night and dreamed of his sister, and the dreams reached into his days.

"She was ... *haunting* me," he said. "I would see her, in the halls at the hospital. Really see her. Not, like, sleep-deprived delusions, Alice. She was there. And she would just stare at me, and shake her head really slowly if I tried to go near. But now I think that maybe she was protecting me. From having to get hardened to all that." Radiation oncology was close enough, anyway, and Kushi was already head resident, on track for his choice of fellowships the following year.

When Alice first met him, she was struck by an immediate, unprecedented desire to have his children. Not to marry him, but to make a person with him, to be and create his family. This longing was so precise and insistent that she felt it physically, a full-body discomfort that radiated up from her pelvis and made rounds with him the worst she'd ever experienced.

"Honestly, I did think maybe you were in over your head," he'd told her, once they were together and she could give the reason for how clumsy and quiet she'd been. When he'd seen her on rounds with another resident, he'd stood in the door, mouth open, stunned by how bright she was, and how eager.

"No one's ever made me quite so incompetent before," she told him later, in bed, and he laughed at this, gestured at his naked, satiated body, said she was stupid competent, and she said he was stupid competent, too, and this became the way they talked about satisfying one another in bed.

"Is Kushi a good dancer, Alice?" Ji Sun asked. The others had been to a classmate's wedding with Alice and Kushi, but Ji Sun hadn't been able to attend.

"Very good," Alice said, and raised her eyebrows. "Ugh, he's *goood*. And let's just say . . . it translates." She closed her eyes and gave herself a little private smile.

"What do you mean? From . . . Hindi? Sorry, is this Hindi?" Margaret looked toward the speakers, music lowered but still on.

"Ugh, no, in *bed*, you prude," Alice laughed. "And I think it's Punjabi. What's it like on the other side, anyway? Married sex, I mean."

"Oh, I don't find it much different from unmarried sex. With Mac," Margaret said.

"And . . .?" Lainey always pushed like this, and though the others were used to it, they were still grateful and uncomfortable both. They were nosy, too, but not quite so willing to pry.

"It's fine." Margaret shrugged.

"Huh. Don't take this the wrong way, M, but why would you marry someone you didn't have great sex with? I mean, at least, like starting out? If it's going to get old, shouldn't it start amazing?" Lainey always needled Margaret, and the meaner she was, the more Margaret sought her approval.

"I don't know," Margaret said. "Maybe I don't think sex is everything in a relationship."

"Well, neither do I," said Lainey. "But it's sure as shit not *nothing*. I mean, Adam, he has, like, cast a legitimate *spell* on me that I cannot break, no matter what."

The stretch since their breakup following Margaret's wedding had been their longest time apart yet, and Lainey was worried now that it would stick. Adam had been dating a fact-checker at the newspaper for long enough that she'd heard they might move in together, news that had made her feel deranged.

"But why would you want to? Break a spell like that?" Ji Sun asked, so tired of her friend's failure to see her good fortune.

This got through, more than Lainey would let Ji Sun know, both the question and the way she asked it, the exasperation that revealed to Lainey, if only subconsciously, Ji Sun's own frustrated desire for that kind of partner, for Adam himself. She would remember the way that Ji Sun had asked it, the look on her face in the mirror, when she and Adam got back together that June, a month before Alice's wedding, and sated by a morning of just the sort of sex she'd missed so much, they wandered out of the apartment in search of ice cream, and she asked him to marry her.

He said yes, and swept her up, smiled his glorious, boring smile, and asked if she'd let him ask her again, maybe on a sailboat, so they'd have a good story to tell his parents, whom he would like to have pay in large part for the wedding. She chafed at how close practicality lay in wait beside romance, but she thought of the salt air and his bright face, a ring she chose for herself, and it dazzled her—let him tell his parents whatever he liked.

But wasn't this a good story, too, surrounded by tropical fruits at their corner bodega, both sweaty and spent and as certain as they'd ever been, as they would ever be, about anything, for the rest of their lives?

CHAPTER 27

B y the second year of their engagement, with no wedding date in sight, the others had begun to call Lainey and Adam the fiancées.

Meeting the fiancées, Ji Sun texted Margaret now, then coming yr way so get out the good stuff.

Margaret had begun working in a perfume store in the East Village, a job she didn't strictly need, but liked as it gave her time to work on *Margaret's Musings*, the blog that had improbably become her job, though the others didn't understand what this meant, and whether she actually made any money or was just paid in clothes and face creams.

She photographed things she liked and wrote little treacly paragraphs about why. Lainey couldn't discern much of a guiding principle beyond this; she might feature a café one day and an aloe vera plant the next. But she had a decent eye and a very expensive camera, and of course she appeared in many of the photos herself, wearing clothes that the reader could imagining layering with that same ease, and maybe they'd spin in the middle of a busy Brooklyn street then, too, and smile so brightly that a taxi driver would be moved to slow down and wave. Soon other websites had begun linking to her blog, and she was back on television, live now, as a Lifestyle Expert who appeared on *Good Morning America* a few times a month to tell women how to spend their money. The owners of the perfume store had hired her after she wrote an entry about their shop, and lovingly photographed Civet, their teacup Bichon Frisé, whom she described as smelling like the pouf in a vintage powder compact.

This was a nice image, Lainey would allow, but it rankled her to no end that Margaret was the one in the group considered a writer now, even though for the most part her prose was clumsy and labored, as well as mind-numbingly repetitive. The word *transformative* appeared in half the posts, and nearly every single one ended with the same invitation to the reader to *Leave a comment if you like; I would absolutely adore hearing from you!*

No one could ever find the door to the perfume shop, and Lainey and Ji Sun struggled even though they'd visited before. They'd lived in New York too long to ask, and though they had maps on their phones now, GPS couldn't account for the way the garden-level shop seemed to retreat further from the street the nearer they got.

Adam finally discovered the door, overgrown with ivy that obscured the faint gold filigree that served as the only indication this was a place of business rather than some eccentric's storefront home.

"How does this place stay in business?" he asked.

"You'll see," Lainey said, and opened the door to the plush, dark room. A dozen footstools in plummy velvet wound a path through the forest of black-lacquered tabletops; any surface not gleaming with gold and glass bottles heaved instead with tremendous bouquets of roses, so large they looked like topiaries, clouds.

"Holy shit," Adam said.

"Only in New York, right!" Margaret beamed from a throne behind the counter. She loved to say this, marveled more than any of them at the city's offerings. *Can you believe this?* About a pork bun, a drag bar, a beatboxer in the subway. *Only in New York!*

"It's easy to see New York as one big amusement park if you've got loads of money," Lainey said once. "Try living here broke." Not that she knew what that was like, either, living as she still did with Ji Sun, but Margaret always seemed to stumble up like this, into still more wonder, oblivious as to why everyone else wasn't doing just the same.

Margaret hugged each one of them in turn, breathed them in.

"Scent-free. Good," she said. "Let me choose something for each of you! I'll make samples." She wore one of her diaphanous tops, wafty layers of pale cream silk that made her look a moth alighting on bright bottles in this basement boudoir.

Lainey lifted a bell jar from atop a seventy-eight-dollar candle, raised the candle up, and let her septum ring clink on the glass. It smelled like honey and cheese and about-to-rot funeral flowers.

"Ooh, let me grab one I know you'll love," Margaret said, and put down her perfume bottles, lifted another bell jar, and held it beneath Lainey's nose. "You don't even need the candle. The scent infuses these."

"Ungh," Lainey said, the smell taking her to another place. "That's *soo* good. What is it? Tea?"

"Lapsang souchong! You have a good nose. Also toasted rice, tobacco smoke, and rose. I get leather, but it's not listed among the notes."

"Wow," Lainey said. "Too bad it's eighty bucks."

"I'll buy one for our place," Ji Sun said.

Ji Sun was generous but unpredictable, her wealth an undercurrent the others acknowledged but tried not to pay too much attention to, as though if they did, something precarious that kept them close across this economic gulf might topple.

"No, don't do that. It's ridiculous." Lainey felt enough guilt at how much Ji Sun subsidized her lifestyle, how little she paid her friend in rent, and how often Adam stayed over. "That price. I would feel physically ill burning a candle that cost that much."

"Okay," Ji Sun said, and put the box back on the table. "Suit yourself." Money became more an issue as they moved away from college, where everyone had lived in the same sort of space, and did the same work, more or less. Now they were choosing or changing lanes—marrying rich, as Margaret already had; coming into trust funds; failing to get interviews for even the poorly paid entry-level jobs that Quincy-Hawthorn had led them to believe were beneath them. Ji Sun wouldn't pretend that the stakes were the same for her, but nor would she be made to feel guilty for her parents' successes. "Margaret, help me choose something to bring to Mac's family."

They were headed together to Mac's grandmother's estate in rural Connecticut at the end of that summer. The trip was still months away, but they talked about it often, their reunion. They hardly saw Alice, even though she and Kushi lived in Brooklyn now, Alice having matched at Langone Hospital in March, and Kushi on a fellowship at Lenox Hill. As a first-year resident, Alice had strict vacation allowances, and they'd planned the trip around when she could get away.

"Are you sure it's not going to be weird, with his cousins? Like we're crashing a family reunion?" Lainey would have preferred to have the reunion with just them, but not having to pay for a full week together was hard to pass up.

"I swear, we will barely even notice them. The place has its own *lake*. We won't even have to see them if we don't want. Except in the pool. Besides, his cousins stay there all summer. They'll be happy for some fresh blood."

"All summer, huh?" Adam said. "What do they do?"

Margaret shrugged. "What does anyone. *Do*."

"You should slap that little anticapitalist koan up on your blog, Margaret," Lainey said.

"I know you're teasing me," Margaret said, "but French people aren't defined by their work the way we Americans are." She took a sleek black bottle from the table, unadorned save a simple sans-serif font, and asked for Lainey's arm, sprayed.

Adam and Ji Sun leaned low and inhaled, the tips of their noses touching near the inside of Lainey's elbow.

Adam laughed and Ji Sun felt lightheaded.

"That's incredible," Adam said. "It's like stone, but . . . alive?" He drew Lainey closer to him, buried his face in the crook of her arm in a way that made Ji Sun sick with longing. She had by now accepted that she enjoyed this particular agony, that her desire for Adam was like a mild but chronic illness, flare-ups inevitable. Rarely did she feel woozy with it, but the combination of the scent, the space, their faces so near—it had undone a bit of the distance she'd put between herself and those feelings.

"I'm starting to get hungry," Ji Sun said. "Can we eat?" There was a ramen place nearby with tables as elusive as the perfume shop's door, but if they left soon they might get lucky. They did, and Ji Sun treated her friends because they didn't expect her to, and so she could order everything she liked without the lengthy scrutinizing of the bill Lainey would otherwise do. While they ate, the smell of that mossy, sacramental stone kept lifting into the air and reaching Ji Sun, who feared she might cry into her broth.

She went back to the shop the next week and bought two bottles of the perfume, one for herself and one for Lainey. Ji Sun only wore it on evenings out, or special occasions, as its power seemed too strong for an ordinary day. It started with a straight-from-the-censer jolt of incense from some chapel where she must have worshipped in a past life. The scent shook something spiritual loose in her, made her reverent for her own skin. Lainey found it lovely but not holy, and wore it on random days, blindsiding Ji Sun over breakfast. They both brought it on the trip to Connecticut, unsummery a scent as it was, perhaps thinking its cool stone might subdue some of the swampy, relentless swelter of late August.

But neither one of them would ever be able to wear it again after what happened in Connecticut. Something turned acrid in the bottles after what Margaret did, and more sour still after what the rest of them failed to.

CHAPTER 28

The Connecticut compound had been dubbed the Warren before Mac's time, for rabbit-related reasons that remained unclear. Mac's father had told him that his grandmother adored rabbits in her youth, planted a whole unfenced field of Bibb and butter lettuces to lure them. Mac's mother said rabbits had swarmed the property in the year after the remodel was finished, claimed her mother-in-law had had them killed by archers. One uncle said there was an underground wing somewhere that no one had ever seen where bunnies lived indoors, cared for by a decrepit butler who read them Richard Scarry books and baked them carrot muffins. If you stood at the lowest point of the land and the weather was right, he said, you could smell burning carrots on the breeze.

Their directions terminated at an ice cream shop up on a high hill, part of a working farm. Margaret had said it was just impossible to find the Warren without an escort, so they were to get ice cream and wait until Mac came to ferry them to his grandmother's place, only two miles away but seeming more and more to be on another planet. Margaret's instructions had listed her top three flavors, and Lainey licked a cone of "Purple Cow," a creamy raspberry with chocolate brittle, and looked down into a valley of actual cows straight out of central casting, none purple, but all alien enough even in their ordinary colors, reminding her as they did of how quickly New York City's streets and vistas had colonized her mind, made her forget there were hills like this, farms, animals untethered to human beings.

Lainey had experienced a version of this exact view on *Margaret's Musings*, where her friend had profiled the shop a month ago. In Margaret's photographs, the valley was greener and the ice cream a

dreamier purple, more lilac and less bluey gray than the stuff melt-
ing onto Lainey's hands now. There were no sticky wrists on
Margaret's blog. In the photos, Margaret sat on the same porch
where Lainey waited now, Adam, Ji Sun, Alice, and Kushi still
inside choosing flavors and browsing produce and knickknacks.
Margaret wore a pair of gold linen gladiator espadrilles in the
photos, paired with short-shorts and a cotton blouse. Lainey wore
espadrilles now, though not in the gladiator style that required legs
for days, and her shorts were even shorter. She wore a gingham
top, steadfast in her belief that the right costume could change
everything.

Margaret had photographed the wildflowers in milk bottles that
sat on the tables, less delightful to Lainey now for having expected
them. She'd been experimenting with her macro lens all summer,
and one photo showed a little sweat bee doing its work, stick legs
garish with hair, face desecrated by pollen, mandibles obscene.

Kushi came outside with a sundae in what looked like a milk
pail.

"I got the Cattle Call! Connecticut's answer to the Vermonster.
If we eat it all, we get a cowbell!"

Kushi had driven them all from New York in an SUV borrowed
from an anesthesiologist friend. The stubble on his face, his
Transitions lens glasses, the sporty Keen sandals he wore—all
conspired to make him look even more like the dad that Lainey
knew he wanted badly to be.

"My hungry herdsman." Alice laughed and kissed Kushi on the
cheek, let the spoons she'd gathered clatter to the table.

The way Alice talked about it had Lainey believing that fourth
year hadn't been just the best year of med school to have a baby, but
the *only* year. Having not gotten pregnant that year—in spite of
"removing the goalie," as Alice put it, right after she and Kushi
were married—had turned her friend pregnancy-obsessed to a

degree that unsettled Lainey, made it seem even more as though Alice was on an accelerated path to adulthood, already married and a real doctor now, trying for babies.

"For real if I'm ovulating on the day we drive there, we're going to pull the car over and y'all will have to get out."

"You know down to the *day*?"

"I know down to the *moment*," Alice had said, and explained to Lainey a little bit about the charts she kept. Even in her women's studies circles, Lainey hadn't heard so much about cervical mucus, ovulatory bleeding, the welcome pain of mittelschmerz, the way the body's temperature, measured precisely, would announce when it was in heat.

"All the time we spend trying to avoid it!" Lainey said, thinking back to their visits to the student health center for Plan B, the abortions she'd avoided thanks to a ready supply of the drug. "And there's just this one little window."

"I know," Alice had said. She'd never been pregnant, to her knowledge, but felt even medical school hadn't prepared her for the intimacy she now had with her own menstrual cycle. "And our timing is already so screwy."

Their ice cream was soup by the time Margaret and Mac appeared, looking like an advertisement for leisure. Margaret wore a linen shift, the string of a white bikini knotted at her neck. Mac was deeply tanned in his tissue-weight Oxford shirt, sleeves rolled up, top three buttons undone, thick hair on his chest one of the few things Lainey found attractive about him. Adam had a patch of soft hair on his rib cage between his pecs, and Lainey realized, looking at Mac's coarse curls now, that she still expected it might spread over his whole chest. But more likely he was done with this kind of growth at twenty-seven, and the hair would stay sparse until it turned white, fell out.

They piled back in the car, Ji Sun in the front seat as she'd been the whole way for reasons related to car sickness none of them had known her to have before this trip. Lainey watched as Margaret wrapped a scarf loosely around her hair, in its usual milkmaid crown. The white chiffon waved like a flag from Mac's little emerald convertible as it sped down the open country road.

"She's wearing a *scarf*," Lainey said to no one. Even Margaret's costume would have to one-up her own, animated, as Margaret's was, from on high.

When Mac made a sharp turn off the main road onto a dirt one, Margaret's scarf floated off her head, snatched up into the sky.

Lainey watched her friend's delayed grasp for it, hands a slight strangle around her own bare neck, before she raised them up in the air, as if expecting the scarf would be spirited back to her on the breeze.

Instead, it whipped onto the SUV's windshield, caused Kushi to make a wide swerve and trundle onto the road's steep shoulder. He'd righted himself quickly, but everyone had jolted forward and been snapped back by their seat belts, save Lainey, who wasn't wearing hers.

"Shit, is everyone okay?" Kushi turned the flashers on with one hand and reached the other back to take Alice's hand.

Adam had grabbed Lainey and she'd only bumped her crotch against the console between the two front seats. She adjusted herself and dug around for the ends of her seat belt, tucked into the cushions.

"Why weren't you wearing your seat belt?" Alice asked.

"It was such a short ride! I'm squeezed in back here," Lainey said. *Sitting bitch*, she thought, a term she loathed.

"A huge percentage of auto accidents happen on short rides!" Alice said, her voice shaky.

"I'm *fine*, thanks for the lecture," Lainey said, and made a show of clicking her seat belt before turning to look at Alice, at the tears on her face.

"Oh, no!" Lainey said. "Are you okay, Alice?"

Kushi had hopped out of the car and was crouched beside Alice's seat now, in the road.

Margaret and Mac approached.

"Oh, my God, what happened? Are you all right?" Margaret opened the door to the passenger seat just as Ji Sun turned around to look at Alice.

Alice gasped, and then Adam, and Lainey, though it was only a small trail of blood on Ji Sun's philtrum. She put two fingertips beneath her nostrils and more blood streamed loose.

"It's the strangest thing," Ji Sun said. "My head barely jerked forward—I don't think it's even related!" She looked at the red blossom of blood on her fingers, and back up at them, as though they might have the answers. Adam found a napkin in his backpack and passed it up to her.

"Should we go to the hospital?" Adam asked.

"For a nosebleed? I'm fine!"

Alice shook her head, "No, no, I'm fine, too. It was just . . . jarring." She had her hands on both sides of her face, and Lainey couldn't tell if she was imagining it, or if Alice's scar was pink, inflamed.

"Sorry I was such a bitch about my seat belt," Lainey said. *Sitting bitch.*

"No, it's fine, I'm fine," Alice said, and started laughing and crying from what seemed like relief. "It was just unexpected. Let's get going." She pointed at Mac's car. "You're stopped in the middle of the road!" She laughed again, and snot flipped out of her nostril.

Lainey watched Adam peel another from his stash of napkins. He must have taken them from the ice cream shop, she thought, and felt a wave of tenderness, only a cresting tip of irritation, how even now, blood and snot all around, he was hoarding a few away. She leaned over and kissed his cheek.

"No one else goes on this road," Mac shrugged. "I'll go really slow this time." He looked at Kushi, who nodded but sniffed.

"It was the scarf," Kushi said. "I don't think—never mind. Great, yes, let's go slowly."

They rode without the radio on, stones popping beneath the tires. Light twinkled from the tree canopy, everything sunny and golden and dappled in honey-washed green. The trees grew taller, but their shadows heavier, so as they drove they felt enclosed by the road, ferried by forest to a place quite distant from the world they knew.

CHAPTER 29

The sensation of being removed from reality only increased once they arrived and sunk into the languor of the long summer days, rotated from the pool to the lake to the house, whose long, lacquered-wood halls led to rooms with beds whose white sheets had high thread counts and a fine coating of the sun dust that comes from lack of use. The closets had lavender sachets on their shelves, along with soft robes and more clean towels than they would ever manage to use.

Mac's grandmother had visited the Gamble House in her twenties, and when she remodeled her Connecticut place, she'd used it as her vision, down to stained-glass trees on the enormous leaded glass doors. Together with leaves from outside winking from the high windows, walking the halls felt like exploring a treehouse mansion in some sleek, Art Deco future.

The lower half of the house hadn't been part of the extensive rehab, and looked more like the 1970s basement of any rich Republican. They spent most of their time together on this lived-in level, its service kitchen better stocked and more inviting in its signs of wear than the one on the main floor. There was a large rec room with sliding glass doors that opened to the pool deck, and a massive fireplace that they sometimes turned on along with the air-conditioning, in a show of excess that Lainey couldn't help but remark upon each time someone flipped the switch and set the glass pebbles alight with blue flames. Mac's cousin Bart and his wife, Clémence, stayed in the guesthouse, but the bedrooms on this basement level were occupied by their children, Colette, seventeen, and Laurent, newly thirteen.

Laurent had had a belated birthday celebration with his American relatives at the house, and there were still crepe streamers and slowly deflating balloons in one corner of the den, half a sheet cake with what looked like Transformers battling cowboys in the fridge.

"Did Laurent choose this theme? Is this a bald eagle?" Ji Sun asked, licking the frosting from her finger at breakfast. She understood the appeal of this kind of sugar bomb of a sheet cake only when paired with strong coffee, couldn't believe her friends enjoyed their slices with milk or juice, ice cream.

"Teenagers," Mac said from his place at the stove. "Who wants bacon?"

Seeing him in his apron softened Ji Sun's sense of him, as had these days poolside, when he'd bring drinks out to the deck for them.

"Living the dream, eh, ladies?" he'd smiled and said to Ji Sun the day before. "I can't tell you how much Margaret has been looking forward to this. She needed this."

"What do you mean?" Ji Sun asked.

"Oh, just that she misses, you know, the gal-pal days. When you all lived together. College. Think it's sort of an ongoing adjustment, you know? To living with me. Being a grown-up." He laughed and showed his overlarge teeth.

"Right," Ji Sun said, and looked at Margaret, floating in the pool on a silver raft. It bothered Ji Sun less that Mac said things like "gal pals" when he kept bringing out bottles of chilled rosé, crisp and nearly clear.

At breakfast now, Mac slid the meat from his skillet onto a tray. Laurent appeared, hair in his eyes, and slunk low into a seat, reached for the bacon.

"Perfect timing, bud," Mac said.

"*Oui, ça sentait tellement bon.*" He looked at Mac, added, "I smelled it."

"*Meillure odeur*," Kushi said, though he didn't eat meat.

"That's so dope!" Mac said, and shook his head at Kushi. "Bacon, bro?"

Despite his heritage, Mac didn't speak any French. Ji Sun tried not to burst a blood vessel at how delighted he was that both she and Kushi did. This was always the case with Mac—she would warm toward him, and he'd promptly unravel her goodwill. It was just so with the way he smelled now, standing behind her. Since Margaret had started working at the shop, Mac smelled gorgeous. He often wore something that skewed feminine, orange blossom and white flowers, and it mixed with his sweat and musk to become nearly narcotic. Ji Sun still didn't want to talk to him much, but she minded standing near him less. Now, neroli and sunscreen mixed with the grease and smoke of bacon, old beer that always rose off his pores, stale coffee breath. He rubbed at his stubble and she felt as though the thick little hairs were loosed into the air, onto her skin, where they itched. The frosting on her tongue turned to paste.

"I wish I spoke French," Margaret said, looking at Laurent. "Still working on English, though."

"Motherfuck!" Mac shouted at the same time there was a loud bang. "Fuck me!"

He'd dropped the skillet, and he bent now to take his foot in his hands.

"Oh, no!" Margaret leaped up from her seat.

"Did it land on a bone?" Kushi asked, and got up from the table.

"No, the pan didn't hit my foot. Just the grease, it splattered," Mac said. "Fuck!" He sucked in a breath. "Pardon my French," he said to Laurent, who had also jumped up when he saw Mac was hurt, strip of bacon still in his grip.

"Oh, good, that's good," Kushi said. "Let me take a look?"

Ji Sun glanced at Mac's foot, specks of blackened meat on streaks of red like the scratch of a big cat along his bones.

"*Ma mère a une bonne onguent*," Laurent said to Kushi. "Biafine? I'll go and find it."

Laurent had slunk in looking like a teenager, but he darted off like a child, lips greasy and limbs scrawny. He wore an oversized Bart Simpson T-shirt that Mac had said used to be his, and swim trunks that hung from his hips. Being around him this week had occasioned them to talk about what they were like at thirteen, for the others to feel a surge of protectiveness and familiarity at how their friends described themselves at that age, to wonder if they would have become friends, alike in their lonelinesses even as they were so different in ways that seemed to matter so much then.

"Looks pretty superficial," Kushi said.

"Hurts like a motherfucker," Mac said.

Alice wrapped ice in a dish towel, and Laurent returned bearing a tube of ointment.

"Put this on it for a bit after you clean it." She handed Mac the ice. "And I'd stay off it for today."

"Aw, man, but we were set for a rematch after breakfast!" He reached for Margaret. "She destroyed me yesterday."

"Oh, love, there's plenty of time for tennis! Today you can put your feet up," Margaret said, her gauzy white swim cover-up transformed to a nursemaid's garment. "You deserve a break anyway."

"I'll play with you," Laurent said, eyes on Margaret as they had been on the bacon.

"He may not look like much, but he's pretty mean on the clay," Mac said. "I'll be line judge."

Laurent watched as Margaret rubbed the ointment into Mac's feet, Kushi and Alice overseeing, a conference of caretakers for this minor grease burn.

Ji Sun remembered the way that Margaret had sliced the underside of her foot in the grass so soon after they'd met, how they'd raced together to the infirmary. She knew that Conner had been there, and carried her friend, but in her memory he had already blurred, was close to vanishing. She saw herself and Margaret, racing through the thick grass of the lawn, holding hands, laughing, Margaret's wound somehow healing itself through the force of their newly forged friendship alone.

CHAPTER 30

Three nights before they were set to leave, as Kushi snored beside her, Alice heard the ping of a text message, sent by Lainey to their group text chain:

MMMmm need nachos. Meet n kitchen?

Lainey, Ji Sun, and Margaret had smoked a bowl of stale weed from Mac's pipe after dinner, giggled, and told Kushi stories about what Alice was like in college. Alice had broken up the fun a bit early to retreat with Kushi to their room, to have sex and put her feet on the wall for forty-five minutes. Neither of them had smoked, swearing off as they had anything that might contribute to compromised sperm motility or a less-than-fecund uterus.

Alice snuck into the hall just as Lainey closed her own door loudly, laughed, and covered her mouth. She took Alice's arm and they approached Ji Sun's room together, heard a rustling, and waited until she came out, wearing oversized men's pajamas that made her look gamine and glamorous.

The three of them snuck through the house like they'd planned a heist.

"Do you think they even have tortilla chips here? Did we bring some? French people have the worst snacks. They don't even, like, *eat* snacks!" Lainey said in her stage whisper. She never could keep her voice down.

"Is Margaret coming?" Alice whispered.

"She didn't write back." Ji Sun glanced down at the glow of her phone. How nice it felt to be together in the night, unencumbered by lovers, on their way to forage for snacks and find more wine.

Margaret and Mac were staying on the other side of the house, nearer the lake.

"We'll just wait for her in the kitchen," Lainey said. "I'm starving."

They passed by Laurent's room, its door partially open.

They stopped before they heard Margaret's voice, or before they could place it as hers. Maybe they heard it as music, or as the voice of one of the lawyers on the cheesy legal drama Laurent liked to watch, and would recap at tedious length whenever given a chance. Each of them had sat beside him at some point on the trip, nodded politely as he summarized the premise of the show, which they'd all by then seen enough of to need no such summary, as he turned it on whenever he was in from outside, lounging in the rec room. Flopped on the couch, soggy from the pool, a bag of corn chips open in his lap, he'd laugh his funny adolescent laugh, snorts teetered just between the abandon of a child and the self-consciousness of a teenager.

But there was a light from the room that seemed wrong, a sense that they shouldn't pass that door without either opening or closing it.

They couldn't help but look inside and so they saw Margaret there, on Laurent's bed, her face and his face—was this, was this a kiss?

"What!" Alice gasped.

It was a kiss. Their faces moved together; they kissed.

Could they have seen what they did?

Alice pushed the door all the way open. Ji Sun and Lainey followed. They couldn't have seen what they did!

"Margaret! What's going on?" Alice cried. "What are you doing?"

The pair flung apart like two north pole magnets, like someone had taken a blowtorch to the air between them, Laurent with such force that he fell off the bed, clutched at his midsection as though he'd been kicked.

Margaret stood and covered her mouth. She ran out of the room, pushed Ji Sun and Lainey, who still stood in the open door, aside.

They watched as she fled in her white nightgown down the dark hallway, its skirt catching blades of light.

"Margaret!" Alice's yell came out like a hiss.

Lainey started laughing again, scraps of giggles she hadn't gotten rid of yet.

"Are you okay?" Ji Sun asked Laurent, who was still on the floor. "*C'est bien*," he said, his face red and wet. "Get out!"

Lainey shut his door and took Ji Sun's arm. Alice was off after Margaret.

"Get back here!" Alice called.

Margaret emerged from the dark hall and came into the den.

"Please stop *yelling*, Alice," Margaret said. "You'll wake everyone up."

"What the *fuck* was going on in there?" Alice said, not lowering her voice.

Margaret stood in front of the fireplace, shook her head, one hand over her closed eyes. She opened her eyes and, seeing her friends still there, closed them and shook her head again.

"Hello, Margaret, what was going on in there?" Alice asked, and then turned to Ji Sun and Lainey. "And you two, can you talk?"

"Please quiet down," Margaret said. "Follow me, let's not do this here." She pointed down the hall, toward an unoccupied bedroom with two small twin beds.

Once inside, Margaret pulled the door closed and paced along the wall, where there was a window seat and a picture window that looked out at the dark black glass of the lake, the mirror of a bright, full moon.

"Stop pacing, Margaret!" Lainey said. "You're making me nervous."

Margaret smoothed her nightgown beneath her and took a seat on the edge of the bed. She put her head in her hands again and began to cry. No one went to comfort her, and after a moment, she spoke.

"It wasn't—it was nothing, it wasn't. Let me explain."

"Please do," Alice said, and glared at Lainey and Ji Sun, who, chastened, sat on the window seat.

"He kissed *me*," Margaret said. "And I just didn't stop it, not fast enough, I mean. I didn't right away."

"What were you doing in his room, in the middle of the night?" Lainey asked. She still felt fuzzy, like this was sort of funny, though she could see on her friends' faces that it was not.

"We were just talking! We ran into each other, in the kitchen."

"Okay, but why did you go in his *room*?" Ji Sun asked again, as though there was any satisfactory answer that Margaret could at this point provide.

"We were laughing, being loud. We just took snacks in there," Margaret said, face flushed deep red, eyes wild. "Please don't tell Mac."

"He's a *child*, Margaret," Ji Sun said.

"He's not a child! I'm a child—I mean, neither of us, I know it sounds so bizarre, but I, I feel like, well, when I was in his room, I felt, I *became* a thirteen-year-old, too, just for that split second and—"

"None of us have any trouble believing that," Lainey said.

"It's not funny!" Alice shrieked. "He's a *little boy*."

"He's not a *little boy!*" Lainey said.

"He is! He is a child! Are you actually *defending* her? Jesus Christ, Lainey. Snap out of it. What if Adam had been kissing Colette? You'd want him in jail!"

"Jail? It's Margaret—"

The red rose in Margaret's cheeks at the mention of jail. She stood from the bed, frantic. "I made a mistake. We only kissed. It will never happen again, and it's never happened before. I just—I just—please just let me try and explain. He's a teenager, and I, I am telling you, I time traveled, I was a teenager, too, when I was in his room," her voice was frenzied, her breathing hysterical, "it was as if I became his exact age when I entered his room, and sat on the edge of his bed, it was like time travel. Truly—"

"No. You don't get to use this woo-woo bullshit anymore. You're twenty-seven years old," Alice said, over Margaret's cries and continued pleas that they not tell Mac what they'd seen.

The tears on her face did make her look like a teenager, and the other three felt as helpless and enraged as children looking at her, bickering about whether or not to tattle.

"Slow down, calm down," Ji Sun said, and, to Alice, "I'm worried she's going to hyperventilate."

"If you're not even going to listen to me—"

"We *are* listening to you, what—"

There was a knock on the door, and Mac entered before they answered.

"Margaret, my God, what's happened? What's going on?" He cast a look of accusation at each one of them, save Margaret, in turn.

"You should sit down," Alice said.

"Alice, no!" Margaret yelped, tears streaming.

Alice didn't look at Margaret, but something passed over her face. "Actually, we're fine, we're handling this," Alice said to Mac. "We're just, we're having an intense talk. It's heated. But we're fine."

Margaret nodded, rubbed her nose on her bare arm.

"Oh, sweetness, what is it? Margaret, what happened?" Mac took Margaret in his arms.

Alice had decided for them, then, that they would not say. Lainey and Ji Sun looked at one another, each one testing whether the other agreed to this.

But Margaret burst out with it before they could decide.

"Mac, he kissed me! It just happened, he was just, I probably led him on, I'm so sorry." She let herself fall onto the bed, and Mac sat with her.

"What? Kissed who? What are you talking about?"

"Laurent. Your teenaged cousin," Alice said, and to his credit, she thought Mac's face displayed a proper horror then, though it passed quickly, as his wife shook and wept on his shoulder.

"What? Laurent? Oh, no. Oh, God, no! He kissed you?"

"It was an accident. It didn't mean anything, he didn't mean it, I mean." Margaret wiped her eyes and looked at Mac. "Of course it didn't mean anything, it just, it just happened!" She wailed again, and by now they heard rustling from other rooms, Colette stirring, maybe, or Adam and Kushi wondering where everyone had gone.

"Jesus," Mac said. "What a mess. Where is he? Laurent? Should I talk to him? That is kind of messed up. He shouldn't be kissing you!"

Alice opened her mouth to speak, raised one pointed finger toward Margaret. But she didn't say a thing. She turned on her heels and left the room, and Lainey and Ji Sun followed. They left Margaret to Mac and they crept back to their bedrooms. Unsure of what to say to one another, they said nothing.

CHAPTER 31

Laurent's parents would never engage in anything as tasteless as a police report, but still, Margaret and Mac were cast out of the house after breakfast, and the others went to their respective rooms and packed as well.

Lainey folded the eyelet negligee she'd purchased for this trip, her stupid Connecticut sex costume, and scowled at Adam.

"Can you even believe this? Margaret! What the *fuck*. Jesus." She'd woken with a brick of a hangover, new to her in the second half of her twenties, and only when she mixed too much wine with pot. Part of her wondered whether she'd hallucinated what had happened. She wanted to talk to Ji Sun and Alice about what they had seen, but she wanted also to believe that she had dreamed it.

"And on top of this we have to leave now, too?"

Adam touched the hem of the nightie as she tucked it away in her bag.

"Well, it's not as though we have to leave this minute." He raised his eyebrows.

"Are you kidding me? You cannot be serious right now."

"I just meant that we have a bit. Alice needs to change her flight." He pulled his duffel bag out of the closet. He looked at ease in this, their own wing, even sullied by association, as he did anywhere, hair in its foppish swoop, his lean, athletic body making even his T.J. Maxx chinos look tailored. She looked at his ass, how adult it looked, how much of a man he was, and felt a pang of remorse for Margaret, that something was so curdled inside her that she could look at a child and feel it was okay to reach for him, kiss him.

She thought, too, of Laurent's older sister, Colette, svelte and seventeen, *coltish*, she'd thought right away when she learned her name, saw her legs, and everyone on the property thought of sex when then they looked at her in her tennis whites, Lainey knew.

"It's so fucked up. So fucked up!"

"Laurent will be okay. They're French! They don't even register this in the way of their Connecticut cousins."

French mouths were different, Lainey would allow. Mouths were how you knew someone was French, she had learned that on the train in Paris the summer after her sophomore year—the shapes their lips made. Even out of earshot it was clear who spoke French, though Lainey couldn't tell, when she saw other foreigners, what languages they spoke, not even English. There was just something to a French mouth, she reasoned, and wrote so in a postcard that she never sent home. She'd thought she would spend the whole summer drunk and kissing artists along the Seine, but instead she smoked and read feminist theory, fumbled through a tormented, jealous relationship with an older British woman with whom she still exchanged recipes over email.

"How can you say that?" She looked at Adam. "How do you know how this will affect him, down the road?"

"I don't know. I mean, I think what happened was deeply messed up, but I don't know that it's going to do lasting damage to Laurent. I mean, I hope it won't."

"What, so teen boys can't be . . ." Lainey looked for the word she wanted. "Assaulted?"

"Assaulted? She said *he* kissed *her*, and she just didn't pull away fast enough!"

Lainey crossed her arms over her chest.

"What, you don't believe her?" Adam asked.

"I don't know. It just, it didn't look quite like that," she said, and tried to call up the scene in her head. Where had their hands been? Why had they looked so enmeshed, for a kiss that wasn't meant to happen at all? What was she forgetting, what was she inventing already? What exactly had she seen?

"Something about it just didn't seem like that." She shook involuntarily, a full body *blech*.

This was Margaret, then, always doing whatever she felt moved to do, and always, by her beauty, getting away with it. Lainey felt no desire to kiss Laurent, but she wondered, if she kissed Colette, would she be forgiven so easily? Lainey knew herself to be pretty, fit, desirable, sexy, Adam told her, *so fucking sexy*, sometimes said with a growl and a look that suggested he was getting away with something, a look that aroused her more than the words. But her looks didn't put her in this category where she would be given soft landing wherever she crashed; she didn't have the sort of face that, even crinkled into guilty sobs, everyone in the house had been conditioned since birth to want to rescue. Would Lainey never get used to this? Now, no longer living with Margaret, seeing her face stunned and stung Lainey anew each time. *Oh, yes, she really is this remarkable to look at; I'd hoped I misremembered somehow.*

Had she imagined then, that Laurent's father looked jealous when he'd learned what Margaret had done? Lainey, hurrying back to her own room after filching a Diet Coke from the kitchen, heard Clémence explain in French what happened, the hard edge of indignation weaponizing even the amorous word *bisou*. Lainey stopped and watched as Bart lifted his espresso cup, and first said Margaret's name, alone, in that dreamy indolent way that better suited her, *Mahgahreeht*, so unlike the way Lainey and her friends did, *Margruht*, the name a toad might say if it could speak.

Lainey watched Bart place his cup down on its saucer, thought she could see him working up an appropriate outrage. But that moment, cup aloft, eyebrows raised, seemed to last forever, his expression of surprise, yes, but also curiosity, jealousy, *pride*. All these things he thought were private, Lainey could see them on his face, feel them radiating off him in that way she'd always been able to read people. It drew them to her, she knew, as people wanted more than anything to be seen, have themselves mirrored back. It was part of what was such a relief about being with Adam, the way he didn't demand this of her, but let her be herself in all her messiness and transition, loved her whatever her mood or hair color, whatever she decided she desired that day: to have, to be.

She looked at Adam now, his duffel bag already zipped on the end of the bed, and she decided she would fuck him one more time before they left this warren after all. It had felt perverse, when Adam first suggested it, but now it seemed like the only way to clean the bad taste from her mouth, shake loose the cloud of what had happened. To not have sex was to sit in the disgust and confusion she felt, controlled by Margaret, forced into feeling whatever shame it was Margaret lacked. Lainey peeled off her top and her pants and kissed Adam, guided him to his knees and did give more thought than usual to the stubble on his face, his man-size hands on her thighs, before his work between her legs made her forget to think of anything.

CHAPTER 32

A lice wasn't thinking of Margaret as she boarded the plane to fly to her conference, but instead, of her own ovaries, organs to which she'd become attuned to a degree she would have previously considered psychotic. She was sure she could feel the right one open, bloom like a flower and send one perfect egg aloft. She knew there was something close to a three-day window in which she could conceive; she was trained as a biologist, for chrissakes, had nearly chosen ob-gyn as her specialty a year earlier, before deciding on family medicine. But trying to conceive, or *TTC*, as the message boards put it, had shaken loose all sorts of magical and demented thinking, and she found herself looking around the plane for someone who looked remotely like Kushi to invite into the tiny bathroom and knock her up, anything not to miss this vanishingly small window of fertility that she knew would close as quickly as it had opened.

An older white man, fat and frail, approached her aisle. She ruled him out as a candidate to impregnate her, laughed to herself, but because she was so serious, not because she was kidding. She might laugh later at how crazed she had become, but it was hard to imagine that now, and she was shocked by how profoundly hormones had already colonized her body and mind, even as she only tried—and failed—to conceive. The man's crotch was at Alice's eye level as he shoved his bags overhead, and she wondered whether there was still sperm enough inside her to fertilize the egg she could feel floating down now. She'd planned to insert a menstrual cup after morning sex, but after the shit show with Margaret, they hadn't had sex at all.

The night before, after returning to her room, she'd navigated to Margaret's Facebook page, looked through her posts as though there might be some answers there to what happened in that room, to what was wrong with her friend. She scrolled through an album of wedding photos and stopped, stunned to see one of Margaret and Laurent, Margaret bent low to get her face right next to Laurent's, both of them making peace signs and goofy grins. In the photograph, Laurent is maybe eight or nine, wearing a navy tuxedo with a bow tie, missing one of his canine teeth. She'd been so upset by the photograph that she decided to wake Kushi, tell him what had happened.

Alice was relieved he was appalled and concerned, not even a little dismissive. She squeezed him so hard that he asked whether she was okay. She couldn't explain why she'd worried that he would think she was making too big of a deal of it. Maybe she wanted to be making too big a deal of it, wanted to be told there was nothing to worry about.

"Yikes, what is wrong with her?" Kushi shook his head.

"She didn't, but, well, she didn't mean to hurt him."

"Yeah, but she can't be kissing thirteen-year-olds, what the fuck."

"No, I know. Of course not! It's just, it's like your family—you can say whatever you like about them, but when someone else does, even if it's true, you get defensive, you know?"

"Right, but that's the case when it's like your uncle is maybe a little bit racist. Not when someone kisses a *kid*."

He was a kid, Kushi was right. He was a child.

They called themselves children, sometimes, still, when they meant they wanted someone to do their laundry and figure out how to organize the piles of paperwork that came addressed to them now, more every year after college. Enough of their classmates had moved back in with their parents after graduating that Op-Eds regularly lamented the endless postadolescence of their genera-tion. But they weren't children, even if they lived off their parents

or their partners' parents, even if they felt like children now, waiting for someone to tell them how to deal with what Margaret had
done. The same way a new baby makes a toddler a giant, Margaret
kissing Laurent showed what an adult Margaret was, even if she
didn't behave as one.

They hadn't even taken off and already Alice felt she might
vomit, but had the irrational idea that doing so would put a potential pregnancy at risk, as though she had to keep all fluids in her
body, even the noxious ones. If she could have physically removed
the memory of what she'd seen, she would have. In a split second,
no question. To not have to recast what she knew about Margaret,
the whole story she told about her friend. Maybe leaving the room
when she had was a version of this anyway, letting Margaret tell
Mac what she liked, letting the shape the story took come from a
person who—whatever the rest of them had seen in their shock
and haze—they could all agree should not be the one to tell it.

"That's me," a lean, tan man said. "You're me." He waggled his
boarding pass in her face.

"Oh, sure. I'm sorry. I was standby—I thought this was me."
Alice felt woozy as she stood.

"Nope. It's all me, honey," he said.

Alice had the urge to sock him in the face, but didn't even say
"Don't honey me." She felt too tender and weirdly frightened to
make her usual stink, to sass and swear, to put this self-important
businessman in his place. She had been rearranged by what she'd
seen the night before, and she resented the creeping worry, didn't
want to give in to the bad feelings swirling in her, convinced as she
was that a positive attitude was also essential for egg fertilization.

Before they began TTC, Alice said having a child was something she wanted to do with Kushi rather than just do for its own
sake, and she could remember saying so, moony and pleased with
herself, cupping her cappuccino with two hands, sunlight on what

felt then like fat, fertile cheeks, telling her friends this, borrowing it from Margaret, really, who'd sat with Alice in the same corner booth and talked about how having children was a "life project" she wanted to share with Mac. Alice had done her same dance of dismissing the notion as goofy before realizing how right and romantic it was, count on Margaret to say aloud things that might embarrass the rest of them, the things they all needed someone else to articulate about their own hearts' truest desires. Of course that was the way one should enter into the work of bringing a baby into the world! Even from a medical standpoint this idea of a life project reflected the sort of environment in which a baby would thrive, cared for by parents who loved one another and yearned for the work of raising a child.

But each month that she got her period rather than the two blue lines, she moved further away from this notion, from anything fuzzy and sentimental, felt the hunger of an animal, reproductive organs voracious, activating areas of her brain that had never lit up before, such as the part that thought it was a wise idea to fuck anyone on this plane who bore a passing resemblance to her husband.

The window in which it would be less of an impediment to her career to have a baby was quickly closing, had already closed, really, once you factored in that any baby not conceived on this flight would be born months into her potential fellowship year, might derail her chances of getting a fellowship, would certainly derail her advancement. If she wasn't pregnant by October, they would get an official diagnosis of "unexplained infertility," and even though she knew this was only for insurance purposes, and so they could try IUI, or explore IVF, it was demoralizing to stare down the official label, the failure implicit in that "unexplained." Wasn't anything "unexplained" her fault? Kushi was so careful to say each month that they couldn't blame themselves, nor each other. And she believed that he wasn't blaming her, not consciously. But she was the vessel. It was her womb that came up short each month; it felt like her mystery.

The tan man beside her was barking into his phone now, though they'd already been asked to put their electronic devices away. Alice could taste his aftershave, astringent and aquatic, like the body sprays marketed to middle-schoolers. She had a sudden, throbbing headache, wondered if anyone in another middle seat would be willing to trade before takeoff. Turning her head made it worse. She closed her eyes.

Where had Margaret's hand been? On Laurent's knee? On her own hip? Behind him on the bed? Nearer to his groin or touching it? His penis? None of them had wanted to ask or wonder. They had seen them kissing, this was bad enough. If it was worse, they were worse still, because they learned in not asking that they were the sort of people to look away.

As a child, Alice had once seen a woman strike a small girl in a grocery store, and she'd tugged at her mother's arm, asked her what they should do. *It isn't ours to intervene*, her mother sniffed, and they hurried out to their car. This was something her mother said often enough that it had been a joke between Alice and her siblings—a box of cereal snatched away, *It isn't yours to intervene!* a report card swiped from the desk, *It isn't ours to intervene!* But there, in public, with the howls of the child still filling her ears, Alice had understood it in a way that would become useful to her later, how decorum and abdication were wed, how willful the former was in rejecting any acknowledgment of the ruinous mess of life, how essential this was not only to her mother's worldview, but to her family's survival. It was a year before what happened with her brother, but she remembers it now as part of the same summer somehow, when she realized no one was ever going to see her brother's cruelty the way she did, when it became clear to

Alice that she was on her own. She thought sometimes that
though the price was too high, she'd gotten out just in time,
before they'd worn her down, before she relented, accepted her
family's philosophy that to look away was the only way. But here
she was now, looking away with the rest of them from what
Margaret did. It was more complicated than she'd believed as a
girl. Or maybe it wasn't. How could she tell which parts of becoming an adult served some greater good, and which were just good
worn down, convenience?

In the car that morning, before they'd dropped Alice at the train
station, they were silent for so long. Adam finally had said, "I hope
she gets the help she needs," and they had all agreed with vigorous
nods and yes, yesses, but no one offered anything specific, or had
any idea what this really meant.

"Do you think," Ji Sun said from the front seat, nearly a whisper. "Do you think we . . . stopped something?" She wore sunglasses,
but Alice could feel that she was on the verge of tears. "If we hadn't
gone by the door, I mean. Do you think."

"No," Lainey had said. "No!"

No one said anything but no. No, no, no. Of course not. It was a
mistake. Laurent had leaned in and kissed Margaret, and she hadn't
pulled away fast enough. One of them could always be counted on
to provide the party line, rehearsing it now as though they knew
they'd be repeating it for the rest of their lives.

The tan man beside Alice was unwrapping a piece of gum now,
his elbow poking into her ribs. His cologne was so like a teenager's
that she thought again of Laurent, tried to call up his face as she'd
seen it in person, not let it be replaced by the photograph that
blazed there, from the wedding, his missing tooth.

She dug for her bag beneath the seat just as they took off. The
movement made her feel much worse, though somehow she didn't
realize she'd thrown up until she heard her seatmates' reactions.

"Ugh, fuck! What the fuck!" The man in the window seat lurched away from her, and she vomited again. Even with her head between her knees, she could hear him smacking his gum.

"Oh, no! You okay? You okay there? Ma'am! Ma'am!" The man in the aisle called for the attendant, who came, bearing a belated air sickness bag.

She heard a voice on the PA ask whether there was a doctor on board.

"*I'm* a doctor," Alice said. It was the first time she'd been aboard a flight where this question was asked—a rite of passage. "I'm a doctor!"

"Yeah, right," the tan man muttered. "What are you, *twelve*?" He reached over her to take a towel from the attendant. "I'm going to need to move seats."

"This is a completely full flight, sir, but we will do our best to completely clean the area."

They bickered and Alice tuned them out, traded her sack of vomit for a cup of ice.

Even though it was too early for morning sickness, part of Alice thrilled at the sick on her hands, took it for confirmation that no, she was not a child, she was grown, competent, *pregnant*—on her way to becoming the most nonchild thing you could be: someone's mother.

CHAPTER 33

B ack in New York three weeks after they'd fled Connecticut, Lainey was on her way downtown to meet Isaac, a friend from college, for lunch. He'd invited her to have an "exploratory chat," as he put it, about how she might help "tell the story" of his fintech start-up, a portmanteau Lainey had to google after getting his message. He wrote that he remembered her being a "really good writer" in college, and Lainey's cheeks reddened to think how many times she'd opened her email in the week since he sent it, just to reread that line.

She clung to the compliment now, telling herself that she needed to make some money at some point, that maybe she could do some good with it, if she made enough, and that anything would be better than another year at the ticket-sales office, now as supervisor, shepherding other would-be playwrights and actors into the drudgery of days spent as middlemen, as removed from Broadway as they would be if they'd stayed in Kansas or wherever else they came from.

Isaac had suggested the location. Lainey didn't spend much time below Tribeca, and had never even heard of Zuccotti Park before that day, hadn't read about the buildup to the protest that she watched now, as hundreds of people streamed down the middle of the street, chanting: *Whose streets? Our streets! Whose streets? Our streets!*

She felt so distant from the version of herself who had chanted in the street every chance she got, but the signs and the shouts, the energy, transported her to sophomore year at Quincy-Hawthorn and she could feel herself shouting *Against our will* about the war, knowing in her bones then and now that the words were meant for other things, too. She began to chant. *Whose streets? Our streets!*

This was the reason she'd felt the small lift of hope at Isaac's email, the sensation of it being meant to be. It was meant to be, to lead her here, not to lunch with Isaac—Isaac was mere collateral to her destiny—but to this protest, coordinated over months by activists whose toil was to Lainey now a parade that stopped her from going to a lunch where she'd finally be forced to learn what a hedge fund did, and have a salad so good that she might consider writing copy that hoodwinked others into learning what hedge funds did, too, so that she could go on eating such spectacular croutons.

Instead, she followed a papier-mâché globe thrust skyward by two women with broad shoulders and buzz cuts.

"Can I join?" she shouted, knowing she already had.

"Hell yes!" said one. "Right on!" said the other.

Lainey unbuttoned her silk blouse down to the black camisole beneath it, shook her hair, dyed pitch black, loose from its low bun. She wore the same black poly-blend pants that she'd worn to every job interview since college, but they were garish now, like a sausage casing printed with the word *Sellout*. At least she'd elected to wear her leather jacket, thinking Isaac would respond to it, familiar enough with founders to know they fancied themselves iconoclasts, badasses. Her pants itched, and she considered darting across the street to Century 21 for a good pair of snug black jeans, *distressed denim*, she thought, as she felt a thunk on the back of her head.

A man dressed as Rich Uncle Pennybags had struck her inadvertently with his sign, CORPORATOCRACY IS A GLOBAL MONOPOLY. GO DIRECTLY TO JAIL.

Jesus, this protest was custom made for her, she was the angel of Occupy Wall Street, thwacked in the head just as she'd considered making yet another offering at the altar of capitalism. She might have course corrected on her own, not ducked out of a protest against income inequality to purchase overpriced even at discount (but at what cost!) *distressed denim* made by underpaid, also distressed, women somewhere in the distant, balmy, inconceivable "Global South." But now, goose egg forming on the back of her skull, she knew she was meant to be in this group, stand with these people, fight against the creep for consumption at any cost in her country and in her own heart.

She texted Isaac: Thank you so much, but I can't make today after all. I can't be part of the global corporatocracy that is bankrupting our nation and planet, even if it is via yr "innovative platform." Her phone autocorrected corporatocracy to "corporate racy" two times before she deleted the line, thinking she really didn't know enough about Isaac's start-up to take this all out on him. She wrote instead, It's just not right (for me). Drinks soon? Xx L

Three days later, Adam and Ji Sun watched Lainey on CNN. She looked filthy, righteous, glorious. Her irises may as well have had lightning bolts down the center. Signs bloomed behind her: *WE THE PEOPLE, PUT THE PLANET FIRST, WE ARE THE 1%.*

"This cannot stand. This simply cannot stand! What does it mean that one percent of the people in this country control nearly half of its wealth? At what cost to our planet this *rapacious* capitalism? To what end? We are out here asking the world to take notice, to join us. We are here on behalf of the planet, and the ninety-nine percent."

"Jesus, she sounds . . . She sounds like *Walker*," Ji Sun said, and her shoulders shuddered, an automatic response now to his name. "But, you know—good." Ji Sun hadn't thought of Walker's lectures for so long, of the way she'd felt about him before everything that happened. How he'd lit her up with questions, made her feel like she could change the world.

"Yeah," Adam said. "She's got that same kind of charisma. Where you want to listen no matter what they really say."

"You don't believe in what she's saying?"

"No, I do. Of course I do," he said. "I just mean. Look at her. She could say anything. I'd buy it."

Ji Sun watched as he turned back toward the screen, eyes shining, dazzled. Lainey, in her leather jacket, hair matted, eyeliner thickly smeared, looked like she had come from the future to warn them. And everyone was listening. Though Occupy took every opportunity to emphasize that they were a leaderless movement, for tonight Lainey was the mouthpiece, her face the star on every screen.

"So she's . . . living there now? In the encampment?" Ji Sun asked.

"Yeah, I brought her down a tent on the first day."

"Guess the prospect of finally moving in with you drove her to tent city instead." Ji Sun pointed at the screen, tents clustered, the long yellow OCCUPY WALL STREET banners wrapped around one corner of the sunken park like caution tape at a crime scene.

"Ha-ha," Adam said, but she could see he was sensitive. "I don't know, maybe we won't move in together until we're married. We're old fashioned that way." He batted his eyelashes in a way meant to be silly, but that felt nearly hostile in its beauty.

"Adam." She thought to tell him not to flirt, not to bat his eyelashes anywhere near her. She had a boyfriend, Roman, and her crush on Adam was more an old habit now than a preoccupation. But with just the two of them there, and Lainey away on her mission to save the world, Ji Sun gave in to the comfort she took in longing for him.

A text came in from Alice: Are you watching this? Go, Lainey! Tell 'em!

Margaret replied: We are the 99%!!!

Are we though? Ji Sun thought to write but didn't. Only she was probably technically part of the 1 percent, but none of them would ever find themselves living in a tent because they truly had no other options.

None had talked to or seen Margaret in person since leaving Connecticut, but they traded texts on their group chain as if nothing had happened.

Ji Sun typed: Or we're the 1% FOR the 99%

Lolololol Margaret responded.

Ji Sun tossed her phone on the couch.

"Should we have done something?" Ji Sun asked. "About what Margaret did?"

Adam lowered the volume on the television, the program now back in a studio where pundits were speculating as to how soon the protestors would be evicted from the park.

"Lainey said she's in therapy," Adam said.

"I know," Ji Sun said. "But. Well, I worry sometimes."

"About?" Adam asked.

"All of it. How troubled she must be. How Laurent feels. How he might feel when he's older."

"Is this about Alexa?" Adam asked.

Asked directly like this, Ji Sun began to cry.

"I don't think it's the same," Adam said. They sat on the huge new sectional sofa she'd ordered when she thought Lainey was about to move out, taking along her few pieces of furniture. The space was crowded now, but the couch so expansive it seemed Adam was in another room. He stood up and moved closer, put his arm around her.

"Why not?" Ji Sun asked, and accepted the handkerchief he handed her, dug out of an inner pocket of his blazer.

"A kiss is different. And he initiated it."

"I think he didn't," she said. "I don't believe it. Or I'm not sure."
Ji Sun hadn't even said this to her friends, and saying it to Adam
felt more loaded somehow, as though she were filing a formal
complaint.

His face crinkled with worry, his eyes narrowed.

"Really?" Adam asked. "Are you—do you think it's possible you
could be misreading the situation? Not that—"

"You weren't there! You didn't see what we saw."

"No, I know, you're right." His hand was still on her back. "I just
mean, the, your guilt about Alexa, is it coming in here? It is not
your fault what happened with her, Ji Sun."

"You mean that she killed herself?" Her voice came out nearly a
shout. "Why do we always talk around it, or ignore it? *What
happened with Alexa, the thing with Alexa*—we don't even have the
courage to *say* suicide."

"Okay," Adam said. "Alexa's suicide was not your fault. You are
not to blame for Alexa's suicide."

Ji Sun was sobbing now, with the relief of having unburdened
herself, and the undercurrent of fear that she might have witnessed
something again, even smaller, even misinterpreted, that would
later fester inside someone, be or contribute to the trauma that
made them want to not be alive. She couldn't let that happen. She
would talk to Margaret. She would find out the truth.

CHAPTER 34

They were all surprised by how quickly the coverage of Occupy Wall Street took on a tone of mockery. They expected it from late-night shows, but mainstream news programs could barely contain their disdain for the movement's representatives they hosted in their studios, clothespins all but pinned to their upturned noses.

Lainey said as much to one of the Comedy Central correspondents who came to the park to do a segment satirizing the protestors.

"Laugh all you want, and it's easy to do. There are as many fools among us as there are anywhere. But what we're saying has merit, and we have momentum. Occupy Wall Street is in over sixty cities around the world already. Even banks would recognize growth like that, no?" She shot a mercenary smile straight at the camera and crossed her arms over her chest.

The show hadn't used the clip, but a producer forwarded it to a friend, who included it in a segment on a morning talk show, and it proliferated, solidifying Lainey as a star in the press caucus, the go-to girl to take down anyone with a microphone and an agenda.

A week later, she came home to shower and change clothes before a scheduled appearance on *The View*.

She came in the door funk first. Ji Sun was out of town, but Adam waited for her at the small kitchen island with his laptop and takeout from her favorite Thai place. Lainey dropped her tote bag beside the door and he applauded.

"It's our anticapitalist crusader! Home from the front lines!"

She laughed, and went to him.

"Hoooooo boy," he said, and fanned his nose.

"It's that bad? It is that bad." She didn't need to sniff her pits; people had inched away from her on the train.

"I don't care," he said. "I love you. I love your stink."

They kissed and had sex before she showered, and he came to the shower with her, so they could fool around some more. She thought, as she watched dirt pool at her ankles, if he could fuck her like this, when she could barely tolerate her own stench, she should find some way to better treasure him.

When they got out of the shower, she said, "Let's get married."

He stood behind her in the mirror, and she spoke to his reflection, his damp, curled hair making him look messier than he had before he'd gotten in the shower. She wound a towel into a terry cloth turban, loosed it again, and held it at her crown like a veil. "Let's go to the courthouse tomorrow. After the interview, before I go back."

"You're going back? For how long?"

"Of course I am," she said. "As long as it takes."

"As long as it takes . . . to what? Like, what is winning with this?"

"What is this, interview prep?"

"No. It's just, I miss you. And I worry about you. It's not safe."

"So, marry me."

"We don't have wedding bands." They did have a wedding license, secured during one of their earlier, aborted planning sessions.

"So what. We'll get tattoos!" She'd wanted a reason to get one.

In college, she'd backed out at the last minute from a scheduled appointment to get *Quod Me Nutrit Destruit* tattooed between her shoulder blades, the tattoo Angelina Jolie had on her lower abdomen. She didn't want people to think she was just some crazed fan, though she did admire and relate to Jolie, her intensity, her refusal to get anything less but the absolute most she possibly could from her spectacular, careening life. A vial of her husband's blood around her neck! Lainey considered getting a version in Vietnamese instead of Latin, but she felt like a fraud using Babel Fish for the translation, and the reluctance she felt to ask anyone pointed to the greater discomfort she imagined down the line, at having to explain herself, this aspect of her identity, over and over, prove to people she didn't even want looking at her that she wasn't some drunk, tacky white girl who'd pointed to the first non-English phrase she'd seen in a book.

"God, Lainey, a courthouse wedding and tattoos? My grandmothers will both disown me."

"Okay, no tattoos, and we have a party this summer wherever your parents want."

"Wow. All right. Yes. Why not? Of course. Hell yes!" He looked so eager there, in the mirror, and she turned around to hug him, stand in the warmth of their two clean bodies, snug together, safe.

Margaret was their witness, along with Adam's friend Evan. Ji Sun was in Belgium and Alice in Boston, and even though Lainey hadn't seen Margaret since Connecticut, she had to have one of her roommates there. When she'd asked via group text, Margaret had responded right away, said she was scheduled to work but that her bosses would understand. She'd written:

What does it mean to witness

Before Lainey could reply, she wrote again:

What should I bring/wear? SO EXCITED!!!!!

When Lainey and Adam arrived at the city clerk's office, Margaret was already there, bouncing on her heels on the steps, all but aloft with the celebratory energy Lainey loved her for. A bottle of champagne nosed up from her huge handbag, open on the ground, its handles tied with a bouquet of peach and gold balloons. She held a heap of white flowers in her arms, heavy as a baby when she handed it to Lainey, along with a flower crown that she'd persuaded the shop's florist to make that morning.

Lainey wore a deep teal suit that she'd chosen for the television interview, giddy with the secret that she'd get married in it later that day. Margaret fixed the flower crown to her head and the scent was so beautiful that Lainey felt woozy, drugged.

"It's tuberose," Margaret said, removing a gold bobby pin from between her teeth. "Isn't it intoxicating? I don't know where Renee got it this time of year, but God, it's gorgeous. Look at you." Margaret stood behind her in the mirror, her hands on Lainey's shoulders.

Lainey wore bright coral-red lipstick and pearlescent powder along her cheekbones. In her stacked, studded heels, she was not as tall as her friend, but nearer. In the mirror now, she barely noticed Margaret. Her own face was so bright with happiness and anticipation, this was the flower queen form of herself, the best version, the one who believed she might change the world. She could marry Adam and still be and become whatever she liked, his ballast a launching pad for her ambitions rather than a cinder block. This was the way she was supposed to feel on her wedding day, and she vibrated with this rare meeting of what she imagined and what was, the two aligned.

Margaret showed Evan how to use her fancy camera, and the two of them took turns taking photographs while they waited for Lainey and Adam's number to be called. Lainey's favorite photograph from the day comes from this time when they were still waiting, before they were married, though she cherishes those images, too, of their triumphant smiles on the steps, of herself in Adam's arms, limbs wild, their two suits, both with ows 1-inch pins on their lapels, Adam's obscured in part by his boutonniere so that in some photos it just reads ow.

The best photo is a close-up of their faces, in profile, looking at one another, Lainey on his lap on the brink of a laugh, smile wide, eyes alight, and Adam gazing up at her with a kind of devotion that she needs to look at the photograph some days to feel like she deserves. They wait, scrunched on one seat, for the fabled "rest of their lives" to begin together, to sign a paper that says they intend to love each other as long as they can, until they die, money and bodies and minds by that time, best case, enmeshed and enervated, but before all that, and in the meantime, to kiss in a government office and feel nothing but hope that they might live up to the vows they made that day, all that promise.

CHAPTER 35

Alice had been pregnant on the plane after all. But now, she was not. She was home from work, her one day off that week, riveted to her BabyHub.com *TTC* message boards, subheading: *Loss;* subsubheading: *Miscarriage;* board description beneath: *Support without judgment only please in this space-loss at ANY stage of a pregnancy can be crushing and this community acknowledges all pain.*

All pain. They were supposed to be grateful for her miscarriage because it meant she could get pregnant, something they'd had no evidence of before this point. Alice resented the rush to celebrate this shitty silver lining, how everyone found a way to tack it on somehow, to their sorrys, even Kushi repeating it like a mantra that morning on his way to work, after both of them woke fresh with grief, wiping sleep from their eyes and remembering that Alice was not pregnant.

"Now we know, now we know we *can* get pregnant, and that's huge," he said, and made her strong coffee. "It will happen again."

She hated the *we* men used in this regard, as though they had anything to do with pregnancy. Fertilization, yes, fatherhood, of course, but pregnancy, don't touch it, how dare you. You didn't feel sick every day and then sicker, so much sicker, to not feel sick the morning before the bleeding began, your tender breasts unignited, returned in an instant to small, unfeeling sacks of fat. You didn't dream of bodies vacating your body, whole marching rows of them, fully grown, enormous, their booted heels stomping on your uterus, yes, but your face, too, your whole body, trampled by the weight of this exodus, flattened, demolished.

Her older sister, Eleanor, who had gotten pregnant the first time she tried, said to Alice on the phone, after Alice surprised herself by blurting out that she'd had a miscarriage, "Oh, I always felt sort of left out of the miscarriage club, really. Like everyone I know has had one and I'd never know what that aspect of womanhood was like. I mean, it's so common, Alice!"

Alice knew this was meant to reassure her, but she was stunned silent by how angry it made her instead.

"Are you there?" Eleanor asked.

"I'm not," Alice answered. "I have to go."

"You're so young," her attending had said when Alice mentioned the miscarriage. This was *the* miscarriage, not even *her* miscarriage, about later ones she would begin to feel both less and more possessive, as though she belonged to the miscarriages rather than them to her. "What are you, twenty-seven?"

"Twenty-six," Alice had answered. She felt she'd aged a decade in the time since she'd had the miscarriage. How even to mark it—from when she felt the first cramps, saw the bright spots of blood, knew? From the day she stayed up all night, the cramps like a cellar door swinging down in the wrong direction, *thump, thump*, off its hinges, down a hole. *Thump.* From when she passed tissue into a toilet the next day, and the day after that, one more piece, golf-ball size, grayish purple, the tissue that was the baby, she knew it, should she have taken it from the toilet bowl with her hands? Should she have buried it? Swallowed it? The doctor flushed it down the toilet, like a goldfish, like waste. The other woman in her, the one ruled by hormones, with the uterus full of named eggs, sat and hugged the bowl, keened, cried, let her tears wash down the toilet bowl, too, at least, let some piece of her crawl in after what she'd lost.

A complete spontaneous abortion. Lucky, too, that she didn't have to get a D&C, so much luck to this loss! Where was her confetti, her bouquet of balloons? Congratulations, at least you can get pregnant. Congratulations, at least it was so early. Congratulations, at least you got to experience this pain at home, away from your colleagues' hands and tools inside your uterus. CONGRATZ!!!!! Margaret's text had come first, its usual spree of exclamation points, received in the moment after Alice had hit send, so fast Alice hadn't understood how Margaret had even had enough time to type this stupid version of the word.

She'd wanted to tell her friends in person, but she couldn't wait. She needed their happiness, and maybe the other woman, the poet, the psychic, the one with a uterus cobbled together out of petals and jellyfish tentacles, had known she needed it right away because she wouldn't get it again like this, the next time it would be tempered with worry, offered with fewer exclamation points. CONGRATZ!!!!! You and Kushi are going to be the most amaaaaazing parents!!! had come next, from Margaret, then, What a lucky, lucky baby. The luckiest.

Margaret was the only one of her friends who might put a cartoon angel graphic below her username on a message board, might call an embryo a baby, give it a name. Alice wished, for the millionth time, that the weirdness after Connecticut could be cleared away, that she could shake her nagging fear that what Margaret had done was a cry for help that they'd barely acknowledged, let alone heard. She was so angry with Margaret, and with the rest of them, their diminishments, their rush to agree that if they'd sat on the edge of that bed and Laurent had leaned over to kiss them, maybe they would have been stunned, too, not gotten up quickly enough, even leaned in, accidentally, instinctually. Lainey had offered this last, over the phone, during one of the few times they'd managed to address what happened head-on.

"Instinctively? Those are some fucked-up instincts," Alice said.

"Not to *him*, to the situation. Eyes closed, forgetting. I don't know."

They worked together to try to believe what Margaret told them, but doubt remained. Alice was the only one who hadn't been drinking or smoking that night, she'd pointed out, and she felt like the way Margaret leaned, the placement of her hand—she couldn't be sure, she didn't know anything for certain! She didn't know. None of them knew. So it was easier to pretend nothing had happened than to try to determine what did. This, at least, Alice understood.

On her message board, nearly every user had a graph beneath her name, an animation depicting how far along her pregnancy was. A little strip of grass and a bounding puppy dog stationed at six weeks, a spray of wildflowers and a butterfly flapping its wings above thirty-four weeks. On the loss boards, women had additional charts, with a different set of graphics: tiny Tinker Bell angels, of smiley faces with halos, bouncing along in a strip of clouds or a long slice of rainbow, no longer announcing how pregnant they were, but how long they had been living with this loss. Most of these women had already named their babies, even at under twelve weeks, and they would include them among their list of children, distinguished by parentheticals and italics, *Gone Too Soon, Angel Since 2007, Here Forever in Our Hearts*. Again Alice felt the yank between her scientist, feminist, intellectual self, the self that knew she'd lost only a ball of cells—not yet even as cognizant as an oyster—and the self that had awakened in this process of trying to get pregnant, the self that wished for herself some concrete memorial, even as ephemeral as a graphic on a message board, where she could mark her loss. Where it would be seen, acknowledged, understood. Where it mattered. She'd had to create a profile to use the site, and it predated the pregnancy by more than a year. She'd felt too superstitious to update her page to include the expected due date, but she'd gone to the page where you could add the loss graphic a number of times, scrolled through the options, all of them stupid, reductive: winky cartoons for cataclysmic pain. She wanted one, but she wouldn't let herself have it. She was fine. She was a doctor, she was not this kind of woman. It had been like an oyster in its texture, too, the thing that she expelled. *It, the thing—* this is what she and her friends, her colleagues, her ilk, would call it, would think of it as. Until it came from their own bodies, and then it would be a baby, at least in some way, as it was for the women on her board, mourning their Aubreys, their Liams, their Samantha Jades. Who could she and Kushi mourn, never having named this baby, never having let it be more than so much cautious promise, so much terrified hope—the opposite of unbridled, so tentative that Alice worried now that her fear may have been a factor, too, that the baby had been expelled in part because it couldn't find purchase in her womb: cagey, skittish, used to keeping its own company, booting out even the would-be baby that was its truest wish.

Was it possible the accident had caused this? She shared a version of this fear with Kushi, made it slightly more logical than it was in her head, said maybe her insides were rearranged in some mysterious way that day, that this was keeping her from getting pregnant and now, from keeping a pregnancy. But her own theory was less that her reproductive organs had been compromised, and more that her whole body was altered on a cellular level that day on the tractor, as sudden as the shove itself, that when she pushed her brother her body said *no*, the line stops here: the source of this chaos is no place to try to form a new human being.

Kushi knew that Alice blamed herself for what happened to her brother, but not that she'd shoved him, not that she meant it. She would never tell him. She was trying to become the mother to his children now, and to do this, she was learning, meant to somehow reconcile the women inside her: the scientist and the one who believed that bodies could change as though struck by invisible bolts of emotional lightning, something doctors who studied trauma might validate to some extent, but not in the way that Alice meant it, not in the way she wanted it, like a cartoon graphic blazing on her body, tattooed on her skin: this many days since I tried to kill someone, this many years since I ruined his life. He lives among us still, no angel. No angel herself.

CHAPTER 36

Her roommates didn't recognize the work it took, to be joyful. They appreciated the results, but not the labor. Margaret knew they sometimes found it tedious, that she was not as bright as they were. But other times they cherished it, how they had so much to teach her. And they were smarter, she could admit, in all the ways they felt mattered most. But there were other kinds of brightness.

Margaret learned about emotional labor from Kimberly, the therapist she'd begun to see junior year of college, unbeknownst to her roommates, who believed they'd convinced her to get therapy for the first time in the wake of what occurred in Connecticut. Lainey was open about having gone since she was a girl, and she'd been the first person Margaret heard say, "I think everybody should go to therapy," though Margaret went on to hear many others say it, even said it herself, just to see how it sounded. Margaret would have agreed to anything to keep them from picking at the scab of what they thought they'd seen, what they imagined she'd done, what she *had* done: kissed Laurent. It wasn't a lie, what she'd told them, but it wasn't the whole truth. The whole truth was that they'd leaned close in the exact same moment, and she had forgotten herself, she *had* been a girl on the edge of that bed, she was still a girl some days, some moments, and her new analyst, Dr. Lowenstein, in whose office she reclined uncomfortably now, was helping her to understand why.

"Sometimes profound trauma creates a kind of emotional stalling point, and a person is stuck in some ways at the age they were when the trauma occurred. This is not uncommon in survivors of childhood sexual abuse . . ."

Margaret's nausea kept her from making any sudden moves, but she felt the urge to bolt upright. It was recognition of herself in his words, but also a feeling like she'd discovered the breakthrough clue on one of Lainey's crime procedurals, and she wished in a way that she could rush into the courtroom, wave it around for her friends: *See, it is possible to time travel. It is possible to get trapped in time!*

But her friends didn't know. There was a moment, after they walked in on her, when she'd thought to blurt it out, her molestation card, never played, this is why I'm broken, but what stopped her, even more than simply not wanting them to know, was her absolute certainty that what had happened between herself and Laurent had nothing to do with what happened to her as a girl. This was true. Even if she allowed that what she had done in Connecticut was wrong, she could not accept that she had hurt Laurent. It had been a kind of love—not even sexual love, but understanding, acceptance, communion—that passed between them; it had been a meeting between two people who felt unseen, seen wrongly, not seen for who they were inside; it had been an offering between them, an assurance. A kiss.

Dr. Lowenstein didn't know what happened in Connecticut, and her friends didn't know what had happened to her as a child. She was split, divided. She rested a hand on her belly.

The people who knew: her mother; her older sister; the anonymous admissions essay readers, maybe, though she'd been oblique, referred to her hopes of fleeing an "abusive environment"; and Gavin, whom she'd told at the ice cream shop the first summer home from college, when the thought of going back to her mother's house after work one night felt like a hand around her neck.

"You could go to the police, still," Gavin had said. "Or you could let me have a run at him."

"Don't do that. No," Margaret said. "Don't make me sorry I told you. I don't want to talk about it. Ever again."

The shop, emptied of customers, felt cavernous, and their voices echoed. She had thought she would have felt unburdened, finally having told someone she knew would believe her: a friend. But she was inflamed with guilt, on fire with shame. It was as though in telling Gavin she became again a girl who asked for it, deserved it, didn't know any better, didn't know how to stop it, didn't know she was not to blame—hadn't even known, for too long, it was wrong. Her face had overheated but the room felt freezing, and she'd shivered. Gavin gave her his Missouri State sweatshirt, Boomer the Bear a shield across her chest, and she'd gone home with him that night, moved in with him the following week.

"You're a grown woman," he'd said. "You don't have to live with your mama anymore."

"But I make like nothing at the shop," Margaret had said, her voice tinged with the same whines children made in line for ice cream when their parents limited their mix-ins.

"Girl, I know exactly what you make, and it's fine. You can pay me when you get it. And you will. I know you're good for it."

She knew he meant that she was trustworthy, but she heard it in her head as him telling her that she was good, and this, even more than a place to sleep, was what she needed.

The last two on her list: Kimberly, and now Dr. Lowenstein. Kimberly had both interrogated and lauded Margaret's ability to compartmentalize, taught Margaret the word.

"Compartmentalization can be a survival mechanism for survivors of childhood sexual abuse," Kimberly had said. Margaret was allowed twenty-six visits per year to Kimberly's small office, tucked in the basement of the student health center, and it had taken twelve before she'd gotten the courage to tell Kimberly the real reason she'd come.

"I don't want to be that. 'A survivor of childhood sexual abuse.'"

"I understand. But you are."

"But I'm not, I don't want to be, you know, *known* as that. I don't want anyone to know. I wish *you* didn't even know."

Margaret liked that Kimberly was midwestern, with a bit of that familiar nasal flatness to her vowels, as well as a warmth that Margaret associated with home. Everyone at Quincy-Hawthorn was so busy all the time, never even smiled at one another on the street. Margaret liked the way that Kimberly was a little disorganized, how she never seemed to be in a hurry, even when she told Margaret that their time was drawing to a close. Margaret believed the invitation to pick up the conversation again next week was eager, and genuine, imagined that Kimberly often thought of Margaret and her problems at home, that she truly cared.

She could not say the same for Dr. Lowenstein, who she wasn't entirely sure thought of her, or her problems, even during the time she was in his office. The idea that she might have stalled at a certain age was the first thing he'd said in the six weeks since she'd started that felt specific to her, not just an all-purpose prompt drawn from one of the big books of dreams and unhappy child-hoods on his many shelves.

"Perhaps we can speak a bit more about that time, Margaret. I've noticed you have been very reluctant to talk in any detail about the abuse."

Margaret didn't like the way her name sounded in his mouth, like she was a child. It wasn't an order, but it was the kind of request a mother made when she was making a big show of her patience. Didn't he understand that to describe it was to go back to that room, her uncle at the foot of her bed, removing his belt and folding his clothes so slowly that she would not have believed it possible that he was doing something he should not have been, that the risk, if caught, was to him, and not to her, as he warned her. That her mother would send her away.

Margaret told her mother when she was fourteen, by which time being sent away had begun to seem more like prize than punishment. She stayed in Missouri, in her mother's house, for four more years. But there was a way in which her mother did send her away.

When Margaret told her, her mother said, "Same thing happened to me, when I was your age." This was the only time she acknowledged the truth of what her brother had done. "It happens to all girls," she said, and ever after she denied that anything had happened at all.

Margaret had asked her best friend at the time, Susie Sherman, if anyone in her family had ever touched her, *touched* her touched her, she said, when Susie first looked confused, and the second *touched* prompted a look of such horror and disgust that Margaret feared again that she might be in trouble, that she had done something beyond saving.

After Margaret's mother told her that what had happened to Margaret had also happened to her, she sent her daughter up to her room. Where did Margaret go then? Upstairs, yes, but also somewhere else. She arrived in another country, one in which she knew her mother also made her home. But across some impassable terrain—a desert or a glacier, an ocean or a universe, something so vast that neither could even make the other out, and it was no comfort to know that her mother was there, since she couldn't see or wouldn't acknowledge that Margaret lived there now, too.

She didn't want to give anyone pictures of that time. She didn't want to see herself in that room, and she didn't want anyone else imagining her there either, not even a doctor. She could believe that they cared, but she couldn't shake the feeling that they were also eager, not to be *entertained*, not so coarse as that, but to be taken out of their lives by this horror from hers. From that first quick pivot that Susie Sherman made, disgust to concern to curiosity, to needing to *know*. The salacious details. Margaret told her nothing happened, but still, the way her friend looked at her changed. They started high school and drifted in different directions, Susie to the ordinary country of high school in a small town, and Margaret to her other country, watching herself in high school as though through a dirty car window.

Salacious was another word Margaret learned from Kimberly. Her roommates had had no trouble believing the weekly meeting was another with Margaret's writing tutor, and sometimes it felt as though it wasn't a lie, she learned so much from Kimberly, took to writing in her own small notebook as Kimberly wrote in hers.

Speak in detail, *salacious* details. She told Dr. Lowenstein no.

"I don't like to talk about it," she said, and then, feeling guilty, "I'm not ready."

"That's fine," Dr. Lowenstein said, and she sensed his body shift. She'd thought it strange when she started that they didn't face one another, that their positions were more like those assumed in her ob-gyn's office, though even there she made more eye contact. But now she turned, to see where he was looking, to make sure he had understood what she said.

"We should of course wait until you are comfortable. There is no rush," he said. His shelves were all books, no knickknacks, but on his desk he had a ship in a bottle and three Ukrainian Easter eggs, deep, saturated hues and intricate designs. When she'd asked about them at her first appointment, he'd said his daughter, an artist, had made them, showed Margaret the hole where she had blown out the egg. He had looked so proud that Margaret felt in that moment both a desperation to trust him and a disdain for his daughter, her luck. "But it is something I believe quite strongly that we will need to explore, to tell your story."

Her story. Why? Why did her story have to start before she made her escape? She had fled that place that threatened to pull her under, left that family behind and forged a new one with the friends she met in a brick palace on a low hill.

Kimberly told her that when a person breaks your trust so profoundly and so early, it can be difficult to trust others, to give over to the abandon that love requires. But Margaret had come to Quincy-Hawthorn desperate to fall in love, and she had done so right away, with Alice, Ji Sun, and Lainey. Then Mac. And they loved her, too. The thought that this love might be threatened by what she'd done in Connecticut, or what they thought she'd done, terrified her.

It wasn't, as Ji Sun had ventured, with a frightened look that made Margaret dizzy, an *urge*. Margaret considered it a precious mistake, an accident almost, and one that she maintained hadn't truly involved *her*, not present-day her. She had, in that moment, time traveled, soul traveled, perched on the edge of Laurent's bed a girl his exact same age, but in a parallel universe, where at that age she had not yet been kissed, let alone touched, *touched* touched, or made to touch.

She knew how wacky it sounded, and it probably wasn't helped by how her friends already thought she was woo-woo for believing that certain fragrances were healing, or that flowers had frequencies, even feelings. But it was a kind of openness, to believe those things, and she cherished it, knew to be openhearted in this world was not easy.

"My story," she said, and shifted on the couch. She thought to reach for the tin of sour lemon pastilles she'd put in her purse earlier in the week, so pretty that she'd already taken photographs for the entry she planned to write about morning sickness on her blog, when her news was safer to share.

"Yes. Part of our work here is to reconcile that time of your life with your life now. That's essential to the goal of seeing yourself as a whole person."

"A whole person?"

Who was whole? She was more than whole, she was making whole new people. Right here, on his couch, she worked, did more without moving than he would accomplish in his whole life.

She knew all mothers failed their daughters, but it would be different for Margaret. For one, she was having boys.

She thought of the good and the bad inside her, the work she did, every day, to look first for the light. *Keep your face to the sun and you'll never see shadows.* Before she left for college, her mother had given her a framed card with this encouragement, bright flower child font superimposed over a photograph of a rainbow and an orange cat that looked like Shambean, Margaret's childhood pet. Margaret had taken the card out of the frame, looked inside for what her mother wanted to tell her but had never been able to say. But there was nothing there, not even a signature.

This office was filled with shadows. So much dark wood, heavy drapes, cavernous shelves. Dust and degrees. Hollow eggs. No plants. What could stay alive in a room like this, built for more shadow collecting? Her mother had let the world tear a hole with its teeth from her daughter's body and said *It couldn't have happened* and *It happened to everybody* and, Margaret knew, believed both.

"I'm unwell, Dr. Lowenstein," Margaret told him. What he wanted to hear. She swung her legs off the couch, got her bearings and sat up. She looked down at her leopard flats, adjusted the scarf she'd tied around her neck—her Upper East Side outfit, Mac called it, though the scarves reminded Margaret more of Ji Sun than of the rich widows who lived in Dr. Lowenstein's building.

She wouldn't make it to the bathroom, but she would spare his lovely rug. She rushed to bend low beside his desk, down into his wastebasket, the closest she had been to his body since shaking his hand when they met. She vomited, then she thanked him, then she turned, and left, and never went back.

CHAPTER 37

P epper spray didn't feel at all like Lainey had imagined. It wasn't righteous, or vindicating. It only stung and burned, and it went beyond her eyes, which she had not known it would. Lainey's whole face felt tight and on fire, like her skin might peel from her skull. She knew she was crying, but it felt more like her head was leaking, something vital pouring forth from her eyes and her nostrils, her mouth. Her friend Santi took her picture, and when Lainey looked at it later, she glowed, lacquered in the flash, bright red and shellacked with her own fluids.

Lainey could feel them handcuff her, hear them shouting at her, but she couldn't make out who was doing it, just sensed dark shapes of uniforms, felt rough shoves of her body back and forth between these forms, less people and more amorphous forces, underworld weather patterns, tombstones circling, like Stonehenge come to life, closing in around her, burying her alive.

Her inability to see the cops was due to blindness and disorientation, but it was complicated by another factor: how difficult it remained for her to reconcile that police officers were antagonists as much as protectors—one had famously joined Occupy the first day, moved like Lainey by the protestor's righteousness, laid down his badge—and even as her vision returned, she found herself thinking that these couldn't be the police, they must be some covert agents. Why would they arrest her, why would they shove her body like this, when she wasn't resisting, she couldn't even see?

Santi was black, from Oakland, and had been among those arrested for protesting against the verdict in Oscar Grant's case. Lainey hadn't remembered who he was when Santi said his name, over dinner one of the first nights in the park.

"Oscar Grant. Remind me?"

"Remind you? Oscar Grant. Murdered by a goddamn Nazi BART police officer? Forced to lie facedown on the ground before he was shot in the back. That Oscar Grant. Remind you."

Lainey was still flooded with shame later that night as she hunched near a charging station with her iPhone, reading everything she could about Oscar Grant, horrified that she'd forgotten his name, that she could afford to, that her comfort and ignorance and privilege had sheltered her from having to keep a list of names like the one Santi knew by heart.

Lainey looked to redistribute her guilt, found an easy rage for Walker, how he'd taught a whole class devoted to resistance against the state and had barely acknowledged ongoing police violence against black Americans, had somehow managed to make it seem as though Howard Zinn had invented Malcolm X. Of course Walker would focus on the heroes who looked like him; the whole class had been in service of his image. She'd fumed, thinking of the fires that had burned in Oakland while he tinkered across the Bay with some code in another glass box of light. Thinking of the fires that had burned in Oakland while, across the country, she touched the glass light of her holy phone, probably on some site that had Walker's fingerprints secreted somewhere in its code. She wept at the charging station, insisted inwardly that her tears were not for Walker, nor for herself, at least not alone. She knew crying didn't change anything, but she let herself feel shame and love and pain and sorrow, tried to remind herself that this was why she was here, in this park, trying to make a change in this corrupt country. Her self-pity did not matter, but her actions might.

Santi had been arrested, too, and Adam and Ji Sun had bailed them both out. Santi went back to the church basement, and Lainey climbed into the backseat of a town car with Ji Sun and Adam. Later, she would often revisit this good-bye, the sort of moment that was loaded even as she experienced it, that didn't need the embroidery of distance or time to feel significant. The sky was orange and purple, and Santi looked as big as a building from Lainey's low seat in the car, bottled water pressed into her hands by Ji Sun, Adam's arm around her. Lainey, exhausted near delirium, believed for a moment that Santi might sprout webs from her wrists, bound up into the sky to look for the signal that told her where to go from here. Instead, Santi adjusted her backpack and seemed to sink like the sun, dusk accelerating as she moved away from the car, headed underground, back into the fight, where she lived and where Lainey had been a visitor.

The photos that Santi had been arrested for taking were all over the news the next day. Lainey had a hard time recognizing herself. She was so red she looked neon, a siren, a warning. Bright beacon of pain. A pain that she could remember feeling, could see that she must have felt, but could not call up in her nerves, could not adequately conjure or even describe now, wearing her softest, threadbare Quincy-Hawthorn sweat suit, wrapped in a white down blanket, sitting on Ji Sun's enormous new couch. Everything felt clean and comfortable, but also strangely sterile. She'd been living outside for two months, and then sleeping mostly in a church basement for another month while they planned their aborted move to reoccupy. Now she knew she wasn't going back, and it was disorienting to look at this photograph of herself, swollen and shining, crying out in pain, and know that that had been the end.

Adam brought her a plate of runny scrambled eggs and a sesame bagel, its edges nearly burned, just the way she liked, and Ji Sun made her Earl Grey tea with milk and orgeat, their favorite comfort drink since college. They sat together and watched the news coverage, talking while Lainey texted. She felt removed from every conversation, though she was central to them all: the one in the room, the one on the news, and the one online.

"They're talking about it like it's over," she said, staring at the TV screen but not seeing it.

"Well, that phase *is* over, right?" Adam said, and rubbed her back. They'd fought about how worried he was, how he believed every news report about sexual assaults and slum conditions over anything she told him about her actual experience of being there. He had been furious when she moved to the church instead of coming home after the eviction, and they'd had one of their biggest fights ever when she'd told him the plans for reoccupation. She'd met him in person, paranoid about being monitored by the police, even in the church basement.

"Lainey, you can't go back! There have to be ways to put forward this agenda that aren't connected to the park. You've said yourself that this is just the groundwork! The park is not safe!"

But she wanted to go back. The church basement felt like sleep-away camp, like a break from her life in the park rather than her life at home. She wanted to hear the birds, smell the mineral outdoor air each morning, fog and cement, before the skunk of weed and BO and damp wool comingled. She wanted to wake up creaky and exhilarated every morning, bone tired and ready to fight.

"Adam, it is safe. There are like eleven drum circles." She was irritated at herself for making fun, but she wanted to get him to laugh, put him at ease.

"I can't stand to see you like this. You are so strung out. You've lost weight, and you're looking around like the CIA is tracking you or something. It's scary."

"Oh, sorry I didn't do my face for you this morning, *husband*. I forgot that my first job as a woman is to look good."

"That isn't fair. You know that's not what I mean."

"You just want me to come home and be your little wife!" She shouted it but didn't believe it. She had so much rage at the way the movement was petering out that she wanted to scream, feel some power, fight everyone.

"I wouldn't mind *living* with my wife, or talking to her, that part is true. If you see her, tell her I'm concerned," he said, before he turned to leave without so much as a wave.

She was stunned, riveted, aroused. She loved how angry she had made him, how he'd been the one to storm away—historically her move. She wanted to race after him, jump his bones, but seemed stuck to the bench, imagining the home-from-the-war movie kiss she'd liked to have given him there on the street, her face less gaunt even in her own fantasy of their embrace.

She'd been glad to feel that desire for him, though she missed sex something fierce. Others took park partners, had grimy sex that Lainey understood as a way to stay sane. The release. But there was a certain utility to not expending energy in this way, to letting it fuel the pent-up rage that just kept building. Lainey wasn't having sex with anyone, but there was an intensity to her relationship with some of the other activists that felt just as treacherous.

Now, on Ji Sun's couch, she observed that familiar energy in the banter between Adam and Ji Sun, one of comrades, partners, not necessarily lovers, but people connected in a way that went beyond friendship. How had she never seen this before? They were talking about her, and she sat between them, but there was an invisible cord that connected their two bodies, and she could feel its vibration.

They laughed at something on the news and she watched them, a visitor now to her own life, unable to comprehend how she would return to this, to takeout containers and television, work clothes and suede couches.

Adam passed her his iPhone so she could see the list of apartments he wanted them to look at, and she clicked through slideshows of little rooms in deep Brooklyn, recoiled at how quickly her mind could return to its old concerns, how small the apartments were, how crummy compared to Ji Sun's. She was the greed she was against, she always would be. There was no way to live in the world without being both, but she still believed she could be better. Her eggs smelled sulfurous now, the burned crust of the bagel toxic. Every room she could imagine would be too small, any place where she wasn't nestled among other people who would walk out of their lives and say it wasn't right, it could not continue.

She didn't want to grow small because everyone said they'd aimed too big. *If Banks Are Too Big to Fail, Are People Too Small to Matter?* This question was painted on a huge sign in the park, had been made a headline in some British newspapers. She wouldn't shrink. She shrugged off the snug cocoon of her blanket, placed Adam's phone face down on the coffee table. She opened her laptop, began to write.

CHAPTER 38

Alice, hunched and hungry, no longer needed to type more than a single letter into her web browser. She typed *B* and Babyhub.com populated, propelled her to the latest *TTC* board she'd visited. She typed *F* and her browser went not just to Facebook, but to backslash *Marit Håkansson*, the profile page of Kushi's former girlfriend.

Marit, to whom Kushi had been briefly engaged, was from an island in Sweden where everyone was six foot something and stunning. Kushi told mordantly funny stories about his visits there, how Vikings would worry whether he'd be okay to go outside in the cold, how they asked if he knew every South Asian person they'd ever met on their travels. The one time he did run into another South Asian man, at a café, they'd actually embraced, just for the relief of it. *Now we'll never be able to convince them we don't all know one another,* Kushi said to his new friend, who laughed still harder and asked, *Should we tell them we're long-lost brothers?*

Marit had gone to the Olympic trials twice for pole vaulting, just missing a spot both times. The second loss contributed to their breakup, as Kushi said her bitterness consumed her. She fixated on the pole vaulter whose spot she considered hers to a degree that Kushi found pretty close to pathological, spending all of what little time they had together, with his resident's schedule, and her training, cataloguing her teammate's failings, not just as a pole vaulter, but as a person.

"And this was from what I could see, and what she told me," he'd said, widening his eyes. "Who can say what she was up to when I wasn't around."

Who *can* say, Alice thought, and wondered whether she needed even type *F*, or if her computer could read her mind, knew she was wondering about Marit, had a feeling. She'd followed Marit obsessively since she had announced her pregnancy two years ago, just as Kushi and Alice had begun trying in earnest to conceive. Alice had watched Marit's belly grow in the "Bump Updates!!" album that Marit curated, starting at eighteen weeks, even the imperceptible increments in those early weeks a taunt to Alice, who back then still believed she might catch up, become pregnant while Marit still was, have a baby born the same year.

"They look like twins," Kushi had said, when Alice showed him the photo set announcing their pregnancy, taken on the porch of a ski lodge. "Egh."

"They look like . . . goddesses. Like fertility gods." The whole portrait had a golden glow to it, the light off her long blond hair, the sparkle of snow in the background.

"I think they are contractually bound to ski one weekend a month," Kushi said, and closed Alice's laptop. "Can you imagine it? Skiing is the worst." Kushi had a populist's opposition to any sport that required more gear than athleticism, and when he'd visited with Marit, he'd insisted on cross-country skiing at this same resort to avoid paying for a lift ticket. Alice had marveled at his stubbornness and also sympathized a bit with Marit having to deal with it, back before Marit had gotten pregnant and, uterus full, vacated Alice's capacity to feel sympathy for her.

But Alice wondered if Kushi ever thought of what his baby with Marit would look like, imagined his face into her husband's place when Alice insisted on showing him one of the photos, as she couldn't help but do maybe once for every twenty times she wanted to.

This morning, before she could even make out the details of the photo, she knew something was up. Most of Marit's latest photos were of Livia, her toddler, and sometimes herself. But in this photograph the whole family appeared, Marit holding hands with her husband, and Livia with one chubby hand on her mother's belly, rounded so slightly it might be mistaken for poor posture, but there was the caption, "We are endlessly excited to share the news that our little family is growing—in a big way. We are 11 Weeks Pregnant with TWINS!"

Twins! Alice thought if Marit was only pregnant again, and on track to have two under two, she would be aggrieved but not obsessed. She didn't consider the logistical and sleep-related nightmares, the madness of three very small children, the toll on Marit's body, bank account, sanity, or marriage, all things that people alluded to or mentioned outright in their comments, populating in a frenzy right before Alice's eyes. Instead, she thought of Marit's womb, this overgrown and fecund place, and of her husband's sperm, absent any mysterious motility issues, how the two of them just coupled and *created*. There needed to be some verb just for this, for fucking when you felt like it and finding that your bodies had made another baby, still more babies, whoomp, an extra! A spare, Alice thought, as uncharitable as she was now toward all fetuses that weren't growing in her own uterus.

At the start of her third year of med school, before her brain saw pregnancy everywhere, Alice had been the first to notice a patient was pregnant. The patient was fifteen, had come in to Urgent Care presenting with persistent stomach pain. Her mother in the room with her, one tentative hand on her daughter's shoulder, as though she wanted to provide comfort but hadn't been granted permission.

The nurse had already drawn blood and said that the patient wanted to be seen with her mother, didn't mention a pregnancy. Alice had seen the girl in the hall earlier, wearing an oversized Patriots sweatshirt, its pocket stretched around what to Alice looked first like a smuggled football and then, undeniably, a pregnant belly. Later, in her hospital gown and striped socks, the girl rested her hand at the top of the slope, which was more angular than most bumps, but still so clearly a pregnant belly that Alice blurted out, "Have you had a pregnancy test?" before even asking about the date of her last menstrual period.

"No," the girl said.

"She can't be," her mother said.

They both dismissed it so easily, as though the question did not apply. Denial was so powerful; Alice knew. But this far along—before she left, they estimated she was thirty weeks—what did she think when she felt movement inside her body? Alice searched the girl's face for some sign that she knew, at least suspected, but she found only fear.

Alice had been startled by her attending's surprise.

"Good catch," she'd said, as though Alice had caught some rare disease. "Cryptic pregnancy. It's not as uncommon as you might think." She went back with Alice into the patient's room, confirmed the pregnancy.

The patient burst into tears. "I'm just so relieved it's not a tumor," she said, wiping her face with the back of her hands.

Her mother appeared so stricken that Alice worried she might say something about a tumor being easier. A tumor, once removed, wouldn't go on to stun you with a secret pregnancy before it was old enough to drive.

"I didn't—when did you have *sex*?" the girl's mother finally said, after a silence so long Alice worried it might swallow the room.

"I only did it once! One time!" She'd sobbed then, and her chubby cheeks, red and wet, made her look even younger, then younger still when she let her mother take her in her arms.

Alice thought of this girl now, as she tried not to memorize the comments beneath Marit's post, wondered what had happened to her, to her baby. Had the girl stayed in high school? Was she with the boy who'd gotten her pregnant? Were they all living together with the baby's grandmother in a triple-decker in Jamaica Plain? Alice imagined briefly the Lifetime movie version of this story, where she tracked this patient down, found that she'd been waiting to give Alice her baby all along. The baby would be a toddler by now, but in the movie playing in her head, the girl hands Alice a newborn, swaddled in soft muslin, gives her a sage nod as if to say, *You've been a mother all along.*

One time. Alice thought, the *first* time! To have sex *once* and become pregnant. No wonder the girl had not been able to believe. How powerful, the mind, to refuse to see what was growing there, to see anything else—a football-shaped tumor! But how weak and worthless that it didn't work the other way, that the force of will, of desperate wishing, couldn't make a baby grow where a body was barren, where there were none.

She wrote *CONGRATULATIONS!!!* under Marit's photograph, thought to add something more but couldn't find any words in her brain that weren't painful. She closed her laptop gently, hurt by it, and in a strange way afraid of it, what it might show her next, and all that it already knew.

CHAPTER 39

S even of them crowded together around a table at an Indian restaurant that Lainey loved, gaudy and greasy, forgettable food but indelible décor: a cacophony of rainbow fairy lights, strung on every inch of wall year-round, neon and novelty, blinking rainbow and bleating white, warm but frenzied, blurring together to give the small room a pulsing glow. It felt to Lainey like being in the bright guts of a cartoon, and this, plus the fact that it was BYOB, made it one of her favorite spots to get drunk.

It was the first time they'd all been together, in person, since Connecticut, and Adam had arranged the dinner to celebrate the publication of Lainey's Op-Ed in *The New York Times*, but said in his email that, hey, they might as well raise a glass to *his* greatest accomplishment, too, which had been marrying Lainey, his warrior bride, activist empress, protestor home from the front lines, her name up in lights now in the old Gray Lady. Reading his email, she'd been embarrassed by how corny he was, and also by how much she loved it. She felt this way again now, as Adam raised his glass, and said, "To Lainey! May she move us all to be better, do more."

Alice, Ji Sun, Margaret, Mac, and Kushi all clinked their glasses, cheered, held eye contact with one another in the way Margaret always insisted they do, to stave off bad luck.

Lainey's Op-Ed had been given the title "After Occupy Wall Street," but the whole piece was devoted to illustrating the ways in which Occupy *wasn't* over, in which it had only begun, how authorities could kick them out of Zuccotti Park, but couldn't boot them out of the whole world, there was too much connectivity, their roots electrified by the internet in a way that past activists hadn't been able to even imagine. The web of lights encircling her made her think of those roots now, and of the friends for whom Occupy wasn't even over in its outdoor iteration, who would attempt to reoccupy the park again in the new year, and again on the anniversary of the protests, some again even after that. Others would reallocate their activist energies in New York, fight stop-and-frisk, lead SlutWalks, move to new church basements and cook for hundreds after Hurricane Sandy. Some would join political campaigns, go to law school, form intentional-living communities. Some left the country to find themselves and some went back to the jobs they'd walked out of when it felt as though they would never return, that they were on the brink of a whole new paradigm, a notion that felt poignant in its naïveté to those who slid back into their cubicles, wondered within weeks whether their time in tents had been a dream. And some, like Lainey, would pursue this polished version of professional activism, byline gleaming in publications across the globe, often enough that it became ordinary, but never failed to thrill her, face back on the news, expert in this new kind of activism that straddled the internet and the real world, expert on this new kind of *human* that straddled those two worlds, too.

"Isn't it funny to toast to this? I mean, you *work* there." Lainey was exhilarated, but wanted to find some way to seem, to be, modest. It was vulgar to think of her involvement in this extraordinary movement as a line on her résumé, to capitalize on her anticapitalist stance! But still, she believed in what she'd written, and had the feeling, the certainty, that she, too, was at the beginning rather than the end of something.

"It's not the same, this is your byline, Laine. It's huge! Look at this freaking glorious illustration of your beautiful face!" He held up the Opinion section of the paper, which he'd been carrying around all day, and Lainey laughed and blushed so deeply that even the maroon riot of light couldn't disguise her pride.

"Oh, do that again, hold up the paper!" Margaret said. "I want to get a picture. The light in here is so luscious. Takes ten years off our faces!"

"Not to get everyone drunk before dinner, but I also wanted to toast to something else." Adam pulled another bottle of wine out of his messenger bag. "If they ever come back around with the cork-screw. We found a place!"

Their friends clapped and shouted.

"Yeah, so cheers to never seeing you Manhattanites again." Lainey laughed. "Our last supper!"

"We'll drink to that," Kushi said, though his and Alice's apart-ment in Fort Greene was near a bookshop, cute restaurants, and a reliable train, while the place Adam and Lainey had found was next to a Subway sandwich shop, and a U-Store-It. Adam was trying to get Lainey excited about commuting by bike, as he did.

Margaret lifted her phone to take more photographs, and her nails, freshly lacquered, caught the light. Lainey watched as Margaret fondled her new iPhone, an eighth guest at the table. It wore a rubber case, and there was a circle around the Apple icon, just a porthole view at the brand, no other function.

"There's a hole in your case," Lainey said. Drinking wine and champagne at once made her happy and mean, and she was feeling it faster since she'd been sober for three months, save the contact high from so much pot in the park.

"What? Where?" She followed Lainey's gaze, turned her phone over. "Oh, ha-ha."

"Seriously, what is the point of that. Does it not compromise the structural integrity of the case? Isn't the whole purpose of a case to keep the phone covered?"

Margaret turned her phone over and over in her left hand, thumbed the case lightly.

"I just got it. It's pretty."

The others laughed, but Lainey was stuck now, felt an urge to reach into the latex lip of that hole and tear it off.

"But why the *hole*. What is the point of that? Everybody knows it's an iPhone! Why do we need this additional advertisement? We know by the shape, the sounds it makes—for chrissakes, we can see the icons reflected in your *eyeballs*."

"Are you done?" Margaret asked. "Do you need me to be here for this rant?"

"It's not a rant! Does it not *bother* you? Why would you choose that case?"

The others piped up now, but Lainey ignored them, heard Mac say, "Girls, girls, no need to fight," and resisted the urge to kick him under the table.

"It's peach! It's pretty. I like it, gosh. Actually, it was a gift."

"Oh, right, for the *blog*," Lainey said, dragging blog into a long ugly worm of a word. She rolled her eyes.

"Why are you being so mean to me? Did you forget how to have a meal at a table?"

Lainey laughed, both delighted and stung. "Fuck you," she said it playfully, but no one could tell she'd tried to shift course.

"Fuck *you*! You think you're the first person ever to, like, discover that capitalism harms people. Wow. Thanks for the insight, let me get on Twitter and let some other people know."

"Whoa, whoa, what is happening?" Kushi said, arms out like a referee.

"I need some air," Lainey said, and grabbed her coat.

Adam stood, but Ji Sun stopped him. "Let me," she said.

Outside, Lainey cried a little, but she wasn't sad. She felt oddly proud of Margaret for having been mean to her, and frustrated at herself for being so petty. There were Christmas lights on the buildings, too, but they looked anemic now. Leaving the restaurant was the reverse of leaving a matinee, after adjusting to such bright light, she couldn't believe the sky could be so dark, other lights so impotent. Margaret was right that she'd forgotten how to behave, a raccoon from the forest in for dinner, used to scraps. She didn't want to fight this idea. She felt feral.

"I'm such an asshole," Lainey said, glad to see Ji Sun and not Adam, who would tell her she was wrong.

"You are," Ji Sun said, zipping up her leather jacket, the knock-off version of which Lainey wore. She moved close to Lainey, bumped her hip with her own. "Why didn't you tell me you were moving out?"

"We've been talking about it for a hundred years! I thought you'd be glad to finally be rid of me."

"No, but that you found a place. That you were really doing it." There was always some toehold for Ji Sun, not just in not having to let go of the idea of Adam—of course they wouldn't be together, even if he and Lainey split—but against this inexorable march toward coupledom, domesticity, an expression of their lives in some version of their final forms, a closing of the door on some possibility that the four would ever live together in the way that they once had. She had believed Lainey, of all of them, might lead the way in some different direction. But here Ji Sun was again, the only one at dinner who hadn't brought a *husband*.

"Yeah," said Lainey, and looked away. "I should apologize. I've had too much to drink, and, you know, somehow she brings it out in me! I don't know, she's still always so *cheerful* and it just, like, activates my nastiness."

Ji Sun nodded, and they were silent for a moment.

"I wanted to ask her, tonight. If she kissed him," Ji Sun said.

"What?"

"I'm going to ask Margaret, did she kiss Laurent. Did she *lie* to us."

"If she did, the worst part isn't really the lie, right?"

"No, I know, but I need to know. What happened. I feel like it's getting worse, imagining it. Worse than it maybe even actually was." Throughout dinner Ji Sun had watched Margaret, whom she hadn't seen since their trip, replayed the way she'd looked that night in Connecticut, frenzied in her pale nightgown, sobbing in the center of the room as though pleading for her life.

"In front of everyone, though? Even Mac?"

"No, after. We're getting drinks just us after this, yes?" *Just us* still meant the four of them, but Ji Sun wondered how much longer it would.

Back at the table, the food had arrived and spirits had lifted. Everyone laughed and ate, save Margaret, who smiled but had her head on Mac's shoulder, looked as though she'd been crying, too. Margaret and Lainey apologized in the same instant, hugged over the table, knocked a mango lassi into Mac's lap.

"Thank God for good breeding," he said, and placed his sodden napkin on the table, stood to show off his clean crotch.

"Yeah, yeah, thank your parents for that penis," Alice teased, prompting a volley of dick jokes from the others, all of them drunker than she; though neither she nor Kushi was on call, they were both lightweights now for drinking so little as they were TTC.

"It's so good to be together, like this," Alice said, and looked at Lainey, squeezed her hand. "I know it's usually Margaret who says corny stuff like this aloud, but I've missed this. Us." She laughed and reached for the bottle, went to refill her friends' glasses. In the same moment that she noticed Margaret's glass was still full, Mac cleared his throat, dinged his knife against his glass.

"We have something to toast, too," he said, and smiled at Margaret, who turned her face away, nuzzled into his shoulder.

Alice knew it. She knew it. She could feel it coming. She braced herself at her seat as though for impact.

"We're pregnant! Well, she is," he said, pointing at Margaret. "But we're having twins, so I'm gonna go ahead and take credit for one of 'em!"

The table erupted in more cheers and claps, with worried glances from all but Mac and Adam at Alice, whose face they could tell had gone white for how much red light it now reflected.

Twins, twins, more twins. Twins more. Twins. Everyone was rotten with babies. Alice had prepared, in theory, for one of her best friends to become pregnant before she did, practiced how she would give herself over to real happiness for them in that moment, feel her sorrow later, alone. But she'd thought she'd have more warning, an email first, or a text. To learn this all together in this room, throbbing and claustrophobic, this acid trip of a womb, she could not take it.

"I have to go," Alice said. "I'm so sorry. I am really, truly happy for you, Margaret," she said, "But I have to go home."

"No, I'm sorry! I wanted to tell you first, I wasn't—we weren't sure we'd share tonight." She gave Mac a disappointed look. "It's still super early."

"Yeah? How early?" No. She didn't want the answer. She imagined Margaret losing the babies, and it wasn't a fear in that moment, but a hope. She was ill at how easily this cruelty came to her, and she started to cry.

"I guess everybody's going to cry at this dinner!" She laughed. *Let me be human.* "I'm sorry, don't get up, no, I'm leaving. I've got to go."

She was out to the door, hair purple and green in the last light it caught.

"Sorry," Kushi said, and stood to leave. He rifled through his billfold for cash. "Look, congratulations for real, you guys. And you, too, Lainey." He bent low to kiss Lainey's cheek before he followed Alice, already gone.

"We shouldn't have shared tonight." Margaret spoke to Mac in a stern voice the others rarely heard. She'd held her tears for Alice, but she started to cry again now.

"I'm sorry," Mac said. "I'm happy! Excuse me for wanting to share our good news!"

I'm not sorry, Ji Sun thought to say, just to break up the apologies. But she was sorry, that they were here, drunk and dissembling at this table, Alice gone, Margaret saying she wanted to go home, too, Lainey and Adam shifting in their seats.

"But the miscarriage!" Margaret said. "I told you!"

"Oh, God, that's right, I'd forgotten," Mac said. "I didn't even think about that."

Alice's miscarriage had not been a secret, but still, to hear her talked about between Mac and Margaret like this felt strange to Ji Sun, a reminder of how their partners were these additional rivulets, information from within their friendship flowing out, away from the source.

Mac seemed to be doing such a poor job of comforting Margaret, and yet Lainey couldn't manage to get up from her chair, go to her. Why were who you wanted to be and how you acted so hard to reconcile, even in such meager ways?

"I'm sorry," Margaret said, crying still harder. "I'm really emotional right now. I can't take her being mad at me."

"No one is mad at you," Ji Sun said, and elbowed Lainey, whose face looked to Ji Sun like a mask of judgment. "That's not what this is about."

"Be mad at me!" Mac said. "I'm the one who spilled the beans." He put his hand on Margaret's belly, protective, and she looked down at his hand there, wiped her face.

"We'll throw you a shower, huh?" Lainey knew she needed to offer something, but she was disoriented. How had they gotten here? She'd only been gone for a few months, and only just discovered something about what she wanted for her future, her life, the direction in which she wanted to point her gaze and forge ahead, and she'd returned to find half her friends looking in a different direction, down, where they all looked now, to Margaret's belly, half hidden beneath the table, but clearly changed now that they knew what was happening there, how the space had been occupied, colonized, claim staked not just by one potential person, but two, and to think it could happen just like that, the dread that it could be catching.

PART IV

THE BITE

NEW PARENTS,

2014–2015

CHAPTER 40

L ainey was in some ways the last they expected to bundle her
baby to her chest like this, wear chewable silicon jewelry,
mortar and pestle baked pears. But then, wasn't this all a bit of a
costume, too, they wondered. Didn't it fit with how Lainey wore
menswear the year she got really into the newspaper, or wedge
sneakers and candy necklaces the semester she spent flopped over
couches at New Jersey warehouse raves? Or, her uniform in recent
years, feminist firebrand and professional contrarian, leather jacket
in the same silhouette as in her Occupy days, upgraded to the more
expensive version, and worn over suits that she had professionally
tailored? Even while pregnant, Lainey had criticized the women
who had gone soft and dunderheaded as new mothers, and here
she was, so soft that the others had the urge to crawl into her lap for
comfort.

When they were with her, as they were now, on a cold morning
in March, two months after Elizabeth was born, Lainey's devotion
to her daughter erased any snide assessments, and all three of
them could see that these were not mere accoutrements—that
Lainey wasn't trying on new motherhood so much as incarnating
the maternal. She had molted her previous iterations, and though
she was older now, and bone tired in the way a new nursing mother
cannot help but be, she had a brushed, raw glow about her, as
though even the dust motes in the air around her had been
sloughed away, and she could be seen clearly now. Even her hair,
which they'd seen every color, and which she'd dyed with henna
during pregnancy in an early nod to the avoidance of toxins she'd
fully embraced now, was finally the perfect color for her, deepest
auburn that framed her face, brought out her few freckles, and

nearly black at the roots, ombré waves so natural they appeared to have been painted on by trees. She had become herself, it seemed, with Elizabeth's fuzzy head peeking out of the raw silk wrap Lainey wore, just a shade lighter than her beige linen dress, so that the whole bundle of the baby appeared not just as part of her outfit, but part of her body.

Lainey, addled as she was by love, was not unaware of how her friends perceived her on this, their first time all together since Elizabeth was born. She knew they could see her devotion, her obsession, really, with Elizabeth, beyond the unhinged plastic clips of her nursing bra and the birthplace coordinates ID bracelet Adam had given her, fat, raw birthstones like screws on either side, placed in a decorative ashtray on the coffee table since she didn't want to risk the stones indenting Elizabeth's head. She'd tossed out or given away any makeup she wouldn't want Elizabeth to ingest, though she kept a bottle of Vamp on a bookshelf, small altar to the woman her friends knew, but could not see sitting before them now.

"Oh, I'm just so happy you're a mother now, too," Margaret said. "It's so special to share this time with you!"

Alice felt a snap in her jaw and unclenched, knew she'd been close to cracking her crown. She'd been wearing her TMJ mouthguard even out of the house on postimplantation days, and it infuriated her that her jaw was now one more thing she could not control. *I am stronger than this!* Crack, pop, grind. She pictured her teeth snapping in half, rocketing out of her jaw, their sharp edges implanting in her friends' fat, happy faces. She had used this mantra as a touchstone before, anytime her body was threatened since the accident. But it was no longer working. It had been a mistake to come. The others had already visited, and Alice had thought that if they came along with her, it might take some pressure off her to perform her happiness. But she could only see

Elizabeth, swaddled and bound to Lainey's chest, the tuft of her dark hair, the iridescent violet shine of her closed clamshell eyes. Elizabeth had slept the entire time they'd been sitting together so far, making catched breath little whinnies from time to time, punctums of Alice's grief.

Alice cleared her throat, more to keep her teeth from locking back together than to speak. But when her friends turned toward her, she bent to collect her purse.

"I should probably get going," she said. She wouldn't cry. She was stronger than *that* at least.

"Oh, I'm sorry, Alice! I didn't mean to be insensitive." Margaret stood, came across the coffee table to kneel before her, take Alice's hands in her own.

"I'm fine! I'm just, I am happy for you, Lainey," Alice said. "She is extraordinary." It was possible to be happy for your friend's joy and miserable for your lack at the same time, but IVF had robbed Alice of the ability to hold these two modes at once. Now she hated everyone with a new baby, Lainey included. This stage, called "embattled resentment" by her therapist, felt to Alice like the place she lived.

That should be my baby, she thought, whenever she saw a baby. *That should be my body*, she thought, whenever she saw a pregnant woman. She had the urge to leap across the coffee table and snatch Elizabeth away from Lainey's body. The bandage-colored wrap, like skin stretched to keep the baby near, appeared so greedy and ghastly in that moment that Alice thought she might throw up.

Alice had hoped that by now she would stop attributing anything bad in her life as a kind of cosmic punishment for what she had done to her brother, but as she got older, she felt this sort of thinking spring up even more often, especially as she'd grown closer to becoming a parent herself, and fallen prey to all the convoluted magical thinking that her failed attempts at procreation inspired.

There had been the bargaining, too. *Please, God, I'll give anything for my brother not to die. Let him live and I will never ask for anything ever again.* These prayers passed through her even on the tractor, became constants in the days that followed, when her brother was unconscious in the hospital. She didn't remember anyone ever using the word *coma* around her, though conversations around when he would regain consciousness were frequent, as were, after the surgery that saved his life, discussions of when he would "come out from under." Alice still remembered the way this phrase had terrified her, how she'd imagined her brother digging himself out of a grave on the farm, back by the smokehouse, where the dogs were buried, and trying to strangle her the moment he saw her, dirt on his face and in his hair. It occurred to her now that he might still come out from under, and what would happen to her if he did?

She was sure she had bargained away her firstborn child during those days when she was begging God to save her brother, but back then she'd only heard about this trade in stories, didn't understand yet what it was like to have believed your whole life that your body would do this thing that you were told women's bodies were made to do, only to find that it would not, could not, and no one could say precisely why.

Have you done everything possible to reduce your stress? well-meaning women would ask. Well-meaning women had many questions: Have you tried acupuncture? Have you tried sensory-deprivation tanks? Have you tried Reiki massage? Have you tried meditation? Transcendental Meditation, though? Medication, though? Rescue remedy, also? Klonopin, just a pinch? Valerian root tea? White pine tea? White wine with peaches, in a plastic glass with ice cubes, poolside at an all-inclusive resort on the Big Island, before sex with your husband, after which you insert a menstrual cup into your cervix, a pillow under your bum, and two yoga blocks beneath your haunches to keep your legs in the air for a full three hours, longer if you can, leave your legs there all night and go out dancing, try to relax and let yourself let go. *The body knows.*

Well-meaning women were also known to offer counsel concerning adoption, which Alice and Kushi had been considering more seriously in the last two years, but which she bristled to see trotted out so often as a means to boost fertility. Everyone's sister or cousin or coworker had struggled for so long, *years*, Alice, they *never* thought it would happen for them, these fertile fools who never seemed to be the ones who struggled themselves would say, and put their hands on Alice's arm. But then, just as these cousin's coworkers signed the adoption papers/touched down in Ethiopia/ brought the new baby home—Hark! a fertilized egg would implant and a positive pregnancy test would knock them sideways. And now their families were so full, these fools would say, and their hearts fuller still.

Did the adoption agency workers have a way of sniffing this out, Alice wondered, through the stink of infertility, the deeper stench of those couples who, in the desperation with which she was deeply intimate, went through all the motions just hoping it might get them pregnant? Could the counselors tell which ones might cut and run, be out the door the moment they got that positive pregnancy test? Alice knew she would have to move utterly beyond thinking of adoption as a consolation prize before she could move further down that path. And she'd delivered enough babies on her ob-gyn rotation to know, absolutely, that if someone handed her one of those babies now, told her it could be hers, she would love that baby with her whole heart. It was only after she and Kushi had begun attending informational sessions on the emotional complexities of adoption that she began to doubt herself, wonder at what point some biological limitation would announce itself, impede attachment. She was a scientist, after all, even if she was one who now believed in something called "sticky baby dust."

After one such workshop, eighteen months earlier, she'd asked Lainey on the phone if she'd ever felt as though her parents loved their two biological children more. Alice wanted to protect against hurting her hypothetical adopted child in this way.

Instead of answering, Lainey had asked, "Did you ever feel like your parents loved any of your siblings more than you?"

Alice felt as though Lainey had slapped her, and the phone burned against her cheek. She'd hung up.

When Lainey called to apologize, Alice felt worse, as it confirmed that Lainey had known just how cruel her question was. But Alice hadn't known that Lainey had just had a miscarriage herself, that she hadn't told Alice she was pregnant so as to protect her, but was steamed now that all their time to talk for what seemed like years had been devoted to Alice's fertility struggles, and, more recently, Alice interrogating Lainey about her own adoption.

Lainey should have told Alice this instead of lashing out at her. But the miscarriage had made her mean and desperate; it had taught her how deep her own well of longing for a child went, even though the pregnancy had been a surprise. Adam had burst into happy tears when Lainey told him she was pregnant, and she hadn't known his face could be so beautiful. The creases around his smile deepened, his dimples seemed to double, and he beamed from every pore. He was radiant. She had not even known she could make someone so happy, and what crushed her then was the knowledge that she would never be able to do so again. That the next time she told Adam she was pregnant, he would be eager, and happy, but he would also be afraid. And even if this paled against Alice's losses, it was Lainey's sadness, and she keened at what they'd lost. Lainey knew it was not always easy for Adam to be her partner, and that she could make someone so good and so steady so happy had been a greater gift than she could have anticipated. She mourned the baby that wouldn't be, but also the wives Adam might

have had, the easier women who would have been able to bring this
unabashed joy into his life more often, who, insides less twisted,
would have gotten pregnant the first time, had it stick, decorated a
nursery while they worked full time and baked homey, healthy
meals. Not sunken into another monthlong depression where she
watched full seasons of *CSI: Crime Scene Investigation* in days,
forgot, even as she watched, both everything that happened on the
program and everything that was meant to happen in her life.

A few days after their phone call, Lainey did tell Alice about her
miscarriage, by way of apology for having said what she had.

"Oh, no," Alice said. "I'm so sorry, Lainey." There was a long
pause and Lainey wished she had waited to tell Alice in person, as
silence on the phone was too easy to interpret ungenerously.

"I didn't even know you were trying!" Alice burst out.

Lainey felt accused. "We weren't, well, not really. We weren't *not*
trying."

Alice hated it when people said this, hated the luck and ignorance they exposed about themselves, that they might just fuck and
find themselves impregnated, like heartland teenagers in towns
that didn't teach about birth control.

"That's the same thing," Alice said. "That's trying."

"I just meant, you know, we aren't, like obsessing about it yet or
anything."

"Jesus, Lainey!"

"I'm sorry, Alice! But this isn't about you! I'm not talking about
your obsession, because I'm not talking about you and Kushi right
now! I'm talking about *me!*"

Another long pause during which Lainey worried that Alice
might hang up. Since Margaret had had her babies, there had been
more pressure on the dynamic between her and Alice, with
Margaret removed from regular rotation, and Ji Sun receptive, but
staunch in her resolve not to have children, making it seem unfair

to burden her with the intricacies of their cervical mucus, though Alice had. Lainey hadn't realized how much better four was for ballast.

She heard Alice take a deep breath.

"You're right," Alice said. "No, you're right. I know I take everything about trying to get pregnant incredibly personally. But I would think, well, I would think that especially now, you would understand that."

Lainey wanted to argue that it wasn't so instant, but Alice was right. Even freshly acquainted with this longing, Lainey had wanted to throw her computer out the window when she saw pregnancy announcements. One of her colleagues had posted a picture of herself and her husband, holding a little pair of tiger-print sneakers in their cupped-together hands, like even the factory-fresh footwear of their future baby required a tenderness typically reserved for just-hatched chicks or live grenades. *Expecting a baby Friedman cub in January!* the caption said, and a growl had issued forth from Lainey's throat in response.

"I do, a little bit. I do understand that. And I'm sorry for taking it out on you. It's just thrown me for a loop. I didn't know how terrible it was. Physically, I mean. I'm so sorry you've had to go through this more than once, Alice," Lainey said, and sucked breath through her teeth. Was there no way to be there for each other and not always be measuring their losses against the others, pitting pain against pain?

The pain Alice felt now was too much to endure. She couldn't be in a room with Elizabeth, couldn't be near enough to smell her, hear her, practically taste the longing she felt for her in the fault lines she was cracking into her teeth. Lainey hadn't offered to unwrap Elizabeth, pass her sleeping body across the table to her friends' arms, let them cradle her, nuzzle the downy tufts of her furry head, breathe her perfect unpolluted scent, and this was a mercy rather than a selfishness, Alice knew, though everything about this room was punishment right now, and she fled, hungry, heartsick, not having remembered to leave the small gift, fishing it out of her bag on the street, tearing the yellow tissue paper from the sack to wipe the sick from her face.

gain Alice had been pregnant, and again her body had announced it with, and rejected it like, vomit. She swung ferociously between the belief that they could not keep doing this, it was too difficult, and the insistence that this was the only thing worth doing, that they could not stop until it worked, stuck, brought them the baby that she wanted even more now, she would admit, since her friends had become mothers. It made sense that Margaret would have babies so young, though that she had become pregnant so soon after the incident with Laurent made what happened that weekend worse in a way, as though Mac had taken her home and tried to fuck her like a proper adult, knock her up. But with Lainey it had come from left field, and Alice couldn't help but take it personally, now that Elizabeth was here, Lainey's pregnancy having been easier to ignore than its successful end. It was so stupid to think *But that's my dream,* as though it was winning a Nobel Prize and not the most mundane desire on the planet.

Kushi wanted to move forward with adoption and take a break from IVF. He was resolute that this was not the same thing as giving up, but thought that pursuing both at once was simply too taxing. When he asked her, a week after the miscarriage, earlier in her pregnancy this time, but worse due to the effort that it had taken to get to that point, all the hands that had been on that one fertilized egg. Alice, even with her medical degree, was continually shocked by how completely hormones ruled her life: her mood, her energy, her skin, her appetites—everything. And looking at Kushi now, in their apartment as he got ready to leave for work, she wondered whether there was some version of couvade syndrome for trying to conceive, a sympathetic miscarriage. His skin was ashy and sallow, his stubble gray in patches that seemed to have sprung up overnight like mold. His tortoiseshell glasses, which always made him look elegant, seemed oversized now on his sunken face, and she giggled to think that he resembled Toby the Turtle from the Disney version of *Robin Hood*.

"I'm not sure what's funny about this, Alice," he said, tucking a file into his work bag. "Alice?"

She'd spun into guffaws, painful coughs of laughter that tore bits from her throat. She couldn't stop.

Kushi had always found her laugh so contagious, but he stood in silence now, looking down his nose at her, even more like the cowardly turtle in his reprove.

"Are you done?" he asked.

"No," she said. "Yes, I mean. I'm sorry." Her throat was sore. "I'm done laughing, but I'm not done with IVF. I want to stick with the schedule."

"I'm part of this, too, Alice."

"It's my body!"

"I know that! Don't you think I know that? I can't forget that. But it seems like *you* can. This is hard on your body, this is too much!" He gestured at her body, now wrapped in a grubby warm-up suit from college that had long since become too tattered for even pajamas.

She was surprised by how angry he was now, how he'd abandoned the sympathy he had in these years endlessly supplied.

"But it isn't, Kushi. We worked up this plan in consultation with Dr. Ferris and Dr. Frisch. This course of treatment is neither inadvisable nor unprecedented."

"Okay, well then it's too much for *me*. Stop talking to me like a reluctant patient. This is our life!"

Was it weakness that made him look like a turtle again? Kushi, like nearly every doctor she knew, didn't lack for confidence, but she loved that he didn't feel the need to walk into a room dick first, clear his throat, and cough up *Doctor,* though he did append the title to all of his credit cards. She'd thought this was cheesy until he explained that he wanted whoever to have to say *Doctor* before they butchered his last name, respect him before they resorted to racism.

But now it made her furious, how he sunk into his shoulders, how his glasses grew. She began to laugh again, this time in a way that she could feel was cruel, but still, could not contain.

"Jesus, Alice, are you losing the plot? Maybe we should talk about this later tonight, after you get some rest. You're not working today, I take it?" He gave her a cold once-over, and she considered what cartoon animal she might resemble, maybe Fievel, or one of the bullying orphans, in her ratty pajamas, poking at others with her same lack.

"You know my schedule," she said, stung by the way he'd looked at her. "I know I'm a mess."

He softened, seeing her sadness, and put his hand under her chin. "I'll bring home Chinese. If you're still up, we can talk then."

He was barely out the door before she pulled up her message boards, *TTC,* subheading: *IVF Success after Loss,* and then her phone, the clinic's number always on her list of recent calls, to schedule the next round of IVF.

CHAPTER 42

N early six months after Elizabeth was born, when Adam summoned them, one by one, then all at once, in the middle of a hot summer night, they feared, of course, the worst. All were friendly with Adam, but none save Ji Sun had the sort of relationship with him where they might receive texts or emails without the others or their partners copied, and even these wouldn't come in the dead of night.

It occurred to each of them, after the flash of car accident, health crisis, assault, after more outlandish or unlikely things, that she was missing: kidnapped, or run away; that Lainey might have killed herself. Even when by all accounts her life was the best it had ever been, when she had wept brightly at the table, their first brunch out together without babies, and said she wasn't crying because she was sad, but because she was so acutely aware that she had never been happier, and she knew it could not last. That suicide crossed all their minds, a barb in their brains—why did this rise to the surface as a possibility?—that she *could*. Maybe it was that Lainey had said so, after Alexa's death.

"Of course I understand it. I could never do it, but I get it."

Lainey had thought about it a hundred times, so many times, yet she would never answer *Yes* to questions about suicidal ideation in any doctor's office. She had everything ideation. Stepping in front of a train, bashing a rock into Walker's skull, traveling to outer space, growing a penis, walking into the sea—none of these were things she could ever do, but nor were they thoughts that popped in unbidden, not voices she heard. They were just things she wondered about as she walked around, a human animal. What she couldn't understand was people who *didn't* imagine everything. What did they think about if not all the ways to live and die?

But Lainey was, since Elizabeth's birth, the most content and grounded that she had ever been. Scrubbed raw and exhausted, to be sure, but also suffused with that glow that was beyond anything people talked about pregnant women having. It was some kind of otherworldly luminosity, like she was a beacon now, and Elizabeth had made her so. A North Star, a lighthouse, dull but visible from any horizon, from any planet.

Adam's text read: Something happened. Please come when you can. As soon as you can.

He didn't answer when Ji Sun called, and neither did Lainey. Ji Sun texted both of them, then Adam alone: What is going on? Is Lainey okay??

He replied right away: Lainey ok but can you get here? I need u

That *u* was obscene. Its shape imprinted behind her eyeballs, white-hot little horseshoes of regret, shame, desire. Ji Sun scooched herself out from under Howie's embrace, his snoring her sound machine. The heaviness with which he slept, the weight of his limbs, flung around her in the night, gave her the deepest sleep she'd had in her life. She wasn't sure how the ping of Adam's text had reached her there, thought it must have been that she was already aware, somewhere in her bones, that something had happened. She sat up and started to write Howie a note, then nudged him awake instead.

"Something's happened. Something with Lainey," she said.

"What? Now? What's wrong?" He lifted his head from the pillow, put his hand on her shoulder.

"I don't know, Adam didn't say. I'm going over. Go back to sleep. I'll call you when I know more."

"All right, are you sure?" He was falling back asleep, but she was grateful for his willingness to wake, for how he never flinched at

Adam's name, even knowing, as he did, that she carried a torch of sorts, as he termed it, for him. She'd been so stunned when he asked her if she'd ever "had something" with Adam that she'd admitted, yes, she once thought they might end up together. She'd asked Howie how he knew.

"I'm pretty attuned to desire," he said. "I think it's what makes me good at my job."

He was a painter, and she loved that he said he was good at it in this easy, unguarded way, the credit he gave his own emotional acuity undermining what might have otherwise felt like a more familiar male arrogance. (Had she ever heard a woman painter say so plainly she was good at her job? Even the dozens who were more attuned to desire than Howie, or any man she knew?) He was good at his job; she thought he was great at it. He painted mostly nudes, but a painting he'd done of Barack and Michelle Obama, based on a photograph of them embracing on a campaign stop in Iowa, gingham and promise and clouds, had gotten him enough acclaim that he'd taken a semester off from teaching. He didn't get jealous, and though he wasn't sleeping with anyone else, he'd told Ji Sun he wanted happiness for her, whatever that meant for their monogamy or future. Her friends found this New Agey, a red flag, but she chafed against how quickly they'd all fallen in lockstep toward creating nuclear families, even Lainey, whom she still thought might find some more radical way of living.

She texted Adam:

I'm on my way. Should I try to reach A & M?

Alice already here. Yes, please bring M if poss

Alice was already there? Ji Sun looked at the time stamp on the group text; it had arrived only ten minutes earlier. Alice couldn't have made it to their place from hers in that time if she flew. Adam must have texted her first?

How, after all these years, bonds assured, could she still feel a pang of jealousy at this jostling? Why would Adam think Lainey wanted Alice first? Would she? Would he?

It wasn't until she pulled up outside their building, and an ambulance roared past, that she thought, of course, Alice is a *doctor*. Alice is a doctor! At that, she flew up the stairs to their lobby. What had happened, why hadn't Adam said? What state was Lainey in? If she needed a doctor, why were they meeting here, at their apartment, rather than at the ER? She nodded at the doorman, who knew her well, and looked at her phone as it pinged another text alert from Margaret.

Elizabeth okay, right? Lainey wld have called if Elizabeth . . .???

Ji Sun had had the same thought, but now she wasn't sure. If anything happened to Elizabeth, Lainey would be so destroyed that Ji Sun couldn't imagine her texting, couldn't imagine her at all. But Adam wouldn't have said Lainey was okay if Elizabeth wasn't.

I'll be there ASAP Margaret texted **But pls text me to say they are okay, when you see**

Please a second, separate text.

Ji Sun understood her desperation, and in the long pause before the elevator opened, she imagined wrenching the doors apart with her hands.

Alice answered the door, looking both haunted and like the ghost that did the haunting. Ji Sun was struck by how drained of color her friend was, but more, to see that she had aged. When she looked at Alice, she still perceived the face she'd seen that first day in their dorm room: strong jaw, perfect teeth, long scar, and cheeks flushed with pink from her latest athletic exertion. Now, she saw a sliver of silver hair mixed in with the blonde, and crinkles in the corners of her friend's eyes. Had all this aging occurred tonight?

Alice pulled her in, hugged her. Ji Sun looked over her friend's shoulder for signs and sounds of Lainey, Adam, Elizabeth. But her impatience lulled for a moment as her friend's body shook against her. She pulled Alice closer, let her shudder.

When she couldn't wait any longer, she pulled away.

"What happened? What is going on?"

Alice shook her head.

"Alice, Jesus. Are you okay? What is going on!"

"Come in, come in. Everyone is okay." She said this very carefully, like she had just learned the words. "Come in and sit down." She took a deep draw of breath. "It's . . . a lot."

"Alice, I am going to lose my mind." Alice's tremors had transferred to Ji Sun's body now, and she shook her arms and shoulders, felt blood pump in her neck in the spot that it always did when she was afraid. She put her fingers in the place, large as an eyeball to her touch, feared it would burst. "Tell me what is going on."

There was a knock at the door: Margaret.

Alice looked at Ji Sun.

"Better not to have to say it twice."

She opened the door and Margaret swept in, enveloped them both in frantic hugs, asked, "What's going on? What's happening? Where is Lainey?"

She hadn't tried to speak quietly, as Ji Sun only noticed now that she herself had done, from habit, thinking everyone might be asleep.

Alice led them to the living room, where Adam sat, clutching a baby monitor in one hand and his phone in the other.

When he looked up from the monitor, Ji Sun gasped again. She went to him. She didn't run, but she took three steps to cover what usually took twelve.

There was the feeling that she shouldn't get too close, that he was fragile and could break. But she ignored it and took him in her

ELIZABETH AMES

arms, pulled him close. He shook on her shoulder and she stared at Alice and Margaret, waiting for them to say what to do, to say what happened.

"Lainey bit the baby," he said, and let his phone clatter to the table, put his hand over his own mouth.

No one said anything. Alice put her hand over her eyebrows like a visor, index finger and thumb rubbing at her temples as though she might be able to reset her brain.

"She *what*?" Margaret's voice was so shrill that Ji Sun felt it coat her tongue, scratch her teeth. "Say again?" Margaret held her hands out like she was waiting to catch a baby that had been tossed down from a high tower. She still stood in the middle of the room like a sentinel.

"Alice?" Adam inched away from Ji Sun, looked at his monitor again, wouldn't meet their gaze.

"Lainey, she, well, Adam said it. She bit Elizabeth." Alice rubbed her temples again. "She bit her cheek." Alice said this last part softly, and put her hand to her own cheek, left it there.

"What do you mean she *bit* her? What is this?" Margaret still stood in the middle of the room, gesticulations as loud as her voice.

"Sit down, Margaret!" Ji Sun didn't understand what was happening, but she needed to do something that gave her some semblance of control.

"What do you mean, though, she bit her? Like she nibbled too hard and it . . . hurt?" Ji Sun looked at Adam.

"No," Adam said, still staring at the screen.

"Why?" Ji Sun said. "Why would she do that?"

"Is she here?" Margaret asked. "Let us see her! This can't be true. I want to talk to her."

"She's here. She's in with Elizabeth," Alice said, pointing her chin toward Adam's monitor, his uninterrupted stare.

"Elizabeth only stopped crying when I let Lainey back in the room with her." He waved his free hand at them as though staving off any action or inquiry. He shut his eyes, hard, like he could force himself not to feel whatever he did. He opened them again and looked back at the monitor. "They're both sleeping," he said, and Alice nodded.

"Oh, my God, how did this happen? How could . . ." Margaret looked around the room, frantic, waiting for someone to tell her this was a bad dream.

"I don't know!" Adam snapped, too loudly. He put his hand over his mouth and leaned back against the couch cushions, less like he was tired and more like he'd been knocked unconscious.

"I'm sorry," Ji Sun said. "I don't understand what happened."

Adam sat up, looked straight at her but also through her, animated by something outside himself.

"Lainey bit Elizabeth," he said in a voice she had never before heard. "Hard. Like an animal. She bit a piece out of her cheek." He shook his face again, unpossessed, back to Adam. "Jesus, I'm going to be sick." He ran from the room.

"I think he's coming out of shock," Alice said. "I should call Kushi. I don't know, I feel like shit. I don't know what I'm doing."

They could hear the sounds of retching from the bathroom in the hall.

"Should we?" Ji Sun pointed toward the bathroom, but Alice shook her head.

"He called me earlier tonight, he didn't want to get CPS involved," Alice said.

"Right, yes, no, we wouldn't want that," Margaret said. "What's that?"

"The authorities," Alice said. "If they'd gone to the ER."

"Was it, was it the kind of thing . . . where they should have?" Margaret said, brows furrowed deep.

"Yes," Alice said, but didn't elaborate.

"It's bad?" Margaret put her hand over her mouth.

Alice nodded.

They listened to the wretched sounds Adam made, looked further down the hall to the closed door of Elizabeth's tiny nursery, tried both to imagine and not to picture what they would see when it opened.

CHAPTER 43

They stayed the night, what little was left of it. Ji Sun and Margaret slept in Lainey and Adam's bed, and Alice slept on the couch. They thought Adam probably didn't sleep.

In the morning, Margaret went to the kitchen. She passed Elizabeth's nursery gingerly, heard a small cry and almost fell down. She heard Lainey's voice, a shush and jostle, a latch and suckle. She heard her friend say, *Shhh shhh, you're okay* and she wanted to open the door, see if it was true, see Lainey, maybe say the same to her.

Margaret had liked being pregnant, appreciated the shift in the sort of attention she received, especially from women, to whom she was rendered less threatening, neutralized by her heaving belly. It wasn't that Margaret saw the babies as parasites, as others—but never she herself—joked throughout her pregnancy. Instead, she failed to see them at all for those first four months, couldn't even make out their distinct shapes; they were one baby, and one she knew could not be hers—surely, if it was, she would feel *something* for it, even a negative feeling, any feeling at all! She recited lines about love that she somehow knew by heart, from books or movies, from other mothers, from being raised a girl in a world that trained her to await this, her arrival as a mother. But none of the lines were felt by her, none were—nothing from that time was—*real*. Now she wondered at what Lainey felt, if she felt so much of what Margaret hadn't felt, so much desperate, unprecedented love, that she was driven mad by it, that she harmed rather than protected her baby. A small, mean part of Margaret felt glad, grateful to Lainey. At least Margaret had never harmed her boys, had never even considered it. She supposed her indifference was its own kind of harm, but she wouldn't dwell on that. She'd more than compensated for it since she came back to herself and recognized them as her babies, felt love in cascading waves that connected her to other mothers, made her understand some of the lines she'd only rehearsed in that first terrible stretch. But still there was the fear that in those first months outside her womb the boys sensed her rejection of them, and would go on to reject her, or all women, or the world. She couldn't yet know.

Mac knew a version of what Margaret had experienced, one called the baby blues that could be allayed by hiring a night nurse in addition to the live-in nanny they'd agreed upon when they learned they were expecting twins.

When he brought the boys to her bedside in the night to nurse, and their wails did not wake her, Mac agreed that breastfeeding twins seemed very difficult.

"Not difficult, Mac. Impossible." She knew she would quit, it was only a matter of how soon she could.

That defeat had been reinflamed by Lainey, too, the way she'd nursed Elizabeth without even a flinch of pain, without seeming to have to adjust anything, their two bodies moving to a harmony no one else could hear, but all could see. Lainey's hand cupped against Elizabeth's tuft of black hair, Elizabeth's small suckling sounds, and a cloud of oxytocin that filled the whole room, everyone moony and fawning, sated.

She could feel this comfort coming from the room now, and when she pictured what was happening on the other side, Elizabeth was unbit, and Lainey had never done the biting. Margaret touched her hand to the door, just the tips of her fingers. She did not turn the doorknob.

When the twins first latched it felt to Margaret like a plastic barrette had clamped onto her nipple, snapped, and sprayed blood. Their gums, her skin, doused with the blood milk, some kind of horror show. They'd pulled tissue through the tiny holes in the silver nipple shield that Margaret's postpartum doula had ordered from France, blood on the bright moon-metal. She'd dropped the bloodied shield in a crystal dish of distilled water, and blood blossomed and swirled like cream in coffee. Her doula had wanted to call another lactation consultant, but the skin through the shield— her own softest flesh like meat in a grinder—was the end for Margaret. I'm done, she said, and looked at the bowl, blood no longer tendrils, just rust red in a filthy dish. Everything around her was sticky with sweat and milk and blood.

"Replace these teas with the ones that stop the milk. Bring the cabbage leaves or whatever. I'm not nursing anymore."

"But we don't want to stop production. You can still pump!"

The hospital-grade pump sat on its bar cart in the corner, hissing at Margaret even when it was turned off. It became a drone, then, and Margaret feared her doula might pilot it toward her in the night while Margaret slept, let its tentacles lash out and suction onto her, do its merciless work on her ruined nipples, already raw and abraded, all to save her sons from the horror of formula.

"Trust me, love, this *will* get easier. If you can pump just to get through, while we work on the latch, keep your supply up for when the twins have learned better how to transfer—"

"No!"

The doula leaped back. Margaret hadn't realized how loud she'd shouted, but could see on the doula's face how wild she must have looked, pale and haggard, a feral raccoon, vicious in protecting the trash of its own body. She wouldn't sacrifice herself for these strangers, these creatures she was not yet convinced were her own! She wouldn't let them bite her nipples off, exsanguinate her, extinguish her!

She fired the doula and insisted she take the pump. Donate it to someone in need, Margaret had said, sick at herself for wanting to help other babies more than her own. Her night nurse helped her with cold compresses, and after finishing her course of antibiotics, Margaret agreed to take a small dose of antidepressants. She thought it might help combat the pain of mastitis, and the pain she still felt at her incision site, throughout her core. Now that she was through with nursing, there was no reason she couldn't take any pill she liked, but she'd long held the belief that antidepressants weren't for people like her, a notion that Mac and his family reinforced, though most of them had medicine cabinets full of psychotropic drugs, and those who didn't abused painkillers they'd been prescribed long after surgeries, or simply felt heavy drinking was the most appropriate course of treatment for any psychiatric ailment.

Margaret realized then that she could drink again, and she did. People gave dirty looks to a mother of two babies holding a glass of champagne, but she'd later learn they'd give dirty looks to a mother of children of any age, to a mother doing anything, so why not drink. She derailed the work of her antidepressants some, she knew, but it was worth it to feel herself in this way, frothing and effervescent, buzzed and alive like she had been so many weekends before the boys were born.

Now, entering the kitchen, she found her hand was out, ready for a coupe of champagne even here, as though they were gathered for a long, boozy brunch and not to discuss how best to manage the burden of this new reality wherein their friend had *bitten off* a piece of her daughter's cheek. She could barely think it to herself let alone say it aloud. She'd spent the night in shock, but now was deep in denial. Margaret wanted Lainey to remain volatile in a less alarming way, her wildest friend, the one who best knew how to enjoy life, even if it meant she also knew how best to find it miserable. Did these things have to go hand in hand? Did loving so much mean you knew more about hatred? Did destruction have to follow

so close on the heels of creation, nipping away, threatening even
the perfect, peach-fuzzed faces of their babies?

Ji Sun and Adam were already seated at the kitchen table, Adam
still in his outfit from the night before, monitor in hand. Alice
came out from behind the fridge with a carton of eggs.

"Adam, please, you can take a shower," Ji Sun said. "We can
watch the monitor."

"I just passed the room," Margaret said, and then she said,
"Good morning," which felt weird since she hadn't said it first, and
since no one replied in kind. "Sorry, I'm, I don't know what's the
right way to behave right now. But they're, she's nursing her, no?"

"You went in?" Alice looked concerned.

"No, no, I could tell. From the sounds," Margaret said. "But . . .
can I, can we see her?"

"She doesn't want to come out," Adam said. "She's ashamed."

Margaret realized when he answered that she'd meant Elizabeth.
She wanted to see Lainey, of course, but her fears about Elizabeth's
face grew worse the longer the baby was kept from them, as though
up in a high tower. Margaret adored babies, had always dreamed of
being a mother not in an abstract sense to a child, but to a newborn,
a baby she could hold in her arms. This had made the alienation
she felt from her own babies worse, and her love for Elizabeth
perhaps more pronounced, standing in as it did for her first enjoy-
able experience with a newborn that felt related to her. Elizabeth
delighted in Margaret, too, preferring her over Lainey's other
friends, even if Lainey's own rankings might have shaken out
another way. Margaret felt grateful to Elizabeth for loving her so
easily, and for bringing her closer to Lainey. Margaret and Lainey
hadn't spent much time together in recent years, what with how
involved Lainey became in her career just as Margaret fell pregnant, and then the inevitable distance and divide wrought by new
babies. But Lainey wasn't comfortable leaving Elizabeth with

anyone other than friends or family, even when she was home, so Margaret had, in recent months, begun to come over a few times a week. She left Anderson and Luc with their nanny and sat with Elizabeth so that Lainey could take a shower, do some emails. Margaret loved these spells with Elizabeth enough that she had started to say to Mac that she wanted another baby.

"Ashamed, of course. And, I don't know, distraught. She's distraught. She's not out of it, though. She's completely lucid." Adam looked to Alice for confirmation, and Alice nodded, but Margaret thought neither of them looked to be in any shape to confirm whether a third party was with it.

"But we were talking, before you got up, about next steps." Alice cracked eggs in a ceramic bowl.

Margaret watched the whites drip from the shells, the bright yolks plop. She knew Alice was used to sleeplessness, familiar with emergency. But something about her movements was robotic, like if she stopped she might power down completely. Margaret had the urge to tell Alice to sit down, let her cook the eggs, but she couldn't will it.

Margaret understood Lainey, which was what none of them would ever grasp. In her jaws, Margaret knew that pull to bite. Once she'd come out of her postpartum depression and fallen in love with the boys, she would pretend to nibble their breadstick biceps, make a long growl to elicit their wild giggles, go again. And she'd feel, in the hollow of her mouth, the urge to bite, not down so much, not through, not into—though these were the only ways to bite, of course. But it was a rounder, fuller wish, a bite that wanted not to hurt, but to devour, consume, contain. People always talked about wanting to take a bite out of babies, strangers on the street! Margaret hadn't known how physical a craving it was, how the wish to nibble would come alive in the jaw and remain there; she could feel it still.

But to bite down. To hurt a child. Margaret could never.

She didn't think about what happened in Connecticut. But when she was forced, she remembered how clearly she had known herself to *be* a teenage girl in that moment. She could believe in time travel, alternate galaxies, astral planes, better than she could accept that she had hurt a child. The therapy with Dr. Lowenstein had been unseated quickly by her high-risk twin pregnancy, the doctor-sanctioned need to avoid any and all stressors, including the good long look at what she'd done, the look her friends insisted she need take.

She could see that they thought she was foolish. No: disgusting. On the occasions they met for coffee or drinks and talked about their days, meetings Margaret always had to initiate, she saw the disdain on their faces, the way they lifted their cups to disguise their lips, curling up. She remembered reading in their freshman psych course that the worst emotion a person could feel about another wasn't hatred, but disgust. That disgust toward a spouse was the most common predictor of divorce. Not the occasional disgust at domestic gross-outs—peed-upon toilet seats, chewed food in an open mouth—but general disgust at the sound of their voice, their posture, their very presence. She had felt degrees of this coming off her friends' skin when she saw them, and she watched it soften, change, in the months after she told them she was pregnant.

Then, the twins came and she wasn't connected enough to the world to know what they thought of her, felt they probably hated her, but it didn't matter because everyone did, she was worthless, and no one's life was any better for having her in it, least of all her babies'.

She operated on some plane outside herself to continue posting to her blog, sharing pictures of the boys, pictures she was so glad to have later, but that she could not recollect taking, nor even being in the room for, pictures of Luc and Anderson wearing the darling matching outfits that friends and family had sent, so many sets from Mac's grandmother, perfect little French things that just about killed the women at her shower who were not yet pregnant but wished to be. The nanny gently wrested their wriggling limbs into the outfits; this she did remember, as there was a time Mac found Margaret struggling to put one in a romper.

"Margaret, you've been in here for forty-five minutes," Mac said, then, seeing her, "Jesus, have you been crying this whole time?"

"I can't get his arm in!" she wailed. "I can't *hurt* him, Mac. I won't hurt him!"

"Of course you won't!" Mac said, and scooped up the baby before taking Margaret in his arms. But the look he'd given her before she buried her head against his chest was one of fear. He'd urged her to let the nanny take on more of the "day to day" while she recovered, though what else was there for a new mother, she wondered, than the day to day, the minute to minute, the tedium that seemed to stretch into infinity even on those days when she opened her eyes to find that it was already dark outside.

On one of the photographs Margaret had shared on Facebook, Lainey had written, *More, Margaret! These babies are the world's cutest, no doubt, but the mama stays in the picture!*

It occurred to her that perhaps Lainey just wanted to see her in her postpartum state, coming apart at every seam, nearer to annihilation than she'd been since she was a child. But then there were comments nested beneath Lainey's, from Alice: *Hear! hear! We want to see the hot mama alongside these precious, precious babes,* and Ji Sun, who'd returned after a years-long hiatus from Facebook just to keep up with baby pictures: *Yes. We can see your beauty in their faces, but we miss your face; we need to see it, too.*

It was this, knowing that they wanted to *see* her, that had let a crack of light into the pitch-dark room. She knew their notes were about more than the album, a photoset of Anderson and Luc at three months. Her friends had sent emails, asked to visit, all of which she'd ignored. They'd met the twins shortly after they were born, but it was easy to retreat back into their own lives after that, and easy for Margaret to beg off as too busy, too tired. But something about their little avatars moved her. There was Alice, beaming, in a years-old picture from her med school graduation; Lainey's photo was outdated, too, but had appeared recently in a big magazine postmortem on the third anniversary of Occupy Wall Street, and showed her, sign aloft, mouth open midshout, cavernous; and Ji Sun's own illustration of a black cat wearing a formal coat.

She felt their pixelated gaze on her, and even in the static images sensed a kind of admonition, but also love. She wanted to reply to their notes, but found she could not, and it was this inability to connect to her friends, rather than the failure to connect to her sons, that prompted her to finally consent to see a postpartum psychiatrist that Mac's mother had pitched to her as having "the utmost discretion."

Margaret considered saying that she thought all doctors were meant to have this quality, but knew the extra reassurance was offered, as it was so often in the case of Mac's family, because they thought her a *rube*, a word she first heard from Lainey and found quite lovely before she learned what it meant.

It infuriated Margaret how rich people thought they had the market cornered on *discretion*, a two-dollar word for ugly secrets. Hush, hush. The ugly secrets Margaret had learned to keep before she started middle school would have made her mother-in-law cower and quake.

Margaret remembered how annoyed Mac's mother had been after Margaret missed two appointments with her fancy doctor.

"This is not a man of limitless flexibility, my dear. He keeps an extraordinarily full calendar."

Margaret had felt a pleasant burble of fury at this, that she could blow off this important man and her mother-in-law couldn't do anything about it—forcing her, kicking and screaming, into a taxi-cab not exactly the picture of discretion. The desire to irritate Mac's mother had been the first blip of motivation that she'd been able to call up in months, and she clung to it. Margaret didn't want to pay another person to hold her secrets, or to imagine them and try to pry them loose. She was done with other people's insistence that to speak pain was the only way to get out from under it.

Her uncle had appeared to her, once, five months after the twin's birth. His shape loomed at the end of her bed, just as it had when she was a girl, and he carefully removed his work boots, as he had always done then, too, a gesture she came to recognize as the most fearsome kind of warning.

The twins were in their bassinets and Mac was at his office. The nanny was taking a shower. Her uncle stood in the corner and said, "Congratulations, Magic girl. You look like shit. Those are two strong and beautiful boys, though." He'd smiled, showing too many teeth, two rows of teeth, like a shark, all of them mossy near the gums from chewing tobacco. When he'd reached for the babies she screamed, and they woke, their squalls joining hers until they were a bloodcurdling chorus, until they scared her uncle off. He vanished and the nanny came running, still wet in her towel.

"A nightmare," Margaret told her. "I was having a nightmare."

But she knew it hadn't been a bad dream or a delusion. He had appeared somehow, to scare her now, to remind her that even though she'd escaped, he could find her, he knew her, what she was. What would it take to be worth something?

She stood on a ring of Saturn, poised to tumble into deep space. How was it that no one could see her there?

Hush, hush.

"But shouldn't Lainey be here for this? While we decide what, what we're going to do?" Margaret asked, looking at Alice and then Adam.

Adam took a sip of his coffee and spit it back into the cup.

"Alice was in touch with a friend, who gave her a recommendation for a place. A private, inpatient facility, upstate."

"Like an *institution*?" Margaret asked. Alice had added shallots to the pan, and the smell was ghastly, less food and more force, it filled the room, reminded Margaret of the smells in the kitchen when her mother used to give home perms.

"You'd have her committed?" Ji Sun said, voice just above a whisper.

"No, no, a treatment center. It would be voluntary. We don't want to set anything in motion, with child services or . . . I don't know. I don't know how any of this works because I never thought it would be relevant to my life," Adam said.

"Lainey is not, she's not *insane*. I mean, she's given to moods, but she's not unwell like *this*. She doesn't need to be in an asylum!" Margaret said, eyes wide, terrified by the idea that people who loved you could sit in a room, in the house where you lived, and decide to send you away.

"But look what's happened! What she's done." Alice clanged the pan on the burner. Even as the only one who had seen evidence of what her friend had done, she struggled to believe it. "Don't you think it's clear that means she's more unwell than we knew?"

"No," Margaret said. "I don't know. I think there are a lot of hormones," this word, she'd learned, the evergreen, inclusive excuse—not that it was an excuse, it was real, but so, she knew, were emotions unbolstered by a medicalized name, and so more easily dismissed, "and also emotions, that come in the postpartum period that—no offense—but I don't know that you would understand."

"Margaret, I'm a *doctor*. And also, fuck you. Try not to make me feel worse about my fucking hellscape of a womb right now, okay?" Alice looked at Ji Sun. "Care to tag in here at any point?"

"I don't know," Ji Sun said. "I really don't know."

"She bit her fucking baby! She took a bite out of Elizabeth's face!" Alice said, and dropped the whole frying pan, still full of food, into the sink. The sound of its heat sizzled and the smell bloomed, sulfurous and sodden and burned.

"But she didn't . . . *eat* the bite," Margaret said.

The room was silent.

"Right? She didn't, like, *eat* a bite!!" Panic rose in Margaret's voice, her hands at her throat. She turned gray then green and fled the room.

"Of course she didn't," Adam said.

"Why didn't you say that before Margaret lost her shit?" Ji Sun asked.

"I don't know. I wasn't there. I'm not sure. But Alice said it's, it's . . . it was two stitches."

Ji Sun looked at Alice, stunned. She hadn't even thought that her friend might have treated Elizabeth, *had* to treat her, but of course she would. What did she think? That Alice had cleaned Elizabeth's face, said it was nothing, suggested Bacitracin and kissed her cheek? Two stitches. How that must have felt. How small Elizabeth was, how much Alice loved her. And where had Lainey been? In the room? Catatonic? Wailing? Forced to wait in the hall, clawing at the walls with her hands? Ji Sun could not, did not wish to, imagine. She felt a wash of gratitude and admiration for Alice, for the work she did that was so foreign to Ji Sun, for the wherewithal to do this work even under these circumstances, when Alice was herself hurt and shaken.

Margaret came back in the room in a hurry, as though she'd been interrupted midsentence.

"But even if she did. Even if she did, and I'm sure she didn't, it wasn't, it wasn't like she meant to. She didn't mean to. She didn't mean to. I mean, she didn't mean to."

Ji Sun thought Margaret might never stop repeating this, so she answered, "No, she couldn't have meant to"—she lowered her voice to a true whisper—"*eat* a bite. We all know this. This is getting nuts."

"Getting nuts! It *is* nuts. It's a completely insane thing for a person to do. But no, of course she didn't mean to," Adam shook his head, "eat the baby. She didn't mean to bite her at all! She didn't mean it. I believe her, of course, I have to believe her. And I know, I *know* she didn't intend to hurt Elizabeth. Not consciously. And that's why I know she needs help." His voice cracked at Elizabeth's name, and he put his head in his hands again, like it might roll off if he didn't support it.

Who knew, Margaret thought, trembling, terrified. It might.

CHAPTER 44

After the aborted breakfast, Alice had to go home and nap, get to work. But before she did, they agreed together that there should always be someone else, that they could not leave Lainey, Adam, and Elizabeth alone. Ji Sun and Margaret went one after another back to their apartments to pack their weekend bags, as though headed upstate for fresh air and a girls' weekend, and not to take Lainey to a mental health facility, where she would self-commit. Margaret arranged for the nanny to stay for three nights, and Mac's mother was ready to come up if she'd be away for longer, always eager to insinuate herself. Ji Sun left Howie, already in his studio, a long note saying that Lainey had had a sudden and serious onset of postpartum depression, and that they needed to get away for a few days, regroup. She couldn't write down what had happened; she wasn't sure she would even be able to say it over the phone. She trusted Howie, but she wanted to protect Lainey, and Elizabeth, too, not tell anyone outside those who already knew what happened. She hadn't even seen Lainey yet—how could she know what to say?

When Ji Sun returned to Lainey and Adam's apartment that afternoon, Margaret was helping Adam pack a bag for Elizabeth while Lainey and Elizabeth napped in the bedroom. Ji Sun went into the kitchen with her laptop to look for a place they could all stay. She found a nearby motel with a run-down log-cabin aesthetic, buffalo check on the beds and a taxidermied moose head that announced its specials. She couldn't tell whether it was kitschy or just seedy, but it would do. She reserved three rooms, not knowing what Adam and Elizabeth would need, and not wanting to share a room with Margaret. She booked them for a week, though she doubted Lainey would consent to stay so long. Adam had talked to

Lainey about the plan while Ji Sun was back at her place. Margaret told Ji Sun that she hadn't been able to make out any of the words, but that she'd heard Lainey sobbing, and then Elizabeth wailed, too. Margaret had run to the door again, but hadn't burst in.

"We're going to see her," Margaret said. "I mean, we're all driving together."

"Who is driving?" Ji Sun asked. Ji Sun didn't drive, and hadn't thought yet of who would. "Adam is wrecked. Lainey can't, of course."

"Oh, I will. Believe it or not, I kind of miss driving, living here. I thought we'd take our car anyway. More room. I just need to move Elizabeth's car seat base."

Ji Sun regarded her friend, how she'd shaken off her horror at breakfast and sprung into action, organized and efficient. Margaret wore a neat seersucker shell, dark jeans, and leather mules the color of toffee. *Mom mode!* Margaret called it, when she'd darted to a nearby liquor store for dry ice and a Styrofoam cooler to pack some of the breast milk that Lainey had stashed in her freezer, already having collected Elizabeth's prescription for antibiotics. "Mom mode!" she said again now, as she stacked the suitcases—all save Ji Sun's, which she'd also packed—neatly in the trunk of her SUV, Tetris-ing the pieces to make room for Elizabeth's travel crib, her bouncy seat, the stroller that Lainey almost never used.

Their proximity to a new crisis gave Ji Sun the idea that she might finally ask Margaret about Laurent. Loss thinned the membrane between day-to-day decency and the darker maw we all avoided, where you looked head-on at the animals you loved and asked them to account for what they had done.

The urgency of her inquiry had faded so much after Margaret told them she was pregnant, and now, with this new horror, Ji Sun struggled to call up her indignation, to see in the friend who'd brought Gatorade back from the liquor store for Adam, insisted he drink one and give one to Lainey, the same woman who had sat on the edge of a thirteen-year-old's bed, lips and cheeks red, and wailed that she couldn't be to blame for whatever happened there, because she was a teenager, too.

Drunk after a baby shower for Margaret, Lainey had been the one to ask Ji Sun if there wasn't some small part of her that felt almost relieved at what Margaret had done in Connecticut—not that she'd hurt someone, but that she wasn't so *perfect*. Though Ji Sun understood that Lainey had long felt jealous of Margaret, the depths of it were revealed to Ji Sun in her friend's question.

"No, not that she was perfect. I don't mean that, exactly. Not that she lacked, like, the *badness*, but the complexity? I don't know, I'm awful," Lainey had said, and belched a sour champagne burp.

How fast champagne could go from golden and effervescent to acrid and sad, flat in the glass, moss on the teeth.

Ji Sun's immediate response had been a stern *No*, and it was true that she'd felt no relief at what Margaret had done. But what Lainey said stuck with her, and in the days and years that followed, she understood that she was guilty of some of that same diminishment, crueler even than to think that your friend was too kind to hurt someone was to think that she lacked the complexity. It took no brilliance to cause harm. But that she and Lainey had thought of their friend in this way was such a failing that Ji Sun hadn't been able to shake it, had the feeling that there were other questions she should ask Margaret, ones where the answers were more for Margaret than for Ji Sun.

What could she ask her now? How could she show she would listen?

Before she could figure out what to say, Margaret slammed the trunk shut.

"Will you run up and tell them that we're ready?" she asked.

Ji Sun turned to go back inside, but when she came out from behind the car, she saw them there.

Adam and Lainey were frozen in place on the sidewalk, side by side but not touching, Adam held Elizabeth in her car seat rather than a pitchfork, American Gothic gone urban, gone haunted. They were so still.

Ji Sun didn't know who to approach, or how. She couldn't move, only stared at them from the street as Margaret swept past her, took Lainey in her arms, hugged her for long enough that someone pulled up and shouted at them to move the car.

Ji Sun realized that she had been terrified to see Lainey. What could she say? How should she act? How could she show her she loved her, didn't fear her, believed her? She was flooded with relief that she even recognized Lainey, that her friend hadn't transformed. Ji Sun realized that she'd still pictured her with blood on her cheeks and chin, had been doing so since she learned what happened. And here instead was her friend, loosed from Margaret's arms now and looking like herself, but smaller, younger somehow, hair pulled back, a few freckles on her cheeks, like a child who someone else had dressed for school, dragged out onto the street. Ji Sun couldn't tell if she was confused or tired or terrified, or all these things. She didn't blink, but she was not so much expressionless as in wait somehow, like even she was not sure how to arrange her face.

Ji Sun looked back and forth between Adam and Lainey until she remembered Elizabeth. The shade on the car seat was pulled down and Ji Sun could only see the baby's tiny feet. Loosed from the muslin blanket that had been draped over her, her feet wiggled, fat as dumplings, and Ji Sun, in spite of herself, thought how badly she wanted to put one in her mouth.

CHAPTER 45

B y the time they arrived, it was nearly dark. They'd been slowed by the need to stop whenever Elizabeth whimpered, to change her diaper, or to let Lainey nurse her.

The first stop, at a gas station just north of the city, Elizabeth's crying had ceased the moment Lainey lifted her from her car seat. Neither Ji Sun nor Margaret had been able to keep themselves from swiveling around to see the baby, the damage.

There was a clean square of gauze on the baby's face, new white tape. The tape was nearly as large as the gauze, but together the bandage covered the fattest part of Elizabeth's cheek, its unbandaged counterpart looking almost obscene in its fleshiness, its immaculate chub.

"Can we have the car?" Lainey asked, the first she'd spoken to them on the ride.

Ji Sun and Margaret went into the gas station, and Adam stayed leaned against the car, still holding his monitor, though it was powered off now.

When they got back on the road, Lainey shushed Elizabeth to sleep, her hand inside the car seat, hidden from Ji Sun's view.

"She's asleep," Lainey said, and shortly after closed her own eyes, the others grateful to have a reason other than fear for their silence.

"Adam, please sleep," Ji Sun said, meeting his eyes in the mirror of her sun visor. "They're both sleeping. Try. You must."

When he did fall asleep, Ji Sun tore into her gas-station bagel, realized she hadn't eaten since the day before. In her haste, she bit the inside of her front lip, hard enough that she cried out. She whipped her hand over her mouth, turned around to confirm that no one had heard her yelp.

"I bit my lip," Ji Sun said to Margaret quietly.

"I see that, my God," Margaret said, and gasped. She reached for a stack of napkins in the center console. "It's just saliva. You know it mixes with the blood so it looks so much worse."

Ji Sun hadn't noticed the blood on her hands, but she wiped her face now, shocked at how badly it hurt, at the power of her teeth, how stupid it was that her body didn't know to stop, that her teeth couldn't sense, somehow, this next bit isn't food, abort mission, turn back, don't do it, don't do it, don't do it!

Napkin pressed over her mouth, Ji Sun turned to look at her sleeping friend. *How* could she have done it? How could she?

Her mouth was throbbing, the blood hadn't stopped.

Ji Sun turned to Margaret, whispered, copper taste of blood on her tongue, "How could she? How could she? How could she do that? How could she?"

Margaret shook her head but didn't answer. Ji Sun watched a single tear trail down Margaret's face, wondered why her own eyes had stayed dry against all this pain.

"She's her *mother*!" Ji Sun said.

"Mothers have done worse," Margaret said, voice steady, eyes now dry.

The institution was on a low hill, ringed by pine trees and blooming bushes of hydrangeas. It looked more like someone's generically impressive McMansion country house than any kind of treatment facility.

Margaret pulled into a spot farthest from any other cars, under a lamp in the style of an old-timey streetlight. They had a clear view of the entrance, but no one moved.

"Here we are," Margaret said, a singsong quality to her voice that she ducked her head to dismiss.

The tears on Lainey's cheeks were Lucite lines, unbroken. Ji Sun realized, in the silence, that she had expected Lainey to fight, to rage, to demand that they turn around and take her home. They had agreed together on a voluntary psychiatric hold, Alice's friend having assured Adam that any place that charged so much would let you leave whenever you liked.

"Oh. Oh, God," Lainey said, so quietly they couldn't be sure of the words.

Of course, everyone knew, they could commit her. But none wanted it to come to that, none would risk it. They wanted so badly not to watch her go inside at all, to be able to pretend that this never happened, proceed to live in a world unbroken by this perforation, free from even the idea that this could occur. Adam had told Ji Sun that keeping Lainey and Elizabeth in separate rooms had been the worst part, that the baby seemed in more pain to be away from her mother than from the bite. He hadn't agreed to let them stay together until after Alice came over, told him to, and until then the only calm in their shared squalls was when Lainey came to nurse Elizabeth, her quiet shushes, Elizabeth's grunts and coos, and sometimes the swallowed sobs as Lainey positioned Elizabeth so that her bandage wouldn't meet any friction.

"I need to nurse her again," Lainey said, her face half lit by the lamp. "Give us a moment." Elizabeth was still quiet, but had begun to stir.

Once, on the drive, Adam had awakened, still sleepy, and said of Elizabeth, "Wow, still sleeping, huh? Guess we should drive around in the city more." In the mirror, Ji Sun could see him come out of his dream, remember. Before her eyes, the way his eyes changed.

Ji Sun and Margaret exchanged a look now. They must have shared the vision of Lainey slamming the power locks, diving into the driver's seat, burning rubber as she blazed away from them, sooner initiating an interstate car chase than sleep in a different building than her baby. Margaret removed the key from the ignition gently, placed it in her pocket.

"After that, we're going to go in," Adam said, so worried that he looked like a little boy, like Lainey's son, more fearful of his mother's silence than of her familiar ferocity, her fight.

Lainey made a nod so slight it was only perceptible in that the course of tears down her face changed, less cage and more cascade, wet drops into her lap, Elizabeth now babbling and awake.

The plan was to tell the doctors that a dog had bit their baby, and Lainey had had a nervous breakdown. They feared for her wellness, worried that she might unravel, wanted to have her talk to professionals, see how she might deal with whatever dark visions had visited her in the wake of this terrible accident, for which she blamed herself.

How could they find out what she needed through this lie? It was the best they could do. What choice did they have?

Adam went in pulling Lainey's small suitcase and returned carrying Elizabeth in one arm and her car seat in the other, like a new father leaving the hospital, disbelief on his face that he could be tasked with the care of a new human in this way. Good luck, man, try not to fuck it up.

He looked like an ordinary man, in his khakis and windbreaker, leaving a house that he might have owned, but as he grew closer they saw his countenance was that of a man escaping a burning building, shocked to have made it out alive, not even sure yet of what he'd left inside, what he'd lost.

CHAPTER 46

B ack at the motel, Ji Sun left Adam, Margaret, and Elizabeth in the adjoining rooms they'd decided would be Adam's and Margaret's, connected by a door. Ji Sun took the third room, a few doors down, the path between littered with cigarette butts and pine needles. She unzipped her bag on the bed but felt too restless to unpack or sleep, decided instead to walk to the dive bar they'd seen on their drive. So much time in the air-conditioned car had tricked her into thinking it was cool, but the air was humid and heavy, the swamp heat of summer, and she stripped down to her linen tank. The bar was less than a mile away, but on a country road with no sidewalk, it felt endless, and she was covered in sweat by the time she arrived.

The kitchen was closed, but after Ji Sun took every bag of chips and pretzels from the wall display and piled them on the bar, the bartender agreed to go in back and see what he might rustle up. Ji Sun's lip still hurt too much to eat anything so salty, but she had the urge to be of use, superfluous as she'd felt watching Adam and Margaret try to set up a space for Elizabeth, passing the baby back and forth between one another, singing to her and distracting her, like parents on an ill-fated getaway, Ji Sun the awkward adolescent stepdaughter.

She drank a shot of whiskey and bought the bottle along with four glasses, so as not to have to drink from the plastic mouthwash cups back in the room. The bartender regarded her with less misgiving than she'd expected, though Ji Sun supposed with the bar's proximity to a place like the one where they'd left Lainey, people had come in looking more desperate than she did now.

On her walk back, loaded down with food, the first few fat rain-drops started to fall, and she waited for the relief of a breeze. But it stayed hot, felt still hotter with the raindrops on her skin, the same temperature as the air, mixing with sweat and leaving her coated with damp and dirt. She needed to shower, but she went to Margaret's door first.

Elizabeth was asleep on Margaret's chest, and Margaret looked close to sleep as well. It was strange to see her, eyes lidded, looking beatific in this run-down room, given everything that had brought them there. But everything felt strange like this now, nudged one over from real life, both hyperreal and fake as a sound stage. Adam sat at the small table near the window, fiddling with the monitor whose camera component he'd propped up on the dresser, aimed toward the bed where Margaret and Elizabeth rested together.

"I guess I'll just sleep there?" He pointed at the bed next to the one where his daughter slept in the arms of someone else's mother.

"Can you eat something?" Ji Sun asked, pointing a slice of soft, cold, bar pizza in Margaret's direction.

Margaret shook her head, put one shush finger up to her lips. Her other hand stayed rested on the dark crown of Elizabeth's hair.

"What about a drink?" Ji Sun whispered, and Adam accepted, took a bag of pretzels from the pile.

"Let's go next door," Adam whispered. "I need to eat something so I don't die. But I don't want to wake her. Them."

Margaret's eyes were closed now, too, and with nothing amiss in this space, Ji Sun followed Adam to the other side.

In his room, the mirror of Margaret's, Adam placed the monitor carefully on the table, and then flung himself back on the bed. He kicked off his shoes and sat up, dumped pretzels into his mouth and chomped, coughed dry salt and slugged the drink Ji Sun had poured him, sat back on the edge of the bed before he got up and embraced her, all so quickly that Ji Sun had barely figured out where she should sit.

"Thank you for getting this food," he said, his breath hot and yeasty. "Thank you for being here." He looked at her, held out his glass. "Jesus. Fuck. Pour me another?"

"Should you . . . can you sleep?" She poured a glass for each of them and pulled a chair from the table close to the bed, where he sat.

"I'm so wired. I slept in the car. Now I'm just, I'm so wired, I can't, I have all this nervous energy." He looked down at his drink. "What is going to happen? What are we going to do?"

"What happened?" Ji Sun asked. When would she learn? Would they ever know? She could not understand.

He knew what she was asking.

"I came home to cries," he said. "Different sounds than what was typical. I don't know, higher pitched. Wails. I can't think of the animal. I still don't know if it was Elizabeth making them, or Lainey." He drank the rest of his whiskey, stood up, and began to pace, as though he couldn't sit still with this story.

"There was blood on her face. On her lips and her cheeks and her chin. Like, Jesus, like barbecue sauce. I thought it *was* barbecue sauce, my brain couldn't register a reason that her face would be bloody like that. When I realized it was blood my first thought was that she'd lost a tooth somehow, that someone had, I don't know, pulled it with pliers from her jaw," Adam said.

"What? Jesus." Ji Sun drank her whiskey, put her hand to her jaw. There was a crack of lightning and the room lit up. Adam went to look at the monitor, placed it back, and resumed his pacing.

"I know. Too many torture scenes on TV. I don't know, I knew something was so wrong that my brain was maybe looking for other ideas. And when I saw the blood on Elizabeth—"

Here he paused for a moment and stared past her. Ji Sun wanted him to put his head in his hands, look down, be overcome in a way that she would not have to acknowledge. But he did not. He shook his head with his eyes open. He looked at her again.

"When I saw Elizabeth, when I realized, I wished Lainey's tooth had been pulled from her jaw."

Ji Sun wasn't sure if Adam meant instead of what had happened or as a punishment for it. He made a slight gasping sound and began to cry. She had never felt the disproportionate sympathy for a man in tears, in part because she rarely cried herself. She didn't think tears were a show of weakness, but nor did she think they were a sure indication of how a person felt. Her roommates cried with relief, with joy, when stressed, when gutted, when exhausted. Everyone seemed to have been crying nonstop since Adam first called them to the apartment, but she knew they hadn't been, it was more that they were in that post-sob state, eyes puffy and bleary, faces drawn, noses red and raw.

She wanted to give him comfort. Where should she put her hand, though. If she put it on his thigh he would know what she was offering, and he would take it. And she would have finally confirmed something about him, trapped him in the lie of what they all believed to be his inherent decency, never more so than now, as he assumed this role of father rescuer, tasked with saving his baby daughter and his wayward wife both.

She didn't want to feel desire like this, in the midst of this. She could blame the rain, so loud on the roof now that Ji Sun looked at the monitor, too, lifted the screen to see them sleeping, Elizabeth on Margaret's chest, her bandage black in the night-vision mode, a square hole on her skin, ghostly gray-blue in the invert color scheme, the soft sound from the small machine of the device almost a purring.

She thought of how the baby must have been giggling, how easy it was to be playful and then go too far. A tickle to a kick. Arms swing out and then push hard. Hands rub, caress, then yank, shove. What did shock even look like on a face so small?

Ji Sun's sister had told her that babies didn't feel pain in specific sites on their bodies, just a diffuse sense of discomfort that quickly passed. Ji Sun accepted this, in part because Ji Eun needed her affirmation, having elected cosmetic otoplasty to pin back her newborn daughter's ears. But she couldn't move past the idea of Elizabeth's little face: terrified, mournful, stunned, confused. What expression would the baby make when next she woke, saw that her mother was not there?

She stood and put the monitor back on the table. Sometimes, when something broke, you rushed to clean it up, piece it back together with care. Other times, you threw your hands up, smashed everything else in the room.

Her window was closing. The lightning cracked again, and Adam refilled his glass. The crazed way people behaved when so near to grief would recede some in the morning, as they figured out how to function in this revised version of the world. She had to touch him now.

She saw her hand on his chin before realizing she'd lifted it. Her cherished rings, raw stones bound in platinum—Lainey called them the brass knuckles a sea witch would wear. Ji Sun wanted them gone, to feel her hand naked against his face.

But he didn't move her hand toward his lips as he had done in her imagining of this moment. He put his own hand over hers, tucked his face into her hand like a child seeking comfort, like some kind of shared prayer. Should she stick her fingers in his mouth? Was there another way to communicate what she was offering, and how he had to accept today? It was still dangerous, and awful, but safer than it would ever be again, anything they did for a few days or hours longer at least could be forgiven as part of this terrible time when they were all out of their minds, standing next to their own bodies.

So she moved closer to him. She crossed another line, and pressed her body against his and kissed him. He kissed her back, and the kissing at the beginning was even better than she imagined because it still existed on another plane, and as long as they kissed, they stayed lifted in the air like this, suspended.

But then their hands became involved, his on her ass, hers on his, both of them forcing their bodies together at the center, needing to fuse together there, collapse all space between their selves. The way they grabbed at each other, their desperation—this was worse in their memory than what followed.

They didn't fall into bed together—nothing about their actions was accidental like that, it was ordained, like the storm outside, inevitable as weather.

Ji Sun would remember later how, before he pulled her onto the bed, he glanced at the monitor. This made her feel both better and worse, this glance, that he was a person who would check to make sure his baby daughter was sleeping before he slept with one of her mother's best friends, and that he was a person who would look at this video of his just-bit daughter, asleep in the next room, and still fuck one of his best friends. That he looked confirmed for Ji Sun that they were in the world, not outside of it, as it felt in the rain and the glow, the strung beads of neon light in the streams of rain on the window, the haze of their exhaustion, and the heat of her body, having waited so long for this.

Her lip stung from where she'd bitten it, but when they kissed the hurt was gone, replaced by a different pain, at how good it felt, how good they were at kissing like this, how many years they'd wasted not kissing like this. If they could just stay kissing like this—

But soon they were taking one another's clothes off, and Ji Sun wouldn't stop him, she wouldn't stop herself, but she did say, like a line she'd rehearsed, "We shouldn't," his face already buried in her neck, one hand on her face, the other between her legs. "We shouldn't," she said again.

"I need to," he said, and "I need to," again, or maybe "I need you," she couldn't tell, it sounded like a growl, and his face was lower now, at her breasts.

They were both drunk but they looked at each other then, eyes whiskey wet, and saw one another clearly, knew what they were doing, had done already.

She came right away, while he watched her, worked at her with his fingers. More than a decade of desire for him, she would have thought it would be the orgasm to end all orgasms, but she felt even in the flood and fever of warmth a kind of urgent need, that upward pull, into the body, even in ecstasy she was asking for more more more right away now more please and he obliged, put his penis inside her. He was so hard, she said, and she was so wet, disgust and arousal at even the familiarity of these borrowed lines, this seedy motel, following some script that she didn't remember learning, surprised even to know words, animal as she felt with him, two wolves wound together, tearing the other apart, so that when she came again, the nightmare of it, they shuddered together, a shudder as ugly as it was exhilarating, a shudder that filled the room. And just like that, he unsealed their bodies, leaped off of her without a word, grabbed the monitor, ran into the bathroom. She found her clothes and as she put them on, she heard a soft cry from the adjoining room. She fled as though burned, before the bathroom door could open, before they would be forced to face one another.

CHAPTER 47

The second morning Lainey woke up in the institution, the pain in her breasts was her first feeling, before the pain of remembering what she had done. She could not remember having bitten, only the love she felt when she kissed and nibbled Elizabeth's cheek, only the shock of Adam arriving home and yanking Elizabeth from her arms, screaming words at her that she couldn't understand, that she didn't believe could apply to her.

She had pumped three times in the night, but she woke, engorged and outraged, the pain in her breasts growing as she waited for Adam to bring Elizabeth, as he had done the previous morning, and promised to do again today, as soon as visiting hours began.

Not allowed a phone in her room, Lainey was forced to remember what waiting had felt like in the days before cell phones, how with each moment your fears and irritations grew in tandem, until by the time the awaited party arrived, you were as relieved that they were alive as you were angry that they weren't unconscious on the side of the road somewhere.

When Adam and Elizabeth arrived, led by an orderly who Lainey felt regarded her with undisguised disdain, Lainey didn't even hear the excuses Adam made, so filled with relief at the sight of her daughter's face, at how, when Elizabeth saw her, she began to bounce in Adam's arms, she *laughed*. Lainey wondered if she would be relieved like this for the rest of her life, every single time her daughter looked at her without fear.

The pleasure she felt holding Elizabeth—her familiar weight, her warm head, her bright babbles, and her fat fingers grabbing Lainey's hair—it was enough to make her forget where she was.

Looking at Adam, her guard and imprisoner, Lainey felt, before the letdown, a rage at how extraneous he was, and at herself, for what she'd done had given him a reason to stand there, watching over them, when he should not be anywhere near. She could recall feeling this way sometimes before what happened, too, when he stood near the glider, to bring her water, or just be near, how she would have the urge to bat him away, how confounded she was that he thought he belonged there.

She loved him more after Elizabeth was born; she loved how he became her family in a way she already felt he was, but was now made manifest on the beautiful face of their baby. She hadn't known how much it would mean, the way she could see his face in Elizabeth's, and her own, and, most exquisitely, a new, perfect face, unlike either of theirs in its abject curiosity, its constant wonder, the most marvelous face she had ever known.

That she had harmed this face remained a shock to her, offset now by the only drug she needed, the rush of love she felt when her daughter nursed, not only for Elizabeth, but for all the world, an openheartedness she could not remember feeling before Elizabeth's birth. The rush of it didn't overcome her as much as it had the first two months, when she would go slack-jawed at letdown, unable to form words, mushmouthed and struck dumb, her brain shut off, her whole body a beating neon heart of oxytocin. Even now, with the blank white of Elizabeth's bandage blazing up at her, she was awash in the relief of her daughter's hunger, her whole self for this moment sated.

Lainey switched Elizabeth to her other breast, touched lightly the clean cheek, and looked at Adam again. The way he leaned in the doorway, his hip at a jaunty, satisfied angle. He looked sexy.

They hadn't had sex since Elizabeth was born, had tried once, too early, and it hurt. Since then, Lainey had had, for the first time in her life, zero interest. She knew it would pass, hadn't been worried, had barely noticed, nor looked up from her daughter's face for long enough to notice Adam making a feline posture like this, if he had, broadcasting his sexual viability in some way that she recognized but to which she could not respond. His body appealed to her in an abstract way, but it seemed garish for him to stand this way in this place, and she suggested they take a walk.

When Elizabeth finished nursing, Lainey wound her up in the light linen wrap she favored in the heat. She felt a warmth toward Margaret for knowing to pack this. As Lainey lifted her baby, she went to kiss her covered cheek, stopped short before her lips grazed the bandage, whipped her neck back so fast that Elizabeth mewled, looked quizzical. Lainey had kissed that cheek a million times, so many times, touched it with no more hesitation than she might her own cheek. Perhaps this porousness had been part of the problem. She didn't know, and she wouldn't find out in this place, the doctors concerned primarily with convincing her that the cocktail of antianxiety medications in their preferred brands were safe for nursing, sure that her resistance was part of the postpartum panic that they believed landed her there.

Though it was a bit early, Elizabeth only ever napped when worn by Lainey, and Lainey hoped it would extend their visit if her daughter fell asleep.

Outside, the pine trees were already baking. She asked Adam how Elizabeth had napped the previous day. He tried wearing her for walking naps in the city sometimes, but she usually stayed alert, eyes wide in wonder, babbling as her papa tried different paces, brisk stride, slow stroll, hip sashay—anything to jostle her into the rhythm she required. Adam would return joking that he'd given the baby another tour of the neighborhood, pass Elizabeth to Lainey, who would wrap her up and go back outside.

He hesitated. "She napped with Margaret."

Lainey swallowed a sob. Elizabeth was still awake, and she didn't want to upset her anymore than she already had, her baby who, before all this, had never slept in a separate bed, let alone building.

"No, I'm glad! I'm glad she napped. Glad that she feels so comfortable with Margaret. That's," she struggled not to cry, "that's lucky."

They walked in silence, the *sh-sh-sh* of the sprinklers and Elizabeth's little birdsong babbles the only sounds.

"Did she wear her?" Lainey could hear in her voice a rising panic so inappropriate for the inquiry, as though she was asking what Adam's lover wore for their latest rendezvous.

"She did," he said. "She borrowed my Ergo."

"With the insert? I think she's still too light to go without," Lainey said. "It can do permanent damage to the hips." She adjusted Elizabeth now, sticky already against her, the heat oppressive in proportion to the frigid air-conditioning indoors.

"It was too stuffy for the insert," Adam said. "Let's not fight about this—no, scratch that, it actually feels really good to fight about this," he said, and offered her the smile that always steadied her, encompassing, authentic, easy. "It's kind of a relief to fight about this."

The day before, they had argued about what happened, in her room with the door closed, while Elizabeth nursed. He'd said that he was going to talk with one of the doctors after she finished nursing, and he wanted to bring Elizabeth.

"So what, I can't be alone with her ever again?"

"I didn't say that! But you have to understand why I," he lowered his voice, "why I am nervous about that."

"But you understand I would never hurt her," she said, and he was silent. "I would never *intentionally* hurt her. Adam, you know that, don't you? You know that's true! It was an accident, I don't, I would never hurt her."

"But you did! And you don't seem to get that. You can't accidentally"—he stopped himself, looked to the door as though the police might burst in—"*do* something like that. Some other force possessed you."

The thing Adam would never understand was that it was *not* some other force, but the same force, the same love so overpowering it teetered into destruction. He hadn't birthed a baby, he didn't know, how Elizabeth had torn out of her, left her gaping, bloody, raw, how every creation is an act of destruction, how the bite was borne out of desire to show Elizabeth how deep her love for her ran, how vast, how endless. They can lock me up forever, they can bury me alive, she wanted to tell her daughter, and the love I have for you will endure. Claw its way out of anything tear down the sky upend the earth erupt from inside its molten core make a black hole of everything, our love the first burst of light.

Lainey understood better now why people wanted to destroy women. In an offhand way she'd always agreed with this notion, that men did so in part out of jealousy or rage that they couldn't grow a human inside their bodies, but she knew now that it was both simpler and more complicated than this, that it was not just their rage and impotence and jealousy, but their awareness, even half formed, that a woman knew something about the connection between destruction and creation that they could never understand, and so some swatted and swatted, beat and raped and strangled women, Lainey knew, out of this impotent desperation to do what she did at that very moment: nurse her baby, give her baby life with her own body, the one that she undid, bled dry, with that same act. This didn't forgive it, and nothing forgave her, it made them worse, really, both the violent men and herself, because with the bite she became like them, greedy beyond reason, wanting so badly to show love, to fight loss, that she'd harmed Elizabeth.

All this but also something physical. She could not remember anything more than the usual nibble, but she had tried in these locked-away days to know, to imagine, to see herself into that horrible scene. Her jaw must have opened, unhinged like a prehistoric beast's, and since she hadn't consciously signaled it, it must have done so on its own, out of time: animal, energy, fat. Not a bone, not a thought. Just the pull to bite, to consume, to have. To swallow Elizabeth the same way it seemed some days that Elizabeth wanted to swallow her, to crawl back inside her, yes, maybe, but that seemed too simple a shorthand for something that went beyond bodies, not one inside the other as in sex or as in utero, just *one*.

"It went too far. I know I went too far. But I didn't mean it," she said, stifled another cry. "It was an accident."

"Lainey, do you really not get that what you did is . . . is psychotic?"

"Now I'm a psychopath?"

"I didn't say that."

"You don't have to! Look around. Only thing missing is the straitjacket." She had waved at her small room, the few half-hearted attempts at making it homey only highlighting how bloodless and sterile a space it was. "When can I go home, Adam. Let me come home."

She'd cried then, while Elizabeth had nursed on the right side, the bit cheek concealed, tucked against Lainey's body. She could feel the tuft of gauze there, the itch. But she could also tell herself it had never happened, and for the length of Elizabeth's suckling, she could believe it.

Now, outside on their walk, Lainey looked down at the bandage, a tiny smudge of ointment glistening in the sun.

"Can I see it?" she asked. The day before, Adam had denied this request, insisting that he'd just changed the bandage and didn't want to expose the wound.

Now, Lainey pointed to a bench in the shade.

"Let's sit here," she said. "Let me look at it."

"Alice told us to remove the dressing as little as possible," he said.

"I *know* that, Adam," Lainey said. "But I need to see. What I've done."

"It's so hot," Adam said. "And we're outside. I don't want, I don't know, a bug to . . ." He sighed. "All right."

Why should he be the only one to have to look at it? The face he made before he followed her to the bench was maybe her first realization that she had done this to him, too.

After they left she could only think of the wound she'd made, how it was still so wet, and angry, and new. The start of scabbing made a thin dark thread of dried blood along the edges of the two pink crescents, each with one neat, tiny stitch. Her cheek was so small and, away from it, it was easy for the wound to grow in Lainey's mind, open wider and wider still, swallow her daughter's face, as Lainey, herself, some version of her, had attempted to do.

What kind of demented person did that to a baby, any baby, let alone her own? Lainey had thought of little else, and still she couldn't reconcile it with anything she knew about herself. She tried to remember that missing afternoon, both a lifetime and a split second ago, could not even insert herself into a movie version of that scene, forced to take Adam's word that it was she who had done this, could not remember anything in her teeth, or, God help her, on her tongue or in her throat. Something in her body and jaw had acted without her mind's consent, brought her teeth down on the world and sliced them both into some other dimension somehow, a needle skip, a parallel universe, this is the version of you that went off the rails. In this time that you were so *in* your life, you somehow fell through it, down into darkness, through the earth and its atmosphere, back down into your daughter's sunny nursery, your husband screaming in the doorway, sounds like you have never heard.

She tested her teeth on her forearm, tried to bite, failed to even break skin. Her breasts were already growing full again, the tingling needles in her underarms insisting that she pump. She hooked herself up, quarantined cattle, and listened to the machine's chant, *mon-stuhr, mon-stuhr, mon-stuhr,* the new word it had learned with this recent increase in use, an accusation she could not deny but that she tried to reshape in her mind, let it sound like, let it be: *mother, mother, mother.*

CHAPTER 48

Their third night at the motel, Adam came to Ji Sun's door again, whiskey bottle in one hand and monitor in the other.

The night before he had done the same, stood there in his stupid khakis, looking both sheepish and ravenous. There was no storm, no excuse. After they spent the second night together, taking their time with each other's bodies, not rushed as they had been the first night, she had been forced to move him into the category with most other men she knew. Now he had betrayed Lainey. She had, too, but part of her was certain of the irony that Lainey would be the only one who might understand why they'd needed to do this, might not even feel betrayed, but grateful in these hollow, desperate days that they'd found some balm against their despair. This was too far, she knew, but still she allowed herself to entertain believing it.

The second night, after, he hadn't darted off so quickly. They'd lain together on the starchy sheets and turned on the television, watched a reality show that Ji Sun had become hooked on during the stay.

"That can never happen again," Adam said.

"Never," she said.

"Never," he said. And they traded more *nevers* like *I love yous*, like *thank-yous*, like *I knows*.

But here he was.

"Never," she said, and she let him in in the same movement that she began to remove his clothes. She wanted to make the mistake again. As long as they were here, in this motel, where they had already done it, she reasoned, it was part of the same mistake.

They didn't say much else to one another, but she was amazed
by the way in which their bodies continued a conversation they had
been having for years, not halting, but curious, not hurried, but
desperate. When would they know enough? How could they stop
asking now, after all this?

"I have to be able to talk to you," he said, wiping his mouth. "I
can't lose your friendship because of this. Your respect, fine. But
not your friendship." He gave a slyer version of the smile she knew
him for, open and easy, affable but not naive. This smile unnerved
her in the same way his glance at the monitor had that first night,
in that it was a nod to an awareness of the circumstances outside of
this room. They fell asleep undressed, in each other's arms, and
when Ji Sun next woke, Adam was still naked, on the edge of the
bed, phone to his ear.

The first light was creeping in the window, his face blue in the
glow of his phone. The panic in his posture took the last of the
sleep from her, and she sat up straight.

"What is it? It's Lainey?"

He tossed the phone down, pulled on his pants, and nodded.

"They didn't say, they didn't say. They just said to come right
away. On the message. Fuck. Oh fuck. My God." He tripped trying
to put his shirt on, knocked his head against the back of a chair.
"Oh, my God, Lainey."

Ji Sun was frozen in place, sheet wrapped around her like a
shield.

"We have to go," he said. "Let's go."

Like that, she would go with him. Of course she would go with
him! She unwound the sheet from her body and sat naked in the
bed, willed herself to stand.

He raced back to his room while Ji Sun got dressed, collected the
keys from Margaret, and told her he would call as soon as he knew
more. He wouldn't bring Elizabeth until he knew what waited there.

The sun leaked its pale white light into the purple of the horizon as they sped to the facility in silence. Adam parked half on the sidewalk and raced inside. Visiting hours had not yet begun, and Ji Sun was alone in the small sitting room. She texted with Margaret and Alice, told them that something had happened with Lainey, she didn't know what. She wanted to call, but couldn't risk being outside when news came, and didn't want to talk in this space, so near to whatever had happened, but knowing nothing.

She was sick with fear. Why hadn't they protected Lainey? Why had they taken Elizabeth from her? Why hadn't they brought her somewhere better, somewhere with more to recommend it than its discretion, its ease of use? If Lainey was dead, Ji Sun would die, too, right in this room, she was sure of it.

When Adam returned, she might have seen on his face that Lainey was alive. But her vision was blurred by pain and fear. She needed him to say it.

"She's okay," he said.

"Is? Did she?" She choked out the question that had been waiting there.

"She bit herself," Adam answered. He held a clipboard in one hand, and he put the other on her shoulder.

"Oh, God," Ji Sun said, and a hoarse laugh came up from her throat. She put her hand to her mouth, tried to catch the laughter she couldn't stop, dry barks tumbling loose. "I'm sorry," she said, still laughing, "I'm just relieved. I don't want her to die."

"I don't either," Adam said, with a look of surprise so earnest that Ji Sun saw it had not occurred to him as a true possibility before this moment.

"Come on," he said, leading her by the shoulder out into the hall. "She wants to see you."

Ji Sun was afraid to go in, afraid to fail. Afraid she would still stink of Adam's sex, afraid she would offer poor comfort, afraid she wouldn't find the right words, any words. She wished Margaret were there. Margaret knew how to comfort, how to grab a trembling hand and hold it in both her warm hands, how to throw her arms around people at the first quiver of their bottom lip. She called them *oh darling, oh love, oh sweet one*; she always started the rounds of *I love you* that they traded when they parted ways. She never hesitated to nurture, though Ji Sun had called upon her less in this regard since Connecticut. After the twins arrived, whatever happened there had been shunted into ancient history, part of an "unhealthy period" in Margaret's life, as though her mistake had been caused by a vitamin D deficiency or not enough centering yoga. In recollecting her own unhealthy periods, Ji Sun saw herself like an undersea creature, all her sumptuous blacks sodden, her hair tentacles, reaching out to try to strangle anyone within reach, and if no one came near enough, wrap back around her own neck. But there were always people near enough.

That's who they were to one another—the ones willing to reach without dwelling on the risk. The ones who would enter the room when it reeked of despair. The ones who would not turn away.

She went into Lainey's room. She saw her friend, white bandage on her forearm to match the one on her daughter's cheek. She looked at Lainey and took her in her arms.

"We have to keep you," Ji Sun said. "You can't scare us like this. You can't leave us!"

Ji Sun lifted her friend's arm, its long bandage in that same place it would be if she had tried to kill herself.

"I would never. You know that. I never would. Elizabeth!"

"Yes, Elizabeth," Ji Sun said. "But us, too. We need you, too." She looked at Adam, who kept his eyes on Lainey. "We need you, too! Promise me." She took her friend by the unbit arm, so they held both hands now, and faced one another. "Promise me!"

"I promise, I promise," Lainey said. She didn't blink. She believed it.

"It wasn't—I told Adam, I wasn't trying to harm—to kill myself." Lainey whispered the last part, looked to the door. "I'm not a danger to myself. I'm not a danger!" She went and sat on the bed, so like a young girl in her loose T-shirt, her lank hair. "I just, I needed to know what pain I caused. I had to know what it felt like. I had to."

Ji Sun nodded, looked to Adam, who seemed now like he could be pulled apart by a single loose thread.

"I can't stay here," she said, and though she had just promised them she was no danger, it was impossible not to hear some threat in her voice, her bit arm cradled, its bandage in that telltale place.

"Will they, will they let you leave, though?" Ji Sun asked. "Isn't there some law, if you, if you are a danger to yourself? Seen as a danger to yourself."

"But I'm *not* a danger," Lainey said again, a sort of fever lost somewhere behind her voice, like she was trying to raise it but couldn't. Ji Sun looked at her again, realized she must have been given a tranquilizer at some point.

"When did you, when did this happen?"

"Last night," she said. "They called you." Lainey looked at Adam with what might have been an accusation, but was tempered by whatever she'd taken.

"I'm fine," Lainey said again. "I barely managed much." She began to remove the bandage, held her arm up for Ji Sun to see.

"I don't, that's—" Ji Sun looked away, and then back at the bite. She thought of how badly she'd wanted to see Elizabeth's cheek, how ghastly it was, that need to see the damage that was hidden from view, and how shameful it was to recoil from that same offering now, when being asked to look at it.

She took a deep breath and went to sit beside Lainey on the bed, take her arm again, look directly at what her friend had done. There were two red crescents, not quite meeting, dark Morse code lines of her teeth, like cave paintings, alien messages, hieroglyphs. What was Lainey trying to say? How could they show her that they wanted to hear?

"See?" Lainey said, her voice still with that slight syrup of sedation, but her eyes clear, looking into Ji Sun's. "It's not so bad."

"You're right," Ji Sun said, and met her friend's steady gaze. "It isn't as bad as I thought."

CHAPTER 49

B ack in Brooklyn, Adam and Lainey sat in their living room with both sets of their parents. They'd been home for three days, having checked Lainey out the same afternoon that they came to find she'd bit herself. Lainey's parents had a visit scheduled, and Adam had decided to invite his own so they could talk about what happened, not have to go through it twice. They'd said on the phone that there had been an accident and that everyone was fine, but rattled, and it would be better to speak in person, that they could use the support. Now, Elizabeth was asleep in her crib, the time for the meeting chosen for when she would be, and Lainey arranged on a ceramic tray shortbread in flavors that she had previously accused of personally gentrifying the neighborhood: lemon lavender, burnt brown sugar, cardamom and bergamot. She tried to call up the ready rage she'd had for the bakery since it opened, its repurposed subway tile, its six-dollar frothy drinks, but she felt instead a wish that the butter and sugar would do some witchcraft, that this pretty pyramid of sweets would distract her parents, keep them from looking for something amiss in her face.

Lainey and Adam were sticking with the dog story, which they hadn't embellished beyond that it happened in a nearby park, early morning, when few other people were there. They didn't talk about what it meant to spend more time guarding the truth than trying to figure out how Lainey would deal with it. They would add that Lainey had been bit, too, and she still wore a bandage, but had put on a light long-sleeve tunic, even in the heat, so her parents wouldn't ask about it right away. Lainey and Adam operated under the shared belief that too much detail gave a lie away, but from whom had they received this wisdom?

Their parents made a valiant effort at small talk, finding a point of entry around their shared disappointment in Obama, who by now they had to accept would not save the world entire. Lainey's parents seemed frustrated for milder versions of the reasons Lainey herself was, that he was more centrist than they'd dreamed, that now, in his second term, his caution would be further hamstrung by a Republican Senate. Why hadn't he done more before? What was he waiting for? Adam's parents' complaints sounded patronizing to Lainey, as though Obama was their child, and he had let them down personally.

Lainey looked at her mother next to Adam's. They were the same age, but her mother let her grays show, and had a face full of lines that she said showed how well she'd lived, how much she'd laughed, but also, Lainey thought, how deeply she worried. How many of those lines had Lainey made, she wondered now. Adam's mother's face had been smoothed stiff by Botox, and she had a paper-doll quality that made her fit in anywhere, chic bob and expensive flats, trade a blazer for sweater or shift, depending on the day. Lainey felt a pang at the way her own mother always dressed up a bit when she came to the city, how she swapped out the leather cord on her reading glasses for a beaded chain, smeared deep magenta lipstick on her thin lips. She worked as an academic research librarian, but had always dressed more like the art teachers in picture books, lots of prints, hair in wild coils, funky jewelry, statement scarves. There was a wide, wet quality to her dark eyes, a way of infrequent, purposeful blinking that she shared with Elizabeth. Lainey wanted to ask her sister, Rachel, whether there was anything in genetics that could account for such a thing, a trait being passed down not by DNA, but in the air, out of love.

When Lainey was four and Rachel was eight, Rachel burned her hands in the bathroom of a diner in the Catskills. The girls had crammed along with their mother into the tiny storage-closet-cum-bathroom, where their mother was helping Lainey on the toilet. She'd perched her handbag on the small sink, and the weight shifted the handle, made the water steam.

"Why would the water even *get* that hot!" their father said as they sped to the emergency room, their mother weeping as Rachel wailed.

Lainey remembered the drive as the first time she'd seen her mother express this kind of agony. Her sister's cries were as familiar to her as her own, and she'd heard both her parents shout, even seen her father cry while looking at old photographs and listening to *Graceland.*

Lainey felt guilty because their mother had only placed her handbag on the sink to better help her on the toilet, Lainey's enduring problem being her need to poop but desire not to; she joked sometimes that she'd needed her mother's help with this through college.

Her mother had been in a low squat, coaxing Lainey, tucking her hair behind her ears, reminding her of the relief she'd feel once she just let the poop go. *Let it go, just let it go,* her mother said, in this practiced poop-strain-specific rhythm that Lainey could still call up. Lainey still remembered how she sweat with exertion, and how the bathroom stank already of recent shits, likely taken with greater ease.

This attempt to poop in public would have blended in with so many others if not for the burn, how Rachel screamed and their mother lifted Lainey from the toilet, pulled her underwear and pants up in one swoop, before Lainey had finished, carried both girls from the diner and into the car as their father collected their coats and raced to catch up. It was hours later, home from the hospital, Rachel asleep in their shared room, that Lainey realized she'd pooped her pants. She found the small, dried disc of poop in her underwear and took it to the bathroom, thinking she would rinse it off herself. But she had the sudden fear that the sink would burn her as it had her sister, so she shoved the underwear into the garbage instead, scrubbed her little butt with a washcloth that she hung back up on the bar beside the sink.

Rachel came to blame Lainey as much as her mother for the burn, during those weeks when it wasn't easy for her to draw, then her favorite activity. And the story served as shorthand for their family dynamics later, with Lainey telling it as a story of how deeply her mother felt Rachel's pain, how she'd wept in the hospital room, cursed herself even when the girls were within earshot. For Rachel, it was a story about their mother being scatterbrained, and while not inattentive, crucially more focused on her younger daughter, the one who was somehow both wilder and easier to love.

Lainey thought of how her mother had had to test the water first, every time, for years, and how the one time she hadn't, her daughter had screamed as if skinned.

She felt as though what happened with Elizabeth was like a faucet nudged too far, from too hot but bearable to scalding, irreparable, how that imperceptible push had happened in her teeth and harmed her most beloved baby beyond measure. How her mother could maybe understand the pain Lainey felt, having made a mistake, an oversight. If she could explain it to her mother in this way, she thought, there was a chance she might understand.

But she never would; she couldn't. Lainey couldn't risk having her mother look at her the way her friends did now, with this blend of fear and worry and rebuke—not like Lainey had a sickness, but like she was one.

The more people she could keep from seeing her like that, the better. They might watch the way she looked at Elizabeth and see only devotion there, no creeping edge of obsession or intoxication, nothing curdled or chemical or offensive in its too-muchness, no besotted poison, no freak vampire-mother out for blood.

When Adam said that a dog had bitten Elizabeth, Lainey swore she could see a flash of doubt cross her mother's face. She remembered a moment, not so much a fight as a disagreement, but worse in the way its aftereffects lingered, when Lainey wouldn't let her mother take Elizabeth in the other room during the first visit, six days after Elizabeth was born. Her mother stopped short of being indignant, but made clear that she was not just hurt, but also insulted.

"I just, I don't want her to be in another room right now," Lainey said. "I need to be able to see her. It has nothing to do with you!" She wanted to shout again, *It has nothing to do with you!* but her mother looked so wounded that instead Lainey just took Elizabeth back in her arms and nursed her by way of further explanation.

It was months before she wanted Elizabeth in another room. Lainey hadn't even slept during the first three days of Elizabeth's life. On the fourth, she did, while Elizabeth slept on her chest. She woke to Adam's kiss and soft applause, but couldn't explain to him, more exhausted than she was, that she didn't need sleep. How electrified her body had been, those first days, attuned in every way to her new daughter, newly aware not just, as everyone rightly said, of how tender and new her baby was, nor even how tremendous the world's threats and cruelties, but more by the need to notice every moment, more by the knowledge of how babies died in the night for no other reason than that first missed breath.

"How could you—how did a dog even get this close to Elizabeth? Where were you? When did this happen? My God!" Her father's eyes were wide behind his glasses, he looked around the room as though for confirmation of what he'd heard.

"Are you suing the owners?" Adam's father asked. "Of course the dog has been put down!"

"Yes, the dog was taken by animal control. To be put down," Adam said. He glanced down at the baby monitor, so he wouldn't have to look at them while he lied.

"It's still alive? It's still out there!?" Adam's mother asked, as though the dog might be just outside the door, scritch-scratching, baring its teeth to bite all their fattened faces.

"I don't—they didn't give us an exact hour, Mom," Adam said. "It's probably dead."

They had been fools not to anticipate the level of detail Elizabeth's grandparents would require.

"Oh, that poor, poor baby! Poor little love." Lainey's mother had begun to cry as soon as they'd told her what happened, and she'd let her husband take her in his arms.

"She's healing well. It happened last week." Adam kept his eyes down, on the monitor, which Lainey saw her mother look to now, too, as though it might hold some answers.

"Last week!" Lainey's mother let out a wail. "How could you wait to tell us?"

"What about infection? I've heard that infections are a serious danger with dog bites." Lainey's father still held his wife, but kept looking around, as though waiting for the real adult in the room to arrive. "What did they say at the hospital, about how to prevent that?"

"We didn't, we didn't go to the hospital," Adam said. They'd decided to be forthright on this front, thought that to hew closer to the truth might make it less difficult to reconcile later.

"We didn't want to trigger anything, with an overzealous doctor or nurse," Adam said.

"Trigger anything?" his mother asked.

"With child protective services. Lainey was—"

"I was worried," Lainey cut Adam off. "That they would blame me. For letting a dog get so close. I do blame myself. It was my fault."

"Darling, you can't blame yourself!" her father said. Her parents had loosed their embrace, but stayed holding hands. Lainey looked at Adam's hands. One held the monitor, the other his phone.

Lainey's mother wiped her eyes, and she rose from her seat to come sit beside Lainey on the couch.

"I didn't want, I don't know—an investigation? Alice saw her. She said it's largely superficial." The word *superficial* stuck in her throat like a ball of warm wax. She could feel herself gag on it, tried to cough it loose.

"Honey, honey, are you okay? Oh, Lainey, love, it's okay! It isn't your fault, dear." Her mother held her, and Lainey tried to turn her coughs to softer, more acceptable cries, but she couldn't, kept coughing as her mother rubbed her back. She couldn't have her mother see how early she had shown her own daughter the very pain it was her one job to protect her from. It was still so new, to be able to cause harm in both directions like this, to disappoint as a daughter, but as a daughter who was a mother herself now, too. She could sense that her mother would find some way to blame herself for what Lainey had done, and that, too, she would protect her mother from for as long as she lived.

"This has been really stressful, obviously," Adam said. "We're glad you could all come in, but we need to rest, too." He stood up. "You can see her tomorrow," he added, before they could ask.

Adam's mother abruptly began to weep.

"Mom, why are you crying?" Adam's family was not demonstrative in this way, and this sudden display brought a look of fear to Adam's face that he had mostly managed to keep from Lainey throughout this ordeal.

"Oh, I'm sorry! Just thinking of her, thinking of her sweet little cheek. If she'll have a scar. It doesn't matter!"

"No, it doesn't," he said, and Lainey could see frustration edge out his fear. His mother was invested in appearances, sent fussy,

starchy little ensembles, offered to pay and decorate the tiny nursery when they'd showed her the plants and paintings they had
chosen with such care.

"No, no, I know. It's just—you understand! It's not the scar
itself, it's just . . ." She waved her hand.

"It's the world touching her," Lainey said. "I understand." If any
of them ever tried to take Elizabeth from her, she would rip the
limbs from their bodies with her now fearsome teeth. She knew
she had done wrong, but she would not forsake the chance to make
up for it, for and with the rest of her life.

Once they were gone, Adam sunk back on the couch. He poured
the rest of a bottle of red into his water glass and drank it.

"Adam, Adam, I am so sorry. Will you ever. Can you ever forgive
me?" She sat beside him, further apart than they'd been when their
parents were there, but facing him now, asking him to look at her.

He didn't answer. He clung to his monitor, fused by now to his
palm. He kissed her lightly and leaned back to observe her horrible
mouth, the first he'd touched it since she had done what she had
done.

"I'm going to bed," he said. "You should sleep. We have to see
them all again in the morning."

The way he said *we*, the team of it, she clung to this even as they
went to sleep in their separate rooms now, Adam in their bed,
alone, and Lainey on the floor of Elizabeth's nursery, like the dog
that hadn't been put down.

CHAPTER 50

Four days later, Alice arrived at Lainey and Adam's to check the healing of Elizabeth's wound. Ji Sun and Margaret had come along, too, as they hadn't seen Lainey since the drive back from the facility upstate. They might have tried to space out their visits, so as not to overwhelm Lainey, but each had her own reasons for not wanting to be without the others.

Ji Sun didn't want to be alone with Adam and Lainey, though more for concern that Adam would feel guilty than that Ji Sun would. The day they drove back to the motel together, having found Lainey alive, all desire for him left Ji Sun's body. Just like that. She felt it evaporate from her skin, mix with the dried sweat there, all that drained adrenaline from fearing for Lainey's life, and the mist of it came off her like steam. She rolled down the window and it was sucked out, a small cloud of vacated desire whipped up into the sky with the rest. The thought of her hands, grabbing, grabbing, and his hands, grabbing, grabbing, made her feel ill. Imagining his breath on her body made her neck hurt. Her head ached. She asked him to pull over, and they fought in a field on the side of the road, near the bar where she'd gone for provisions that first night. They agreed they could never tell Lainey, not ever but especially not now, that there was no excuse for what they'd done, and that they wouldn't ask her for one. Then he went on making his excuses anyway.

"I needed to think of something else. I needed to think of nothing."

"It wasn't nothing! I'm not nothing!"

"That's not what I mean. You know what I mean. We were—I was obliterated. I needed," he said, growling again, a different growl altogether from the ones he'd made in the motel, its rooms designed for hunters, not for the wild animals themselves, not for the wolves they'd been in those hours, ouroboros of this same obliteration he shouted about now, "I don't know, further obliteration."

She wanted to obliterate him still further for saying as much, for making her feel so used, and worse, for making her feel as though she had used him, taken advantage of his state, though she allowed that she had.

"But it wasn't nothing. It was something, something real. I don't mean—let me be clear. I don't mean I want it to happen again. But I am not sorry that it did. That we did."

She felt this way still. But if guilt would come for her anywhere, it would be here in their home. She was relieved to find that Adam's face confirmed her belief that what they had done was a service, defanged the desire that had for so long existed between them, so that when she embraced him now and said, "Welcome home," she felt no pull to be nearer his body, no wish to stay longer in the warm scent of his skin.

He thanked her for coming, and she felt from his hug that he was genuine, but could see from his expression that he was worried. She wondered if, when he saw her, he pictured the indecent things they had done, which to her felt already like they had happened in another life, to another woman. The other woman.

Margaret watched Ji Sun and Adam embrace. She lifted her hand, palm up, as though she might shove them together to the ground. She wasn't sure what they had done during those nights in the motel, while Elizabeth slept on her chest, while she woke to warm her bottles, to shush her back to sleep, but she knew they had been up late, drinking, talking, and laughing, trying to comfort one another. Maybe they had kissed, but that wasn't the intimacy she envied. Margaret had wanted to come all together less for not wanting to come alone, and more from her wish for any opportunity for the four of them to be together that wasn't a formal gathering or an emergency. She longed for a kind of everyday togetherness, to sit close beside the others without any thought to when they would have to go. There was a way in which, when they were all together and the twins were at home, she could call up in her body what it had felt like to live with them, what it felt like to still be forming, free from their own parents, and not yet mothers themselves. It wasn't nostalgia, but a kind of conjuring, and when it worked she could blur her eyes and make Lainey's couch the window seat, imagine that the window behind it looked not out onto a city street, but hovered above the grass and trees of an empty courtyard, everyone else in the world asleep.

Alice had most feared coming alone. She didn't want to open the door to Lainey's apartment again and flash back to that day, only two weeks earlier, when she had raced over and found them all inconsolable, blood on their hands and necks, blood on Elizabeth's cheek, bloody washcloth in Adam's hand.

She had arrived then to find the scene both worse and not as bad as she imagined. The way Adam had sounded on the phone, it was as though the baby's head was hanging on by a thread. She felt relief to recognize Elizabeth, to see that she was harmed but okay, but after that relief was revulsion in a rush that she could not release until she'd left their apartment, let herself feel the anger and disgust and fear and sadness that she could not when she was there, providing care. She'd felt that coming with Margaret and Ji Sun might guard against all of this coming back for her, and she'd been bolstered when Margaret arrived outside with a bouquet of yellow ranunculus, for which she'd already found a vase in the kitchen, where they all crowded together now.

"It's healing nicely," Alice said, and Margaret clapped like this was a party to celebrate an infection-free face bite, rather than whatever it was, which Alice supposed she did not quite know. They were all in the kitchen together, having all seen Elizabeth's face by now, and wanting to be there, to know what they could hope for, how to move forward.

"What are you going to tell her? When she's older?" Alice asked, lifting Elizabeth from the countertop changing pad where she'd examined her, and passing her back to Lainey, who bounced her and cooed at her, quieting the cries she'd made when Alice hovered over her with her penlight.

The stunned look on Adam's face told Alice that they hadn't talked about it, maybe hadn't even thought about it.

"That a dog bit her," he said. "Of course. We can't tell her that her mother, that her mother . . ." He trailed off, looked at Lainey, who had her own face tucked low, over Elizabeth's, as though to protect the baby from hearing what they decided.

"Bit her face," Alice said.

"Yes, Alice, we all know what happened," Ji Sun said, looking back and forth between Alice and the baby.

"But she'll need to know the truth," Alice said. "Someday, I mean. Don't you think?"

"Uh, no," Adam said. "I don't."

"Doesn't it seem wrong, though, for us to know this thing about her that she will never know? People have trauma," Alice said, "when they don't know the story of their own lives."

"Not everyone has your damage, Alice!" Margaret said, an abrupt edge in her voice that caused Alice to turn and face her. "And besides, it's not up to us."

"Sometimes you just . . . you can't have it in the house," Adam said.

"But it's here! Even if you pretend it isn't, blame it on some dead dog. You're going to live with it." Alice was angry enough to cry. She knew that with enough time, even those who knew the truth would

believe the lie. Even Kushi thought Alice's scar came from an accident. Wouldn't they tell their children the same? How many generations to make it true?

"Dog or truth," Ji Sun said. "You're going to live with it either
way."

"Dog or truth?" Alice looked at Ji Sun, aghast. "Truth! It's not
the same! Keeping that kind of secret, it can cause not just stress,
but physical degradation in the body. There are studies about
this."

"Okay, Alice, calm down. What are you, a trauma psychiatrist
now? Can you back off a bit?" Adam spoke in a tone that only Lainey
and Ji Sun had ever heard, and which made Ji Sun consider how he
might struggle to guard his own secrets.

"No one knows everything about anyone. Not even themselves.
Maybe least of all themselves." Lainey spoke now, looked up from
Elizabeth's head, which rested against her chest.

"What would you have them tell her? That her mother bit her?"
Ji Sun asked Alice, wanting to take the heat off Adam.

Lainey would never say aloud how large a part of her wanted to
answer yes to this, that this was the story she wanted her daughter
to know, to tell. She could imagine how the scar would be almost
imperceptible in the future, faint lines of shine, and only those
people who looked at Elizabeth for a very long time, or held her
face in their hands, would notice and wonder, or ask. And what,
Elizabeth would tell some tale about a pit bull? This tormented
Lainey to consider, that people would think Elizabeth had parents
who left her unattended in a park or a yard, how they would not
know, hearing this story, that Lainey had never been far enough
from her daughter's face during that part of her life for a dog to
come anywhere near.

The story of how her mother bit her was truer to reality, of course,
but also truer to what kind of mother Lainey was: consuming,

voracious, insatiable, and in love. Deranged by love, she had told Adam, after the institution. I'm not depressed, but I am deranged.

Rearranged by love. Lainey had always been a fierce defender of the belief that people without children didn't have some compromised experience of love, that to suggest a life was incomplete without a baby was yet another way to control women's lives. No one knew what it felt like to love anyone else, no matter who they loved, and she didn't truck with these people who thought loving a child granted you entry into some true human club. You could know a love as rich and as deep without a child, maybe richer, maybe deeper, who could say? How deeply you drank from the well of human experience did not depend on any one person, even one you helped to create.

And then she had Elizabeth and realized most everything she'd said was utter garbage. She did know another love now, and it wasn't a different speed in the same lane, it wasn't a new key for the same song, it wasn't a variant on anything she'd ever known. She hadn't known a thing. It wasn't any adjective she knew or could name, though she tried: encompassing, consuming, transcendent. Could love be transcendent when it knit her to the earth in a way she had never known she could be, when she felt herself so elemental but still otherworldly, like she both lived on and had become some new planet, and no one could visit but Elizabeth, who didn't know enough language yet to speak about this place.

How could she have been the one to bring them back down to planet Earth? She was meant to shield her daughter from the muck and ugliness of this place for as long as possible, for as long as she lived, and that she had failed so spectacularly, already, only redoubled her dedication to not let further hurts touch her baby, to remake the world. Elizabeth's future lovers should know that there was someone who loved her more than they could ever even imagine themselves capable of. They should know this and treat

Elizabeth accordingly. If love and protection, even warped, had led Lainey to bite down into the soft flesh of her infant daughter's face, they would know to fear her power. They would have been warned.

CHAPTER 51

They were not all together again, not truly, for nearly a year, a stretch during which they were so busy in their own lives that it was difficult to meet even in permutations other than the four. But Margaret made a plan for a reunion, saying if they didn't establish it as a yearly tradition now, they never would. She arranged for everyone to come to the beach house that she and Mac rented in Montauk, and over a lengthy chain of emails they agreed on a long weekend in late spring to congregate at the end of the world.

They had all been gathered once in the interim, for a party celebrating Alice and Kushi's adoption of a son, Tej. But there had been so many people in attendance that it was easy to get swept up in other conversations, and Margaret had been distracted chasing her twins, Lainey feeding Elizabeth blackberries, and Ji Sun busied in her role as godmother. Alice had asked her, though only nominally Lutheran, and in spite of the fact that she knew Ji Sun had turned down this same request when Margaret made it, after the twins were born. Margaret had thought of it as almost a gift to Ji Sun, who did not plan to have children of her own.

"But you know, I don't want children," Ji Sun had said, and wished that Margaret had asked her over the phone rather than inviting her to this "special lunch," a designation that might have warned Ji Sun, but which she'd brushed off as special for other reasons, since the two of them almost never met alone, and hadn't once since the twins were born. "In the event that . . . that the unthinkable happens, I still don't want to raise any children." Ji Sun busied herself with her silverware.

"I hadn't really thought of it like that," Margaret said. "Of course that is what I'm asking. But I suppose I was just thinking how you'd stand up at the baptism, be the special auntie."

"I'll be a special auntie anyway. Their *imo*, their only one," Ji Sun said, feeling guilty as she always did when called to defend her lack of desire for children, even to her friends. She was always quick to say that though she didn't want her own, she loved children. This was not true. She didn't love children, not all children, not as a group. She loved a few, specific children: her nieces, her nephew, and now, her would-have-been godchildren, Margaret's newborn sons. But she didn't wish to live with any of them.

"And I could, God forbid, if anything happened to you and Mac, I could help financially, whoever does raise the boys," Ji Sun said, still feeling guilty. It was harder, somehow, to say no to such an enormous favor, than to a minor one. Major mistakes were made simply by being caught off guard, unprepared to decline with grace.

"Oh, no, that's not, that isn't a consideration," Margaret said, though Ji Sun's wealth had in fact held appeal to Mac when Margaret told him that she wanted to name Ji Sun godmother.

At the party for Tej, Ji Sun had hoped somehow not to acknowledge this awkwardness, but Margaret had broached it off the bat.

"Oh, hello, godmama," Margaret said, and knocked her hip against Ji Sun's. Margaret smelled of cut flower stems and lemon rind.

"It's just the one," Ji Sun said, and blushed. "Maybe I could manage it. Before I ship him off to boarding school."

"Not to worry," Margaret said. "Alice is indestructible. She'll probably live to be a hundred and four."

Ji Sun bristled at this fast-forward, pained already by how quickly the years had begun to go, how they'd accelerated for her, even without the physical yardsticks for measuring time that now lived in her friends' homes, their children.

"And Howie, too," Ji Sun said. "We're a package deal this time."

"Even unmarried!" Margaret said, adding, "Sorry, you know what I mean."

"Even unmarried. I know what you mean."

Kushi and Alice's son was black, and Alice had, after an adoption counseling exercise using dried beans to represent her and Kushi's closest friends' ethnic backgrounds, told Ji Sun that she hoped to enlist Howie, also black, as a role model, even if he wasn't comfortable with the formality of being godfather.

Ji Sun had been a little reluctant to convey Alice's request, embarrassed at its intimacy, and its racial contours, so frank that they felt crass. But Howie clapped when she asked him, and pulled her into one of the tight hugs he sometimes gave when he was surprised.

"Of course I will, are you kidding? I'm honored," he said. "I love Alice. But she's white as hell."

Ji Sun had laughed then, and been grateful for his embrace of the title, how it meant that no matter what happened between them, they would remain connected in this way, godparents to a baby that they would never wish to raise, but loved without reservation before having ever glimpsed him.

Now, on the beach together, Howie was holding his godson while Kushi took a photograph. Mac was chasing his feral sons, and Adam trailed close behind Elizabeth, newly walking, as she navigated the sand with her own two feet for the first time. Lainey sat between Alice and Ji Sun, empty baby wrap loosed around her like an overlong scarf, her eyes on Elizabeth. Though it was sunny, the wind was brisk and they all wore long sleeves. The water was two months away from being inviting, but Margaret was in the ocean. She insisted that this kind of bracing off-season dip was the key to health and longevity, and they watched her now, shivering but somehow radiant even in the shadow of her hat. She was pregnant again, but in the water up to her breasts, so Alice didn't have to consider her stomach.

Alice had told Kushi she was ready to adopt the same weekend that she'd stitched Elizabeth's cheek. Biology was no guarantee. You could birth a baby, your own, and take a piece from her face. You could try to push your brother by blood to his death. Why, knowing this as she did, had she insisted there was some greater safety in a baby she and Kushi might make with their bodies? The best love she had given so far in her life was to women to whom she was not related, and to Kushi. The best love she had been given, too. She'd fled Lainey's apartment that morning as though chased by the cresting wave of a tsunami, faster than she had ever run in her life. She knew Kushi was waiting for her, that he would help her bear the weight of what she carried home.

She'd collapsed on their couch and stayed there all weekend, tucked in a blanket and lulled by the smells of Kushi cooking his big batch of Sunday biryani; the hum of their turned-low television; the reassuring weight of a book tented open at her ankles. She knew this place could be a shelter. She didn't know yet the ways she would fail Tej, but she could feel, in the room with Kushi then, the comfort she and Kushi could offer, the safe harbor of the space between them on the couch, even if, against all that waited outside, it was only a scrim. When she told Kushi over dinner that she wanted to call their adoption counselor first thing the next morning, he cried, and she felt a relief unlike any she had felt before, save the once, that deliverance she would always return to, when she saw her brother come back from the dead. The relief of not having killed him, just before the terror of watching his eyes open, wondering what he might say when he saw her face. She lived there still, between the relief of not having killed him, and the terror of what he might one day show her that he knew. But Alice knew by now that most people lived in that same place, that everyone around her was just between escaping something and not knowing what might come for them next. All they could do was find those people whose hands they would hold fast when they ran.

Alice looked at Kushi now as he adjusted Tej's tiny sun hat, lifted him from Howie's arms into his own. When she, Kushi, and Tej were out together, people never failed to point out how alike Kushi and Tej looked, their matched black hair and bright brown eyes, Tej's brown skin lighter than Kushi's, but darker than Alice's, even when she'd spent whole summers on a boat. She thought Tej and Kushi did share a kind of irrepressible adorability, a charisma that people responded to, and that Kushi teased her about saying a baby could have, even as he agreed that their baby did. But she also believed Tej looked objectively more like her, his jaw strong like hers, his gaze intense like hers, at times forbidding. Tej had a birthmark on his neck, below his jaw, on the opposite side and not quite aligned with where her scar fell, but near enough that Alice recognized it immediately as a connection, a matched mark they arrived to one another already bearing. A question others would ask of them. Answers that, if offered, would not satisfy. What they were born with, what the world wore away.

Kushi pointed out prior to their adopting Tej, when they'd agreed early on that they were open to transracial adoption, that if Alice were alone with their hypothetical, mythical, biological baby, she might get versions of the same reactions, the same curiosity as to whether she was, or could possibly be, their baby's mother. She knew Kushi was right, but still, she wished for strangers with better imaginations. She wanted the kind of easy congratulations that any mother got, not ones that came with pity, or any kind of extra commendation, the suggestion that what she was doing was for anyone other than herself. People had babies because they wanted to. She was the same. Just before this trip, Alice had worn Tej face-out in his carrier to the co-op, his neck newly strong enough to see the world this way. In line to check out, a white woman somewhere between Alice's age and her mother's had approached, put her hand too close to Tej's face, nodded, and said, "So brave," shook her head in apparent awe. Alice had felt in her fist that if she didn't have Tej strapped to her chest she might have socked the woman, but then, of course, she wouldn't have been given a reason. Instead, she pretended not to hear her, wished she would have thought to volley back, "You, too! So, so brave," so that the woman would spend all night wondering what courage Alice commended, what deformity or depravity Alice had seen or sensed. She would find better ways to answer or ignore the questions people asked or tangled themselves up in knots not to. She would learn to be better, and the world would, too; it had to.

Alice thought of the thrill she'd felt when Hillary Clinton announced her presidential campaign just a few weeks earlier, and the debates they'd had already on this trip about her. No one would ever convince Alice to vote for anyone other than Hillary, there was not a chance, but she didn't mind letting Lainey try. A few of Lainey's Occupy Wall Street friends were working for Bernie Sanders, and they'd invited Lainey to come write speeches for the senator, who was preparing to announce his own campaign, who promised revolution.

Lainey was not ready to throw herself into such work, but the heat she felt discussing it, the desire to, even the ability to find space in her mind for attention up and out, held a kind of painful promise. In the months right after what she'd done, she couldn't even read her emails, couldn't write a thing, could some days barely speak. Her role in her own life, as Elizabeth's mother, felt so precarious and provisional that to even glance in any direction other than down, at her daughter, seemed obscene.

Her mistake had hurried that work, toward breaking their bond, a rupture she knew would one day come, but needn't have occurred with such violence. Now Elizabeth took a bottle from Adam in the night. Now she could nap in another room. None of these were things Lainey wanted her to do, not yet, maybe never, but she'd been the one to put that distance there, and now she would need to learn to live in it, to watch her daughter from across space as she did now, Elizabeth on her brand-new land legs. She did not so much toddle as careen, Adam close behind. Lainey let the warmth from her friends' bodies keep her from leaping up, let their chatter keep her from calling out, tried just to watch as Elizabeth careened, careened, careened, not near the water's edge, but headed in that direction, toward its depths. Adam scooped her up and she squealed in his arms, her laughter a sound that Lainey could hear above any crashing wave.

Lainey was both of these women: the one who would never bite her daughter, and the one who had. She wanted to be able to explain this to someone who understood.

Ji Sun leaned closer to Lainey as her friend called out to her husband, watched along with Lainey as Adam caught Elizabeth, lifted her into his arms. Ji Sun thought of how, before the bite, Lainey had told her that Adam's daily runs had begun to look like he was fleeing something rather than enjoying the exercise, how she'd looked down from their window and seen him sprint away, how he *flew* from the door, liberated. He'd escaped his wife and daughter's oppressive love, the smells of their milk and shit and skin. Ji Sun remembered picturing him—his long legs, his easy gait—she had thought of him running toward her. That she had imagined this so recently, so vividly—a crowded street, all the other people falling away, the exact faded navy of the Quincy-Hawthorn shirt he wore—was more painful to her than what she had done with Adam in the motel. Those nights were somehow easier to file away as fantasies than the ones she'd had during daylight hours, and she yearned to be able to long for him in a harmless way, or a way she'd believed benign. She felt split, like Lainey, both the woman who would never hurt her friend, and the woman who had. She rested her head on Lainey's shoulder, longed, too, for an earlier iteration of her friend, one whose wildness felt risky but not perilous, one whose pain had seemed in some ways so like her own. It was not possible to rescue anyone, she knew by now, but you could recognize her. You could see what she showed you, flinch and keep looking, let her find in your own face the truth.

Ji Sun looked past Adam and Elizabeth at Margaret, still in the water, even as clouds crept half over the sun, smudged and diffused the light, made the sky dimmer and brighter both, somehow, a color more like the sand and less like the sea.

From Margaret's vantage, her friends so near to each other, legs leaned one to the next in such a way that if you didn't know which fabric each favored, you might mistake one's legs for another's, joined there at the knees. Margaret wished she had brought her camera into the water, to capture what they looked like from this distance, so like the girls she met when she entered their common room, its window seat a ticket to another world. She remembered one of their first evenings together, how they'd been in their own rooms and heard a loud sound at the window. They rushed out, kneeled close together on the bench, and cranked open one of the windows, tighter in summer, the seam sealed stuck with ancient layers of paint. They disagreed on the source of the sound: crack of a rock or thunk of a bird? There had been no swain, Lainey's word, there in the empty courtyard, no small body of a hurt bird. Lainey popped the screen and leaned all the way out, knew she would find someone fleeing with their flowers, the song they'd been too cowardly to sing. Her two braids, dyed candy apple red then, dangled out the window and Alice lifted one, called out *Rapunzel, Rapunzel, let down your hair!*

Ji Sun said that birds didn't always die when they hit glass, and Margaret hadn't believed it, had said she learned growing up that they always do, that they hit their heads and if they don't die right away, they die later. Everything dies later, one of them answered, and they had laughed at that, everything funny and fearsome then, when they shared that room. Maybe the sound had been the building settling, maybe it was nothing, maybe they had all imagined it.

Margaret wasn't ready to go in just yet, as eager as she was to be wrapped in a warm towel, to smell her sons' skin, to sit beside her friends and listen as they wondered and worried and argued and laughed, decided what to do next. She hoped they'd build a bonfire, stay on the beach until it died, until their children fell asleep in their arms, until they were close to sleep themselves. They still had time. She waved. She would go in soon, tell them how they had looked to her.

ACKNOWLEDGMENTS

M any people helped me realize this dream of having a book with my name on it in the world. My enduring, ecstatic, and enormous thanks to those named here, and to every reader who chooses to spend time with this book.

Lisa Grubka and Laura Tisdel, Midwest dream team, for changing my life before we met, for leading by example, and for loving this book with a ferocity and tenderness that humbles and heartens me.

Lisa, thank you for convincing me you knew exactly what to do, and then doing it, and for everything you've done for me and this book since. All future daily Michigan sightings will remind me of how glad I am to be on this path with you. Laura, thank you for making me laugh until my cheeks hurt, for beautifully balancing vulnerability and strength, and for championing this book beyond what I could have imagined possible.

Thanks to everyone at Fletcher & Company, Viking Books, and Penguin Random House who has read, supported, and labored over this book. What a thrill to work with people who so love books and are so brilliant at their jobs.

Thanks to those individuals and institutions whose belief in me has been a sustaining and necessary force, especially to the University of Michigan Helen Zell Writers' Program, and my generous teachers there: Peter Ho Davies, Nicholas Delbanco, Laura Kasischke, Matt Klam, Eileen Pollack, and Nancy Reisman. Thanks to my earlier writing teachers, who made whole worlds possible: Dr. Steve Behar, Jesse Lee Kercheval, Judith Claire Mitchell, Aimee Nezhukumatathil, Amy Quan Barry, Ron Kuka, and Ron Wallace. For your dedication to making space for art in the world, thanks to Kerry Eielson and John Fanning at La Muse Artists and Writers Retreat. Thanks to Julie Barer for that first corsage. Thanks to Cill Rialaig Arts Centre, the Helen Riaboff Whiteley Center, the Vermont Studio Center, and the University of Wisconsin-Madison's Program in Creative Writing.

Thanks to Quincy House at Harvard University, in whose Qube Library much of this book was written and in whose company I found true community.

My wholehearted thanks to the women who cared for, sang to, and loved my child while I wrote this book. Rama Nakarmi, for my first precious, tentative steps out the door. Everyone at Snowdrop, especially Megan Pentz and Anna Brabazon: I could not have done my work without the grace with which you do yours.

This is a book about friendship, and in friends I have been very rich:

For a lifetime of showing me what friendship means, this book is for Jenny Di Meo. Thank you for seeing me.

An MFA offers the time and space to write, but if you are truly lucky, you will meet lifelong friends and readers in the process. Natalie Bakopoulos, she of the fierce intellect and nougat heart, whose counsel, encouragement, and example is worth more than any fellowship, and without whom this book simply would not be: thank you. For years of Sundays, support, and clear-eyed love, thanks to Britta Ameel and Preeta Samarasan. For showing me what real writing—noun and verb—looks like, thanks to Jesmyn Ward. Thanks to Celeste Ng for your words on the page and off. Thanks to Dargie Anderson, Charlotte Boulay, Christina McCarroll, Jeremiah Chamberlin, Ray McDaniel, Joel Mowdy, and Marissa Perry.

Thanks to every friend who has cared all these years about the answer to the How's-the-writing-going question, including: the Friday Club, the Moms of Camberville, Brandon Abood, Jocelyn Ellis Abood, Tina Chang, Dorothy Cronin, Patrick Egan, Elisa